We hope you enjoy this book. Please return or renew it by the due date.

You can renew it at www.norfolk.gov.uk/libraries or by using our free library app.

Otherwise you can phone 0344 800 8020 - please have your library card and PIN ready.

You can sign up for email reminders too.

NORFOLK ITEM

30129 083 181 231

D1464828

Bill Rogers is hereby identified as author of this work
in accordance with Section 77 of the Copyright, Designs
and Patents Act 1988

Cover Design by Dragonfruit www.dragonfruit.it
The book cover picture is copyright to Inmagine Corp LLC

First published by Grosvenor House Publishing 2009
Copyright © Bill Rogers

Caton Books
www.catonbooks.com

ISBN 978-1-909856-10-3

Acknowledgements

Chief Superintendent Brian Wroe, former Divisional Commander, Greater Manchester Police, for his meticulous attention to detail. Anthony Phillips FFS.DIP, former Senior Scene of Crime Officer at New Scotland Yard, and Visiting Lecturer at Thames Valley University, for making sure that I didn't stray too far from reality. Vicky Rosin, Assistant Chief Executive, Manchester City Council; Kathy Oldham, Assistant Director, and Rob MacNeill, Town Hall Facilities Manager, for allowing me access to the roof and clock tower of the Town Hall. My primary readers, Joan, Barbara and Brian, for their patience, insight and wisdom.
And finally … to the City of Manchester itself, for providing such a magical backdrop and stimulus to my writing.

Chapter 1

Albert Stephen saw the lights first. Blue flashes erupting in the rear-view mirror; hard on their heels, the wail of a siren. His heart began to race as adrenalin surged through his veins. He braked gently, pulled into the curb and took a deep breath. The van swept past towards the bottom of Cambridge Street, where crimson brake lights momentarily marked the roundabout. It swayed ominously, veered precariously to the left and disappeared up the ramp onto the Mancunian Way.

He exhaled slowly, as he had been taught. The young policeman in the nearside passenger seat – one hand braced against the dashboard, the other clutching his personal radio – had not so much as glanced at him. The costume and the make-up would, in any case, have left a vivid image; easily recalled, but for purposes of identification of no practical use whatsoever. Had they stopped to check him over, however, it might have been a different matter. He was confident that his story would hold up. The mere fact that he was sober – indeed, completely alcohol free – at this time in the early hours of a city Sunday morning would have impressed them. The contents of the van were easy to explain. A quick check with the Police National Computer would reveal that the vehicle was not stolen, the road tax was paid and the driver comprehensively insured. But Albert Stephen knew that it would only take an astute or zealous officer, even one simply bored enough to want to liven up the graveyard shift, and then it might be over before it had barely begun.

He dug deep in the voluminous trousers and mopped his forehead, eyes and upper lip with the handkerchief. The skullcap wig, with its grotesque side growth, had caused him to sweat profusely. He folded the handkerchief meticulously along the original creases and placed it carefully back into a pocket. He calmly checked the nearside, offside and rear-view mirrors, depressed the clutch, slipped into first, checked the rear-view mirror once again and pulled slowly away from the curb. There was no reason to hurry. As he reached the roundabout, Albert Stephen began to sing softly.

'Hush, little baby, don't say a word, Mamma's gonna buy you a mocking bird. If that mocking bird don't sing, Mamma's gonna buy you a diamond ring. If that diamond ring turns to brass, Mamma's gonna buy you a looking glass...'

Chapter 2

Caton slung the jacket over his shoulder and stood for a moment, looking out of the window at a frosty Manchester morning. It had been a slow night. The reason he had come in on a Sunday; to catch up on paperwork and search the databases. Nothing but a series of dead ends. The consolation was that he had been able to take DC Woods, undisturbed, through his abysmal interim review.

'I'm off,' he said as he headed towards the corridor that led past the communications suite and out onto the car park.

And now, a rest day of sorts. Straight to bed, followed by a decent brunch and a spell at the gym. He might even make the reading group. Then a full night's sleep before an early start.

'I'm afraid not, boss.'

He turned wearily towards Woods, sitting on the edge of his desk, phone in hand, the sympathetic smile belying the hint of satisfaction in his voice.

'It's A Division. Got a funny one, back of Byrom Street. They're asking for you.'

Caton dropped his jacket over a chair and took the phone.

'Tom Caton... that's right, Detective Chief Inspector Caton... I'll hold.'

It was interesting how many cases had been

marked down as 'funny ones' in the three months since the squad was formed. Specialist Detection Group had become a euphemism for problematic, time-consuming and unrewarding. All the messy cases the rest of the Force Major Incident Team didn't want. Not quite what Hadfield had in mind when he called Caton over to Chester House. Chief Superintendent Martin Hadfield – head of FMIT – had opened the door himself.

Superintendent Helen Gates was already sitting at the boardroom table, smiling broadly. Something of a first for 'Iron' Gates. Caton had thought it strange they'd chosen GMP Headquarters, since nobody else had joined them. He soon realised it was just for a bit of gravitas; applying that little bit of extra pressure.

'The Chief Constable is four square behind this, Tom,' Hadfield had begun, Gates nodding vigorously in support. 'Even with a squad of three hundred dedicated officers you know how thinly spread our capacity is. And to cap it all, we've just been asked to second a small team into the Historical Enquiries Team cold casing the unsolved murders in Northern Ireland. There are too many cases taking up a disproportionate amount of time simply because our officers don't have the time to reflect … to think laterally.'

Nothing new there then, Caton had thought.

'We intend,' Hadfield continued, 'to create a small specialist detection group within the team to deal with some of the more telling cases. Think of it as an experiment, a pilot. Just you, two DIs, two sergeants and two DCs. You'll have a chance to negotiate who with Helen here. You can draw on the normal resources of the rest of the squad as and when. But we expect you to be resourceful and highly economic. You make this work, Tom, and there'll be no stopping you; all the way to the top.'

They had stared at him. Identical smiles of encouragement, their eyes searching his face for some spark of connection, a hint of ambition. It hadn't come and they had both found it difficult to hide their frustration. Hadfield's back had straightened and his voice firmed up.

'It's a great opportunity, Detective Chief Inspector, and it makes sense. Some quality time on the more challenging cases, and some extra flexibility in the team for detection.'

For challenging read bloody impossible, for flexibility read dogsbody, and for resourceful read resource-less. Caton had thought that at the time, and the last three months had simply confirmed it. He heard the click as the call was patched through.

'Tom? It's Gerry ... Gerry Sarsfield.'

'What are you doing at Bootle Street, Gerry?' Caton asked. 'I heard you'd been made up to Inspector at Stockport.'

'Last-minute switch. They had a vacancy, so here I am.' He adopted a serious tone. 'Got a nice one for your lot here, Tom.'

'Your timing's off, Gerry,' Caton told him. 'I've been in all night. I'll send Gordon Holmes over; he's on his way in as we speak.'

Caton could see him getting out of his Mondeo in the car park, trying to find a vacant bay this side of the barrier.

'Sherlock Holmes? Is he in your squad, Tom?'

'Inspector Holmes to you, Gerry; and yes, he's my DI.'

'With all due respect to Gordon, I think you might want to make your own mind up on this one, Tom ... whether it is one for your lot, or not.'

'You mean I have choice?' Caton barely managed to keep the frustration out of his voice.

Up until now, whoever had wanted to pass the parcel had suggested the Specialist Detection Group. Since SDG had been set up, the other seven senior investigating officers in the murder squad had enjoyed more time on the most straightforward cases, and a faster clear-up rate. From that point of view it might look as though the experiment was working, but it was Caton's squad that was becoming stretched.

'It came in as non-suspicious,' Sarsfield continued. 'And our lot were happy to let it stay like that.' He paused for emphasis. 'But the senior SOCO's got a feeling about this. I really think you should have a look.'

Out in the car park DI Holmes paced up and down. The thought of having to leave his six-month-old pride and joy outside the safety of the compound was getting to him.

'Hang on a minute, Gerry,' Caton said. He pushed the window open and called out, 'Gordon! Give me a minute and you can have mine.'

Holmes beamed like child in a sweet shop. Caton closed the window, cutting out the sound of the pneumatic drills that had just started up around the new block.

'Go on, Gerry. What have you got?'

'A body, in St John's Gardens; male, IC1, no obvious cause of death.'

'So?'

'We can't be certain on account of the temperature overnight, but it's looking like the time of death was somewhere between 1 p.m. and 4 p.m. yesterday.'

'Yesterday afternoon … in St John's Gardens?'

'Precisely!'

'So unless we've got a string of passers-by on the other side, and not one Good Samaritan in sight, he was dumped there,' Caton observed.

'Placed there, actually.' He paused as though a thought had just come to him. 'Very carefully indeed. I thought you'd be interested. And there's something else, but I think you should come and see for yourself before they ship him off to the mortuary.'

Caton looked at his watch – 6.20 a.m. The traffic would still be relatively light, just building up to the 7 o'clock early starters.

'I'll be with you in ten,' he said.

The chill November air hit him as he stepped out into the car park. Caton slipped his jacket on as the security lock clicked shut on the door behind him.

Twenty metres away Holmes stamped his feet and rubbed his hands together. Each exhalation produced a puff of steam from his nostrils. With his broad shoulders and stocky legs he had often been referred to as 'bullish'. This morning it fitted him like a glove.

'Come on, boss, it's bloody freezing out here!'

'We'll go in yours,' Caton said. 'It'll save time. I'll just get my gear.'

He walked to his own car, releasing the boot with his electronic key fob, and reached for his incident bag. He thought about bringing the whole bag, but decided against it. He took out a set of scene of crime gloves and shoe protectors, and closed the boot. The rest he could always get from the scene of crime officers. Holmes was already behind the wheel of the Mondeo.

'Where are we going, boss?'

Not, *what's the shout?* Caton noted, opening the passenger door and sliding with difficulty into the leather Recaro sports seat.

'Upper Byrom Street – St John's Gardens to be precise, and don't worry, Gordon, the area will be swarming with North Manchester Division right now.

Your precious car will be safe. I warned you not to get a flashy number for work. Look at it; titanium and racing seats. The drug barons will laugh their socks off, and the kids on the estates will have a field day lobbing bricks off the walkways. You're already a nervous wreck. I can't check if there's secure parking every time we get a call-out.'

Holmes gunned the engine and reversed towards the barrier at speed.

'Don't worry, boss,' he said, 'it's only the novelty. And I've got plenty of insurance; it cost enough … five hundred quid excess!'

Caton rubbed with his sleeve at the condensation forming on the windscreen.

'I hope you've got plenty in the bank,' he said. 'Those excesses are going to mount up.'

'Don't do that, boss!'

Holmes pulled Caton's arm away and clicked a switch on the console. A blast of cold air bounced off the screen, hitting Caton full in the face. At the same time the car braked erratically as Holmes realised he'd misjudged the speed of the gently rising barrier.

'For God's sake!' Caton snapped. 'This one has been dead for some time. I've no intention of joining him.'

They drove in silence up Stockport Road, locked in the queue of early starters.

'The Big Yin is back – Billy Connolly at his best!' screamed the posters outside the Apollo. Up onto the Mancunian Way, floating in the early morning mist between the university faculties and halls of residence, the low winter sun reflecting harshly off the glass and steel towers as they dipped down to the Cambridge Street roundabout.

Holmes gave in first.

'So what have we got, boss?'

'All I know is that it's a male IC1 who has been dead since early yesterday afternoon, and was most likely dumped in St John's Gardens sometime during the night.'

'Bit risky,' Holmes said. 'I thought it was locked at night on account of the down-and-outs?'

'The homeless, Gordon, or rough sleepers,' Caton said. 'The Down and Outs are a Liverpool punk group. You're right, though, it is locked, and there are those iron railings all the way round.'

Caton hung on to the handle above the door window as Holmes made a sudden right against the traffic down by the side of the Hacienda apartments. He took a quick left under the GMEX Bridge onto Trafford Street – the forty-seven-storey Beetham Tower soaring high above them – and up to the junction with Deansgate. The traffic was heavier here, and they had to wait for the lights to change. Then it was a quick right turn onto Deansgate, a left into Camp Street, another sickening right into Byrom Street and a screech of tyres as the Mondeo pulled up behind the line of official vehicles outside the gardens.

Heads turned; precisely what Holmes had intended. Caton shook his head as he unbuckled his seat belt. He pulled on the elasticated shoe protectors and slipped the pair of plastic gloves into his jacket pocket.

'Come on, Inspector,' he said. 'Playtime's over!'

Holmes chuckled as he fished his incident bag from the boot, locked the car and followed him in the direction of the gates.

The young WPC guarding the blue and white police tape that weaved in and out of the railings and across the entrance recorded Caton's name on the log, and lifted the tape for him to duck under.

Inside the gardens he stopped for a moment to get

a mental picture and let Holmes catch up. A small group of people dressed in white or blue Tyvek all-in-ones were huddled beside the central cross. A handful of officers guarded the perimeters. Ahead of him a line of tape marked the sanitised route to the body. He half turned as Holmes arrived.

'What do you see, Gordon? Not the people... the rest.'

Inspector Holmes was getting used to Caton's methods. Taking mental photographs, drawing pictures, walking the scene, visualisation, creating narrative and more, all on top of the extensive and proven techniques of crime scene investigation. But he got results. Holmes took a deep breath, scanned the gardens and began.

'Public gardens, surrounded on three sides by iron railings set into a stone base. Green railings, pointed on top, making a fence some five feet high; too narrow to squeeze between. There are gates with locks at each end, and another pair on the north side where they open onto a narrow alley which runs east to west, between Byrom Street and Lower Byrom Street. The fourth side is bounded by continuous high walls and the sides of buildings which abut the gardens. Mature trees and shrubs line the inside perimeter on all four sides, as does a metalled path about a metre wide, with wood and wrought-iron benches at intervals of about five metres. The garden consists of three main sections. The first, closest to Byrom Street, has formal flower beds in the form of a ten-metre square with a circular bed at its base, surrounding an engraved Celtic cruciform stone cross. To the south of the cross there is another shaded and grassed area about ten metres wide by twenty metres long.' He paused.

'Go on, Gordon, you're doing fine,' said Caton.

'It's just that I can't actually see up to the top of that

section, but I know what's there…'

'That's alright, just visualise it and play it back.'

'Well, at the head of that section, almost up against the wall, is a stone memorial to … John Owens – founder of Manchester University – whose gravestone, bounded by a single iron railing, lies in front of the memorial.'

'Very good, Gordon,' Caton said. 'I think you'll find it's Victoria University, and his wife Elizabeth is buried there, too.'

If he had a fault, and he admitted to several, Caton could not resist displaying his considerable knowledge of Manchester's rich, if recent, history; a seed sown in the local history society at MGS.

Holmes carried on.

'To the west of the cross, the garden continues as a grassed area for a further thirty metres or so down to Lower Byrom Street. To the south of this part of the garden is another shaded and grassed area almost matching the first, but with several wooden picnic tables and benches. To the north is a path leading to a pair of smaller gates set into the railings. On either side of the path, partly obscured by shrubs, are two wooden shed-like constructions.'

'And how does it feel?'

'Bloody cold, boss. About three or four degrees centigrade. There's heavy dew on the grass – which could be melted frost – a slight mist and damp in the air. And before you ask…' He thought about it for a moment. 'Cheerless.'

Caton nodded. It was the word that had been hovering on the tip of his tongue.

'Come on,' he said, setting off between the tapes marking the area already searched. 'Let's see what they've got for us.'

Inspector Gerry Sarsfield was bent down, his back

towards them, deep in conversation with someone obscured by the cross. When Caton tapped him on the back he turned and straightened, grinning from ear to ear.

'Tom, it's great to see you; thanks for coming.'

He nodded to Holmes, and signalled two PCs in bright yellow jackets and a man Caton recognised as Jack Benson – a regular crime scene manager, in a white protective suit – to step back off the path. He led Caton around the flower bed surrounding the cross to its west side, where a portable screen had been erected.

The deceased was seated at the base of the cross. His back was straight up against the column, arms thrust out and down on both sides, hands pressing into the fading white and yellow chrysanthemums in the flower bed. His head was thrown back, the rictus of the face muscles forcing sightless eyes to stare straight up at them in disbelief. Nobody spoke, waiting for the chief and his inspector to take it in.

'Who found the body?' Caton asked eventually.

'The park attendant,' Sarsfield answered. 'They always open up early because of the number of people who use the gardens as a short cut onto Deansgate.' He pointed towards the wooden sheds. 'You'll find her over there having a cup of tea. I've got a woman officer with her.'

'Is this how he was when he was found?' Caton asked.

'That's it,' said Sarsfield. 'Rigor mortis was well set in, so there was a limit to how much he could be moved. Just enough for the FME to give us likely cause and time of death.'

'The force medical examiner?' Caton said. 'Where's the duty pathologist?'

'At the Royal Infirmary. Had an accident on the way in. A couple of youths in an Impreza jumped the lights, hit him broadside and sped off. Reported stolen. Traffic are on to it. Mr Douglas wanted to be brought straight on here, but the paramedics insisted on a check-up. Sounds like concussion and some bruised ribs. So we thought we'd better ask the duty FME to do the initial assessment.'

'Where is he now?' asked Holmes.

Sarsfield grinned. 'She got tired of waiting out here in the cold, Tom. It's Carol Tompkins. You'll find her sitting in her car on Lower Byrom Street.'

Caton grimaced. It wasn't like him to reinforce stereotypes. In the early days, behind his back they used to call him the 'pc' PC, until the new chief constable began to shift the culture and others began to catch up. Still, it was good to know that the principal police surgeon was on the case.

Caton studied the body closely. Before it had been cut short this life had been heading towards middle age. No more than seven years older than himself. Forty-four max. Hair cropped short – a number two, or three at best. The torso was covered in a black and white hooped half zip top, fastened up to just below the chin. The bottom half was clothed in fashionable blue denim. He slipped on a pair of protective gloves and fingered the designer label just visible over the right hip pocket. Lee Dillon Jeans, it proclaimed. He recognised the distinctive armadillo-like articulated soles and cross straps of the Nike 'Free' cross trainers. He had considered buying a pair for himself.

'Smart gear, boss,' Holmes observed over his shoulder. 'Sporty, too.'

Caton nodded thoughtfully. This was no rough sleeper. The clothes were still relatively new and unmarked. There was something else, too. They were strangely ill fitting, far too loose. The top hung from the shoulders like a scarecrow. He wondered if it could be the rigor mortis simply accentuating the bone structure. He sat back on his heels to get a better perspective. The lengths of the top and the jeans were fine. Balancing himself with his left hand on the ground, he leaned forward and gently placed his right hand on the victim's left thigh. It was thin, almost matchstick thin.

'Bloody hell!' Holmes exclaimed. 'He's anorexic.'

Caton half turned, the rebuke evident in both his expression and his tone.

'Anorexia is a condition, Inspector. Whatever he had, he hasn't got it any more. Let's wait and see what the pathologist has to say, shall we?'

He was about to turn back and ease up the left sleeve a few centimetres when Jack Benson put a hand on his shoulder.

'Please don't do that, sir. We haven't finished processing him.'

Caton stood up. 'Any ID on him?'

The SOCO shook his head. 'Nothing so far; no wallet or papers that we can tell.'

Caton pointed to the gold and silver watch hanging loosely from the painfully thin wrist.

'If I use a spatula, can I have a look at this?'

Benson shook his head ruefully, but reached into a pocket in his overalls and handed the chief inspector the thin plastic tool. Caton used it to turn the watch at an angle and then flip the clasp open. The watch fell loose and came to rest where the base of the hand was locked open. He lifted it gently, just enough to see the stainless steel back.

'No sign of an inscription,' Caton remarked, handing the spatula to Benson and rising to his feet.

He scanned the flower bed and the seven-foot-high cross. Apart from the corpse, there was nothing unusual.

'They've done a fingertip search of the flower bed,' Sarsfield informed him. 'And an initial look at the perimeters and the rest of the garden. Nothing so far, apart from a few sharps, a couple of cans and some bottles.' He picked up on Caton's expression. 'It looked like they'd been tossed in from the outside. No indication that anyone had actually been in the garden.' He nodded towards the body. 'Except for him.'

'Well, he didn't wander in on his own,' Holmes added caustically.

'They don't call you Sherlock for nothing,' Sarsfield bristled.

'Take it easy!' Caton addressed it to the two of them.

They were going to have to work together. At the very least he would have to rely on some good will from Division to continue to secure the scene while the Tactical Aid Unit completed the forensic search of the area. He still had to assess the demands this one might place on FMIT, and whether or not it was one for his own team. The only flexibility Chester House wanted to hear about was making existing resources stretch further.

'Can you give us a couple of minutes, Gerry?' he asked. 'I just want a word with the FME, and then I'll leave Gordon to work out how quickly we can replace your night shift here. We'll be as quick as we can, but can you make sure you preserve the scene in the meantime?'

'Don't worry, Chief Inspector, at least there's a fence around this one. It shouldn't take more than half a dozen to keep this sewn up till your lot get here. And there will be plenty who'll be glad of the overtime coming up to Christmas … while they still can!' he added ruefully.

'Thanks, Gerry.'

With a brief nod of his head, Caton invited Gordon Holmes to join him as he set off west in the direction of Lower Byrom Street.

They found the forensic medical examiner sitting, head down, in her Nissan Micra, typing notes on a laptop. Caton could see that strands of silver had begun to invade her jet-black curls since he saw her last. She wound her window down and smiled up at them. World-weary blue-grey eyes that had seen it all, and had long since ceased to try to make sense of any of it.

'At last, Detective Chief Inspector,' she said. 'In ten minutes my eighteen-hour shift on call comes to an end. Have you any idea how much it's going to cost you if I go over?'

Caton returned her smile. 'Believe me,' he said, 'I don't want to keep you any longer than I have to.'

Carol Tompkins leaned back to reveal an earnest young man in the passenger seat. In his late twenties, he wore a dark overcoat with a grey scarf around his neck.

'This is Doctor Mark Patterson; he's a trainee FME getting his hours in the hard way.'

'Doctor,' Caton nodded politely, and turned his attention back to Carol Tompkins. 'What can you tell me, Doctor?'

She ran the cursor up to the top of her screen.

'Probably not much more than you've already heard from Inspector Sarsfield.'

She referred back to her notes.

'The victim is in an advanced state of rigor mortis. It's at least twelve hours since maximum stiffness was reached, probably more. Death could theoretically have occurred up to thirty-six hours ago. Body temperature is less reliable at this stage till we have some certainty on how cold it was out here last night. All in all, I would suggest that death occurred somewhere between 10 a.m. and 4 p.m. yesterday afternoon. I can't be more precise than that, but the pathologist should be able to narrow it down when the rigor retreats.'

'When will that be?' Gordon Holmes interjected.

The principal police surgeon turned to her colleague.

'Do you want to tell them, Mark?'

He leaned forward keenly.

'Rigor mortis typically lasts in a temperate climate for anything from thirty-six to forty-eight hours, and depending on environmental temperature can last for as long as seventy-two hours. After that, general tissue decay and leaking of lysosomal intracellular digestive enzymes cause the muscles to relax.'

Caton had a feeling the young man was enjoying this a little too much.

'Seventy-two hours! We can hardly wait another two days to find out what happened to the poor beggar,' Holmes muttered.

'Don't worry,' said the FME, 'the pathologist will be able to begin the post mortem. The sooner the better, as the time of death will be increasingly hard to determine. He can break the rigor, but it will mean tearing those muscles that are under tension.

'And you wouldn't have a stab at possible causes?' Caton already knew what her response would be.

'You know me better than that, Chief Inspector. I can do a bit of eliminating, though. There's no evidence of cuts, stabs or gunshot wounds that I can tell, and don't be misled by the contraction of the facial muscles – that's entirely down to the rigor mortis. Unlikely, therefore, that the deceased suffered severe trauma. No sign of damage to the head either.'

She paused and looked directly at him with a penetrating gaze, her eyes watching for his reaction.

'He does appear, however, to have lesions on his arms, and on his abdomen and lower chest.'

'Lesions? I didn't notice any when I looked at his watch.'

'They are there, Detective Chief Inspector,' she said firmly. 'And in the nasal passage. Kaposi's Sarcoma to be precise.' She let it hang in the air.

Gordon Holmes broke the silence. 'AIDS? He had AIDS?'

'Not necessarily, Inspector, but the most common occurrence is in patients with acquired immuno-deficiency syndrome.'

She saved the file she had been working on, shut down the computer and began to close the lid, pausing as though she'd had an afterthought.

Then she added, 'There was just one other thing.' She had them both on tenterhooks and knew it. 'I think the pathologist will find that there's a recent injection site on the inside of the deceased's left arm, just below the elbow. With the thinness of the arm, and the rigor, the bruising is clearly visible.'

She closed the laptop with an air of finality, placed it on the rear seat and pointedly gripped the ignition key.

'I'll email my report over as soon as I get back; copy to the chief pathologist.'

Caton watched deep in thought as the car pulled out and turned immediate left down Great John Street, taking the short cut past the Granada TV Centre. Technicians and extras slowed noticeably to gawp as they passed by on the other side of the street, heading for the red-brick studio leading to the Coronation Street set, just yards away. It would only be a matter of minutes before the Granada news team had a reporter and camera up here, and with the Manchester Evening News headquarters only round the corner in Spinningfields, Caton knew that someone had better talk to the press office. He turned, ducked under the tape and strode back towards the cross.

'AIDS, boss. Are you thinking what I'm thinking?' Holmes asked as he struggled to keep up.

Caton had been happy to inherit Gordon Holmes when he put the team together. An experienced detective who had managed to stay sharp and committed. The only reason he had never progressed to chief inspector was his Achilles heel: a tendency to jump to conclusions. The oldest member of the team, he still shared something in common with some of the others; he was work in progress.

'Let's not make any assumptions, or rule out the possibilities,' Caton replied. 'It's not certain that it is AIDS, and we've no way of knowing if the deceased was gay or straight. In any case, transmission to heterosexuals is possible through blood transfusions or use of dirty syringes, or medical needle stick injuries. You know the permutations as well as I do. So let's not assume a homophobic motive just yet. We'll just not discount it.'

They arrived at the cross just as Gerry Sarsfield emerged from behind the screen.

'The woman from the Parks Department, Tom … do you want a word with her?'

Caton was dead on his feet, and despite the challenge this case already promised, he knew there was little he could do at this stage that he could not safely leave to others.

'No,' he replied, 'Gordon can do that. I'm going to ring headquarters to check they want us to handle it, and then get off. I suggest you two begin the handover procedure, and get a press statement sorted sharpish.'

Caton turned to face Holmes, who already had his notebook out.

'If we get the green light, you can use our incident room at Longsight. Check all the CCTV cameras. There must be dozens of them in this area with all the solicitors' offices and barristers' chambers, not to mention the city centre main street and arterial route cameras. He must have used a vehicle to get the body here. We need a fingertip search of the perimeter on both sides, especially the iron railings. He had to have got that body over somehow … unless,' he added as an afterthought, 'he had a key. Better investigate that possibility. And make sure the photographer gets a full set of shots, including all of the inscriptions and any graffiti in these gardens, especially on that cross.'

It took him five minutes to get hold of Superintendent Gates. And half that time for her to decide this was one for the Specialist Detection Group.

'I know we would normally have given it longer,' she said, 'but we've got five on the go at the moment, Tom, and another three in court. If this turns out to be straightforward we can easily review it, and you can hand it over to one of the other investigating officers, but from what little you've told me it sounds as though this one's got legs.' She paused for emphasis. 'Keep it low profile, Tom. You can imagine what the press could turn this into.'

Never mind that his team was still struggling with the Chinatown murders. This was all about fast clear-up rates for the rest of the squad. With ninety per cent of killings domestic, or at least murdered by a known acquaintance, and with a full-time specialist murder squad homing in on each one, it wasn't surprising that the statistics were looking good. The downside was that everyone else got to celebrate their success on a regular basis while his team laboured on. Still, it was more of a challenge, and a damn sight more interesting. And that was the irony. The rest of them were actually jealous of the SDG. Just one of the curses of being called 'specialist'. The grass is always greener, he mused as he walked back down the path to give them the good news.

'This one's ours, Gordon,' he said. 'Superintendent Gates has agreed we can have a dozen DCs and two extra SOCOs from FMIT, and some time-limited support to work through the CCTV tapes. Forty-eight hours in, there'll be a review to decide on the size of the investigation team. Give Amit Patel a ring at Chester House to set it up. And you don't need to give me a lift back, I'm only two minutes from the flat.'

He saw the disappointment on his DI's face and knew it was more his parking space that Gordon would be missing than the company of his DCI.

'And don't page me unless it's an emergency,' he threw over his shoulder as he set off. 'I'll ring in when I'm compos mentis.'

It was a standing joke in the squad that Tom Caton tried to get his team to find some semblance of work–life balance, and did his best to model it himself. Many attributed the slowing down of his promotion, after a meteoric rise, to just that. What he knew, and they didn't, was that much to the chagrin of the top brass it was his choice to stay out of the rat race. And it didn't mean a lack of motivation for the work. He got results. He just didn't believe it was necessary to grind his team into the ground to achieve them.

As he passed the stone cross, Caton glanced briefly at the inscription on its east face. He already knew what was written there: *St John's Church, which was taken down in 1931, was built on this site in 1769 by Edward Byrn, around the remains of more than 22,000 people.*

Plague, cholera and starvation had haunted the past of every city, and for too many they still afflicted the present. But mankind's capacity for evil seemed to Caton of a different order altogether. He recalled a poem by an anonymous local poet he had seen in the Manchester United trophy room.

As Satan was flying over Clayton for Hell
He was chained in the smoke, likewise the smell,
Quoth he: I'm not sure in what country I roam,
But I'm sure by the smell, I'm not far from home.

Caton shook his head, turned up the collar of his jacket and strode towards the west gate.

Chapter 3

The winter sun sent shafts of light spearing in all directions off the steel sphere at the entrance to the Museum of Science and Industry.

Caton turned up the collar of his coat and weaved his way in and out of the river of people streaming into the city centre. He crossed to the other side of Liverpool Road, where the licensee of The Ox, whose gastropub menu and guest beers ensured that Caton was a regular, was busy fixing the watering system for the hanging baskets. Caton wondered how many people in the Whitbread Empire knew that the inn, formerly The Oxnoble, was named after a potato, not an ox. Come to that, would they be pleased to learn that a building at the rear had opened in the 1870s as the Manchester and Salford venereal diseases centre? Would that have threatened or boosted trade, he mused? Out of the clinic and into the pub. Just what they'd need. A good stiffener.

A discordant clash of tubular bells caught his attention as he passed Potato Wharf. Three brightly painted narrowboats nestled close in the basin. Beside them, a gang of men at the foot of the stepped arena were unloading scaffolding poles from a wagon. Whatever the event, he hoped it wasn't going to be as loud as the last one. He turned left down Old Medlock Street and immediate right into the gated community of faux Georgian houses and apartments. The car park was almost empty as he opened the door to his apartment and tapped a code into the alarm pad. He elbowed the door closed, picked up the small pile of mail and made his way through the lounge to the open-plan kitchen, where he tossed them, unopened, on top of the bread bin. He poured a glass of water and made his way through to the bedroom. It took him less than a minute to hang his jacket in the fitted wardrobe, draw the blinds, undress and climb, exhausted, into bed.

The dream was no stranger. Darkness, a sudden jolt and a stomach-wrenching sensation. He fell faster and faster. There was a blinding flash of light as he fought to flee an empty, featureless white landscape. But he was rooted to the spot. The silence was as terrifying as the sensation. It seemed to last forever.

Caton woke as always in a sitting position, bathed in sweat, thrashing wildly with his arms, his legs locked rigid beneath the sheets. He forced himself to slow and deepen his breathing, to bring his hands down to the bed and to focus where the wall and ceiling met. Gradually he regained control and sank back onto the pillows.

He lay there for some time, gazing at the shimmering halo of light around the blinds, listening to the occasional ringing sound of metal on metal and the murmur of voices as the stage neared completion in the Castlefield arena.

The first time he had admitted to these flashbacks was several months after the crash, and only then because his screams had woken the rest of the youth hostel. The school doctor had been right when he predicted they would become less frequent. He rarely experienced them now. The last had been over a year ago. Caton had already worked out that they were always triggered by some completely unrelated traumatic event. He managed a grim smile. The murder squad was probably not the best place to avoid them. No one in the force had any idea that he experienced them, and he was not about to tell them. He knew enough about post-traumatic stress disorder to know that he should have sought counselling years ago, but it wasn't available then, and he was not going to ask for it now. It didn't affect his work, he reasoned. He was on top of it.

He threw back the sheet, stepped over the duvet where it had slipped into a pile on the floor, picked up his discarded clothes and padded to the bathroom, where he dropped them into the basket. He went through to the wet room, the floor walls and ceiling immaculately tiled in emerald mosaic. Caton would not normally have showered before setting off for the gym, but the stench of fear still clung to him.

The bedside radio clock said 2.05 p.m. He slipped on a pair of jeans and a clean T-shirt and selected his worn but comfortable leather jacket. Pulling his ready-packed kitbag from the wardrobe, he walked through to the kitchen area, poured a glass of orange and cranberry juice, and started to peel the one remaining banana in the vegetable rack. Glass in one hand and banana in the other, he walked across the lounge to the area which doubled as his study, drank half of the juice and placed the glass on the side of the desk. His computer was always on, but password locked. He checked his emails. Two Virgin Wine offers, a 'Late Rooms' update, two 'Trace your ancestry.com' messages – the constant legacy of a brief flirtation with family history – what looked like an Old Mancunian circular, an electronic greetings card and a reminder from Nick Bateson about The Old Nag's Head

Reading Circle. The first three he deleted, the remaining three he kept as new. Then he closed the screen down and logged off. He finished the banana, washed it down with the remainder of the juice and accessed the voice messages button on his answer phone.

'Thomas? It's Marilyn here… We decided to send you an email card for your birthday this year… Alan has just found out how to do it, so you're our guinea pig … so to speak. Well … I suppose you're as busy as ever… Give us a ring sometime… Bye now.'

His aunt never forgot his birthday, but found it as hard as ever to move beyond the veneer of conventional politeness. Caton understood. It had been just as hard for her, losing her sister that way, and he was a constant reminder. He arrowed down to the final message. Nick's voice piped up cheerfully.

'Hi, Tom! The lads have decided to change this week's meet to tonight to fit in with your shift. Bangkok Huskies were supposed to be doing a set in the function room, but they've had to cry off … flu or something … so we're sorted. Have a good kip and get yourself over here for 7.30. I've emailed you the list of questions … so no excuses! See you later…'

Caton sighed. He had been hoping for a quiet evening before he was sucked into this new inquiry that he sensed would lead him to break his own rules, and pull him into that cycle of long days and bleary nights. He checked his mobile to see if there was anything from Gordon Holmes. Two spam messages, a service call, and a short text from Nick telling him to check his emails. That decided it. He wasn't needed. A night at The Old Nag's Head it was. It might be his last for some time.

He took the glass through to the kitchen and threw the banana skin in the pedal bin. At the front door he reset the alarm, closed the door firmly behind him and walked the hundred yards or so to the gym.

Caton had joined the old YMCA in the city centre in his final year at university and had good memories of pounding out the miles on the wooden suspended track high above the hall. When the club closed and moved to the brand new premises attached to the Castlefield Hotel, he had moved with it. And then the apartment came available as one of the first regeneration developments around the Castlefield basin and he'd snapped it up, mainly because of its proximity to the Y Club. The bonus was that the apartment had tripled in value.

Saskia, the pert blonde Polish receptionist, took his membership card and, smiling broadly, swiped it through the computer link.

'Thank you, Tom. It's a lovely day, isn't it?' she said as she handed it back with full-on eye contact.

Caton had not yet worked out if she really had memorised his name or read it each time from the computer. Either way, he was impressed. He felt obliged to respond.

'It's certainly an improvement on yesterday,' which, he reflected, was true on several levels. 'What will it be like in Krakow this time of year, Saskia?'

'Much the same, Tom,' she beamed. 'A couple of degrees colder, that's all. I was speaking to my parents last night. I'm going back for a break at Christmas … now then it *will* be cold, and real snow! You'd love it!' She let her meaning hang playfully in the air, waiting for his response.

As a tourist or boyfriend? he wondered. Flirting was something he wasn't good at these days, but was frequently confronted with.

'I'm sure I would,' was the best he could muster as he tucked his card into his bag and set off, struggling with the zip to hide his embarrassment.

He didn't know if girls – make that women – were becoming more predatory, or he was becoming more sensitive to it. Either way, it irked him that these days he was finding it bloody hard to deal with.

The changing room was empty, but it still took a while to find an empty locker with a hanger in it. Too many members – despite a recent purge – had reverted to leaving their kit in the lockers after they'd finished training and then walking off with the key. That way they didn't have to trawl their kitbags to work and back for the evening session. Caton couldn't believe that it was the little things like this that really made him angry. Why not the terrible injustices he dealt with day to day? It had been explained to them once on a course at Bramshill. They called it diversionary projection! Most officers, whether they were aware of it or not, had joined the police out of a strong sense of social justice. Ironically, simply in order to be able to do their job they had to control the anger they might reasonably feel about the real and often horrific injustices they would inevitably come across. Not just man's inhumanity to man, but also when the legal system set the guilty free. They could expect that repressed anger to surface somewhere else, often when they least expected it, and over the smallest trifle. Caton had seen that played out among his colleagues, too often contributing to the breakdown of their relationships. He just had difficulty relating it to himself.

The aerobics room was equally deserted. Ten minutes into a spin session the leaden feeling in his legs and the tension in his head had leached away as the endorphins kicked in. A further forty minutes, divided between the cross trainer and the rowing machine, left him feeling energised rather than exhausted. He moved on to the weights machines. This might be the last full session he could squeeze in this week, and Caton had promised himself a good one.

Half an hour later he made his way up to the running track – an exact copy of the original in the old YMCA – and put in ten laps on the springy boards before the tight bends and steep camber began to tell.

He made his way down to the changing rooms, slipped on his shorts and dove into the empty pool. The cool blue water closed over him like a friend, and he lost himself in the rhythm of the stroke.

It was already dusk as Caton exited the Castlefield Hotel and Y Club through the café. His watch said 4.30 p.m. The stage was finished, and the crew had gone. Lights from the bridges, Y Club and three remaining narrowboats threw curtains of colour dancing across the water in the canal basin, gently agitated by the chilly evening breeze. Through the floor-to-ceiling windows of the swimming pool he could see the first batch of city workers exorcising, length by length, the stresses of the day, waiting for the rush hour crush to ease before venturing onto the ring road.

There were no messages on his mobile, but one fresh one on his answer phone from Gordon Holmes.

'Hi, boss. Not too much to report. The incident room is set up. The physical search is complete. We've made a start on a pile of CCTV discs and tapes – you wouldn't believe how many – and we've started collating the returns from face-to-face interviews of those night workers we could track down. I've got ten officers on that tonight as well. The post mortem is fixed for 10 a.m. tomorrow, and the lab's promised to give us what feedback they can on the rest of the physical evidence as soon as they can. There's nothing

*more to report, and everything's in hand. So don't come in
… and don't bother ringing in either. Get a good night's
sleep, and we'll see you in the morning. See you, boss.'*

Holmes went up a notch in Caton's estimation. He
had obviously rung because he knew that if he didn't,
his chief inspector would either ring in or, worse, be
tempted to come in. Well, he was right on that score,
and he also seemed to have everything in hand. What
was it that Chinese proverb said of great leaders? 'Of
a great leader they will say, we did it ourselves.' If
only it were that simple.

There were two new emails: the first was from Olives
et al, confirming delivery of two packs of Moorish olives
that had been out of stock; the second, as promised, was
from Nick, with the questions for tonight's meeting
attached. Caton downloaded the attachment, pressed
print and walked through to the kitchen.

The mail lay where he'd tossed it. A half-yearly bill
for the maintenance contract, the quarterly telephone
bill, three advertising circulars, and a reminder about
the Police Charity Dinner and Dance. The final
envelope contained another offer to buy his car park
space – the third this year. What the hell did they think
he was going to do with his own car? The best offer so
far was fifteen thousand pounds. He knew of at least
one neighbour who was getting one thousand six
hundred a year rent for hers, in advance. It was getting
crazy. The bills went back on the granite worktop, the
rest straight into the bin.

He checked the faded scribbled list showing the
contents of the freezer, secured to the fridge with a
magnetic Manchester City crest. It was a habit he had
acquired several years previously, having discovered
two shelves of meals which had been in there long
enough to interest archaeologists, let alone health
inspectors. He chose the remaining dish of chilli from

the batch he'd made the previous week. As he opened the fridge, Caton observed that his mail was a sad reflection of the way his private life had become perfunctory, and that word Holmes had used – cheerless. He had fought to preserve his personal space from the way in which his work threatened to expand to fill every hour available; but for what? Maybe, he decided, soulless was nearer the mark.

While the meal cooked in the microwave he collected the sheet of paper in the printer out tray, selected 'Brassed Off' from the rack of DVDs below the wall-mounted flat-screen TV and slipped the disc into the player. Armed with his chilli, a glass of water and the list of questions, he pressed play on the remote control and sat back on the sofa.

True to form, Nick had omitted the names beside each question. Caton enjoyed identifying the author of each, although it was becoming increasingly predictable. The first, he decided, was definitely Nick's own teaser.

Consider the relationship between fifty-year-old Alberto and fourteen-year-old Sophie. Is there a subtext here which owes more to 'Lolita' than to Socrates?

Only an established teacher would open with 'Consider'. It was typical of Nick to assume that the rest of them would be happy to respond to an examination task.

How does Gaarder compare with Umberto Ecco?

That would be Craig Lloyd's. Craig was one of the three – Nick, Jamie and himself – who played for the Didsbury Beavers football team, and by far the most widely read. As an English teacher, Nick tended to read with one eye on his role. Lots of fiction, and mainly recent and modern classics. Craig, on the other hand, had an amazingly eclectic taste, and of the five of them could be relied on to propose some of the most interesting and unusual reads. Caton found the remaining two less easy to decipher.

Why has Jostein Gaarder used the device of a book within a book ... within a book?

Which Philosophy best represents you ... and why?

Eventually, he decided that the first was Jamie aspiring to match Nick's inquisitorial style, while the second was typical of Jerome's mischievous probing of the psyche of this random group of men brought together through the most tenuous of connections. The remaining question was his own.

How does the author keep what could have been a really boring book moving along?

As always, he felt dissatisfied with his offering. Somehow it lacked inventiveness, and depth, but at least it would get them talking about the book itself. Caton normally enjoyed his sessions with the Alternatives. Not least, because paradoxically they all had so much, and so little, in common. They were united by their status as unattached male city dwellers on the cusp of middle age. On the other hand – and this was the real plus – none of them worked in the same occupation. Above all, he was the only policeman. Apart from the books, their conversation spanned beer, sport, food, television and films, even art sometimes, and ... women, except in Jerome's case, although perversely, he seemed more knowledgeable about women than the rest of them put together. All of this, and a little intellectual stimulation, more often than not made for a decent night out. These days it was about as good as it got.

Caton put the plate and the paper on the coffee table, and turned up the volume on the remote. The haunting sound of Rodrigo's 'Concerto De Aranjuez' wafted over him through the 360-degree surround-sound speakers.

He closed his eyes, summoning an image of his father, standing tall on the stage of the Free Trade Hall, his tenor horn to his lips, his mother sitting proudly beside him in the stalls. He could see the faces of the band, the detail of their uniforms, the peeling paint on the underside of the balcony, the curve of his mother's lips as she smiled down at him. Insidiously, the combined effect of the training and the chilli kicked in, his eyelids fluttered and closed, and Caton slept.

Chapter 4

Albert Stephen slid the remaining sheet of vinyl from the worktop and placed it carefully against the side of the van. Starting with the left-hand corner, he eased the upper edge to match the faintly pencilled guideline. When he was satisfied that both the upper corners and the left side were in place, he used a new sponge block, working from left to right to smooth out the sheet.

Not until he was sure that all of the bubbles had gone did he step back to admire his work. Slowly circling the van, he checked for the slightest flaw or inconsistency. After three circuits, he was satisfied there were none.

Along the sides of the van the word 'Manchester' stood out boldly in red, followed by the words 'Environmental Services' and the city coat of arms, all on a dark-blue background. Across the rear doors – one discrete sheet on each panel – ran the current City Council's exhortation: 'This is *Your* City. Help *Us* to Keep it Clean'.

Satisfied that no one would easily distinguish this from the real thing, he put the tins of vinyl glue, the sponge and the packaging in which everything had come into a big black wheelie bin. He then picked up the number plates from the garage floor, wrapped them in sacking and placed them in a long grey canvas workman's holdall resting on top of the workbench.

He doubted that anyone would have seen him drive the van in, but it was not worth taking the risk that someone might register the transformation. He took a well-used dust sheet from the rear of the van and threw it over the back portion, effectively obscuring the licence plates and signage.

Albert Stephen then took a long brown anorak from a hook above the workbench, slipped it on and pulled the hood low over his head. He pressed a button at the side of the door, which quietly and effortlessly rose to reveal through the rough brick arch the gathering gloom of early dusk. Pushing the bin ahead of him, he wheeled it to the corner of the row of railway arches where a cluster of bins waited to be emptied the following morning. He took simple pleasure in the knowledge that the Environmental Health department would be disposing of the evidence. It was the kind of symmetry that appealed to him.

Back in the garage he closed the doors, peeled off the thick plastic gloves and placed them in the holdall. From his pockets he retrieved a pair of new leather gloves and slipped them on.

Hefting the holdall over his right shoulder, he collected a foldaway mountain-style bike propped up against the wall, opened the doors again and wheeled the bike out onto the roadway. He took a moment to scan the garage for anything he might have missed. Satisfied, he used a small remote pad attached to the van keys to set the wireless alarm and close the door. Then he mounted the bike and rode away.

Had anybody been following Albert Stephen – and he took pains to check that they were not – they would have wondered at the circuitous nature of his route. As with everything that Albert Stephen did, behind it there was a simple, if devious logic. Although only a handful of the many garages, workshops and small industrial premises held much of significant value, all of them were of value to their owners, and prey to petty vandalism; sometimes serious criminal intent, including arson. The route that Albert Stephen took had been carefully researched some months previously, and minimised the likelihood that he might be caught on one of the many security cameras. Even if he was, there would be little indication of where he had come from, or where he was going.

Fifteen minutes later he arrived at the newest of several Eastlands building sites, where speculators capitalised on the second wave of demand generated on the back of what even he had to admit had been a spectacularly successful Commonwealth Games.

Albert Stephen threw the holdall into the back of a three-year-old Peugeot 406 estate he had parked there earlier that morning, and folded and placed his bike in the boot, together with his anorak, overalls and over trousers. He was, to all intents and purposes, a decorator finishing his shift.

He smoothed down his jeans and sweatshirt, took a pullover from the back seat and slipped it on, before climbing into the driving seat and pressing the central locking switch. You couldn't be too careful. Carjackers and mobile phone snatchers lurked in the most public places, even at traffic lights. Now that the city centre had been flooded with city wardens and police support officers, as well as traffic wardens and beat policeman, these petty, but very nasty and unpredictable parasites had moved out to the inner suburbs. It was time something was done, Albert Stephen reflected. But first things first. He checked his mirrors, switched on the ignition and set off towards the bright lights of the burgeoning city skyscrapers.

Caton jerked awake. The pain was excruciating. His right calf was knotted with cramp. He swung his feet to the floor and massaged his leg roughly, angling his toes towards the ceiling until the tension eased and the pain subsided. The television flickered blankly. It was dark outside. He looked at his watch. Already ten to seven. He switched off the TV and went to pull the blinds. Down on the quays, noisy revellers would already be making their way to Dukes 92, Barca, Albert's Shed and Jackson's Wharf. He decided the jeans and T-shirt would have to do. He had a quick shave and brushed his teeth, slipped on his leather jacket, picked up his mobile phone, wallet, keys and warrant card from the bedside table, switched off all the lights other than the one by the door on an automatic timer, set the alarm and ventured out into the cold night air.

However cold and inhospitable the weather, there was, for Caton, an ever-present warmth about the centre of Manchester. He put that down, in part, to the fact that he had been born at Manchester Royal Infirmary, had lived just a mile and a half away in Chorlton, had gone to school first at Oakwood High and then, after the accident, at Manchester Grammar. Three years at Manchester University and then straight into the GMP. It was all he had ever known. It was home.

As a child, some of his earliest memories were of trips to the art galleries and museums. The Christmas Grotto in Kendals, and pantomimes at the Opera House, the Palace and the Library Theatre. Matches on a man and boy ticket with his dad at Maine Road, and some of the biggest matches at Old Trafford when Lancashire were the kings of one-day cricket.

His life was inextricably linked to Manchester. He had seen the terraced streets and mean concrete crescents in Hulme demolished, to be replaced by the smart new flats, linked houses and apartments designed to attract a different social mix. In his first year at university he had skirted the embattled streets of Moss Side during the short but fiery riots, in which the police station on Greenheys Lane, close to his student hostel, had been laid to siege. He had been part of the 'MadChester' scene, frequenting the Hacienda at its height before the drug barons and the gangs behind the doormen formed the unholy alliance that led inexorably to its premature closure.

When the IRA bomb exploded in June 1996, he had helped to achieve the near miraculous evacuation of the city centre before being swept from his feet by the blast as it funnelled, a quarter of a mile from the epicentre, down the wind tunnel that was St Mary's Gate. He had seen the city rise like a phoenix and, through it all, what had struck him most was the resilience and humour of his fellow Mancunians. He smiled even now at the memory of the night right here on Potato Wharf, when the second Olympic bid had gone to Athens. The crowd around him bursting spontaneously into 'Always Look on the Bright Side of Life'! That spirit and optimism had been repaid with the Commonwealth Games. He had not been ashamed to shed a tear or two at the opening ceremony as he watched from the Operations Centre at the City of Manchester Stadium. For sixteen years his own life had been professionally fulfilling, but, by any stretch of the imagination, an emotional wilderness. Caton was convinced that it was this inexplicable feeling of warmth that folded around him like a pair of arms each time he returned from a trip away that kept him sane as he picked his way, day by day, through the dark underbelly of the city.

He turned into Jackson's Row. The freshly painted

sign of The Old Nag's Head beckoned halfway up the narrow street, rising gently before him. Caton had much preferred the original sign with its wicked caricature, somewhere between the witch in Hansel and Gretel and a hooked-nose crone straight out of Dickens. He understood why it sat uncomfortably in a city committed to equality, but the sad and aged horse's head which had replaced it could never inspire the same affection, or reflect the true history of Manchester's past, except perhaps to represent a phase of safe, and edgeless, conformity.

Halfway up the adjoining Bootle Street there would be a line of police vans outside the garage entrance to the nick, preparing for the invasion of clubbers, stags and hens who had survived the previous two nights and had the stamina for one more frantic round. Caton had not used the city centre incident room for some time, and had no problem with the handful of officers and civilian staff that frequented the Nag, the majority preferring the Abercrombie. He confined himself to the usual pleasantries, refusing to get drawn into routine gossip and the occasional vicarious probing of his latest case. He knew that many of them regarded him as standoffish, arrogant even, but he judged that infinitely preferable to getting drawn into the careless exchanges and boozy camaraderie.

'Hang on, Tom!'

Fifty metres away on the opposite side of the road, Nick hurried towards him. True to form, despite organising their meetings, Nick could be relied upon to be late.

Caton waited in the doorway below the sign. He could have sworn the horse gave him a knowing wink.

'Glad you could make it, mate,' Nick puffed as he

reached the pub. 'Never the same without you.'

Caton pushed the door open, and they stepped into the pub. It was like entering another world; like passing through the wardrobe into Narnia. Already it was heaving. Jean was busy serving one group of testosterone-charged males while fending off the advances of another. Tall, curvaceous, brunette and self-confident, with a winning smile; by general agreement, one of the most attractive barmaids in Manchester. She caught his eye and smiled, nodding towards the stairs. He waved in acknowledgement and hurried towards them, conscious that DS Watson had also spotted him and was about to stop harassing Jean and try to engage him in conversation. Taking the steps two at a time, Nick panting behind him, Caton finally emerged at the door of the function room to be greeted by a chorus of mock applause, and a pint of guest beer. He accepted the one graciously, and the other with real pleasure. He had forgotten just how thirsty he was for a good pint, and normal company.

Less than half a mile away, Albert Stephen cruised the city. He left the Mercedes in the only empty space outside Shimla Pink, the diners inside displayed like a cage full of tropical birds against the hypnotic backdrop of alternating pink and blue neon lights. He knew that in the past the narrow streets off Bridge Street had been a favourite haunt of his latest prey. He recalled the down-and-outs sprawled in the narrow alleyway between Bradley's Court and Wood Street, taking advantage of the steam and heat from the open kitchen door of the Olympus Café, and fighting over the scraps of food dumped outside for collection. But not tonight. The urgent drive to cleanse the streets of detritus, and those who lived off it, which had begun with the first Olympic bid and had climaxed with the

Commonwealth Games, had had a dramatic effect. With enough accommodation for every rough sleeper, no excuses were accepted, and the police and community support officers were consistent in their targeted approach.

He found the doorways at the rear of Kendals equally empty. The time when the fabled 'bag lady' had graced the front doors, let alone the rear, were long gone. He cut through Parsonage Gardens and down onto St Mary's Parsonage. A pair of ageing dipsos on a bench in the square on Motor Street took turns to swig from a bottle wrapped in a supermarket bag. Albert Stephen crossed into Wood Field, deactivated the alarm on his car and climbed in.

He took the mini map of the city centre from his glove compartment, spread it out on his lap and began to visualise the most likely points of displacement. The purge on the retail and cultural centre had, he knew, simply pushed the hardened cases out towards the fringes, concentrating them as much as dispersing them. There was a place, if he could just remember it.

The rap on the front nearside window took him by surprise. A small burst of adrenalin ran through his veins. A young man with shaven head and a gold tooth grinned inanely at him through the passenger window. Albert Stephen pulsed the electronic window switch.

The intruder had to turn his head a hundred and eighty degrees to speak through the two-centimetre gap.

'Are you leaving, pal, or arriving? 'Cos if you're done, we could do with your space. We're already ten minutes late, and I don't wanna lose the eff'ing table…'

Albert Stephen had never regarded himself as a 'pal' or a 'mate'. Nor did he take kindly to this mixture of assumption and aggression. He fixed the stranger with a chilling stare, somewhere between threat and contempt, and pressed the button again.

'Shit!' said the young man, the rest of his invective lost as the window closed.

Out of the corner of his eye Albert Stephen watched him in the wing mirror as he flung open the passenger door of the stationary Subaru, just beyond his offside wing. He watched as the driver began to back up towards Bridge Street, all three of his passengers straining forward to gesticulate.

Somehow the incident had sharpened his mind. He knew immediately where he would look next. His finger traced a direct route through the city, a matter of Store Street, hard by Piccadilly Station. He waited until the Subaru had disappeared, then started the engine and pulled away.

'Come on, Nicky, you must be joking!' Jerome was on a roll. 'Where in Sophie's world is there anything remotely resembling a middle-aged novelist who marries his sex-starved – and frankly very scary – landlady so that he can get his hands on her fourteen-year-old daughter?'

'Twelve year old!' Nick cut him off. 'And leave off with the Nicky, alright?'

'Fourteen year old.'

'Twelve year old!'

'Fourteen year old,' Jerome batted back. 'I thought you were the English teacher, Nicky?'

They glared at each other across the table as the other three steadied their glasses in anticipation of a sudden spillage.

'Come on, girls,' said Jamie. 'It's just a matter of perspective.'

They turned to look at him.

'Have you actually read the book, Jerome?' he asked. 'Or did you get a copy of the film from one of those dodgy sex shops in the Village?'

'How very dare you?' Jerome mimicked. 'I most certainly did not!'

'Funny, because that would have made sense.' Craig paused for effect, twirling the remains of his beer around in his glass. 'You see, they upped her age from twelve in the book to fourteen in the film, to try and win over the censors.'

'Well, I've never seen the bloody film. I wasn't even a twinkle in my mother's eye when it came out.'

Suddenly, Jerome had dropped the petulant pose and was deadly serious, hurt, believable even.

'You could have seen it on tele,' Jamie pressed. 'It was on about three months back, which was when I saw it.'

Craig sat back in triumph. Nick and Jamie nodded in agreement.

'Well, I didn't!' Jerome exploded.

'On the other hand,' Caton casually let drop into the circle of judgment, 'you could have looked for a summary of the book on the Internet when you saw Nick's question, and ended up with one of the film instead.'

Guilt flooded Jerome's face. He held up his hands in a dramatic pose of surrender.

'Got me, Officer, fair and square! Do take me to your little cell. I promise to ... come ... quietly.'

'You stupid prat,' said Nick warmly. 'Go on, it's your round.'

Caton heard the insistent ping, and eased the urgently vibrating mobile from the holder on his belt. He stood up and moved a short distance from the table, something the rest of them had got used to and to which they never took offence. It was Gordon Holmes.

'I'm sorry, boss, but there have been developments.

I think you might want to get down here.' There was a trace of barely contained excitement in his voice. 'You're not going to believe what we've got on the CCTV.'

Jerome was at the door, miming an invitation for another pint. Caton shook his head and looked at his watch. It was 10.30 p.m. Whatever it was, it had caused them to stay late.

'You'll have to send a car, Gordon,' he said. 'I'll walk up to Barton Street.'

'Thanks, boss. I'll see you shortly.' Holmes sounded relieved.

Caton thanked them for the evening, made his apologies and left. They had known better than to quiz him.

Downstairs the bar was now packed wall to wall, standing room only. He had to push his way carefully through the throng; it was too easy at this time of night to spark a confrontation. Jerome, busy insinuating himself into the middle of the queue at the bar, failed to acknowledge his parting wave.

Outside, the air was sharp and clean, heralding the coldest forecast winter for a decade. His breath formed a trail of steam as he crossed over the road and walked through the rubble-strewn car park at the side of the synagogue, turned left and set off up the hill past the colourful windows and noisy entrance to the Abercrombie. He wasn't going to give a patrol car the satisfaction of collecting him from outside a pub. The stereotypic detective's slow decline into oblivion. He vowed it would never come to that.

Chapter 5

The first thing Caton noticed was that the blinds in the empty office next to his were up, and the lights were on. He found DC Ben Willis pushing a display panel against the right-hand wall. Over his shoulder he glimpsed a group of photos from the Chinatown investigation.

'What's going on here, Ben? I thought this was earmarked for the MMAG Team.'

The Manchester Multi-Agency Gangs Team had had some sustained success, especially in targeting siblings of known gang members at risk of getting sucked in, by engaging them in diversionary activities. Longsight was a tough nut to crack – so was the whole of South Manchester, come to that – and Caton knew that the C Division commander wanted more joined-up working between the MMAG team on his patch and his regular beat teams.

Willis turned to face him, surprise and exhaustion etched on his face.

'Gordon blagged it for us, sir. Rang CS Hadfield and persuaded him to put some pressure on the divisional commander. Bit of a Barney by all accounts ... but here we are!'

It looks like Gordon's really on a roll, thought Caton.

'You look knackered, Ben. How long have you been

on duty?' he said.

Willis glanced instinctively at his watch.

'Since eight this morning, boss.' He recognised the look on Caton's face and grimaced wryly. 'Sorry, boss. We just got carried away.'

Caton adopted the tone of stern housemaster. 'Well, now you can carry yourself off, before your wife starts sticking pins into a doll with my face on it!'

He stepped back into the corridor and almost collided with his inspector.

'What's the hurry, Gordon?' he said. 'Nice piece of work here by the way; I've been trying to colonise that office ever since we moved in.'

Holmes grinned mischievously. 'Don't get carried away, boss, it's a temporary arrangement. Soon as we clear one or other of these two up, we've got to get out sharpish.'

'In the meantime,' said Caton, 'you've established a precedent, and possession is…'

'Nine tenths of the law.'

Holmes took him by the arm and steered him down the corridor towards the incident room.

'Seriously, though, we've made some real progress on this one … you're not going to believe it.'

'Try me,' said Caton.

There were still five members of the team working away at their desks, and a sixth standing at the projection console typing commands on the control panel. Caton nodded to DS Joanne Stuart and DS Nick Carter, both of whom had spotted him entering with Holmes. The others were too engrossed in their work to notice. He looked around the room, which had already been transformed from one dramatic scenario to the beginnings of another. One whiteboard already held an extensive duty roster. Another had what looked like a series of tasks, some of them struck through with notes beside them. A third had a burgeoning mind map with circles and squares, and as many question marks as connecting arrows. On a pinboard along the right-hand wall a number of photos were displayed. Caton recognised some from that morning's crime scene. The body crudely splayed at the foot of the cross; the gardens quartered; the gates and railings; long shots of the alleyway, St John Street, Byrom Street and Lower Byrom Street; close-ups of the victim's face, and of the panels on each face of the cross, as he'd requested.

Gordon Holmes motioned Caton to sit on the desk facing the angled projection screen, and took up a position between the screen and nearest of the whiteboards.

'Scene of Crime have done three sweeps of the area now, and just about exhausted the possibilities,' he began. 'To be honest, we weren't getting anything, and it was beginning to look like the perpetrator had been really careful. Then the tapes and DVDs came in. You wouldn't believe how many security cameras there are on St John Street. Those law practices must have a lot to hide.'

They all grinned at that.

'I started one team off on the traffic cameras on Deansgate, Quay Street and Liverpool Road, another team on the public order ones on the same streets and a third on the only camera we could find on Byrom Street.'

'What time did you ask them to start running their searches?' Caton asked.

'Given those streets are busy on a Sunday night, right through to 3 a.m.,' Holmes said, 'and quite a few of the Castlefield residents – and even some out as far as Ordsall – use both Byrom Streets as a shortcut, I thought we'd start at 2.30 a.m. Then we might catch him doing a reccy.' He paused for dramatic effect. 'And guess what?'

Caton was rarely given to guessing.

'Surprise me,' he said.

Holmes nodded to his co-conspirator at the control console, who Caton now recognised as Kerry Ann Stuart, a civilian audio-visual technician who had just been assigned to his team. Joanne Stuart and Nick Carter got up and joined their chief inspector, each perching beside him on opposite corners of the desk. They had obviously seen it all before, but it was equally obvious to Caton from the broad grins on Nick's face and the grim expression on Joanne's, that they believed it was worth seeing again, and again.

It had been, he recalled, a cold night and consequently free from cloud cover. The usual haze from light trapped downwards was absent from the remarkably sharp pictures that appeared on the screen.

'This is Byrom Street,' said Holmes. 'The camera was on a property on the bottom left-hand corner of St John Street.'

The street was empty, with the exception of two cars parked to the left of the park gates. The chronological time scrolled in hours and minutes in the bottom right-hand corner of the picture. It was 3.17 a.m. Two uniformed figures – one male, one female – appeared in the bottom right of the screen and crossed diagonally into Byrom Street.

'Tut-tut … jaywalking,' said Carter quietly.

'That's two of Met Division's community support officers,' said Holmes. 'We've contacted the beat office, and the beat sergeant's going to send them over as soon as they come on shift.'

Just past the entrance to St John's Passage, the two officers moved out of the camera's field of vision in the direction of Quay Street. Thirty seconds passed. Two young women, supporting a third evidently the worse for wear, appeared from the direction of Quay Street. Tottering on high heels, they staggered on and out of sight towards Liverpool Road.

'Look at the state of that,' Joanne Stuart bemoaned. 'Freezing temperatures, and not a coat between them. And they've just come out of a hot, sweaty club, drunk and probably dehydrated! God knows how they keep it up.'

'If they take a coat, odds on it'll get nicked. At least they've got the sense to stay together,' Nick Carter replied.

'Shush,' said Holmes, 'here comes our friend.'

A white van appeared, cruising slowly from the direction of Quay Street. It slowed as it approached St John Street, indicated left, then turned into the street and off up towards Deansgate.

It was a fairly standard Transit, Caton noted, three years old. Holmes read his mind.

'It's a Ford Transit 300 MWB High Roof,' he said.

A minute passed and the van appeared again, this time from the direction of Liverpool Street, continuing towards Quay Street.

'He's quartering the area,' Caton reflected out loud. 'Making sure he won't be disturbed.'

'Maybe he's had military or security training,' said DS Carter.

'Or he's just very careful,' added DS Stuart.

'I don't call dropping a dead body off in the town centre on a Sunday morning particularly careful,' Carter responded.

Holmes nodded to Kerry Ann and the film fast-forwarded until the van came into view for the third time. Caton noted that a minute of real time had been telescoped.

'This is it, boss,' Holmes said.

The camera picked up the van as it reached the bottom of St John Street and turned right into Byrom Street. It came to a halt in the middle of the road, outside the gates to the gardens, a full car length beyond the second of the parked cars. Slowly, the van turned ninety degrees until it was facing away from the gardens, then backed up towards them until it was about a metre and a half from the gates. The driver's door opened and someone jumped out, closing the door behind them.

Caton leant forward disbelievingly.

'Bloody hell!' he exclaimed. 'It's a clown!'

The others nodded, grinning inanely. Kerry Ann Stuart pressed the shift key and the picture zoomed in to capture someone in a traditional clown suit. A white ovate face had huge woollen outgrowths on either side like earmuffs, a large round nose, high arching eyebrows, dark shadows painted beneath the eyes, and a wide and wicked grin for a mouth, exaggerated by a pair of grotesquely protruding rabbit's teeth. A long check coat with wide cuffs, secured with two large buttons, topped a pair of baggy trousers with matching turn-ups. On the feet were a pair of oversized floppy shoes, at the neck a massive bow tie and on the hands, incongruously, what looked like white gloves.

Caton watched as the figure walked confidently to the rear of the van. A man's walk, even in those floppy shoes. Between one metre seventy-four and one metre seventy-seven, about five foot eight or thereabouts in old money – it would be easy to calculate against the known height of the van. Medium build, Caton thought; allowing for the clothes, probably around seventy kilograms, or eleven stone. They watched intently.

The clown opened the rear doors and disappeared from view. He re-emerged carrying a large circular bundle, which he carried to the park gates. He appeared to attach a part of the bundle to the top of the gates and then pushed the rest over into the garden. It immediately unravelled into what was clearly a ramp.

'It's called a Ramp 2 Roll, and it's for wheelchairs and scooters,' Joanne Stuart informed him. 'I found it on the Web.'

As though to prove the point, the clown climbed into the van and emerged seconds later with the front end of a second ramp, which he attached to the first where it sat on the top of the gates. They watched as he climbed back into the van and emerged with a wheelchair, which he proceeded to push along the first of the ramps towards the gates. In the chair was what appeared to be a mummy, wrapped in layers of bandage, legs sticking out horizontally, arms straight down on either side of the chair. There was a moment when the chair appeared to catch at the point where the two ramps met, and then it was free and moving down into the gardens, the clown leaning back and straining to prevent it slipping away. As soon as it came to rest on the path the clown walked back up the ramp, jumped down onto the pavement, released each ramp in turn, rolled them up, placed them inside the van and closed the doors. Then he climbed back into the van, started the engine and backed into a parking space just beyond the gates, facing north towards Quay Street.

Caton looked at the elapsed time on the screen. It had all taken less than two minutes.

Nick Carter broke the stunned silence. 'Now this is really interesting, sir.'

As the driver opened the van door, two men – the

shorter of the two supported by the other – appeared at the bottom of St John Street and began to turn left, until one spotted the clown jumping from the van. He grabbed his colleague's arm, pointed, turned and steered him towards the gardens. The clown was rounding the side of the van when he became aware of them approaching him. He turned to face them at precisely the moment that the least steady of the two appeared to spot the wheelchair. For a split second the clown seemed to freeze. Then he threw his arms out sideways, performed a series of sidekicks, a skip and a dance, and finished with a flourish, one foot and one hand in front of the other.

'He's not very good, is he?' said DS Carter.

'He's got a bloody nerve,' retorted DS Stuart.

The more sober of the two men began what looked like a mock applause, but the other pointed persistently at the figure in the wheelchair. The clown turned and raised both arms, miming surprise and shock. Then he pointed down the gardens towards the statue, pretended on tiptoe to push the wheelchair towards it, stopped and put one finger to his lips. It's a secret!

'He's been watching too much bloody Batman,' muttered Holmes. 'Some Joker!'

How could they fall for this? Carter wondered incredulously.

The taller man appeared to put his finger to his lips and nodded conspiratorially. Then he pulled his companion's arm over his own shoulder and, taking some of his weight, turned and began to head back towards Camp Street.

Holmes shook his head.

'It's a Sunday night, you've had a few bevies; if you weren't of a naturally suspicious frame of mind would you really believe that someone dressed as a clown would be depositing a body, dressed as a mummy, in broad moonlight, in a city centre garden? It has to be a stunt. Or the end of a stag night. It's pure bloody genius.'

'It's pure evil,' Joanne Carter added softly.

'That too,' Carter agreed.

The clown watched them go. He turned to check the street behind him was clear, and then used both hands to clumsily vault the gate into the gardens. He grasped the handles of the wheelchair and began to push it down the path towards the cross. After less than three paces he was out of sight. Carter began to motion the technician to fast forward, but Caton put his hand on his arm.

'No, let it run,' he said.

They watched in silence as the minutes passed. A solitary car – a Skoda Octavia – came into shot from the direction of Liverpool Street, drove past the van and disappeared towards Quay Street.

Holmes broke the tension. 'He took his time.'

'He had all those bandages to unwind. That can't have been easy,' Caton mused.

Three minutes had passed when the clown appeared again, pushing the wheelchair. They could see the bandages piled up on the seat. He stopped just short of the gate, collapsed the wheelchair and lifted it over the gate, placing it carefully to one side. Then he vaulted clumsily over the gate, retrieved the wheelchair, opened the rear van doors and placed the wheelchair inside. Without bothering to check the street behind him, he climbed into the driver's seat and pulled the door to. The van remained stationary.

'He's not in any hurry, is he?' Carter remarked.

'Cop this, boss,' said Holmes.

The van pulled out from the kerb, made a U-turn – its front wheels crossing the opposite pavement – and cruised slowly towards Camp Street. As it drew level with St John Street it slowed, and the driver looked directly up towards the camera and smiled.

Carter stated the obvious. 'The bastard knew the camera was there all the time! He's taunting us.'

'More like a performance,' said Caton thoughtfully.

The van picked up speed and disappeared from sight. Caton noted that just nine minutes forty-five seconds had elapsed from the time they had begun watching. Holmes nodded to Kerry Ann, and the screen went blank.

'Did you pick up the van on the city centre cameras?' Caton asked.

Holmes moved over to a display board on which was pinned a large-scale map showing a five-mile radius from the city centre.

'We did better than that,' he said. 'We picked him up here, on Deansgate.' He pointed to the map where a route had been marked in red felt-tip. 'He must have come out of Camp Street and turned right. Then he made a left into Whitworth Street West, and right into Medlock Street. We tracked him all the way down Princess Road as far as Mauldeth Road, where he turned left. Then he made a right into Palatine Road, and a left down Wilmslow Road. We lost him somewhere between the Christie Hospital and Fog Lane. Wherever he went after that, it was off the radar as far as traffic cameras are concerned. Harry…' He nodded towards a young DC transfixed to a computer screen in the corner of the room. '…is going through everything we've got on Kingsway, Stockport Road and Heaton Moor. It's not as bad as it sounds, because we have a pretty small window to search in. Nothing so far, but we think we know why that is.'

Turning to Joanne Stuart, he invited her to pick up the story. She got up off the desk and joined him at the display board.

'The first thing we did was check the licence plate. The vehicle is registered to a John Barrett, at 79 Clifford Street, Burnage, M19.' She pointed to a red circle on the map. 'Just here, about half a mile from where we lost track of the van. Nick ran a PNC on him and he came back clean … just a couple of parking tickets, not even a speeding offence, and let's face it, that's as good as a miracle in this city!'

Carter nodded sagely.

'What else do we know about him?' Caton asked.

'He's 48 years old, a plumber, married, with no children. He bought the van from new four years ago. His mortgage has ten years to run. He's got a good credit rating, and less than average debt. His wife is a school meals assistant at Burnage High. She's as clean as a whistle.'

Caton shook his head slowly. 'It doesn't sound right, does it? He goes to all this trouble to disguise himself and then calmly drives home, his licence plate there for all to see, knowing full well we've got cameras all over the city.' He turned to Holmes. 'Where is he now?'

'The van's in the drive, and we're pretty sure he's in the house. I sent an unmarked car down as soon as we got the address … about an hour ago. The lights were on in the downstairs lounge and a man and a woman appeared to be watching tele.' He looked at his chief inspector. 'We've got to pick him up, whatever. We don't have an option, do we, boss?'

Caton knew he was right. 'What else have we got?' he asked.

Nick Carter pointed to a set of photographs displayed around a blown-up map of St John's Gardens, each of them attached by a coloured thread to a spot on the map.

'Not a lot, boss,' he said. 'There's a small piece of cloth that was snagged on a railing on top of the main gates, probably consistent with the bandages we saw on the body, and some fag ends and a tissue retrieved from the fingertip search of the area outside the gates, right by where we know he parked the van. On the other hand, we would probably have noticed if he'd emptied his ashtray out of the window. And would he be that stupid?'

'Stupid, is what solves most murder cases in the end,' Caton reminded him.

Unabashed, Carter continued. 'The rest looks like the kind of litter you'd expect to find in the gardens, but we won't know till forensics have given it all a good going over.'

'What about footprints?' Caton asked.

'Well, with it being a hard surface, any that might have been evident in the frost had melted away. SOCOs have got a few, but they're most likely to belong to the park keeper. Small prints, like a woman's, and we already know he was wearing those floppy clown's shoes.'

Caton clasped his hands behind his head, an unconscious habit which told the others he was going into summary mode.

'So,' he began, 'we've got an unidentified victim, a clown, a piece of cloth, a suspect vehicle complete with partial route, the registered keeper and a complete registration number.'

Nobody answered; it was a statement, not a question. He turned to Holmes.

'We're still watching?'

'Yes, boss,' Gordon replied.

'Okay. Then we keep a night watch. Nobody makes a move unless he leaves during the night, in which case they simply report in and follow him. Find out who the duty magistrate is, Gordon, and get a search warrant. We've just about got due cause. Then the three of you can make a morning call. No forcible entry, unless there's a big delay in coming to the door.'

He turned to Joanne Stuart.

'I want you to talk with the wife while Nick leads the search team. And let's get the van straight to the lab. And make sure it's a full lift to preserve any evidence on the tyres and underside.'

Joanne Stuart made a hasty note in her pocketbook as Caton turned back to his DI.

'Gordon, I want you to bring him in, and we'll conduct the interview together.'

He paused for a moment, running a mental checklist. He realised he hadn't seen a newspaper or watched the news all day.

'What was the press reaction?' he asked.

'Good job it's Sunday; we're waiting for the early morning papers off the presses,' Holmes replied. 'There was a mention on GMR, and on the 10 o'clock regional news on Granada. Both of them followed the press release – an unidentified male ... no obvious signs of injury ... the police are treating it as suspicious at this stage. Nothing on the BBC – they're probably waiting for the post mortem results.'

'How long will it be before those two blokes put two and two together?' Carter chipped in. 'We'll have the press swarming around like flies as soon as that happens.'

'When they do, I want Chester House press office dealing with them,' Caton said. 'I don't want this team fronting anything until we've something to go on. Let's keep it as low-key as possible for as long as possible.'

He turned to Gordon Holmes.

'As soon as you've got the warrant, I want you to

go home. The rest of you, all of you, go home now. We've got an early start and I've a feeling this one is going to run and run.' He paused and looked at each of them in turn. 'And well done,' he said. 'You've made a good start.'

He waited until he was sure that they had logged off the computers and were preparing to leave, then rang the transport pool for a car. As he waited, his head buzzed with possibilities. The only thing he was certain of, was that there was no way this was going to stay low-key beyond lunchtime tomorrow. He knew it, the team knew it and so did the perpetrator. He had a premonition that somehow that was what all this was about.

Showtime … with the clown as the ringmaster.

Chapter 6

Albert Stephen turned left out of Boad Street, into Store Street, and pulled up a few metres further on. Just enough to avoid the attention of any of the many minions of the law that recent policy had spawned, and far enough from the soup kitchen under the railway bridge ahead of him to avoid suspicion. He switched off the engine and the lights, eased himself down in his seat and waited.

It was a longer wait than he had anticipated. In the halo of light from the hatch of the mobile catering van he could see the huddle of figures shuffling forward to receive a cup of steaming soup. Occasionally, a tram swung past the entry before disappearing into the bowels of Piccadilly Station; the interior lights throwing the homeless in their uniform army greatcoats into sharp relief, like a glimpse of a far-off gulag.

In ones and twos, they began to leave in the direction of London Road. Albert Stephen began to wonder if he had miscalculated. With the engine off for so long, he was beginning to feel the cold.

When it seemed as though his luck had run out, one of the three remaining vagrants turned away from the van and began to head in his direction. This one was smaller than the rest, and as he passed momentarily beneath the arc of a street lamp it was apparent that his head, unlike those of his fellow travellers, was shaven close, and in place of the usual matted beard there was stubble on his chin. Albert Stephen checked in his mirrors that the street behind him was empty, opened his door quietly and slipped out.

Head down, disconsolately swinging a plastic bag, the man was almost level with the bonnet of the car when he became aware of someone standing directly in his path. He flinched and adopted the defensive cower of one who had been here before; the frequent victim of mindless bullies.

Albert Stephen raised his hands slowly, with his palms facing outwards. He spoke softly, reassuringly.

'My friend, it is a cold night. I wondered if you would like a warm bed, a hot meal, a drink and a little company?'

The down-and-out – for in Albert Stephen's eyes he was precisely that – unwound to his normal height, still a good nine inches shorter than his predator, his watery eyes full of suspicion.

'Don't worry, it is neither a mugging nor a pick-up,' said Albert Stephen. 'I've been where you are. I came into some good fortune, and now I'm rattling around in a large empty house. You would be doing me a favour … and none asked in return.'

'How long for?' The voice was rough and wheezing, the breath sharp and rancid.

Albert Stephen flinched involuntarily, and then composed himself.

'One night, a day or two … it's up to you,' he replied.

Capitalising on the spark of interest, he opened the front passenger door and invited the man to get in, which, after a moment's hesitation, he did.

As he rounded the bonnet, Albert Stephen casually scanned the street in both directions. Inside the car he found the man squirming uncomfortably on the plastic-covered seat, trying unsuccessfully to fasten his seat belt. In this confined space the combination of stale sweat, alcohol and urine was almost overpowering. Loath as Albert Stephen was to reach across and help him finish the task, he did not want to risk being flagged down. As soon as the belt was secure he started the engine, turned the air conditioning up full and set off.

The route he chose was necessarily circuitous. He judged the likelihood of anyone assuming that his victim had been picked up so close to his last known sighting to be limited, but then again, the police would have to start somewhere.

'You can't be too careful,' muttered the vagrant.

Albert Stephen glanced across at him, wondering if his thoughts were being read. Head down, the man was fiddling with the plastic bag dangling between his legs.

'We're always gettin' offers,' he continued. 'Those posh bitches are the worst. Coming down 'ere for a bit of rough between business meetings.' He chuckled inanely. 'I'd give 'em rough!'

'Businesswomen?'

Encouraged, the man warmed to his theme.

'With their snotty accents, high heels an' bloody power suits. I'll give you a tenner for a funnylinctus. What they take us for, povvies?' He chuckled again.

'This has happened to you then?'

'Not me ... I'm too quick for 'em. I see 'em coming. But lots of the others ... happens all the time.' He grinned at Albert Stephen, his teeth yellowed and broken.

Another urban myth, or one more example of the double standards Albert Stephen had come to hate, and to which he had finally fallen victim? It was not relevant.

'What is your name?' he asked. It would make it easier to retain this creature's confidence until it was no longer needed.

'On the street they call me Whistler ... but you can call me Barry.'

'Do you whistle a lot?'

'I can't whistle at all!' Barry's chuckle morphed into a frenzy of convulsive coughing.

Albert Stephen turned the radio on and concentrated on the road ahead, threading his way through the side streets and cutting neatly across the arterial routes at points where he knew there to be no cameras.

Albert Stephen arrived home. It had taken fifteen minutes to complete what should have been a five-minute journey. But for a string of parked cars, the street was deserted as he swung the Mercedes into the curving drive and stopped behind the high yew hedge.

He watched his victim devouring his doorstep cheese and chutney sandwich, and slurping his mug of whisky-laced Lapsang Souchong. Given that the liquid GHB he had added to the mug was both colourless and odourless, there had been no need for the smoky-flavoured tea. But Albert Stephen was a creature of habit.

The alcohol, he knew, would accelerate and deepen the effect of the drug. Sure enough, within fifteen minutes Barry was beginning to show signs of intoxication. Complaining of nausea, he attempted to push himself up from the table, but only succeeded in slipping forward, knocking the mug to the floor, where it smashed on the dull red quarry tiles.

Albert Stephen stepped behind him, grasped the

shoulders of his greatcoat and hauled him to his feet. Half carrying and half dragging his victim, he hauled him to the cellar door beneath the stairs, kicked the door open and manoeuvred him down into the bowels of the basement.

By now, Barry was comatose. Albert Stephen stripped him of his clothes and dragged him up onto the plastic-sheeted metal bed frame. Ensuring that the head was propped up higher than the chest, he fastened a series of leather straps across the width of the bed, pinioning his victim.

He stepped back and appraised the situation. The man – there was no longer any need to acknowledge his name – was snoring deeply, but there was still a risk that he might be sick. A premature death from choking would undermine his plans. There was, he knew from the literature and from experience, an outside chance that his captive might have a seizure, or even respiratory failure. Tonight at least, he would keep close watch.

He bundled up the clothes, rammed them into a black plastic bin liner, tied it tightly and threw it in a corner. He took a can from a shelf on the back wall and sprayed his victim from head to foot. Then he retraced his steps to the kitchen, where he tidied up meticulously, rinsing the plate three times before putting it in the dishwasher, and switching it on. Having switched off the lights in downstairs rooms, he made a final check on the rough sleeper, locked the cellar door and climbed the stairs to the shower room on the second floor, where he stripped off and scrubbed himself with soap and a loofa until his skin was livid.

Fifteen minutes later, dry and dressed in a white cotton dressing gown, he retreated to his study on the first floor.

This room was where he spent his nights, and many of his waking hours. In one corner was a beech wood futon with a stone-coloured mattress, on which he snatched the occasional nap. He rarely slept, and always with the light on. From an early age he had cultivated the ability to survive without sleep, until his mother had finally caught on and thrown her husband out of the house. Now he managed on a daily ration of four or five twenty-minute naps which he could take at will. The blind over the only window was permanently down. A series of bookcases and a large filing cabinet dominated one wall. Along the main wall a long broad beech-veneer desk held a computer with flat-screen monitor, a printer and a digital cordless phone nestling in its cradle. Above and to the right of the desk flickered a bank of three CCTV monitor screens.

Albert Stephen sat on the high-backed office chair and glided close to the desk. He checked the monitors one by one.

The first showed his Mercedes parked by the front door, and an empty street beyond his high yew hedge. On the second he caught a sudden movement across the middle of the garden. In the moonlight, an urban fox – a regular visitor – slunk head down across the lawn. With its ragged brush and sorry manner, it reminded Albert Stephen of the man in the cellar as he had made his way towards his nemesis on Store Street. The final monitor captured the man he now knew as Barry prostrate on his bed. Albert Stephen pushed the slide on a small black volume control box beside the computer mouse.

The sound of the man's breathing filled the room, heavy and irregular, occasionally erupting into a full-blooded snore. Albert Stephen brought the volume down to background level, flicked the monitor screen on and entered a password into the computer keyboard.

His fingers moved rapidly and effortlessly across the keyboard. Within seconds the computer monitor was filled with a bank of smaller screens, each capturing the random movement of vehicles and the occasional pedestrian or cyclist on one of the city's streets.

He typed in an alphanumeric code and a new bank of screens appeared. Selecting a screen in the top right-hand corner of the monitor, he used the mouse to zoom in. Satisfied at last, Albert Stephen relaxed into his chair, watched and waited.

Caton checked his watch as he entered the incident room. It was only 6.30 a.m. and already a hive of activity. Gordon Holmes spotted him and hurried over.

'Morning, boss,' he said. 'It was a quiet night, and they're pretty sure he's still in there.'

Caton held up his hand. 'Hang on,' he said. 'Let's go into my office, it's bedlam in here.'

Once inside the office, he closed the door, motioned his inspector to take one of the chairs arranged around the low coffee table and drew up another for himself.

'That's better,' he said. 'Now, where are we up to?'

'Like I said,' Holmes began, 'he hasn't left the house. The tele went off at 11.45 p.m. and the two of them got up and left the room. Five minutes later the lights went off in the downstairs room and the hall, and then the lights came on in the front bedroom and a room on the side, which looks like the bathroom. Both those lights were off at 12.36.'

'And the van hasn't moved?'

'No, and nobody's been near it.'

'Did you manage to get a search warrant?'

Holmes grinned. 'It was a bit touch and go. The affidavit was thin, and she wanted to know why we couldn't try a "consent to search" first. When I pointed out this was a real nutter, the case was likely to go high profile and we couldn't risk evidence going AWOL in the first days of the investigation, she relented. She's limited the search, though.'

'What have we got exactly?' Caton asked.

Holmes took the warrant from his inside jacket pocket and handed it to Caton. He recounted the contents as his chief inspector read them, a habit that never failed to irritate Caton.

'Search the premises at Clifford Street, Burnage, on Monday, 21 November 2005. Search and seize a van specified in the affidavit for this warrant, and its contents, and any materials and clothing reasonably suspected as pertaining to the events recorded on CCTV number 1f77769 on the morning of Sunday, 20 November 2005.'

Caton sensed Gordon preening himself.

'She doesn't exactly believe in carte blanche, does she, boss? Limited the search, and hasn't even given us the normal twenty-eight days,' Holmes added.

'I wasn't aware you spoke French, Gordon,' Caton said, looking up. 'This will do for now.' He tapped the document on the table. 'The important thing is that it gets us in there; anything we find after that is fair game.'

'I've got a team standing by,' Holmes told him. 'Are you sure you don't want to come?'

'I'd rather stay here and get up to speed with the rest of the investigation. In any case, it would be best if he was confronted with a new face in the interview room.'

Holmes nodded. 'The papers are on your desk...' he said pointedly. 'You might want to have a look.'

Caton got up and walked over to his desk. Splayed out across them in a fan were the Manchester Evening News, The Guardian and The Independent. The Manchester Evening News had a front-page picture taken with a zoom lens from Lower Byrom Street, looking up the gardens to the east. It showed a small group of scene of crime officers and technicians in their Tyvek suits clustered around the screen that covered the base of the cross. Several were on their hands and knees, one kneeling and the remainder standing. This strange scene, partly shrouded in mist, reminded Caton of a number of exhumations he'd been party to. Too many, he reflected wryly, and still only a month shy of his thirty-eighth birthday.

The headline was predictably dramatic: 'Police Puzzle over Body Dumped in St John's Gardens'.

The text was a rehash of the statement issued the day before, with one important exception.

The body, which we understand to be of an unnamed white male, appears to have been dumped overnight at the foot of the cross commemorating St John's Church which formerly stood on this spot, and the flagged graveyard which used to surround it. Police are reported to be unclear as to how the body got into the gardens, since the gates remained locked until they were opened by the park keeper at 6 a.m. The park keeper found the body and immediately contacted the police…

Caton quickly checked the other two papers. The Guardian had a shorter version on page two; The Independent had only the original statement.

'How the hell did they find out it had been dumped there?' he asked.

'Probably the park keeper,' said Holmes. 'Then again, any one of the uniforms from Division could have picked it up and let it slip. It was only a matter of time. If nothing else, it means those two guys who saw the clown are going to put two and two together and get in touch.'

Caton knew he was right. 'So long as they get in touch with us first, rather than the papers. What about the news broadcasts? Do they have any more than this?'

'It doesn't look like it. Arthur Bewick wants to do an interview on GMR Today with the investigating officer. We referred him to Chester House, like you asked.'

'Good. He's sharp enough to cut himself, but he won't get much joy out of that lot,' said Caton. 'The trouble is, there's enough in this story already to get all of them sniffing round us. I didn't see anyone on the way in, but you'd better send someone out to check before the team set off. The last thing we need is a press cavalcade turning up in Burnage.'

He sat on the edge of the desk and looked at his watch.

'Have we a time for the post mortem yet?'

'Later this morning I think, but they promised to confirm the time asap. Are you going to attend, boss?'

Caton thought about it for a moment.

'It depends on what comes out of the interview. Let me catch up, and we can decide later. Are you ready to go?'

Holmes nodded. 'I'll send Robbie out to make sure the coast is clear, and then we'll get going.'

They pulled up behind the unmarked Volvo estate. Holmes kept the engine running while Carter got out to check. He spoke briefly to the officer in the driver's seat and then slipped back into the Mondeo.

'Looks like there's still just the two of them. The lights went on fifty minutes ago. There are only the downstairs lights on now and they've had plenty of time to have their breakfast. There was bit of a flurry in the hall just before we arrived, so they might be planning to set out for work.'

'What about the rear of the house?' Joanne Stuart asked.

'It backs onto the school grounds. There's a six-foot-high fence, and the school has its own fence just inside the perimeter to stop balls and such going over into the gardens. There's a gate in the Barretts' fence with a Chubb lock. Probably so she doesn't have to go all the way round to get to work.'

'So she could already have left?' said Holmes.

'They reckon not. The other team has been parked up opposite the school drive with a clear sight of the back of these houses. But there's only one way to find out for sure.'

'Okay,' said Holmes, 'let's do it.'

He started the engine and pulled out past the observation car, stopping forty metres ahead on the opposite side of the road. The following convoy of a marked car and a black van pulled in behind him.

Holmes led the procession towards the path of what looked like a former council house. It was neat and well kept, with new double glazing and a faux cobbled drive in coloured concrete. The net curtains moved in the downstairs front room and the pale face of a woman briefly appeared, no doubt alerted by the successive slamming of the car doors.

They heard her anxiously calling out inside the house, her tone fearful.

'John! John!'

'The double glazing's not much cop then,' said Carter.

Holmes accelerated towards the front door, which opened just as he reached it. He thrust his warrant card in front of the startled face of a man in his mid forties, of medium height and slim build, wearing a set of blue overalls under a three-quarter-length anorak.

'Mr John Barrett?'

The man looked in amazement, first at the warrant and then at Holmes.

'Yes,' he stumbled on the words, 'I'm John Barrett, but I don't understand…'

'John Barrett, I am Detective Inspector Gordon Holmes. I have a warrant to search these premises. May I come in?'

'I thought he was supposed to give him a chance to consent to a search?' whispered Joanne Stuart.

'Not much point with this lot charging up the drive. As if he'd think he had a choice!' Carter replied.

As though to prove the point, Holmes had already pushed past John Barrett, leaving Nick Carter to take him gently by the elbow and guide him back into his own hallway.

Framed in the doorway of the kitchen at the end of the hall stood Mary Barrett, her hand to her face, her mouth wide open.

Holmes turned back towards her husband, who had begun to compose himself.

'Look, Inspector,' Barrett began, 'I've no idea what this is all about. Whatever it is, it's a mistake.'

Holmes cut him off. 'Mr Barrett, we have reason to believe that your van has been involved in an extremely serious incident.'

Behind him, Mary Barrett began to scream hysterically.

'What have you done?! John, what have you done?! No, no, no, John … what have you done?!'

Holmes waved Joanne Stuart past them. She was just in time to catch Mary Barrett as she crumpled.

'Take her in the kitchen, Sergeant, and calm her down,' said Holmes.

He turned and placed a large hand in the centre of John Barrett's chest as he strained to reach his wife. With his other hand he took over from Nick Carter, grasping Barrett's right arm and guiding him into the front room.

Over his shoulder, he shouted, 'The warrant, Nick … follow the warrant. Neat, tidy and thorough!'

Chapter 7

Caton was in his office clearing a backlog of emails when he was told that they were on their way in.

He had got up to speed with the investigation and could not fault the energy with which the enquiries were proceeding, or the direction. Gordon, Nick and Joanne made a good team, he reflected, probably the best he'd worked with since he joined the murder squad. All of them relatively young and still enthusiastic, but with a lot of experience under their belts. More importantly, they were a team. No inflated egos, unbridled ambition or maverick instincts getting in the way. Unique, in his experience. Not like detectives at all. And certainly nothing like Chester House. One of the reasons, he reminded himself, why he had continued to resist the constant pressure to go for promotion. He realised that he really enjoyed his work more than he had in a long time.

His one concern was that the Chinatown investigation – officially Operation Panda – was on the back-burner. But then it had virtually been a cold case when it was handed over to the Specialist Detection Group, and he knew that the next step would have to be a trip to Shanghai. Something he could not put off much longer.

He heard Holmes coming down the corridor and rose to meet him. He hated holding conversations while having to looking up at his colleagues, whatever the rank. They had taught, back on the initial training course at Bruche, what he had already instinctively known: looking down on someone during a conversation or interview automatically placed you in a position of authority; power, if you liked. It even worked over the phone. He could now tell if someone was standing up by the degree of assertiveness their voice carried. But that was only part of the reason Caton liked to get out of his chair. He had a counter interpretation, which was that making them stand was a lot like playing head teacher. What's more, it was a damn sight easier to read body language at eye level.

There was a sharp rap on the door, and before he could answer it had swung open and Holmes was inside.

'Come in, Gordon!' Caton said.

The irony was lost on Holmes, who launched straight into his report.

'They're both downstairs, boss, in the custody suite. We kept them apart and brought them in separately. He's in number one interview room and she's in number three. She's in a right state. I thought at one point we'd have to sedate her. Stuart's with her, and I suggest she and Carter get her statement on the record as soon as he's finished up at the house.'

Stuart and Carter all of a sudden, Caton noticed, not Joanne and Nick. Where's that come from? he wondered. Misreading the look on Caton's face, Holmes rushed ahead.

'I cautioned him, but he doesn't want a solicitor. All he's worried about is his wife, and frankly I don't blame him. In fact, when we arrived on the doorstep she went hysterical, and I got the distinct impression she wasn't the least bit surprised he'd been up to something.'

Caton thought about it for a moment. 'Get him the duty solicitor. We can't risk any appeals on procedural grounds. I want it done absolutely by the book.'

'What about the wife?' Holmes asked. 'We can't really use the same solicitor with both of them.'

'I don't see why not,' Caton replied. 'It's not as if it'll be their own solicitor. As long as we don't allow the solicitor to have a private chat with each of them in between the interviews there shouldn't be a problem. Get the wife a drink, and get a female officer to sit with her, just to calm her down and keep an eye on her. No discussion of the case, no bland reassurances, just a holding brief. Then let's find out what he's got to say for himself.'

The duty solicitor turned out to be Jaswinder Singh, experienced and worldly wise. A staunch defender of his clients' rights, but nobody's fool. Caton thought he'd have made a good detective and been a credit to the force. Probably would have made a greater contribution to the common good into the bargain, but he knew he'd never have convinced him of that.

John Barrett looked up nervously as Caton and Holmes entered the room.

Caton said nothing for a moment, taking it all in. Barrett had dark hair, already receding from the temples, with a few flecks of grey and the beginnings of a widow's peak. His eyes were brown, not unlike Tom's own, but his nose was shorter and flatter. His mouth was wide above a broad chin, and there were beads of sweat across his forehead. He was breathing nervously through his mouth, exposing crooked teeth, stained yellow at the tips and brown where they crowded into the gums. He was dressed in a blue boiler suit, as though ready for work. It was difficult to tell with him seated, but Caton estimated Barrett as between one metre seventy-two and one metre seventy-five tall, medium build, somewhere between sixty-nine and seventy kilograms. Well within the parameters for the clown.

As the silence continued, Barrett became agitated. He looked first at Caton and then at Gordon Holmes.

'I don't understand,' he said. 'I don't know why you asked us to come here. And I keep asking to see my wife. Why can't I see her?' He turned towards the solicitor, appealing for his support. 'She isn't well. Why can't I see her?'

Jaswinder Singh nodded reassuringly and leaned forward. 'Mr Barrett and Mrs Barrett volunteered to accompany the officers. I understand they have not been charged, and that they cooperated fully with the search of their premises, which Mr Barrett assures me they would have consented to, had they been asked.'

Caton glanced at Gordon Holmes, who gave a little shrug and continued to stare at Barrett.

The solicitor continued. 'Mr Barrett has continually requested to see his wife, and to know why they have been asked to assist you with your enquiries. That seems to me to be a wholly reasonable request, Chief Inspector.'

Caton addressed his response to John Barrett.

'Mr Barrett, I am Detective Chief Inspector Tom Caton; this is Detective Inspector Gordon Holmes, whom you have already met. We are investigating an extremely serious incident, and when we get to the details I am sure you will understand why we have asked you here to help us, and why it was necessary for us to search your premises. But before we begin, you say your wife is ill?'

A little of the tension began to leach from Barrett's face.

'Well, when I say she's ill, she's not ill as such …

but she has real problems with her nerves, and she's prone to panic attacks.' He looked at Gordon Holmes. 'You saw her at the house.' He turned back to Caton. 'She's been under the doctor. I'm really worried about her in here. Anything could happen.'

'Go and check on Mrs Barrett please, Inspector,' Caton said to Holmes. 'If you are in any doubt at all about her condition, arrange for the duty doctor to have a look at her. Give her that option in any case.'

As Gordon made for the door, Caton turned back to Barrett.

'I'm afraid that I can't let you speak to your wife,' he said. 'Not until we've had the opportunity to speak to each of you. You could be in the position of providing an alibi for each other, and I'm sure you wouldn't want to prejudice that in any way.'

Jaswinder Singh smiled wryly as Barrett tried to work it out. Caton carried on.

'And if, as you claim, you are innocent of any wrongdoing, then neither you nor your wife has anything to fear. The sooner we manage to get these interviews over, the sooner you'll both be back home again.'

It took only a couple of minutes for Gordon Holmes to establish that Mary Barrett had calmed down. A cup of tea, and the sympathetic if neutral ear of the WPC, had had a dramatic effect. There was no question of her needing the doctor, and Holmes reported as much. Barrett was sufficiently reassured and eager to get the interview over with. Caton switched on the tape.

'Mr Barrett. I understand that Inspector Holmes cautioned you during the search of your house. I am going to repeat that caution for the sake of the tape, and to be sure that you understand. You do not have to say anything, but it may harm your defence if you do not mention, when questioned, something which you later rely on in court. Anything you do say may be given in evidence. Do you understand?'

'Yes,' said Barrett. 'But I haven't done anything … I don't understand why you've brought us here.'

'We asked you here to help us in our enquiries into an incident which took place in the early hours of Sunday morning.' Caton paused, looking for a reaction. He could sense Barrett's mind racing, trying to remember where he was. 'Between 2 a.m. and 4 a.m. to be precise.'

Barrett's eyes flicked down to the right.

Holmes took up the questioning.

'Can you tell us where you were at that time on Sunday morning, Mr Barrett?'

The eyes flicked up to the right. A smile crept across his face.

'That's easy. We watched tele until about 11.30 p.m., then we went to bed. I did a small job for a neighbour on Sunday morning, and Mary and I went shopping that afternoon at the Trafford Centre. Bought a load of Christmas presents. We had dinner, watched a bit of TV and went to bed about 10 p.m. To be honest we were both knackered and went straight to sleep. That's why I was so pissed off when the phone rang.'

Holmes leaned closer. 'When the phone rang?'

'There's a group of us take it in turns to be on call for emergencies at weekends. It was my turn. An elderly couple, on the border with Tameside, had a burst in the loft.' He shook his head despairingly. 'No lagging on the pipes, or the tank.'

'When was this exactly?'

'1.45 a.m. I know because Mary woke up really mardy. "What time is it?" she said. So I told her. Quarter to two! She said, "Well, you can sleep in the spare room when you come back. I don't want you going waking me up at some ungodly hour when you come in".' He turned to Caton. 'It was a right mess when I got there. They didn't know where the stopcock was till I helped them find it over the phone. Their bedroom and bathroom were flooded and the ceiling was bowing in the kitchen. I was just in time to stop the whole lot coming down. I emptied the system, thawed out the pipes and replaced a whole section. Then I helped clear up ... well, make it liveable at least. It was gone three when I got home.'

'Can you be a little more precise, Mr Barrett?' asked Holmes.

He thought about it for a moment. 'Well ... it was about five to three when I left the house. I know because I looked at my watch and checked it again in the van, on the dashboard clock. It took about twenty minutes to get home, so that would have been about quarter past. I just dumped my clothes on the landing and went straight to bed.'

'And did you sleep in the spare room?' said Caton.

'Yes. It took me a while to get to sleep, though ... head buzzing and all that. Mary brought me a cup of tea up about eight the next morning.'

'What route did you take to get home, Mr Barrett?' asked Holmes.

'The same one I took going. Mauldeth Road, onto Heaton Moor Road, Green Lane, Bowerfield, Belmont Road to the roundabout with Lancashire Hill, then onto the M60. Came off at the next junction ... 25. Then I went up Ashton Road and turned right into ... what's it called? Err... Two Trees Road ... no, Two Trees Lane. That takes you down into Haughton Green. Moondale Road's on the right near the T-junction. I just did that in reverse.'

Caton and Holmes looked at each other. They both

knew this would be easy to check out. There were cameras on at least three of the sections, including the motorway, and at a quiet time of the morning with very little on the road.

Gordon Holmes continued the questioning.

'Do you have the name of the occupiers and the address with you, Mr Barrett?'

'Mr and Mrs Tyldesley. 14 Moondale Road, Haughton Green. You don't forget when you've been called out at that time of the morning, I can tell you!'

Barrett was beginning to relax, reassured to be telling a story in which he was clearly confident.

'Actually, I've got their number in my mobile.' He began to unzip the breast pocket of his overall. 'I always get their number in case I get lost.'

He retrieved the number from the phone's memory and read it out as Holmes copied it down.

'How long have you had your van, Mr Barrett?' Caton asked.

'I got it from new just over four years ago ... from Manchester Central, just off Ashton New Road.'

He searched the faces of the officers, hoping they might explain the reason for these questions. When none was forthcoming, he ploughed on, desperate to get back to what he saw as the key issue – his alibi.

'So you'll check with the Wallaces and we can go?'

'It's not quite that simple, Mr Barrett,' Caton replied. 'We will check what you've told us, and we'll still need to speak with your wife. But I can promise you, we'll do that as quickly as possible. In the meantime I'll arrange for you to have another drink. If you could just bear with us a little longer?'

John Barrett looked at his solicitor, who nodded his agreement.

'Alright, as long as I can see my wife as soon as you've finished speaking with her.'

Barrett was becoming quietly assertive.

Caton matched his tone, reminding him who was in control.

'I can't promise that, it all depends on what she has to say and whether we need to check it with you. But I repeat, we'll get you both out of here as soon as we're satisfied.'

He looked at the clock above the tape machine.

'This interview was suspended at 9.27 a.m. precisely.'

Reaching across Gordon Holmes, he pressed the stop button.

'Thank you, Mr Barrett. The officer will get you both a drink, and we'll be back shortly.'

He rose and left the room, closely followed by Gordon Holmes.

'What do you think?' he said.

'He's obviously telling the truth,' said Holmes. 'You couldn't make up a story like that and hope to get away with it. And his whole manner, his body language, says innocent. And I'm the first to wish it didn't.'

'I agree. So let's eliminate him as quickly as possible. Take Joanne in with you and check his story out with his wife. Find out if she heard him come in. I'll ring the Tyldesleys, and then find out what Nick's got from the search.'

The Tyldesleys were home, and not only confirmed the story, but wanted to tell Caton what a brilliant plumber John Barrett was. How polite, efficient, hard working, uncomplaining he was. How he had helped them clear up and made sure they were comfortable before he left.

It took him nearly a minute to convince them that he wasn't the man's employer and to explain that someone would come to take a statement, and to extricate himself from the conversation without appearing rude.

He instructed DC Wood to get hold of the tapes for Stockport Road and that stretch of the M60 at the time in question, reasoning that if both of those came up trumps, there was no way the van could also have been in St John's Gardens at the time registered on the tapes they had already viewed.

Wood had been busy tracking down the supplier of 'Ramp and Roll', and didn't hide his irritation at being pulled away for a pretty routine task. Caton heard him delegate the job to the team collator, and was just about to pull him up when Nick Carter burst into the room.

'Boss … a word,' he whispered, like a conspirator.

Caton led the way to his office.

'The house and the garage are clean,' Carter began. 'And the van has racks fixed to the inside walls, stuffed full of tools and lengths of piping. Most of them have been welded on, and from the state of the welds it looks like they've been there ever since he bought the van. So there's no chance he could have added them in the past twenty-four hours. We brought the van in anyway, in case you want SOCO to have a good look at it.'

'That's it then,' said Caton. 'His alibi stacks up, and if his van turns out to be where he said it was, then we let them both go, and he can have his van back. Do me a favour, Nick, chase up DC Woods. He's been tracing the Ramp 2 Roll suppliers and distributors, and I happen to know he's just palmed off my instruction to get some traffic tapes on to Duggie, who has better things to do with his time.'

Carter grinned knowingly. 'Leave it to me, boss.'

Mary Barrett's story matched her husband's version more or less exactly. Except that hers was punctuated with sobs, and sips of water.

'I heard him come in and I looked at the clock. I always do. It was 3.17. I was glad he'd gone in the spare room because he's taken to a snoring like a steam train. It was a relief to have a few hours undisturbed, especially after being woken up like that. So I turned over and went back to sleep.'

Joanne Stuart consulted her notebook.

'Mrs Barrett, when we came to your house, why did you call out, "*What have you done?! John, what have you done?! No, no, no, John … what have you done?!*"'

Mary Barrett looked decidedly sheepish.

'I always seem to expect the worst. I just can't help it. It really gets to John. Sometimes I think it's the only reason he'd ever leave me.'

DS Stuart pressed her. 'But what exactly were you thinking he might have done, Mrs Barrett?'

'Well, I thought he must have been involved in an accident, even though he's never had one in thirty years of driving, never even a speeding ticket.'

They let them both go, and since a close inspection of the van in the workshop confirmed Nick Carter's impression, they let him take that too. Caton thanked them with genuine expressions of gratitude for 'finding the time' to help them with their enquiries. The massive relief for the Barretts, of being together and of no longer being suspects, was enough for them to accept this with good grace, even to feel that they had made a real contribution.

'I doubt they'll feel that way when they get back and see the state the house is in,' Joanne Stuart said ruefully as she watched them go.

Caton's core team were gathered in his office. The

four of them sat around the small table he used for these brainstorming sessions that political correctness required they now call 'thought showers'.

'I don't think any of us really believed it was going to be as easy as that,' he said.

Holmes, Carter and Stuart nodded in unison.

'The trouble is, it confirms what we suspected as soon as we saw the perpetrator grin up at the CCTV camera on St John Street. He's playing with us. And he's clearly cloned John Barrett's licence plates. And not only has he chosen an identical van, but Barrett even matches the height and size he must have known we'd pick up from the camera. If it hadn't been for the emergency call-out, Barrett would still be downstairs sweating, and we'd be wasting valuable time trying to work out why we couldn't see the racks in the van on the video footage.'

'He's gone to a lot of trouble, sir. But he must have known we'd eliminate Barrett eventually?' Joanne Stuart observed.

'I'm sure he did, Joanne, he's just enjoying putting us through it. Either that or he wants to gain a little time. Either way, what does it suggest?' He looked around the table, inviting comment.

'He's a nutter!' said Gordon Holmes.

'I think that goes without saying,' said Caton. 'But what kind of nutter, exactly?'

They thought about that for a moment. Joanne Stuart was the first to respond.

'A severe personality disorder?'

'And given the way he dumped the body, one with sociopathic tendencies,' added Carter.

'And pretty delusional, if he thinks he can get away with playing these kinds of games,' Holmes joined in, anxious to make up for his earlier response.

'Exactly,' said Caton. 'And what does that suggest?'

They spent longer thinking about that one. But all three of them came to the same conclusion; Nick Carter got there just a fraction ahead of the others.

'He's likely to do it again!'

'We could be dealing with a serial killer,' Holmes added thoughtfully.

'So what does that mean for us?' Caton pushed on.

'We'd better get a quick result. The press and Chester House will be down on us like a ton of bricks, running interference, generally getting in the way,' said Carter.

'And more people could die,' DS Stuart reminded them.

'And we might just need some more support, specialist support,' Caton suggested.

They looked at him and at each other, none of them wanting to second-guess him.

'Like what, boss?' asked Gordon Holmes.

'I think we'd better alert the regional office of the National Crime Squad.'

'Isn't it a bit soon for that, boss?' asked Carter.

'Well, strictly speaking, if we've gone forty-eight hours without a clear suspect, we're supposed to do that as matter of course. And, in the event that we do have a potential multiple murderer on our hands, we are going to need a forensic profiler, and NCS will source one for us.'

'But we don't know for a fact that we do, do we, sir?'

'No, Joanne, we don't. But I have a feeling the post mortem will firm that up for us, one way or another. In any case, the whole clown thing, the performance and the taunting … a profiler has got to be part of our approach. And whilst as a team we've had some multiple killers before, we haven't had a serial killer. Come to that, FMIT hasn't had one for the past four years.'

He paused and looked at Gordon Holmes.

'I've just had a thought. Have we requested a search for this particular MO in the National Crime Intelligence Service HOLMES database? There can't be too many MOs involving clowns, ramps, public dumping and displaying.'

'I don't know, boss, but if we haven't, I'll get Duggie to do it. To be honest, I'll be surprised if he hasn't done it as a matter of course.'

Caton reached across to the flipchart behind him and picked up one of the marker pens.

'Okay, let's just run through the most urgent next steps.' He lobbed the pen to Nick Carter. 'Nick, you can capture this for us.'

Nick got up and stood beside the flipchart.

'Find out who copied those licence plates, and who sold him the Ramp 2 Roll. There can't be many of those in circulation; I've never seen one before,' offered Holmes.

'And where did he get the clown outfit from?' asked Joanne Stuart.

'And where the hell is the van?' Nick Carter added as he raced to get it all down. 'And have forensics come up with anything new?'

'And who exactly is our victim?' said Caton, at which they all nodded sagely. 'And what more will we find out from the post mortem?' he added finally. He pushed back his chair. 'And that's where I'm going to start. Joanne, it's a while since you've been to a PM, I want you to join me. The rest of you can decide if we've missed anything out, raise actions for each of those bullet points and then agree with the allocator who is going to chase what. And make sure they go in the incident room manual. I've had complaints about people forgetting.' He looked at his watch. 'Let's meet back here at 1 p.m. Working lunch.'

He closed the door firmly behind him. This was going to be a real test for the team, and for him. One half of him was beginning to relish it, the other repelled at the thought of where it might lead.

Chapter 8

'Why don't I drive, sir?' DS Stuart asked as they left the building.

'That's fine by me, Sergeant,' Caton replied, maintaining the formality as two officers stood aside to let them out.

But then Joanne Stuart always addressed him as sir. Was it a gender thing, was she naturally polite, conscious of rank, or was it a defence mechanism of some kind? Was she maintaining a distance between them? Unlikely to be that, he decided, with her sexual orientation; something she had always been open about from the moment she joined the force.

It must have been hell at training school, and probably not a picnic on some of those early postings, especially given that she was such a strikingly attractive woman. Not that she ever referred to any problems, and never a hint of sexual harassment or sexual orientation complaints on her files. She was a very strong, independent and confident person. Good at her job, and brimming with emotional intelligence. Just what the top brass valued most these days. Caton was certain she had a bright future in store.

She opened the front passenger door, conscious that his long legs would never fit in the back.

'I'm sorry about the mess, sir. I haven't had a chance to clean up.'

The car was spotless, just an empty supermarket bag on the parcel shelf and a pair of spare shoes behind the driving seat.

'I wish mine was half as clean as this,' he said, adjusting the seat and pushing it back as far as it would go. 'You know where we're going, Jo?'

She nodded and started the engine.

'I know where it is, but it's the first time I've been to this particular building. It's a brand new extension, isn't it?'

'The Home Office finally came up with funding. The PCT was never going to on its own. You can't blame them. The hospital morgues are kept pretty busy with the flow of their own patients, "accidentals" and sudden deaths. This way, suspect cases and criminal investigations get the priority they need, and there's a purpose-built facility for training and research on behalf of all of the North-West Primary Care Trusts. More like an operating theatre than a morgue.'

The lights were on green at the junction on Stockport Road. She turned right into tree-lined Plymouth Grove and headed towards the University Precinct and the hospital complex.

'I wonder why they are called operating theatres?' she said.

'Have you ever been along the South Bank when you go down to London with Abbie?'

'It's our favourite Saturday morning jaunt whenever we're down there.' She smiled at the recollection. 'We usually start at St Catherine's Dock, cross over and wander through Butler's Wharf. Have a coffee at Gabriel's Wharf, browse and shop at Hays Galleria, and lunch at Borough Market snacking off the stalls. Then there's the Globe, the Tate Modern…'

Caton laughed. 'Alright, you've convinced me,' he

said. 'But have you ever been to the Old Operating Theatre?'

She kept her eyes on the lights as they approached the junction with Upper Brook Street, and shook her head.

'It's right opposite Guys Hospital, just before you get to the Clink. It used to be the Herb Garrett and Operating Theatre for St Thomas's Hospital – originally a delivery room for poor and unmarried mothers in Southwark. There's a plaque on the wall. It says "Miseratione non Mercede", which loosely translates as "From Compassion not for Gain".'

They pulled up at the lights as they changed to red, and he paused to check that she was still listening. She glanced across at him.

'Go on, sir.'

'Well, it's the oldest remaining operating theatre in Britain … only as a museum, mind. Climb up the stairs and you come out in a room clad in broad panels of seasoned deal and pine. You're standing at the top of four tiered rows of semi-circular wooden terraces, each divided from the next by a chest-high wooden rail supported by black cast-iron poles. A bit like the concrete terraces at the old football stadiums. Except that instead of looking down on a pitch, you're looking down on an original deal operating table. At the foot of the table is a blood box – a sand tray one of the assistants moved around to catch the blood. On the wall behind it there's a blackboard. Overhead, a wrought-iron chandelier supports two gas lamp holders, and extra light comes directly onto the table through a skylight in the roof. White aprons, like those that butchers wear, hang from pegs by the door through which the surgeons and the patients came. There's a small table with a porcelain washing bowl. Only they used to wash their hands after the operation, not before it. And there was no anaesthetic of any kind.'

DS Stuart visibly blanched.

'Christ!' she said, turning to look at him. 'There must have been a hell of a mortality rate. It certainly puts MRSA into perspective.'

An impatient hoot from the car behind reminded her that the lights had changed. She released the hand brake and made a quick left onto the A46.

'The point is,' Caton said, 'this was where the doctors and the surgeons learned their trade. Every time there was an operation, the students would rush across to the operating theatre and fight their way to the top of the stairs, pushing and jostling to get as near to the front as possible. They had to employ men to keep order, and eject anyone getting over-boisterous or fainting.'

'So, as well as the unendurable pain, these poor girls had to put up with the indignity of a bull ring?' Joanne Stuart was visibly upset.

'I'm afraid so, Jo, though I guess that was the least of their worries. But the point is, this was a theatre, and the surgeon was performing, hence…'

'Operating theatre!' She grinned ruefully. 'Well, thanks for the history lesson, sir, but frankly, I'm sorry I asked.'

The reserved places outside the mortuary were taken and they hunted in vain for a car park space, settling for a pay and display three minutes' walk away. Security was tighter than she remembered it being in the old building, and despite their warrant cards, and the fact that they were both expected, it took another two minutes before they were finally ushered into the viewing gallery.

A chunky, distinguished-looking man in his mid fifties smiled briefly at Caton as they took their seats behind the glass window, but let his gaze linger on DS Stuart. Her well-proportioned figure, rich brown hair, bright hazel eyes and full confident lips had this effect on men regardless of their age. She was well aware that she was being scrutinised and avoided his eyes, focusing instead on the surroundings.

The room was brightly lit, and spacious, with far more equipment than she had expected. Apart from the stainless-steel post mortem table on which the body lay, there was a portable trolley on which it must have been wheeled in, and a mobile trolley on which a number of instruments were laid out. All of the other units were fixed to the floor. There were two work units within a few metres of the post mortem table, and others sited along three sides of the room, some of them with wall-mounted cupboards above them.

She thought she could make out at least three refrigerators, and a vertical freezer. The pale-blue floor covering continued halfway up the wall, and part of the way up all of the fixed units. The ceiling was honeycombed with what looked like air conditioning vents, between which ran specialist lighting tracks. Security alarm detectors blinked intermittent red in each corner of the room, and high-spec digital video recorder cameras monitored the proceedings from three different positions above the post mortem table. The proceedings were displayed in real time on a whiteboard on the wall opposite the viewing gallery. All in all, it reminded her of a cross between a science lab, an operating theatre and the hard-chip manufacturing lab she had visited as part of their previous investigation.

The post mortem was well under way, and Caton had difficulty in identifying the people in the room.

All four were wearing personal biological protection suits with clear plastic face shields. Not the full spacesuit model, which would have been too clumsy for the occasionally delicate work involved, but good as a barrier against the three contaminations most feared by surgeons and pathologists – AIDS, tuberculosis and Hepatitis C.

The person hovering a couple of metres back from the table holding an SLR digital camera was almost certainly the photographer, who seemed to assist most of the post mortems Caton had attended. He didn't remember his name. The tallest of the four, standing well back from the table, he recognised as Benedict, the technician. Eager to take his turn at the table, like a greyhound in the stocks, Benedict had always struck him as highly competent whilst emanating that solitary and intense morbid fascination which seemed to characterise all mortuary technicians.

A woman with her back to them was carefully placing a specimen jar beside a dozen or so others on one of the tables. The pathologist was bent over the body, peeling the skin, muscle and soft tissues away from the chest wall with a scalpel. That finished, he pulled the chest flap up over the face, exposing the front of the rib cage and the muscles across the neck. He stepped back and nodded to the technician, who came forward clutching the electric saw and began to open up the rib cage.

As the pathologist turned towards the gallery, Cayton recognised him. Sir James Flatman, one of the most highly respected Home Office pathologists, who had performed post mortems on a number of cases he'd worked on.

'Welcome, Chief Inspector,' Flatman said. 'Better late than never. Have you met Dr Hope, my assisting pathologist?'

The woman turned back from the work table and nodded up at them. It was almost impossible to get an impression of what she looked like behind the shield, but he could just make out a pair of serious brown eyes.

'Benedict and Zahoor I'm sure you've already met. If he hasn't already introduced himself, the bored-looking gentleman to your right is visiting Professor Michael O'Brien from the University of Melbourne, who is over here to see how it's done.'

Caton glanced at O'Brien, who grinned his approval of this introduction.

'He's taken the Hippocratic oath,' Flatman said, 'and he's performed enough post mortems to know that whatever he hears or sees in this room stays in it … except, no doubt, for my mistakes.'

They all laughed at that.

The images on the whiteboard captured Benedict cutting either side of the chest plate before beginning to detach it, with a scalpel, from the tissues sticking to its underside. Professor Flatman watched for a moment and then moved a little closer towards the viewing gallery.

'Who's that you've got with you, Chief Inspector?'

'This is Detective Sergeant Joanne Stuart, Sir James. She has been to a number of post mortems before, but none of yours, and this is her first time in this theatre.'

'Then you're in for a treat, Miss Stuart. This is a state-of-the-art theatre, and I'm a state-of-the-art pathologist!' Flatman smiled broadly behind his face shield, oozing the charm and arrogance to which Caton had become accustomed.

'Take this table for example.' He gestured towards the post mortem table. 'Fully adjustable to raise and lower not only the whole body, but also the head or chest, to make it easier to carry out our work. An integrated down-draft system to minimise the smell, and more importantly, to reduce the spray effect from fluids released from the body. Do you know where the word post mortem comes from?' He didn't wait for a reply, and waved imperiously at the overhead cameras. 'It's from the Greek autopsia, "to see with one's own eyes". But now we have these DVR cameras which make it possible for us to zoom in at will, to keep a perfect voice record, to carry out all sorts of search functions, to download you the videos electronically and email still pictures instantly. It wouldn't surprise me if Zahood was looking for a new job soon!'

Caton looked for a reaction from the photographer, but saw none. He had probably heard this thoughtless remark a few times since the theatre opened, but it must still hurt. The professor changed tack.

'But I suppose you want to hear what we've found so far? The external examination gave us very little beyond what you already know. His body weight is low, but consistent with someone with a serious illness. There's no evidence of malnutrition. No significant scars, only a few historical ones such as the falls and cuts you'd expect to see in a man of his age. And there are no major cuts or blunt instrument wounds or burns anywhere on the body. The X-rays show no indication of recent bone injuries, but some evidence of early onset osteoporosis. His hands and fingers suggest a white collar rather than a manual worker; oh, and he's probably been playing some kind of stringed instrument recently – possibly a guitar – judging from the calluses on his fingers and the shorter length of the nails on his left hand. Nothing unusual about the deposits under his fingernails or toenails. His hair is his own, and not dyed. It's in poor condition, and the growth pattern has all the hallmarks of heavy drug use – particularly consistent with chemotherapy, Jean?'

He paused and looked across to Jean Hope, who was now seated at a work table looking down a microscope. She looked up and nodded her agreement.

'And probably radiotherapy too, and quite recent at that.'

As she returned to her task, Flatman continued his narrative.

'If the fingerprints turn up a blank, his teeth give you your best chance of identification. He's had a lot of work done over the years.'

He paused for a moment to check Benedict's progress, and then continued.

'The blood pooling confirms that he was moved post mortem, at least eight hours after his death. From the ambient temperature records your chaps sent me, his body mass and fat distribution, and the degree of rigor mortis when we began to examine him, I'd say Dr Tompkins got it about right. Somewhere between 2 p.m. and 5 p.m. on Sunday afternoon. Impossible to be more precise than that because we don't know what temperature he was stored in before he was deposited in the open. He wasn't in the open long enough for insect activity to provide us with any clues, especially in those low temperatures, and – although it remains to be seen – I doubt that his stomach contents will narrow that window any further.'

He paused again and shifted his position for a better view of the post mortem table. The saw had been replaced by what looked like an enormous bread knife, which Benedict was using to slice through some of the more inaccessible tissues adhering to the chest plate. Michael O'Brien spotted DS Stuart's rapt attention.

'The large gross sectioning knife,' he explained helpfully. 'Those long grooves you can see on either side of the blade create an air gap to prevent vacuums occurring in the tissues which would otherwise cause the knife to stick. Great for steaks from the barbie, even better for smoked ham!'

Joanne Stuart was still trying to shake off the nightmare vision of the women in the Old Operating Theatre, and O'Brien's commentary was less welcome than he could possibly imagine. Down on the theatre floor, Flatman continued his report.

'The lesions Dr Tompkins noted are definitely Kaposi's Sarcoma, and quite an extensive spread. There are lesions in the mouth and upper parts of the larynx, and I fully expect to find it has spread to the lymph nodes and some of the organs. Having said which, there is evidence that he's had a line inserted in the recent past, which suggests that he's been receiving chemotherapy as well as the radiotherapy indicated by his hair condition. If it is HIV/AIDS related – and we won't know until we've seen the blood results – then he'll have been having anti-retroviral treatment, which would also have been delaying the spread. But this is speculation, and Professor O'Brien will tell you there's no place for that in a post mortem examination.'

Caton leaned forward and spoke into the microphone dangling down from the roof of the gallery.

'So the bruising and puncture wound on the left arm was where a line had been inserted?'

Flatman shook his head and responded with all the feigned tolerance of an indulgent parent.

'I'm afraid not, Chief Inspector. The sites where lines had been inserted – and there were three of them altogether – were barely visible to the naked eye. Between a fortnight and three months old, I'd say. Expertly done.' He chuckled to himself. 'Probably an oncology nurse, well practised and much more careful than your average consultant. The bruise, on the other hand, was caused by a clumsy and much more recent puncture wound.'

He paused for effect.

'Certainly no more than an hour, and probably minutes, before death occurred. And before you ask me the obvious, yes, it could have been the vehicle for the cause of death, but we won't know that until we've finished the post mortem and received the toxicology results. But I will say that the blue tinge around the lips and on the fingernails does tend to suggest some kind of poisoning.'

He noted the police officers' surprise, and added cheekily, 'Oh, didn't I mention that earlier? Must have been before you arrived.'

Before either of them could respond, he turned back to the post mortem table, where Benedict had removed the chest plate revealing the heart and lungs. Taking a scalpel from the table, Flatman cut open the pericardial sac and the pulmonary artery at the point where it exited the heart. On the screen they could see him insert his finger into the pulmonary artery, seeking evidence of a blood clot as a possible and frequent cause of death. Satisfied, he turned his attention to the point where the abdomen met the rib cage. Swiftly dissecting the muscle from the rib cage and the diaphragm, he flipped the two sections of the abdominal wall to the left and right respectively, exposing the abdominal organs. He placed the scalpel down on a separate tray and stepped back to be replaced by Jean Hope. The assisting pathologist found, and tied off, the carotid and subclavian arteries, tucking the long ties into the neck and chest cavity before severing each artery in turn.

Joanne Stuart turned to Professor O'Brien.

'Why do they use such long ties?'

He smiled. 'So that the embalmer will be able to find them easily when it's time to inject the embalming fluids.'

Jean Hope was now cutting above the larynx prior to pulling the larynx and the trachea downwards and free from the neck. She stopped abruptly.

'Sir James, there's something here.'

Flatman walked around the table, stood opposite her and bent forward to peer into the entrance to the trachea. After a moment he stepped back and selected a pair of long tweezers from the instrument table. Turning back to the table, he waved the photographer forward.

'Zahoor, I'd like you to get some shots of this please.'

The photographer stepped nearer and began to focus his camera as Flatman moved closer to the head to give him a better view. On the screen, the video zoomed in. It was obvious that somewhere outside of the room there was a remote operator following every move. Jean Hope held both trachea and oesophagus steady as the pathologist inserted the tweezers.

'There is a foreign body lying horizontally across the head of the oesophagus, approximately two centimetres from the point where it would have met the larynx,' he said for the sake of the video record.

Very carefully he began to retract the tweezers until the object appeared. As Zahoor took his first set of photographs, the video camera focused sharply. To their amazement, they realised that they were looking at the unmistakeable shape of a horse. A small, yet perfectly formed horse.

'Bloody hell,' whispered Michael O'Brien.

'We appear to a have a model of a horse,' the pathologist said smoothly. 'A white horse, constructed from a hard material.'

He waited until the photographer had finished, held the horse up and turned slowly for the sake of the camera, and then took it across to one of the workbenches where he laid it on a microscope slide. First rinsing his hands, clad in two pairs of surgical gloves, at the nearest sink, he dried them before returning to the slide. Moving the object around from time to time with the tweezers, he made fine adjustments to the microscope. After a minute or so he carefully placed the object in a plastic self-seal bag and put it alongside the line of exhibits awaiting the attention of the Forensic Science Services. Finally, he stepped back and turned to address the cameras above the table.

'The horse is constructed of a smooth polymer-based material. It has no significant markings. It is twenty-eight millimetres from head to tail, ten millimetres high and five millimetres wide – from shoulder to shoulder.'

He moved back towards the post mortem table and nodded to his assistant.

'Thank you, Jean, you can remove the organ block now.'

Jean Hope, assisted by Benedict, began the process of freeing the abdominal organs prior to lifting out the entire set of organs in a single block. Sir James moved closer to the viewing gallery.

'You'll have some questions for me, Chief Inspector?'

'Is there any possibility he might have choked on this object, Sir James?'

'No. It was lodged in his oesophagus, not his trachea,' came the swift reply.

Caton considered that for a moment. Joanne Stuart seized the opportunity.

'Is there any possibility it could have been coated

with a poison?' she asked.

The pathologist was struck by the novelty of the question.

'Ah … like a Trojan horse! What a fiendish idea, Detective Sergeant. I think that highly unlikely, and there are easier ways of dispensing a toxic substance. However, we'll have to await toxicology analysis to rule it out completely.' He looked up at Caton. 'Chief Inspector?'

Is this becoming one of Flatman's 'Twenty Questions' sessions? Caton wondered. Why the hell doesn't he just tell us what he's waiting to hear? Then it struck him.

'Sir James,' he said, 'was the object actually lodged in the pipe … stuck, as it were?'

Flatman grinned broadly.

'Now that's a really interesting question. As it happens, it wasn't. Not nearly big enough. And that of course leads to the question, why hadn't it moved further down into the stomach?'

He left the question hanging in the air, enjoying his own performance.

'We might have expected normal involuntary spasms of the muscles around the oesophagus to have sent it inexorably on its downward path. Alternatively, the normal human reaction in such a case, given that there was no way of reaching it manually, would have been to wash it down with a glass of water and hope for the best. Unless…' He paused dramatically, inviting them to respond.

'He was already dead!' the two police officers declared simultaneously, as much to each other as to the pathologist.

'Bravo!' said Flatman in the manner of a lecturer whose students have finally grasped the obvious. 'Now,' he said, turning his attention to the organ block, which had been laid across the separate dissection arm, suspended above the table, 'let's see if there are any more little surprises in store.'

Twenty minutes later the organ block had yielded nothing of significance. The brain had been found to have moderately advanced lymphoma, which Flatman thought consistent with the traces of radiography, and the likelihood of HIV/AIDS. Probably the most useful observation he had made was that given the degree and sites of the tumours, they may well have presented as tiredness, memory loss and loss of coordination and balance. Their victim could have been walking awkwardly, stumbling, having trouble keeping his balance. That at least was something to go on.

They walked to the car in silence.

Chapter 9

Caton's head was spinning. The right side of his brain was working overtime on the possible meaning of the object in the poor man's gullet. The left side struggled to bring order to chaos, itemising the next steps to be taken as soon as they reached the office. He closed his notebook and looked across at DS Stuart, her eyes fixed firmly on the road ahead.

'It gets *me* like that sometimes,' he said. 'I'm not sure I'll ever get used to it. I'm not even sure I want to.'

Joanne Stuart gripped the wheel tighter and gave the appearance of nodding in agreement. For once, he had got it wrong. During the post mortem her thoughts had kept slipping back to the cockpit in that garret room, and the procession of young women brought there to strain on that simple wooden table to bring a new life into the world, and with luck survive the process. Joanne was comfortable with her sexuality and took solace in the fact that she and Abbie planned to adopt, probably from abroad, when they both were ready. They had talked interminably about the alternatives, such as fostering, IVF by donor, even supplying their own eggs to a surrogate mother. In the end, adoption was the only one for them. They would make great parents, she was certain of that. But she knew that there would always be a void that nothing could fill.

She eased off the accelerator, conscious that she was well over the speed limit and that Caton was still looking at her, this time with concern. He was a good man, more emotionally intelligent than many women she knew, but she didn't know him well enough to share these thoughts. Not yet. She forced a smile.

'I've been meaning to ask you, sir, are you doing anything over lunchtime on the 9th of December? It's a Friday.'

Caton's curiosity was aroused. 'I shouldn't think so. I'd have to check. And you know anything could happen, especially if we don't get this one sorted. What did you have in mind?'

Her face lit up and a slight flush came to her cheeks as she smiled and half turned towards him, eyes still on the road.

'Abbie and I are signing our civil partnership at the Town Hall, and I … we would love you to be there.'

He was surprised and touched. Surprised because she had never mentioned it before, although as soon as the law had been changed he had expected that they would want to solemnise … regularise – neither of those seemed right – to celebrate their relationship, and publicly commit to one another in the eyes of the law. He was touched, because he knew how important this day would be to her, and he'd assumed she would have wanted to keep it to her family and friends.

'I'd be delighted to come, Jo,' he said. 'It would be a real privilege. But are you sure you want the plod ruining your special day?'

She laughed brightly. 'I'm asking Nick and Gordon, too, although I'll be surprised if Gordon actually turns up.'

Caton realised that they were actually becoming a family. Working closely together in stressful, emotional and sometimes dangerous situations, they came to rely on each other in ways that people outside of the forces and emergency services seldom did. He just hadn't realised that Joanne Stuart felt it that strongly. He was glad of it.

'I'll be surprised if he doesn't find a sudden excuse to cover his embarrassment,' Caton said. 'But you never know with Gordon. There's a heart beating somewhere under that big chest of his; he's softer than we think.'

Holmes pulled in as near to Gerry's Motor Supplies as he could get. It was always a nightmare on this stretch of the Rochdale Road, but he managed to squeeze into the space between a delivery van and the zigzags of the zebra crossing. As he locked the car, he checked his bumper wasn't over the line. The wardens were mustard and it wouldn't matter that he was police. He could still come out and find it whisked off to the pound at 'Fort' Collyhurst, just a mile or so down the road.

As Holmes entered the shop, Gerry Nelson was handing a package and some notes to a young man in his late teens dressed in trainers, black jeans, a black flight jacket and a two-tone black and grey baseball cap.

They both looked up at the intruder, and Holmes spotted the furtive look that passed between them. Even in plain clothes he knew he gave off the unmistakeable musk of a police officer, which was why he'd never attempted to go undercover. He stepped back to let the young man, head down, shuffle past to exit the shop. He turned his attention to Nelson. A short, scruffy bull of a man, who wouldn't have been out of place in a pub rugby league team, standing with both hands gripping the counter in front of him. Just a little too firmly, Holmes thought.

He flashed his warrant card. Gerry Nelson's pupils contracted and his knuckles whitened.

'What can I do for you, Officer?' He exuded a combination of arrogance and anxiety.

'Mr Nelson is it?'

'As it 'appens, yes, it is.'

Holmes placed a piece of paper on the counter.

'Well then, you shouldn't have any difficulty confirming whether this registration number was one for which you were asked to provide copies.'

It was a statement, not a question. Nelson held the inspector's gaze, not bothering so much as to glance at the number in front of him.

'I suggest you 'ave a word with Mr Lounds.'

'Mr Lounds?'

'Detective Inspector Lounds. Everybody knows Mr Lounds.' The corners of his lips lengthened into a sneer.

Holmes refused to be drawn. 'So Mr Lounds would know if you had been approached with reference to these registration plates, would he?'

The sneer broadened into a grin. 'Search me.'

Holmes reached under his jacket, pulled out his mobile phone and began to dial a number.

'Fair enough. That's precisely what we will do.'

Gerry Nelson, shocked out of his comfort zone, pushed himself back from the counter.

'You can't do that. You've gotta speak to Lounds first!'

Holmes entered the final digits and put the phone to his ear.

'*Mr* Lounds to you. And I can do anything I like. This is a murder enquiry, so whatever you and Detective Inspector Lounds happen to have in common, I think you'll find this takes precedence.'

He half turned away and began to speak into the phone

'Frank? I need a search warrant, fast as you can...'

He was interrupted by Nelson, both hands raised as if in surrender.

'Alright, alright, there's no need for that. I didn't know it was a sodding murder, for Christ's sake. You should've said.'

Holmes turned and looked at him for a moment, then pretended to continue his conversation.

'Put a hold on that, Frank. It looks as though we won't be needing it after all, but I'll get back to you either way.'

He pressed the exit button, cut off his imaginary colleague, flipped the phone shut and slipped it back inside his jacket.

'Well now, Mr Nelson, that wasn't too difficult, was it?'

He pointed to the piece of paper on the counter between them and raised his eyebrows expectantly. Gerry Nelson reluctantly picked it up and stared at it briefly.

'I don't recognise this one,' he said. 'Two thousand and two reg. Stockport. I'll have to check.'

He made his way sullenly into the back of the shop, pushing the door closed behind him.

Holmes used the time to have a look around, but the scant display of licence plates in different formats and colours – some legal, others very much not – and the shiny chrome rims, custom wheels and aluminium spoilers suspended from the low ceiling, gave nothing away, and caused him to keep ducking like a Christmas turkey as he moved around the cramped display.

Gerry Nelson emerged from the back of the shop and went straight to the computer next to the cash register. He looked at the slip of paper, typed in the registration and pressed return. It suddenly occurred to Holmes that if the information was all on the computer he'd had no need to go into the back office at all. Well, it was too late to do anything about that now. Nelson handed him the paper and shook his head.

'I'm sorry, I can't help.'

'Is that can't, or won't?'

Nelson was clearly rattled. 'Look, I've done what you asked. That registration ain't been made up here. I checked backed to November 2001, and there's nuffin. Now please, you're going to get me a bad reputation.'

Holmes resisted the temptation to laugh.

'If I wanted to get a set of plates made up, and I didn't have the original plates, or logbook, where would I go?' He resisted adding, 'other than here'.

Nelson laughed. 'You're out of touch, Inspector. You can go on the Internet and order whatever you want – no questions asked. Even on the supposedly kosher sites, all you have to do is pretend you want them for a showroom or off-road driving, and you can choose and design whatever you like. But don't go telling anyone, it's buggering up my business as it is.'

Holmes had barely got as far as Queen's Park when he spotted them. It wasn't difficult; they were practically up his exhaust. Two up, and one of them, the passenger, was suspiciously familiar. So that's what Nelson had been doing in the back room, calling for reinforcements.

He signalled left, turned into Lathbury Road and stopped. In his wing mirror he watched the black Volvo pull in behind him. He stayed in the car. The bastards can come to me, he decided.

Dicky Lounds placed one hand on the roof and waited patiently for Holmes to lower the window. He leaned in and flashed a Hollywood smile that was more of a grimace than a greeting.

111

'Now then, Sherlock. What the fucking hell are you doing on my turf?'

'You want to be careful, Dicky; with teeth like that they'll spot you coming a mile away.'

'Very funny, Gordon. What isn't fucking funny is that you could have just blown an operation we've had going for over six months!'

'Shame you didn't let us in on the secret then.'

'Some fucking secret that would have been!' Lounds could see this wasn't going anywhere, and changed tack. 'Look, why didn't you back off and call me when he offered my name?'

It was a reasonable question, Holmes decided.

'Normally I might have done, but this is a murder enquiry, and he'd already seen the registration number we're interested in. While I was wasting time contacting you, what was to stop him getting rid of the evidence?'

Lounds had to think about that, briefly. 'You must have known that if we had some kind of arrangement, I could get him to tell you what you wanted to know,' he said.

'Maybe, but under the circumstances I wasn't prepared to risk it.'

'Circumstances? What fucking circumstances?'

'That body in St John's Gardens? Well, we don't think it'll be the last. So we haven't got time to prance round skirting the cracks in the pavement!'

Dicky Lounds placed his other hand on the roof and leant in closer. Close enough for Holmes to decide that teeth whitening was no substitute for dental hygiene.

'For your information, Detective Inspector Holmes, this particular pavement marks our way into the biggest drug operation in North Manchester, and one of the biggest in the North-West. And if you want to start comparing body counts, I'd say our lot already beat your man hands down! So just stay the fuck away from Nelson. Stay the fuck away from the shop. And stay the fuck off my patch!'

He thrust his right hand into Holmes' face.

'Now give me the bloody number, and I'll find out if he's on the level or just jerking you around.'

Holmes reached into his inside pocket and produced the slip of paper. Lounds snatched it, and with an ironic, 'Thank you!' stood up and made his way back to his car. Holmes watched as the Volvo backed up, did a U-turn and sped off. At least I'll find out if Nelson's on the level, he told himself. And I've ruffled Dicky Lounds' feathers into the bargain. All in all, he decided, a good outcome.

Caton was unhappy about the post mortem. The placing of the object in the victim's throat simply reinforced his hunch that this was only the first move in what might become a pattern of killings. As he and Joanne Stuart entered the station, his day got worse. DC Woods met them in the corridor.

'Larry Hymer's down in reception, boss,' he said. 'And he's got those two guys with him who spotted our Mr Bojangles.'

'It was only a matter of time, sir. You said so yourself,' Joanne Stuart reminded him.

'I know,' said Caton, 'but I had hoped they might come to us first. This is too good a story for Hymer to pass up on, and we're not ready to have our hand forced just yet.' He turned to his DC. 'Ian, you carry on. Detective Sergeant, you come with me, and we'll see what we can salvage from this.'

'Mr Bojangles?' Joanne Stuart asked as they made their way to the main reception.

'You must have heard it. The down-and-out with

worn-out shoes who'd dance for you. A Jerry Walker classic, but everyone's sung it. It was even on The X Factor,' he said. 'Something of a mystery in his own way, Bojangles. But that's about where the likeness ends,' he added as an afterthought. 'Our man has size 16 shoes, brand spanking new.'

'Trust Woods to introduce levity to a cold-blooded killing,' said Stuart. 'Still, you've got to admit, it's uncannily close.'

'Do me a favour, Jo,' he said. 'Find out which interview rooms are free.'

Two Jo's in one morning, she reflected as she headed for the custody suite.

Larry Hymer advanced to meet them. The senior crime reporter on the Manchester Evening News was short and wiry, with tiny bright blue eyes and sharp features that neatly fitted his reputation for ferreting out a good story. His grey trousers and black anorak hung loosely, despite his ability to eat heartily and drink copiously; attributes to which many a detective could ruefully attest.

Hymer grinned and held out his hand.

'Detective Chief Inspector Caton, how are you?'

Before Caton could decide whether or not to shake it, Hymer placed it firmly on his shoulder and started to guide him towards the two men in the process of rising from the bench behind him.

'Let me introduce you to Mr Jason Roberts and Mr Dean Riley,' he gloated.

Inwardly, Caton seethed. It was bad enough having Hymer get to his witnesses first, but this matchmaking performance was way over the top. He knew that he had to bite his tongue if he was going to broker a deal. Hymer knew it, too.

On the video both men had looked to be in their

thirties, but these were much younger, in their mid twenties. He had the strong impression that they were both nervous and embarrassed. Probably because they had gone to the press first and were wondering how he would respond to that. Not such a bad thing, he decided; it might make them more desperate to please.

'Thank you for finding the time to come in and help us with our enquiries, gentlemen,' he said, with just enough irony in his voice to keep them on the back foot.

Joanne Stuart mimawed 'Room 3' at him through the security glass door that led to the interview rooms. Caton stared hard at Roberts – the taller of the two – and then at Riley.

'Please follow me,' he said.

As he reached the doorway, he became aware that Hymer was still with them.

'I'd like you to wait here, Mr Hymer,' he said. 'I'll be happy to have a word when we've finished interviewing Mr Roberts and Mr Riley.'

'I assumed, Chief Inspector,' the reporter retorted, 'that since I was the person who persuaded them to come in, and since they don't have a solicitor with them...'

Caton cut him off in mid-sentence.

'You assumed wrong, Mr Hymer. Firstly, as I know you are now well aware, this is a serious incident we are investigating; secondly, since you were not in the vicinity of St John's Gardens on Sunday night, I doubt that there is anything you can add to these gentlemen's evidence; thirdly, they are neither under arrest nor under suspicion and therefore have no need of a solicitor; fourthly, even if they did, I was not aware that you were so qualified?'

He knew that he was sounding pompous, but he had to create a breach between these witnesses and their self-appointed mentor. From the looks on their faces, he could see it had had the desired effect.

Leaving Hymer in his wake, he ushered the witnesses through the doorway and down the corridor towards the interview room, outside which DS Stuart stood waiting for them, her face suitably grave. A nice touch, Caton noted, a very nice touch.

Jason Roberts' right leg stuck out at the side of the table, heel off the floor, hammering up and down at a rate of knots. The fingers on Dean Riley's left hand drummed on the tabletop as he tugged nervously at his T-shirt with the other. For a moment, Caton wondered what it would sound like on the tape.

'Why don't you go first, Mr Roberts?' said Caton. 'Tell us about your night out.'

'We were out celebrating a mate's birthday,' he began. 'We had a meal at the Comedy Store, then worked our way round Day Seventeen of the Central Manchester slow pub crawl.'

He paused to check that the two detectives knew what he was talking about. From the blank expression on both faces, it was clear they did not.

'It's a website. Everybody follows it. Bloody brilliant.'

He turned to Dean Riley for support, found him nodding tentatively and was encouraged to continue.

'We started at the Fat Cat Café, then the Café Bar, then Baa Bar. That was the ones on Deansgate Locks ticked off. Then we crossed over to the City Road Inn on the corner of Albion Street. We stayed a bit longer there because Dean got on the *Hyperolympics* games machine and we couldn't get him off it.'

Riley chuckled briefly beside him. He carried on.

'We couldn't get in The Briton's Protection because it was heaving, and the doormen were working a one-in-one-out policy. Besides, there were six of us, and they wouldn't allow a group. So we headed up to the Pitcher and Piano, which was pretty quiet; then we turned down Peter Street and got in Barracuda. By now we'd split into pairs and staggered our approach so that we wouldn't get turned away. You were certainly staggering,' he said, nudging Dean Riley and grinning nervously at his own wit.

Caton interrupted the flow.

'How much were you drinking in each of these pubs?' he asked.

'A pint normally, that's our rule. We've got a couple who drink a bit faster, and they might have managed a couple of pints, or a chaser. To be honest, I wasn't keeping count.'

'If you were drinking that much, how come you can remember exactly which places you visited?' DS Stuart asked him.

'I told you,' he said, looking at her with the undisguised disdain of a sexist, 'we were following the route from the website. We do a different one every week. Plan it like a military operation. If we miss one of the pubs out, it's like a bloody disaster.'

'Go on,' said Caton.

'Well, that was more or less it. We got into The Gallery in the Novotel, but Dean here was in danger of knocking the table over. We only had the Ibis Hotel bar to go. I doubted we'd get in there the state he was in, so I brought him out.'

'So by now you'd had seven pints, plus whatever you started with at the Comedy Store?' Joanne Stuart suggested.

Roberts grinned wryly. 'Well, to be honest we'd both had three or four before we left the Store, and Dean had a couple of chasers along the way. That was a fairly normal weekend tally,' he added hastily. 'You'd be surprised how you build up the tolerance.'

Tell that to your liver, Caton was tempted to respond. His sergeant leaned in.

'So what happened to you then, Dean, dicky tummy?'

The hapless Riley shrugged and attempted a little bravado.

'I ordered a *special* cocktail for Mickey – it was his birthday – but he wouldn't touch it. So I offered to split it and drink my half at the same time as he drank his.' He grinned manically at his partner. 'Like being bitten by your own dog!'

Caton was becoming impatient.

'Mr Roberts,' he said, 'just tell us what route you took to St John Street, and what you saw as you reached the junction with Upper Byrom Street.'

'We went down Portland Street, up Princess Street. Then I suppose we must have gone down Moseley Street, and across St Peter's Square. I know that because Deano was sick there. We just made it to the garden area before he threw up. Then I think we went straight down Peter Street. Just as we got to Deansgate, he started looking queasy again and said he wanted a slash. We would have gone down Quay Street, but I could see there was one of your heavy mob's vans parked up outside the Opera House, and I didn't want him getting picked up drunk and disorderly, or worse, so I turned left into Deansgate, crossed over and nipped down St John Street. Dean had a piss in a doorway. Then, as we started to turn the corner, I heard a sound behind us and turned round. This bloke dressed as a clown had just jumped from the cab of a van parked up outside the park gates. He must of seen us cos' he looked in our direction and stopped still. I don't know who looked more surprised, him or us. I started to walk towards him, hauling Dean here with me.'

'Why did you decide to go towards him rather than just stop and look?' DS Stuart asked.

Good question, Caton thought, but she should have saved it. Let him tell the story his way first.

'I don't think I did decide. I was drawn towards him … curious I suppose. It's not every day you see a clown on the city streets at that time of the morning. Plenty of girls dressed like French maids and nurses and such, showing their arse and falling down drunk, but this was different.'

'Tell us what happened next, Jason,' Caton said before DS Stuart could ask a follow-up question.

'Well, he stood there for a moment, grinning. Then he saw Dean looking at this mummy in a wheelchair on the other side of the gate and suddenly started kicking his legs up in the air, touching his heels together like clowns used to at the Blackpool Tower circus. Then he did a bit of a dance, and finished with a sort of bow.'

'Did he say anything?' Joanne Stuart asked.

'Not a word. I asked him, I said, "What you doing, mate?" But he never said a word. Just grinned back at me. Dean kept pulling my sleeve and pointing at the mummy. So this guy does a sort of mime, like he's pushing the wheelchair down the gardens. I thought it was some kind of stunt. Maybe a stag night, with the bridegroom done up like a mummy and left in the gardens. Beats being chained to the railings in the nude like we did to Dean here.' Reid grinned sheepishly.

'What happened then?' Caton prompted.

'Well, he wasn't for saying anything. Dean was getting heavy, and I was freezing cold. So we left him to it and carried on home.'

'Which is where?' said Caton.

'Ordsall. Peregrine Street. Just by Ordsall Hall.'

Peregrine Street? About as unlikely a name for that estate as you could get, thought Caton.

'And you went straight there?'

'Yeh, straight down to Regent Road. Never looked back.'

'And what about you, Dean? What did you see?'

Dean Riley stopped tugging at his shirt and shifted uneasily in his chair.

'To be honest, I was out of it. It was like Jason said. I don't reckon I can add anything at all.'

It was unlikely, Caton decided, that they would get anything from him, and the state he must have been in, how reliable would it be anyway? He shifted his focus back to Roberts.

'Can you describe him for us, Jason,' he asked. 'Give us your first impressions, then any details you can remember.'

Roberts gave it some thought. 'He looked really big, but when we got up close I could tell it was the costume. He was about my height – five eight, maybe five nine. Probably a bit slimmer than me. Bald on top, with masses of white hair over his ears and down the back of his head. You could see it was a wig, though. His face was made up like those clowns you used to get in a jack-in-the-box.'

He paused for a moment and Caton watched his eyes slip up to the left as he accessed his visual memory.

'His eyebrows were made up massive. He had big yellow shadows painted under his eyes, a big Red Nose Day nose and big red lips curved almost from ear to ear. When he smiled, he had a large pair of rabbit's teeth. Although Dean reckons they were more like Dracula's, and he should know.'

He grinned at Riley, emboldened by the concentration with which they hung on his every word.

'His clothes, tell us about his clothes,' Joanne Stuart said.

He looked again at Riley, this time for inspiration, but found none. His eyes scanned upwards.

'A jacket, a big baggy jacket. Yellow, with a blue check. And matching baggy pants, and great big floppy shoes.'

'And gloves,' said Riley suddenly.

They all turned to look at him.

'That's right,' said Roberts, 'tight white gloves … like surgeons wear on the tele. I remember thinking it was strange. They didn't match at all.'

'And the eyes,' Dean Riley said, as though to himself. 'His eyes were green. They stood out against the whites of his eye, and that make-up. And his smile was crooked … and…' He searched for the word. 'Cruel.'

He looked straight at Caton, who noted the sudden pallor of his cheeks.

'But his eyes were cold and empty,' Riley added, 'like the lights were off and there was nobody home.'

Chapter 10

'How did you get on with Hymer, sir?' Joanne Stuart asked on their way back to the incident room.

'I got him to hold off till tomorrow's morning edition. He's already got all he needs from Roberts and Riley, and after the way we read them the riot act about prejudicing any future trial, they're not likely to take their story anywhere else. In any case, they know the interest will hot up when the trial's over, whenever that is.'

Caton paused to hold the fire door open and waited for her to go through.

'I convinced Hymer that he would be doing us a real favour, and in return I promised to give him an unattributable statement. It won't be that brilliant, and it won't prejudice our work in any way, but it'll be enough. Better than the one he's going to get from Chester House. I've just contacted the press unit and they're working on a suitably anodyne script; part appeal for witnesses, part confirmation of what's already been in the press.'

Stuart held the door to the incident room open for him.

'What did you think about Riley's description, sir? After all, on his own admission he was "out of it".'

'On the other hand,' Caton replied, 'he was the one who spotted the wheelchair. We know that from the

CCTV. And, judging from the look on his face, it must have come as quite a shock to find out that the wheelchair almost certainly had a body in it. That would be enough to trigger some recall – and why not the part that made the most impression? At that time of the morning, and the state he was in, it would have scared the hell out of me.'

They found Gordon Holmes with his back to them, waving a slip of paper in the air at the same time as doing a poor impression of a tap dance. He finished with a flourish, mimicking the one they'd seen the perpetrator perform for Roberts and Riley. Everyone in the room but Holmes had spotted them enter, and was looking to see how Caton would react. He waited for Holmes to cotton on and turn to face them. The smile on the DI's face evaporated.

'Sorry, boss. Didn't know you were there.'

Caton let him sweat.

Holmes waved the paper in his hand nervously. 'We just got a breakthrough, sir,' he said in desperate justification. 'The licence plates … we know where he got them from.'

'Let's continue this in my office, Inspector,' Caton said, careful to keep his tone neutral.

He turned and led the way out of the room. Let them make of that what they will. They would assume that Gordon was in for a bollocking. And they would note that it was going to be in private. Just as it should be. Caton was quick to praise and slow to blame, but he demanded professional behaviour in the office – especially from his sergeants and inspectors.

He'd enough experience of cavalier detectives in the early days not to countenance an insidious macho culture more appropriate to Sunday league football. It led to narrow thinking, sloppy evidence gathering, dubious convictions and, at its worst, fostered corruption. That was why there were only two long-service detectives on his team. And if Woods didn't shape up, there would be just one. He opened the door to his office, leaving Holmes to follow him in.

He perched himself on the edge of his desk and waited for Holmes to close the door. He held up his hand to save him the trouble of repeating his apology.

'Come on, Gordon. When I'm not there it's even more important for you to set an example, not take it as an opportunity to clown around.'

They both smiled at his pun.

'You know that, so let's just leave it there, shall we?'

'Thanks, boss.'

Holmes proffered the piece of paper he had been waving triumphantly in the air.

'Dicky Lounds came through after all. It seems there was nothing on Gerry Nelson's system for two reasons. Firstly, he was paid in cash, and he always hides the majority of those from the taxman. Secondly, these were supposedly off-road plates that don't have to be checked against DVLA to see if they're legit, or be backed up by a logbook. But he does remember them, because they were more or less standard, except for the bloke asking him to leave a space where the year of registration would have been. He knew it was fishy, but not strictly illegal. He keeps a separate book for show plates and off-roaders, but he just wanted me out of there as quickly as possible. The Drug Squad have turned him, and if any of the gangs he supplies with false plates find out...'

He left the obvious unsaid.

'I don't think he'd have given us anything if Lounds hadn't leant on him, and he only did that to stop us screwing up his operation.'

'So, armed with these plates, our Bojangles simply had to buy a couple of black number 2s, and stick one on the front and one on the back?'

'That's it, boss. Couldn't be simpler. He was taking a risk, though. There was a good chance a patrol car would have picked them up as amended, even if the registration did come back as legit.'

Caton read the note several times. 'The height and build fit, but this description doesn't take us much further. When did he say this customer collected the plates?'

'The customer didn't. He ordered them in person alright, but he sent a young lad in to collect them with the cash. He was obviously taking no chances that he might have been sussed. He went in to order them on the 17th of October. Just about a month before he put them to use. They were collected the following day. There was no CCTV in the shop. Nelson's regular customers would go ballistic. He relies on mirrors to catch shoplifters, and on his reputation to deter them.'

Caton handed the note back. 'Okay, Gordon. Get him in to have a look at the mugshots, and work with the e-fit team.'

Holmes looked doubtful. 'Lounds won't be happy with that, boss.'

'He must have known we'd have no option but to follow this up. And he can complain all he likes. His boss can take it up with Superintendent Gates.'

As Holmes turned to go, Caton threw him a reminder. 'And get them to concentrate on the eyes, Gordon. On the eyes.'

Caton was in the middle of a backlog of emails when the call came through from the front desk. Superintendent Gates was on her way up. Caton had a lot of respect for Helen Gates. She was a good cop who'd made her way through the ranks on merit. During her spell in Moss Side she'd been responsible for sorting out the turf war on the estate by putting away both sets of ringleaders for a good stretch. And she had all but eliminated muggings on the university students and school kids in the area. She was tough as a bag of nails to boot.

He replaced the phone and began to order his thoughts. Gates would normally have preferred him to make the trip across town, so the odds were that she'd got wind either of the post mortem results or, more probably, that Larry Hymer had been in touch looking for the press statement. Either way, she would be on the warpath. He decided it would take some of the steam out if he met her halfway.

The fire door flew open and she came pounding down the corridor towards him; hat in hand, her normally immaculate chequered cravat awry, cheeks still red from the cold. Caton pushed open the door to his office and stepped aside to let her sweep imperiously in. As she wheeled to face him, he gently closed the door.

'What the hell's going on, Tom?'

At least it was Tom, he reflected. Just a hint perhaps, that they were both in it together.

'Why don't you sit down, Ma'am?' he said, indicating the only easy chair in the room.

She sank reluctantly into the leather upholstery, lobbing her hat onto the coffee table as she did so. Caton wheeled his chair out a little from behind his desk, just enough so that it wouldn't look like he was hiding, sat down and reached for the phone.

'A drink, Ma'am?'

'I'll have a tea – and make it camomile. Refreshing and reviving I don't need!'

He pressed the intercom.

'Ian, I've got Superintendent Gates with me. She'd like a camomile tea, and I'll have the usual please.'

Caton sat back and decided to let Helen Gates get it off her chest. She ran a hand through her hair, loosening the natural black curls squashed by the regulation hat. Her fierce chocolate-brown eyes were capable of boring into the mind of suspect and colleague alike, but as she lifted her head, Caton could see that she was tired, or stressed, or more likely both.

He vaguely recalled a phrase from Maestro Benjamin Zander's *The Art of Possibility*. Something about everybody in the presence of possibility having shining eyes. Helen Gates' eyes had ceased to shine the minute she joined the higher echelons. That was precisely why he'd resisted all attempts to get him to do the same.

'The Chief Constable called me in, Tom, to ask about your investigation,' she said. 'Apparently, he'd been in the press office on an unrelated matter and overheard several of them discussing a press release. His ears pricked up when the words clown, murderer and Hymer were used in juxtaposition. Larry Hymer may behave like a clown at times, and there are others when any one of us could cheerfully murder him, but you can imagine the chief's response when they explained.' She fixed Caton with a stare just this side of steely. 'And you can imagine my response when he asked me to bring him up to date, and I hadn't a clue where you were up to!'

Caton took a deep breath, but she was simply changing gear – from fourth into overdrive.

'And if that wasn't embarrassing enough, in the time it had taken him to get back to his office and contact me, he'd had Assistant Chief Constable Gerry Parker on the phone complaining that you have compromised a sensitive drugs operation.'

She sensed Caton's hackles rising and raised both hands to placate him.

'I know, he had no right going over my head, or over CS Hadfield's for that matter, but you see the position you've placed me in.'

Mercifully there was rap on the door and DC Woods entered, two cups and saucers and a jug of hot water balanced precariously on a metal tray covered with gaudy canal art roses. The barely disguised smirk suggested that he had overheard just enough. Woods placed the tray on the coffee table and handed Gates her cup of tea.

'Ma'am.'

He filled the other cup with hot water from the jug and handed it to Caton.

'Sir.'

'Thank you, Detective Constable,' Caton said through gritted teeth. He placed his cup straight back on the coffee table. 'I don't want to be disturbed for the next twenty minutes. Can you see to that?'

'Certainly, sir. Ma'am.' Woods smiled gratuitously at the superintendent.

She pointedly ignored him as she blew on the surface of her camomile tea.

Caton waited until the door was closed and Helen Gates had started to sip her tea before judging it prudent to mount his defence.

It took much of the twenty minutes for Caton to explain that he had held off from updating her piecemeal until he had interviewed the witnesses, and seen the interim forensic report. He agreed, in hindsight, it had been a mistake, although even she recognised that it was just bad luck that the chief constable had been in the press office at that moment. As for the complaint from the Drug Squad, there was no love lost between them, and it was clear that they were overreacting. In his place, she admitted, she would have insisted on an e-fit. It was just a pity

Lounds had stirred up the assistant chief constable and, in particular, the National Crime Squad liaison officer, because that was where they both agreed Caton needed to turn next.

Helen Gates reached for her hat and stood up.

'You're right to contact NCS, Tom. This has all the hallmarks of a potential serial killer. If you haven't told them, and brought a profiler on-board, before … if he strikes again, there will be hell to pay.'

Caton crossed ahead of her to open the door.

'Would you like me to show you the incident room, Ma'am?'

She smiled wearily. 'It's alright, Tom. This is your show. If it looks as though I'm poking my nose in it won't help you in the slightest. Quite the reverse. I'm happy with our agreement. I'll ring you early morning and late afternoon. You will contact me if anything major crops up in between.'

They left it at that.

Before he made the call to the National Crime Squad, Caton went through to the incident room to find Duggie Wallace, the team's senior collator, crime intelligence analyst and liaison with the Serious Crime Analysis Section at CENTREX. It was still early days, but given this was now a murder enquiry, with no obvious motive and an increasing list of bizarre aspects, all the more reason to find out if there were any similarities with previous offences. Duggie was rattling away on his keyboard as Caton approached.

'Give me a second, boss. I don't want to lose this.'

A protected file name appeared on the screen. He punched in a password and pressed the return key. A database appeared filling half the page. Wallace speed-read it, shook his head, gave it a file name and saved it into a folder. Caton couldn't help noticing the folder name – Bojangles. It looks as though the team has christened the investigation, he decided. Me and my big mouth. Wallace swivelled round to face him.

'Can't see there being much there, boss. The more I narrow it down, the less I get.'

'What are you using, Duggie?'

'Body displayed post mortem; displayed in a public place; foreign object placed in or on the body; miniature plastic white horse; perpetrator dressed as a clown,' he replied. 'There's no previous MO involving a combination of more than two of the five in the HOLMES historical or active files. And I used my contacts to run it through their Violent Crime Linkage Analysis System. If they can't find anything in VICLAS, we're not going to find it anywhere.'

Caton pulled up a chair and sat down.

'So what combinations are coming up so far?'

'There are just two: displayed post mortem in a public place, and displayed post mortem with a foreign object in or on the body. There are seventeen in the first category, although whether they were really displayed is always open to interpretation. Only five in the body were planted, or got there accidentally – it isn't always clear. And not a clown in sight. Except as a victim. Interestingly there were two of those: a crime of passion in a Polish travelling circus twenty years ago, and a drunken brawl in Leeds town centre three years ago. I'll check those out for a possible revenge motive, unlikely though it is.'

He looked up at Caton.

'Be easier if we had a suspect.'

'What have you got?' Caton asked.

Wallace plucked a post-it note from the side of his laser printer.

'Half of them are deceased, the rest are in prison. Except for two unsolved: one in Cannes in 1997, linked to a Russian mafia feud, the other in Paddington in

1979. So unless our perpetrator started when he was in nappies...'

'It's beginning to look as though this could be his first.'

'I'm afraid so, boss. Unless...'

'Go on, Duggie.'

'Well, since the lifting of the border controls for the ten countries which joined the EU in 2004 we've had a major influx of East Europeans – including the former Balkan countries – and I'm afraid their records are far from complete. Some disappeared – lost and deliberately destroyed – during the wars in that region. VICLAS has access to the Interpol database I-24/7, which covers all one hundred and eighty-four of its member countries, but it's the same old story: garbage in, garbage out. Or in this case, nothing in, nothing out.'

Caton pushed back his chair and placed a hand on Wallace's shoulder.

'Stick at it, Duggie. I'll try and bring you a bit more to go on.'

He stood up and looked around the room. It was still a hive of activity. Officers on the phone, at their monitors, leafing through files. If anything, the tempo had risen since word spread about that small white horse. None of them knew what it meant, but they knew where it was leading. There was a distinct whiff of anxiety in the air.

The phone call to the NCS took longer than Caton had anticipated. Neither of the designated liaison officers was available, but irritatingly he was kept on hold for five minutes before someone promised to arrange a ring back. He was ploughing through a stack of reports from his team, to approve and countersign, when the call came through.

'Chief Inspector Caton? This is Detective Inspector Derek Wheatley. What can we do for you?'

'Thanks for calling back, Derek. I am heading an investigation into a suspicious death, which I expect tomorrow morning's post mortem report to confirm as a murder.'

'When was the body found, Chief Inspector?'

'Sunday morning at 6 a.m., but the body had been dead for at least fifteen hours.'

'So your investigation is less than thirty-six hours old. Isn't it a bit early to be notifying us?'

'Not when it's shaping up the way it is.'

Caton took a deep breath. He knew just how ridiculous this was going to sound, and didn't relish retelling it for the second time in an hour. Each time it sounded even less believable. When he'd finished, he waited for a reaction.

Wheatley took it in his stride. 'We're talking about the body in St John's Gardens? We got copies of the media reports in our latest update. Nothing about a clown, though. When are you intending to go live on that?'

'We don't have an option. The witnesses decided they were on to a good thing and went to the press first. There will be a statement shortly. Expect it on the evening news and in tomorrow's papers.'

'Are you fronting the statement?'

'Thankfully, no. I believe this is going to get worse before it gets better. I managed to persuade Headquarters I need to keep the pressure off my team as long as possible. If I have to stand up there, I want to be sure we've got something more substantial to go on.'

'So how can we help?'

'This has all the hallmarks of a serial crime in the making. I want to get an offender profiler on-board as soon as possible.'

'You want a behaviour profile and a criminal profile?'

'That's it.'

'I had a feeling you were going to say that. I did some checking here, and with CENTREX, before I called you back. Give me a second.'

In the background Caton could hear muted voices and the sound of fingers rapidly moving across a keyboard. Forty seconds later, Wheatley came back on the line.

'You're out of luck. The two current designated Home Office profilers are out of the country. There's a major five-day conference over in the Schevenegen and The Hague, and they're not the only ones attending. Everybody from the Midland's Centre for Criminology and Criminal Justice and from the North West Forensic Academic Unit seems to be there, too.'

He paused for a moment to let that sink in.

'However, there is a note on Professor Stewart-Baker's out-of-office reply.'

'Go on,' said Caton, sensing the hesitation in his voice.

'Apparently, he's suggesting that any requests should be referred to his assistant, Kate Webb. According to our records, she's a senior lecturer in his department – the taught MA course on Investigative Psychology. She was with him on that kidnap and extortion case in Preston a few years back. I seem to remember she was one of his PhD students at the time. She is showing up as licensed, but we haven't used her before so she's likely to be a virgin profiler. Do you want to risk it, or wait till the others get back on Monday? Not that there's any guarantee any of them will be able to drop everything straight away.'

Caton thought about it. 'I don't suppose it can do any harm to have a word with her. See what she thinks. At the very least she may be able to nobble Stewart-Baker as soon as he gets in.'

'Okay, I'll email her contact details over now. Incidentally, what are you calling your investigation? I'll set up a file and reference.'

Caton realised that they still hadn't given it a name. At least not officially.

'Bojangles,' he said. 'We're calling it Bojangles.' A bloody sight better, he decided, than Coco the Clown.

Chapter 11

They gathered round the progress board. Against each key task the name of the senior detective responsible for progress chasing was written in green. The first on the list read 'Clown Outfit'. Nick Carter led off.

'I had one DC ringing every costume supplier in the region, starting with Manchester and working outwards, and another checking out Web suppliers. We've got them sending us a list of any customers for Bojangles' particular combination in the last two years. I've also had a check run on circuses performing in the region in the past year, and reports of lost or stolen.'

'Why two years?' Caton asked.

'Same reason as starting in Manchester and working out. See if we can get a recent hit close in, and then widen the net if we have to.'

Caton nodded his approval.

Carter continued.

'We got lucky quite early. This man rang Julie's Balloon Décor in Bolton this August. He specifically wanted cash on delivery. She said she needed a credit card number to secure the order. He refused, and asked for the names of other suppliers. Which he didn't get. She came up with the time, date and incoming phone number. The call was from a pay phone in the University Precinct. And before anyone asks, yes, it is covered by a CCTV, and no, they don't keep the tapes longer than a week. However,' the pause was triumphant, 'on the same day a series of bids were made for the very same costume, on eBay.'

'From the university?' Gordon Holmes asked.

'From the Internet café on St Anne's Square.'

'Don't they have to provide credit card details?' Joanne Stuart wondered out loud.

'Let's allow him to finish the story, then we can ask the questions,' Caton said, which he realised was a bit rich since he'd been the first to interrupt.

Carter carried on.

'Normally you're talking PayPal, and/or a credit card. Some sellers accept an international money order. In this case, the buyer was offering cash up front, and prepared to take the risk. The bid was accepted – nine pounds ninety-nine as it happens – plus six quid postage. We've just traced the seller, and she still had the delivery address on her computer. We've got a name: Alexander Westerby. And guess what?' Another of Nick's rhetorical questions. 'The address is known to us. It's that new homeless hostel in Hulme that was picketed by local residents protesting about the concentration of hostels in the area.'

It was clear Carter had finished.

'And you haven't been round there yet?' Caton asked.

'No, boss. The address only just came through.'

'The name will be as false as the plates on the van, but run a check on it anyway.'

'That's in hand, boss.'

'Thanks, Nick, and well done,' said Caton. 'Who's next?'

'That'll be me,' said Gordon Holmes, stepping up to the smart board situated next to the progress board.

He'd been on a training course to maximise the use of the technology, and had started using it at every opportunity. It seriously ruffled the feathers of the rest of the team, but they were also secretly impressed. Except for DC Wood, the resident Luddite, who had to be reminded to check his emails every day.

Holmes tapped the board twice and a rich picture appeared, part mind map, part storyboard. In the centre were the words Ramp 2 Roll. Holmes began his presentation, tracing a route around the board, starting in the centre and radiating out to follow each fresh connection.

'Once Joanne had identified the make of this ramp it was pretty easy to track down,' he said.

'Hang on, Gordon, who did the tracking exactly?' Caton asked.

Holmes looked distinctly peeved to have been interrupted just as he was getting into his flow.

'Well, DC Wood did most of that, sir,' he replied.

'Let's get him over,' said Caton. 'Presentation is one of his new performance goals. Better he starts with something he knows about.'

They waited for Holmes to bring DC Wood over. The inspector looked put out, the DC distinctly apprehensive.

'It's alright, DC Wood,' Caton said. 'I gather you've done some good work tracking this ramp down. I'd like you to tell us what you discovered. Take your time.'

Dave Wood approached the board hesitantly.

'I started by looking this up on the Internet,' he said, tapping the title in the centre of the board.

Immediately the screen went blank, and then a second page appeared headed 'Next Steps'. Caton, Wood and Stuart couldn't resist smiling. Holmes grunted in thinly disguised disgust. Wood turned to the board to see what they were grinning at and immediately coloured up.

'I'm sorry, sir...'

'It's alright, Dave, it happens to me all the time,' Caton said. 'Show him, Gordon.'

Holmes tapped the bottom corner of the board and the original page reappeared.

'Forward ... back ... forward ... back,' he said brusquely, indicating a pair of arrows.

Then he stepped back.

'Go on, Dave,' Caton encouraged.

Ignoring the rest of them, DC Wood focused his gaze on Caton.

'Well, as I was saying, I started on the Internet. The firm came up straight away. It's based in the US. They were brilliant. Emailed me a complete list of their customers in the UK since they started to export, which is just three years ago. Nationally there have been one hundred and seventeen delivered.'

He traced a line diagonally across the board to a hub headed Greater Manchester.

'There were ten in the GM area; seven for industrial and commercial use, and three for personal use. We thought we'd start with these first.'

He paused to check they were still with him. Then he carried on with growing confidence. He touched a small box at the side of the hub and a new page appeared. The heading was Industrial and Commercial, and a list of the names of firms and their addresses appeared. Against each was a series of tick boxes; some ticked, others empty.

'As you can see,' he said, 'we've done a first trawl on five of these. All of them are still in use at the premises, or in one of their vehicles. Inspector Holmes has assigned a DS and a DC to go and double-check. Especially the vehicles, the staff using them, their rosters, whether they had the ramp with them on the night in question, etcetera. The other two we're still pursuing.'

He was beginning to sound impressive, feeding off their rapt attention. He touched the forward arrow, and the page jumped to a list of just three names and addresses.

'Surprisingly they're all within ten miles of the city centre. Inspector Holmes is just about to pay the three of them a visit,' he said, deftly returning the screen to the opening page.

'Thank you, DC Wood. Good work,' said Caton. 'And that was a smart presentation … excuse the pun.' He turned towards Holmes. 'Why don't you take DC Wood with you, Gordon? Looks like he's earned a break from his desk.'

Holmes nodded sourly. Dave Wood returned, with a spring in his step, to his workstation.

'So that leaves you, DS Stuart,' Caton said.

'Thank you, sir.'

She directed them back to the progress board.

'First, the identity of the victim,' she said. 'Up until now, we've not had a lot to go on. We've put his description through Missing Persons and drawn a blank. The dental records are our best bet, unless we're lucky enough to get a DNA match – and we're waiting for a result on those any time soon.'

She paused and shifted tack.

'Now the van. We've got all of the distributors sending us a complete list of sales of that particular model. DVLA has sent us a list of matching registrations, re-registrations and changes of owner or keeper. It's going to take the team a while to sift through it all. Like Gordon and Nick, we're starting with those in the GMP area. We've also got an alert out for our van to all divisional officers across the entire GMP area, a general alert nationally, and specific search teams in the Metropolitan, South and Ashton Divisions. I suggest we consider extending that to North and Salford Divisions, sir, if we draw a blank.'

'Thank you, DS Stuart. And let me just check, all of this data from the different strands is also going into the common database so that we can get crossmatches automatically flagged up on Duggie Wallace's computer?'

They nodded in unison.

'Is there anything we're missing?' he asked.

'What about the pathology and forensic reports, sir?' asked Joanne Stuart.

'I'm going to follow that up right now. DI Sarah Weston has been assigned as our forensic liaison officer for the duration.'

Nick Carter whistled softly. Caton chose to ignore it.

'She's just gone straight from giving evidence in that horrific arson case in Trafford, to Chorley,' he continued, 'to find out what forensics have got for us, and then back to Manchester to collect Professor Flatman's report. Then a session with our lab here. So give her some slack when she gets here. I should also tell you I've spoken with NCS, just to make sure that further down the road they don't think they've been left out of the loop. I've got a bad feeling about this one, and I'm going to bring in a Home Office profiler. Better to build up a profile as we go along than to wait until it becomes pressing, and then have to go over a load of old ground. Any more questions?'

'Are you thinking of extending the roster, sir?' Carter asked.

'No, I'm not. I'm concerned there are people working far too late as it is. The more tired we become, the less effective we are. I've told you before, sleep deprivation is cumulative; if you don't make it up, it catches up with you big style. Anyway, late evening there's less likelihood of any reports or essential data coming in. And even if it does, there'll be no one to task. It'll be another matter if all hell breaks loose. Until then, let's leave it as it is. Unless some of you are missing shift work?'

There was a hurried shaking of heads and he heard Gordon Holmes mutter, 'Not bloody likely.' They all missed the overtime pay unique to uniformed officers – although not for much longer – but certainly not the shifts. On the other hand, when the shit hit the fan, weekends and rest days went out of the window. Swings and roundabouts.

'In that case,' he said, 'let's get to it.'

Albert Stephen checked monitor number three. The man remained dead to the world, his breathing shallow but regular. He flicked the switch on his console and watched as all three screens dissolved, logged out of his computer, picked up his key ring from the desk and left.

DI Sarah Weston looked distinctly flushed as she entered the room. If anything, the colour on her cheeks enhanced an already stunning appearance. Tall, willowy and athletic, with shiny blonde hair feather cut into a bob, bright blue eyes and a perfectly shaped mouth that revealed Beverley Hills teeth every time she smiled. Caton had often wondered why she had chosen the police when she could have been a model, or with her mind virtually anything she wanted. A late entrant at twenty-eight, the fact that she was already married to a property developer was the only thing that had prevented the entire cohort of unattached officers, and some of the married ones, making a play for her. She and Caton had taken their inspector's exams at the same time, and had been friends as well as colleagues ever since. Nevertheless, he continued to be bowled over by her appearance and her presence.

He fixed his eyes on hers as he stood to welcome her. It was a strain keeping his peripheral vision in check at moments like this, but he was ever conscious of the example he had to set. Like there was a guardian angel constantly on his back.

'Come on in, Sarah,' he said. 'And take a seat. You must be knackered.'

'Thank you, sir, I am.'

She flopped down into the easy chair, placed a black zipped document case on one of the arms, undid the single jacket button on her navy suit jacket and crossed her long legs.

Caton was relieved that she had chosen a trouser suit. Much easier on the concentration. The swell of her breasts under the white blouse, however, was another distraction entirely. He wondered if he was turning into a stereotypic lecher, or if this was the perfectly normal reaction of a healthy single man. He shook himself out of it.

'Would you like a drink, Sarah? I'm just about to have one.'

'That would be brilliant, sir. Can you make it strong black coffee? I need a lift.'

'No problem, and let's drop the sir in here, shall we? You'd have made chief inspector long before me if you'd wanted to. We both know it.'

She laughed, but didn't contradict him. Comfortable in her skin and well aware of her ability; modest with it.

Caton rang through for a coffee and some hot water, and then scooted his chair out from behind his desk.

'How was the trial?' he asked.

'Difficult,' she said. 'I was hoping they wouldn't call me as well as the FSS, but the defence team was pretty desperate and clutching at straws. Tried to suggest the evidence could have been contaminated by us or by them. Not a hope in hell of proving that, because it didn't happen. But it meant I had to relive it all over again.'

'I'm sorry I raised it,' Caton said. 'You must just want to put it behind you.'

'No, you're alright, Tom. It was good of you to ask. You can't just put something like that away in a box in the attic. Not when there are children involved. You have to work your way through it; you'll understand that.'

She looked down at her feet for a moment, and her fingers moved slowly back and forth along the arms of the chair.

'A bloody sight worse for the relatives,' she said. 'Those poor grandparents.'

Mercifully there was a knock at the door and the drinks arrived. Sarah took a sip of her coffee, put her mug on the table and unzipped the document case. She removed two copies of a report, each spiral bound with plastic pockets containing the pages of text and accompanying photos.

She handed one to Caton and opened the other at the contents page.

'This is Professor Flatman's post mortem report. I thought we'd have a look at this first, and then at the preliminary findings from the Forensic Science Service. Is that alright?'

Caton was already scanning page one. He nodded in agreement.

She carried on.

'Flatman told me you were present at the PM, and

you've already received the FME's report at the scene and his own initial findings, so I suggest we skip to page five. That's where it gets really interesting.'

Caton found the section and read it.

'He died of a morphine overdose. Injected into his right arm. So he could have committed suicide?'

'Unlikely, Tom, given how I gather he was brought to the gardens. Can't rule it out, though. However, when you see the forensic report I think you'll find it even less feasible.'

Caton flipped the page and read on.

'He was in the advanced stages of cancer, especially Karposi's Syndrome and AIDS-related cancer, and most of his organs had been infected, including his brain. We knew that much on the day.' He read on a little further. 'Ah ... but Flatman now estimates that he had less than two months to live.' He looked up. 'That would be a reason to kill himself.'

Sarah Weston picked up her cup and drank deeply.

'Like I said, Tom, wait till you read the FSS report.'

It took another five minutes for Caton to finish the report. He put it down on the table, picked up his mug and had a drink of what was now seriously tepid water.

'All the indications are that he was a sexually active homosexual...'

'Or possibly bi-sexual,' Sarah Weston suggested.

'Or possibly bi-sexual. But no evidence of any recent sexual contact. Hardly surprising, given the state he was in. There were no signs of any restraints.'

She reached into the document case, withdrew a second report and handed it to him.

'Read the forensic report.'

He took it, but left it unopened on his lap.

'Take me through it,' he said.

She opened her report, but had clearly committed most of it to memory.

'Part one: the scene of crime. Compiled by our lab. There were fabric hairs all over the deceased's clothing. They are all consistent with having come from the clown's costume, the artificial hair he was wearing and the bandages. There were no signs of any bodily fluids – semen, blood, saliva, urine, faeces – at the scene, on the body or on the clothing, other than those belonging to the deceased...'

Caton was listening carefully, although a part of his brain registered the incongruity of this matter-of-fact account flowing from the mouth of such a beautiful woman.

'...Nothing special about the dirt taken from the soles and uppers of the shoes, apart from a fine layer of cement dust. The heels were scuffed incidentally, suggesting that the body was dragged across a surface coated with the dust. Several partial footprints related to the suspected perpetrator were recovered, but, since they were likely to have been made by the massive clown shoes evident on the CCTV footage, and the path was too firm to give any indication of relative pressure across the sole, they won't be much use, unless you can find the shoes. Basically, our perpetrator was exceptionally careful.'

She paused to check that Caton was giving it his full attention. He nodded, and put his mug back down on the table. Satisfied, she continued.

'Particles of the same dust were found in the hair and on the surface of the skin, but in small concentrations. Also under the nails. Analysis of the stomach contents suggests that his final meal – very shortly before he died – was tomato and basil soup, and a little dry toast. The contents of his bowel suggest a light chicken meal, probably on Saturday evening. Part two: the samples taken for toxicology during the post mortem. That's where the Chorley labs came in.'

She looked up at him.

'This is the really interesting part. Not only did they establish that the body contained a high concentration of morphine, but also that the deceased had ingested Rohypnol.'

Caton sat up straight and opened his copy of the report.

'Rohypnol?'

'Roofies, Ruffies, Ruff up, Roach 2, R2-Do-U, Ropies, Rope, Circles, Mexican Valium, Forget-Me-Pill, Forget It...' she intoned as he searched for the page. 'The best-known date rape and predator drug on the market.'

He read the brief paragraph and looked up.

'I know that, Sarah, and I know that you know that I know that. But I thought that when the drug manufacturer responded to worldwide concern and changed the formula to cause it to change colour in liquids, it fell out of use in favour of GHB?'

'It's true that it moved down the popularity charts, but it's still fairly easy to find in its original form, if you know where to look.'

'But I thought it left the system within twenty-four hours?'

'That's an urban myth. Based on the fact that it leaves the victim so disoriented and uncertain as to what did or didn't happen, let alone whether or not they were a willing partner in the act, they often leave it too late to report it. The reality is that it does leave the bloodstream within that time period, but it can still be found in urine samples for up to forty-eight hours. Particularly if you've got scientists who know what they're looking for. Just as well Mr Clown didn't leave it another day, and that samples were taken before the post mortem.'

'*Bojangles*, Sarah,' Caton said, realising that it didn't

sound any less bizarre, 'we're calling him *Bojangles*.'

Sarah Weston smiled softly, her lips pursed, acknowledging the underlying seriousness of case.

'Well, it's unlikely that the deceased took Rohypnol and then injected himself with morphine. Why go to all that trouble when the morphine is going to put him to sleep anyway? So that rather puts our Mr Bojangles back in the frame, don't you think?'

Caton had to agree it did sound more likely.

'Is that it then?' he asked.

'Not at all, Tom. There's a good chance we can narrow down the identity of the deceased. You'll find it in the next section.'

Caton found the relevant paragraph.

'Trace elements of the following drugs were found: Ritanovir, Combivir and an unidentified GSK protease inhibitor. Ritanovir and Combivir are commonly used together, or in combination with other drugs, in the treatment of cancer and, in particular, AIDS-related and immunosuppressive-linked Kaposi's Sarcoma.'

'How does this help us with identification?'

'I showed it to Professor Flatman, and he says it suggests that the deceased must have been involved in a new trial. Almost certainly here in Manchester. He offered to ring round some of his contacts and get back to us. This means you stand a good chance of getting a name, and of talking to the doctors and other staff who were treating him up until shortly before he died.'

'Once we get a name we can really begin to motor,' Caton said.

'I nearly forgot,' she said. 'Flatman asked me to tell you that he's been elected President of the Pathological Society of Great Britain, and this year they are holding their centenary celebrations in Manchester to mark the first meeting of the society.

He wants to know if you'd like to come to the opening ceremony at the university. He's invited me, too.'

'Typical surgeon; the desire to present. Wants us to hear his speech no doubt.'

He glanced at his watch. It was nearly 5 o'clock and he suddenly realised how hungry he was.

'Look, I've not eaten since breakfast, and I'm willing to bet you haven't either?'

'You're right, I haven't. I couldn't even face breakfast this morning. I'm starving.'

'In which case, how do you feel about visiting the Curry Mile? We can be there in five minutes. Call it an early dinner. We both know your Jack will be working late. Then you can get off home.'

She began to raise her hand in protest, but he brushed it away.

'Yes, Sarah. I'll fill you in on progress so far, and then you can get off home. I want you in bright-eyed and bushy-tailed tomorrow morning.'

She stood, placed her copies of the reports in the document case, zipped it up and brushed her trousers down.

'I'll tell Jack you said that,' she replied artfully. 'He's still doing martial arts, you know.'

Chapter 12

Gordon Holmes closed the door of his car and checked that it was locked. He stepped onto the pavement and stood looking up at the block of canal-side apartments. He couldn't for the life of him imagine what use a Ramp 2 Roll would be in a building like this. The old warehouse had been transformed. The stone exterior sandblasted; the windows double glazed and tinted against the sun, and curious passers-by; secure parking in the old basement.

The Northern Quarter shops and restaurants were a spit away. Just fifteen minutes into the city centre. He wished that he had bought one when they first came on the market. Eighty thousand for a two-bedroomed apartment six years ago, and now they were going for a hundred and ninety-five. He could easily have got a second mortgage to make the initial investment, and rented it out to cover the mortgage. He would have made a killing. Just didn't have the balls to go for it, and Marilyn never missed an opportunity to remind him.

The wind began to bite, carrying with it a hint of freezing drizzle. He turned up the collar of his jacket, climbed the stone steps to the entrance and pressed the button for number twelve. A voice replied almost immediately, tinny yet crystal clear. Probably watching from the window, or more likely there was a camera somewhere.

'Hello?'

'Mr Soaper?'

'Yes?'

'It's Detective Inspector Holmes. We spoke on the phone.'

There was the briefest of pauses.

'Of course, come on up. It's the second landing, first on the right.'

John Soaper was waiting at the doorway to his apartment. As Holmes climbed the final two stairs and made his way across the narrow landing, he made a quick assessment. About five foot seven, slim to medium build, mousey hair and brown eyes. Late forties to early fifties. Blue jeans, beige sweatshirt and trainers. Ordinary looking, easy to miss in a crowd. Near enough to our sketchy Bojangles, he decided, apart from the eyes. Soaper stepped aside to let Holmes enter first.

The apartment was smaller than he had anticipated. He stepped into an open-plan living area. Oak laminate flooring, white plastered walls, large steel-framed windows almost floor to ceiling and a breakfast bar – cleverly built around one of the original iron pillars – leading through to an offset kitchen.

This room was sparsely furnished. Matching brown leather reclining chair, small leather sofa and footstool. A twenty-eight-inch flat-screen television and two electric storage heaters. Vertical Venetian blinds at the side of the windows.

John Soaper watched him taking it all in.

'Would you like to see the rest of it, Mr Holmes?'

He was quite well spoken, with a trace of a Manchester accent. More Trafford than Clayton, Holmes decided.

'Why not.'

Soaper led him through into a kitchen area that was much larger than he had anticipated – practically the same size as the living area. A series of base and eye-level birch units, a stainless-steel oven, hob, extractor and sink took up two of the three walls. The third contained a large walk-in storage cupboard, and a wall-to-floor American-style fridge freezer. Half-concealed halogen light fittings showed above and below the wall-mounted units and along the length of a beam supported by a second iron pillar.

'The washing machine and the dryer are behind these units,' Soaper told him, indicating the cupboards adjacent to where he leant on the work surface. 'And these tiles are Italian, apparently,' he said, tapping the floor with his foot. 'Impressive, isn't it?'

He led the way back across the living area and through an oak-veneered door complete with a long vertical stainless-steel handle and three glass portholes. They entered the single bedroom. Half the size of the kitchen, it held a single pine bed with a slatted headrest, a single free-standing pine wardrobe, a small chest of drawers and another of the iron pillars from floor to ceiling. A narrow window, partly obscured by anonymous beige curtains, provided a shaft of watery blue light. The bed was neatly made; a red and green tartan blanket folded across the bottom, on top of a beige cotton duvet. Soaper wouldn't be having guests to stay, Holmes decided, unless someone slept on the sofa.

Immediately off the bedroom was a shower room with a large glass shower cubicle, and a white toilet and sink. Apart from the roll of toilet paper, this room held only one barely used bar of soap, a shaving mirror and a glass with a single blue toothbrush. Spartan, Holmes decided as Soaper led him back into the living area. Not really impressive at all. Just like one of the thousands of canal-side, riverside, town centre, urban village apartments that had sprung up in the past ten years. But in this case, characterless. A bit like Soaper himself.

'Holmes. That's an interesting name for a detective. You did say it was Detective Inspector?'

'That's right, sir, I did.'

'So, what can I do for you exactly?'

'I understand you own a Ramp 2 Roll, Mr Soaper?' said Holmes, watching closely for a reaction.

Soaper's brow creased and his eyes expressed mild surprise.

'Owned, Inspector. I did own a Ramp 2 Roll. It was for my mother. She was crippled with arthritis in the final ten years of her life. I sold it shortly after she died.' He looked around the room. 'After all, it wouldn't be much use here, would it?'

'Funnily enough, that's what I was thinking, sir. So who did you sell it to, and when exactly?'

Soaper had to think about that.

'Let's see. My mother died last February, so it would be sometime in April. I can check for you if you give me a minute?'

'That would be very helpful, sir.'

'Would you like a drink while you're waiting, Inspector?'

'Thank you, a cup of tea would be very nice,' said Holmes.

It wasn't as though he was thirsty, but it was surprising how much people loosened up over a cuppa. And he needed to spend a little more time here. Just to get the measure of our Mr Soaper.

'I've found it,' Soaper said, waving a couple of pieces of paper.

He sat down on the sofa next to Holmes, who took another sip of his tea and set his mug down on the coffee table. Soaper handed him the first document. It was a copy of an advert in Loot, the free ads paper: 'Ramp and Roll, good as new, Manchester Region. £999'.

'A thousand pounds?' said Holmes. 'Seems a lot to me.'

Soaper took the advert back.

'It's nearer fifteen hundred brand new, and demand has soared, especially from retailers now that shops are being sued under the Disability Discrimination Act. I could have asked for more, but I just wanted rid. Too many memories, and not enough space.'

He handed Holmes the second piece of paper. It was a copy of the receipt for the advert, dated 6th April 2005. Holmes inspected the signature; it was indecipherable.

'Do you mind if I hang on to this, sir?' he asked.

'Not at all. And if it would help, Inspector,' Soaper said, 'I could search my bank statements and show you when I deposited the money from the sale. I bank online, but I'm sure I could dig it out.'

'That would be very helpful. And did you meet the purchaser, sir?'

'He came to collect it. Didn't try to haggle the price down, and paid in cash. In fact, he came with a thousand and told me to keep the change. I remember laughing at that.'

'Did he give a name?'

'I asked him for one when he phoned to arrange to come over and see it. He seemed a bit reluctant, now I think about it. Paused just a little too long, if you know what I mean? Jackson, or Johnson; something like that.'

'And can you describe him for me?'

Soaper looked dubious. 'I can try, but it was a long

time ago, and to be honest I didn't have any reason to remember him once he handed the money over.'

'It would be really helpful if you could try, sir.'

Holmes took out his notebook and a biro from his inside pocket.

Soaper folded his arms, closed his eyes and leant forward, his face tightening with the concentration, as though squeezing the image out. He opened his eyes and turned to Holmes.

'Well, he was in his mid forties, my height, slightly taller perhaps. Bit of a paunch. He had a black leather jacket on with a white T-shirt underneath. I remember that because it was quite a cold day for the time of year. And black trousers, I think. His head was smaller than you'd expect for his frame, and his hair was quite striking, almost ginger. But not as striking as his eyes.'

'His eyes?' Holmes had difficulty concealing his excitement.

'Yes, Inspector, they were green; not your usual weak, insipid green, but a really vivid dark green, with flecks of brown. It's funny how it comes back to you once you get started. But I wouldn't have forgotten those eyes.'

'Was there anything else about him you remember?'

'I don't think so. His manner was brusque. He just wanted to see the ramp, pay for it, load it up and go.'

'What did he come in? It must have been big to take the ramp. An estate car, or a van?'

Soaper had to think about that.

'It was a white van. I couldn't tell you the make; I'm not really into that kind of thing.'

'And what kind of vehicle do you have, sir?'

'I used a Peugeot 406 estate, Inspector. It was a bit of a squeeze, but the wheelchair folded down and you'd be surprised how little room those ramps take up. I sold it when Mother died.'

'So what do you have now, sir?'

'A Mercedes, Inspector. An E-class saloon.' He saw Holmes' eyebrows rise almost imperceptibly, and smiled weakly. 'I sold the house when Mother died and bought this apartment. I decided it was time to indulge myself a little, hence the car. But it was second hand, a demonstrator. I could never have justified a brand new one.'

'What line of work are you in, Mr Soaper, if you don't mind me asking?'

'I was in computing, but shortly before Mother died she had a win on the Premium Bonds. A big one. What with that and the sale of the house, I live quite comfortably.'

'Doesn't it get a bit boring with nothing to do all day?'

'Far from it. I read a great deal. I have an interest in local history; I still go to the Central Library several times a week, and I help out at the local hospice whenever they need me. On reception, or in the gardens. When you've been both a carer and a full-time employee you'll jump at the chance to get off the treadmill. Anyway, it beats working for a living.'

Holmes still enjoyed the job, but there were times when he'd felt the same way. He stood up.

'Well, you've been very helpful, Mr Soaper. And I wonder if you could help us some more? I'd like you to come in and have a look at some photos, and also to help one of my colleagues see if he can't put together an e-fit of your Mr Jackson, or Johnson. He'll do a sketch, and use a computer to generate a couple of likenesses. Can you do that for us?'

Soaper got to his feet and stepped round the sofa towards the door.

'Certainly, Inspector. As soon as you like. Where

would you like me to come?'

'Longsight Police Station. Just off Stockport Road, back of Plymouth Grove. Check in at reception. A Mr Knight will be expecting you.'

Soaper opened the door and Holmes stepped out onto the landing.

'If I think of anything else, is that where I should contact you, Inspector?'

'That's right, sir.'

'And if you're not there?'

'Ask for Chief Inspector Caton, or leave a message with the major incident room. And thank you again, sir. You've been most helpful.'

Holmes was about to descend the stairs when Soaper called after him.

'Inspector! I was meaning to ask. I'm intrigued about why you want to know about my ramp. What is it in connection with exactly?'

Holmes turned slowly and scrutinised Soaper's face closely as he answered.

'We have reason to believe that a ramp similar to yours was used during a serious incident, sir. So we are questioning anyone in the area who has purchased one.'

'A serious incident?' Holmes could see Soaper trying to work it out. 'You mean like a ram raid?'

'No, Mr Soaper, much more serious than that; to be precise … a murder.'

As he headed down the stairs, he left Soaper standing with the door ajar, his expression caught somewhere between shock and incredulity.

The wind had picked up, and the driving rain stung his face as Holmes hurried to his car. Thankful for the electronic key, he flung the door open and threw himself inside. He sat back for a moment, switched on the ignition so that he could activate the heated front seats and leaned back on the headrest. He always liked to take a moment after a visit, to check his notes and to tune in to his gut instincts. He took his notebook from his inside pocket and flipped it open. His thoughts began to tumble.

Soaper's story made sense. It was neat and tidy. Like the apartment. Why did they insist on calling them apartments? A couple of rooms on one floor. It was a flat. A very neat flat. Spartan was right. Sparse. Come to think of it, if he read a lot, where were the books? And if he banked on the Internet, where was the computer? Could be a laptop in one of the drawers. Was he just a bit too quick to show me around the flat? Handy having the advert and the receipt. How many people would have kept those? I know I wouldn't. The wife would have weeded them out months ago. But then he hasn't got a wife. Living all that time with his mum, I suppose.

Poor sod. Not so poor now, though. Big win on the Premium Bonds. How big I wonder? So what? He flipped back a page. Good description, though. Very good. And it tallies. His memory came back fast. What was that? Some kind of visual memory trick, like the boss keeps banging on about? Green eyes! That's special. You would notice those. No make on the van, though, and no licence plate. Have to see if we can get him to work on that.

He clipped the biro back into his pocket and slipped the notebook behind it. Then he gunned the engine, cursed as the wipers smeared a greasy film across the windscreen and sped off towards the city.

Chapter 13

Two miles away, as the crow flies, Nick Carter pulled up outside the hostel. The three-storey red-brick house would have been a veritable mansion a century ago. Probably some wealthy self-made man growing rich on the fruits of the industrial and commercial revolution that propelled this city onto the world stage. Now it sat on the border of Hulme and Moss Side, between the new apartments and office blocks, a fading testimony to the time when cotton was king and goods were made, not merely shunted round for profit.

Carter alarmed his car and crunched up the gravel driveway, head down against the sleet. He rang the brass bell and waited inside the porch, watching the water drip from the pitched slate roof and run in rivulets down the wooden pillars, diverted from their paths by the slashes of peeling paintwork. He felt like that most of the time; bounced from one objective to another like a human pinball. But that's what he was addicted to. The uncertainty. Never knowing from one moment to the next. His ruminations were interrupted by the sound of a bolt being withdrawn on the door behind him and successive locks released. The door swung open and a man in his late fifties, short and distinctly overweight, squinted at him through thick prescription lenses.

'Yes?' said the man, wiping his hands nervously on his blue overalls.

Carter held up his warrant card.

'Detective Sergeant Carter. I would like to speak with the hostel warden.'

'Hostel manager,' the emphasis a rebuke. 'That'll be Mr Jennings. He's not here.'

Truculent, Carter decided, would be an understatement.

'And you are?'

'I'm Harman, the caretaker, handyman, dogsbody.'

He placed one hand on the door, the other on the door jamb. The message was clear.

Carter placed a foot into the doorway and stood his ground.

'If a parcel was delivered here for collection, who would deal with it?'

'Mr Jennings, I suppose, though Mrs Obong would probably be the one to take it and put it in the safe, or a filing cabinet. Depends how big it was.'

'Is Mrs Obong in?'

'She's on the bog, that's why I answered the door.'

'In that case, I'll come in and wait.'

Before Harman could object, Carter levered up on his front foot, applied his weight to the door and, as it swung free from Harman's grasp, pressed past him into the hallway. It wasn't his usual style, but the caretaker was really pushing his luck. Ahead of him the hall opened out to a space from which a broad staircase ascended and a passageway, with doors on either side, tunnelled deep into this Tardis of a house. Noticeboards along the walls carried rules and regulations, contact numbers and useful addresses. A small poster invited residents to a free StreetSmart meal event at the Choice Bar and Restaurant in Castlefield. There was a disturbing smell of damp clothes and disinfectant. The doorway closest to the stairs had a sign saying Administration. Below it a notice proclaimed: 'All visitors MUST report to the Office'. Suddenly, the door swung open, and a large and formidable woman of African heritage appeared in the doorway.

She had a remarkable face, strong and intelligent; high cheekbones, and a hint of humour in the wrinkles around her mouth and eyes. Almost certainly Nigerian, Carter decided, and without doubt architect of the notice on the door. Her voice boomed and echoed around the confined space of the wood-panelled hall.

'How can I help you?' she asked.

As Carter struggled to find his warrant card, Harman waddled down the hallway.

'I told him Mr Jennings was out, and you were otherwise engaged,' he panted.

She acknowledged Carter's credentials with a nod, and dismissed the caretaker with a wave of her hand.

'Thank you, Mr Harman, you can get back to your bins.'

What a put-down, Carter reflected, warming to her as she ushered him into her office. She turned to face him and remained standing, hands on hips, like a prop forward waiting for a maul. He was only just inside the room and she was closer to his personal space than he would wish. Part gatekeeper, part enforcer. She'd stand no nonsense from the residents, whatever their record.

'What can I do for you, Sergeant?

'I understand that earlier this year a parcel was delivered to this address for collection by an Alexander Westerby.' Carter consulted his notebook. 'The last week in August?'

Her face creased in a mixture of amusement and puzzlement.

'I remember it distinctly, Sergeant. I answered the door and had a bit of a barney with the postwoman. You see, although the name sounded familiar, we didn't have a Westerby staying or passing through; not then, and not since. And we can't have this place used as a drop-off for God knows what.'

'So you refused to accept it?'

'Oh no. Most of our guests don't have a place of their own – that's the whole point. If someone does need to send them something, they'll give the address of a hostel. But you have to be careful. I agreed to accept it on condition that I could see what it contained.'

The surprise was evident in Carter's voice. 'And she let you?'

Mrs Obong chuckled, and her bosom rose and fell like a tidal wave.

'Certainly not. Tampering with the Royal Mail?' Mrs Obong winked mischievously. 'She said she needed to check her bag for a moment – the trolley was at the bottom of the drive. When she got back, I'd taken a peek and was happy to sign for it.'

'And why was that?'

'Because, Sergeant, the parcel contained a clown outfit. You're not going to tell me anyone is going to smoke that?' She chuckled again, and the waves threatened to breach the sea wall where Carter was standing.

He stepped back a pace and felt the door handle hard in the small of his back.

'And did someone collect the parcel?'

'Oh yes, Mr Westerby himself. Or so he said.'

'Why do you say that, Mrs Obong?'

'Because nobody gives their real name if they can help it. In this case, he didn't look or sound like an Alexander, if you know what I mean?'

'Tell me.'

'Well, for a start, he was wearing a great smelly trench coat, with a few layers of pullovers underneath, and a pair of those black boots with steel toecaps. I couldn't see much of his face because he was wearing a woollen balaclava. In August, for heaven's sake. Still, we see all sorts here.' She paused for a moment to let Carter catch up with his shorthand. 'He had a strong Mancunian accent, and a hacking cough; like he had tuberculosis.'

Carter looked up. 'Did you ask him why he gave your address?'

She pulled a face, her nose crinkling up. 'To be honest, with the smell and the coughing, I couldn't wait to get rid of him.'

'Did you ask him for any identification?'

She began to laugh. The handle dug deep into Carter's back.

'Identification? Nobody who comes here carries identification. Maybe the odd photo or two, but never of themselves.'

'How tall would you say he was?'

She thought about this for a moment.

'About your height, I'd say. Probably a bit fatter than you. Hard to say with all those layers on.'

'And you'd never seen him around here before?'

'Neither before, nor since.'

Carter closed his notebook.

'Thank you, Mrs Obong. If you think of anything else, perhaps you'd let me know.'

He handed her his card and began to edge sideways, searching for the handle. He eased the door open and began to squeeze through. She smiled with amusement at his discomfort. He had almost made it to safety when she stopped him in his tracks.

'You didn't ask me about his eyes, Sergeant.'

'His eyes?'

'Well, his mouth and eyes were all I could see beneath that balaclava. His teeth were black and rotting, but his eyes were remarkable. Most of the men we get in here, their eyes are clouded and watery. Sad, soulless and weary. His didn't fit.'

'In what way?' Carter probed.

'They were clear and bright, and green, Sergeant … vivid green, and flecked with brown.'

It was mid afternoon and they were in Caton's room. Just the three of them: Holmes, Carter and Caton himself. DS Stuart had just nipped out to take a message. DI Weston was expected.

'So let me get this straight, Gordon,' Caton was saying. 'All of the ramps are accounted for bar two: one on the back of a lorry somewhere, heading back to the depot in Wythenshawe, and another which was sold on in August?'

'That's right,' Holmes agreed. 'But I've got a good description of the buyer that matches with the one Reilly and Roberts gave us. Only this time, it's a hell of a lot more detailed.'

Caton turned to DS Carter. 'And the man who collected the parcel, which is now confirmed as having contained an identical clown outfit, was of a similar build, and with the same green eyes.'

Carter nodded.

There was the briefest of knocks on the door and Joanne Stuart hurried in, notebook in hand. Her eyes were shining and there was a telltale flush to her neck and cheeks.

'The dental records came up trumps, sir. We've got a name.'

She slipped into the chair she had recently vacated and placed her notebook on the table, angled so that both she and Caton could read it.

'Stephen Davies, forty-five years old, and he has an apartment in that new complex down on the canal behind Whitworth Street.'

Funny, Caton reflected, how some people continue to speak of the victims as though they are still living, until they've been buried or cremated.

'That's a fantastic building. Must have set him back a bob or two. What did he do for a living?' Carter asked, confirming that most rules are general, not absolute.

'As far as they can remember, he was a graphic designer. He would always talk about things he was doing: Web designs and brochures, magazines and advertising, that sort of thing.' She turned the page in her notebook. 'They think he worked for a small firm somewhere near the Gay Village.'

'So he walked to work and play,' said Holmes.

'Thanks, Joanne,' Caton said. 'What about the horses? Does anyone know where Duggie is up to on that?'

'I checked this morning, boss,' Holmes replied. 'There was nothing on HOLMES. Not a single MO remotely similar. As far as bodies displayed is concerned, the normal patterns – if you can call any of them normal – involve trophies removed, and messages left either on the body, in blood, or on the walls or floor. There was one where a bronze horse had been used to hit the victim over the head. But that was domestic, and no display involved. She rang the police and turned herself in.'

'She?' said Stuart.

'Wife. Been married thirty-six years and caught her husband about to leave her for a long-term mistress she didn't know existed.'

'What about the Web? Something must have come

up on that,' said Caton.

'According to Duggie, "white horse" alone brought nearly thirty million hits on the Web and over three million on the UK Web. He's tried to narrow down the search by building in permutations, and he's got a couple of helpers ploughing through them. Nothing so far.'

There was a double rap on the door, and a pause for Caton to respond.

'Come in!'

DI Sarah Weston breezed in and cast a winning smile around the room. She looked more relaxed and fresher than she had done the day before. As he stood to introduce her, Caton wondered how she managed to look so elegant in a simple workaday pinstriped suit. Carter and Holmes were already halfway out of their seats, not something he'd ever seen them do before for anyone below the rank of superintendent. He pointed to a seat at the far end of the table.

'Welcome, DI Weston. Come and join us. Gordon you know. This is DS Carter and DS Stuart.'

She shook hands with each of them in turn and sat down.

'Good news, sir,' she said. 'We've got a name for your victim.'

The lack of reaction around the table spoke volumes.

She raised her eyebrows quizzically as she added, 'Davies, Stephen Davies. And why do I get the impression this doesn't come as a surprise?'

'I'm sorry, Sarah,' said Caton. 'I'm afraid Joanne beat you to it by a full three minutes. The dental records came through. But it's good to have it confirmed from another source.'

She smiled graciously. 'Sir James called. His reasoning was spot on. One of his contacts at the

Christie Hospital is working with the consultant conducting a new trial specific to patients with advanced forms of AIDS-related cancers. The trial matches the toxicology analysis, and Stephen Davies is a patient who fits our description exactly. And what's more, he's missed his last three treatments.'

'When was the first one he missed?' asked Holmes.

She consulted her notebook. 'Monday the 28th.'

'The morning he was found,' said Carter.

'And the last one he actually attended?' Caton asked.

'Wednesday the 23rd.'

'Which suggests that he may have been abducted sometime between the 23rd, and Saturday the 26th, when he was killed,' Carter chipped in.

'We can't assume he was abducted,' Holmes interposed.

They all turned to look at him.

'Okay,' he continued, 'so he held on to the body after he'd killed it, and before he dumped it in the gardens. But it's still possible that Stephen Davies met up with him of his own volition. In fact, that's always going to be the most likely explanation if he was drugged. It's one thing to be supporting an apparently intoxicated female from a pub or club, but quite another to be doing that with a man.'

'What planet are you on, Gordon?' Stuart asked. 'Not only would it be perfectly normal in the Village, but come to that, what about Reilly and Roberts? What's to say one of them couldn't have been drugged?'

Holmes took it well. He shrugged his shoulders.

'I s'pose.'

Caton looked on, noting yet another subtle change in the relationships between his colleagues since the team had been put together. A few months ago, there was no way DS Stuart would have been so direct, and as for Holmes, he would have been simmering, and it would have shown.

'Either's possible, so we cover both,' he said, moving swiftly on. 'Let's have another look at that e-fit. DI Weston hasn't seen it yet.'

Nick Carter pulled the image out from the folder in front of him.

The face that stared back at them would have been unremarkable but for the eyes. The head looked to be on the small side, with a short-cut cap of mousey ginger hair and matching eyebrows. Taken together with the unmemorable ears, nose, mouth and cheekbones, this face would have had the anonymity of a dummy in a high street store. But the eyes were mesmeric. Slightly larger in proportion than the rest of the face might suggest, the irises were an unusual shade of green. Somewhere, Caton suspected, between jade and emerald, but with a hint of yellow. And both eyes had small irregular flecks of brown, such that they were not identical.

'That's incredible,' said Weston. 'It's like looking at … at a pair of jewels.'

Caton scratched his head.

'He's using those eyes to distract attention away from the rest of his features. My bet is he's using contact lenses. Everything he's done so far has been measured, calculated. If he really did have such unique eyes – and I doubt that's possible – he'd wear dark or tinted glasses, or a contrasting set of lenses to throw us off. I think it's all part of the game he's playing.'

'Actually, boss, they could be real.'

They looked at Carter, fishing in his folder. He found the papers he had been looking for and placed them on the table.

'I couldn't believe it either,' he continued, 'so I went on the Web. The colour of the iris comes from the pigment in your eye, and that's determined genetically. If there's no pigment at all, you're going to have a pink iris. Just like albinos. A little bit of pigment and the iris appears blue, like Inspector Weston's. A bit more, and you get green, and then hazel like Joanne's, and then brown. If you've got a lot, they're going to look almost black.'

'But these have got green and a bit of yellow, and brown,' Holmes pointed out.

'That's possible,' Carter replied. He consulted the first sheet of paper – a printout. 'There are two pigments responsible for eye colour: melanin, which is basically brown, and lipochrome, which is a yellowish brown. And although it's rare, one iris can be a different colour from the other, and even more rarely, one part of the iris can be a different colour from another. And we all know that there are already biometric security systems using iris recognition, because the colour and patterns of each person's iris are as unique as a fingerprint.' He put the paper down with a flourish. 'It's all down to your genes.'

'But if this kind of combination is rare, then the odds would still be on contact lenses?' asked Caton.

Carter picked up the next two sheets of paper, and passed them, one to the left and the other to the right.

The sheets were covered with individual eyes sporting contact lenses, each of them a shade of green, some of them with a second colour for the pupil. The names beneath each well chosen: gremlin, green envy, cat's eye, creepers, green reptile, jade green, emerald green, hazel green, turquoise... There were at least a dozen on each sheet.

'But if he wanted to make a point, why didn't he choose one of the really scary ones?' DI Weston wondered, staring at the green panther.

'Good question,' said Caton. 'I still think they're more likely to be contacts.'

'So you don't think we should use the descriptions?' said Holmes.

'On the contrary. If I'm wrong, then it would be a big mistake to ignore it. And if I'm right, not releasing a description would let him know what we're thinking.'

Caton picked up the e-fit and had another look.

'And let's face it, if he really does look like this, we should have a hit within twenty-four hours.'

He passed it to DS Carter, who was busy placing the Web sheets back into the folder.

'Well done, Nick. At least we've got a clearer idea of what's possible. Before you get this circulated I want you to check it out with Reilly and Roberts, and with the hostel manager.'

Carter looked like a rabbit in the headlights. 'Do I have to, boss?'

'Come on, Nick, she can't be that bad,' chuckled Holmes, giving him a playful nudge.

'I tell you what then, why don't you go?'

'Because I've got to see a man about a ramp.' Holmes glanced at his watch. 'He's due back from Bristol about now.'

Sarah Weston leant forward.

'The consultant won't be in till tomorrow morning, sir. If it's alright with you, I'll file this lot and bring my paperwork up to date.'

'That's fine, Sarah,' said Caton. 'And Joanne and I will visit the victim's apartment, and then head up to Canal Street, see if anyone in the Gay Village can tells us a bit more about him.'

They began to leave the room, Holmes and Carter racing each other to hold the door for Sarah Weston, who winked at Caton and sped off towards the incident room, leaving them wedged in the doorway in their haste to follow her. DS Stuart hovered uneasily.

'Yes, Joanne, what is it?' asked Caton, looking up.

'It's just … you and me, going up to Canal Street. Why me, sir? It's not just because I'm the only gay in the Village, is it?'

Caton smiled, but knew better than to laugh it off.

'Don't be daft, Sergeant. It's because I need a keen pair of eyes and a smart mind. I'll arrange for the force LGBT liaison officer to meet us there. He can do the introductions, then you can concentrate on what you do best – detecting.'

'Thanks, sir,' she said, the relief palpable. 'I'm sorry to appear so touchy, but you wouldn't believe what I had to put up with in uniform. And in any case, we don't get into the Village that often.' She turned in the doorway. 'It's full of queers, you know.'

Caton heard her laughter echoing down the corridor. He went to his desk, collected his notebook and phone, and followed her. As he closed the door behind him he reflected that he couldn't wish for a better team, or need one like this as much as he did right now.

In the shadows beneath the trees, Albert Stephen waited patiently in his car watching the police cars come and go. Sooner or later Chief Inspector Tom Caton would emerge. He was surprised how many seemed to inhabit this modest building; scurrying, antlike, to and fro. He chanted the words like a special incantation. It was as though they had been written specially for him.

'…*But mine enemies are lively, and they are strong: and they that hate me wrongfully are multiplied.*'

Chapter 14

They walked the towpath, deep in shadow. The late afternoon sun cast a golden hue on the underside of heavy grey clouds, tinged pink in an otherwise leaden sky. Rich hues of bronze, red and green shimmered on the surface of the canal, embracing the reflections of the stately warehouses and modern brick and steel apartment blocks edged with sorbus, and hedges of box.

A heron glided past them, landed on the far bank, extended its neck and nonchalantly surveyed a scene that was at once beautiful and sinister.

DS Stuart broke the silence.

'When I started walking this beat, the canal was full of weeds, mattresses and bits of junk. Most of the warehouses were derelict. We never walked the towpath on our own. Look at it now. One of the coolest locations in the city. I wouldn't mind living here myself.'

Caton had just had the same thought himself.

'This is it,' he said, turning off the towpath and up the gentle incline beneath cylindrical V-struts that seemed, miraculously, to support the smart new glass and steel building clad with white glazed terracotta tiles.

To their right, an Italian-style piazza stretched out between the canal and Whitworth Street. A discrete sign by the side of a pair of huge glass double doors proclaimed simply that this was indeed 'The Lock'.

On the left, beyond the doors, a man in his early fifties, smartly dressed in a dark suit and silk tie, sat behind a long counter, a telephone cradled to his ear. He gave them a wave to show he'd seen them and courteously raised two fingers to show that he would be with them shortly. For want of anything else to do, they pressed their noses against the glass, and peered in like children at a sweet shop window.

Behind the doors stretched a wide boulevard, along the left side of which beds of pure white pebbles were planted with low-growing evergreens. Rising from the pebbles, a series of five angled columns, edged from ceiling to floor in alternating strips of pink, purple and blue neon lighting, supported a succession of glass and steel walkways, similarly lit, that criss-crossed the boulevard and rose beyond their line of sight. On the right-hand side, a sheer wall, punctuated by glass panels along the corridors, had at its base a panel of glass, crossed at intervals by staircases leading to the first level. The panel, bathed in blue light from below, gave the impression of a river. At the far end a bank of creamy yellow elevators beckoned invitingly. They were still taking it in when the concierge rose from his desk, released the doors and came to meet them. They held up their warrant cards as they stepped into the gentle warmth of the boulevard.

'I am Detective Chief Inspector Caton, and this is Detective Sergeant Stuart. We are investigating the death of one of your residents.'

The concierge looked shocked. 'I wasn't aware that there had been a death,' he said, leading them over to his desk.

'I believe a Mr Stephen Davies is the registered

owner of an apartment here?' Caton asked him.

The face of the concierge betrayed a gamut of emotions: surprise, puzzlement and finally, sadness.

'Mr Davies?' he said. 'I can't believe it. I mean, I could tell he was ill, but he had been looking so much better. He was such a nice man, polite, well mannered. I wondered why I hadn't seen him coming and going.'

'How long had he been a resident here?' Caton asked.

'He was one of the first. Bought it off plan four years ago and moved in at the end of August. He got a bargain too. A lot of people have bought them as investments, and the price is bound to soar. Not that that's any good to him now,' he added as an afterthought.

'We need to see his apartment,' Caton said.

'I'm not sure about that,' said the concierge, straightening up.

Ex-serviceman, Caton decided, probably a warrant officer.

'I'll need to ring head office.' He reached for the phone.

'In which case, you'd better tell them that this is a murder enquiry. We'll return with a warrant if we have to, but time is of the essence, and I don't see Mr Davies objecting, do you?'

The concierge froze, the telephone suspended in his hand.

'Murder? Mr Davies? I can't believe it.'

'Given that we didn't find Mr Davies' body anywhere near this area,' Caton began, 'I don't see any reason why it should affect the reputation of this complex in any way. Of course, if we have to get a warrant...' He let it tail off, his meaning clear.

The concierge replaced the telephone in its cradle and walked into the office immediately behind his desk. They heard him punch numbers into a digital pad, the sound of bolts withdrawing and the operation repeated in reverse. He returned, a small set of keys in his hand.

'I'll have to tell head office,' he said. 'But I suppose I ought to know a bit more first.'

Caton nodded. 'You lead the way, and I'll tell you what I can.'

They followed him down the atrium, craning their necks to look up at the maze of suspended walkways crowned by a skylight ten stories up, flooding them with natural light. Joanne Stuart plucked Caton's jacket and pointed to the right, where a slight bubbling sound confirmed that the river of blue was actually water, lit from below, flowing gently down the boulevard.

'We call this the street,' said the concierge, conscious of the effect which first impressions of this building unfailingly had. 'The building is basically two blocks of apartments, separated by the street, but joined by these suspended galleries. You wouldn't believe it, but there are eight apartments immediately above us supported by those columns.'

Stuart looked up. He's right, she thought; I don't believe it.

'Secure parking, rubber flooring under natural wood, zoned-controlled under-floor heating throughout and concrete dividing walls. Must be the quietest building in Manchester,' he said proudly as they neared the lifts.

'Are you on commission?' Stuart asked.

He laughed. 'I wish. You can't help being enthusiastic about a place like this.'

The lift door opened and they followed him in.

'Mr Davies is on the eighth floor,' he said. 'Two bedrooms, and a very nice view across the canal.'

He punched a button, and the doors closed with a sigh.

'Why did he wait so long before moving in?' DS Stuart wondered out loud.

'Ah well, he didn't have a choice really. It took five years to complete these apartments.' He smiled at the incredulity on their faces. 'No sooner had they started than they found a massive great pumping station where the foundations were supposed to go. Apparently, it used to pump water to the mills that lined the canal. They had to remove it piece by piece, much of it by night, because there's a professional recording studio next door. Still, it was worth it. Apparently, there isn't another building like it in Europe. I've heard there's one in Australia, though.'

Caton was still waiting for the lift to begin to move when the doors suddenly opened, eight stories up. They stepped out onto the central gallery, stretching back down the length of the street far below, from which walkways split at intervals to the left and right, where entry alcoves and porthole windows punctuated the walls. Up here the natural light was stronger, heightening the sense of airiness and space. The ribbon of blue shimmered far below them, visible in the gaps between the intersecting walkways.

'Mr Davies is down here,' said the concierge, heading north towards the canal side. 'You were going to tell me what you could?' he reminded them as they followed.

'Which isn't much I'm afraid,' Caton replied. 'Mr Davies' body was found in a park near the city centre early on Sunday morning. We suspect that he had been murdered.'

The concierge wheeled to face them. 'In St John's Gardens? He was murdered by that clown?'

Caton and Stuart looked at each other. It was the

inevitable conclusion everyone would be making, not least themselves.

'That headline in the Evening News,' he continued. 'I've just this minute read about it. The bastard! Why the hell would he want to kill a man like Mr Davies?'

'We don't know that he did, sir, we just need to find him as soon as possible, which is why we're here,' said Caton, eager to get on.

The concierge angled right onto one of the walkways and led them into a small alcove that harboured the entrances to an apartment.

'This is it,' he said, opening the door.

An insistent beep told them that the alarm was on. He stepped into the narrow hallway apartment and punched a number into the keypad alongside a video entry screen, with instant effect.

'Apart from the alarm company that maintains these, my relief and me are the only ones that have an override code. For emergencies,' he said.

'Quite a responsibility,' DS Stuart said.

He looked at her closely, trying to work out if this was an observation or a pointed comment.

Unable to decide, he sniffed huffily and said, 'Don't worry, they run a police check on us every twelve months. We're a damn sight more reliable than your average security firm any day.'

'I'm sure you are,' she replied, not wanting to lose his cooperation.

Caton took the initiative. 'I'm afraid I'll have to ask you to wait here, Mr...?'

'Johnston, Harry Johnston.'

Caton took a pair of plastic gloves from his pocket and began to put them on. DS Carter followed suit.

'There may be evidence here relevant to our investigation. We won't be removing anything, and there will be a scene of crime team here within the next hour or so. It's better if you let us find our own way round.' It wasn't negotiable.

They divided the search between them: Caton taking the master bedroom, en suite, bath and shower room; Joanne Stuart heading for the kitchen, utility room, living room and second bedroom.

Caton took in the master bedroom. A series of signed chrome-framed designs on the walls confirmed Stephen Davies' occupation. He was good … had been good, Caton decided. The bed was made. A white coverlet, illustrated with geometric designs in black, covered the duvet and pillows, on top of which a Spencer teddy bear with a sad expression stared back at him. A bedside unit held a radio alarm, and a copy of *BERLIN: The Downfall* by Antony Beevor.

Caton checked the alarm. It was set for 7 a.m. He opened the drawer and found five medicine dispensers, each of them with the days of the week printed along the top. He tried to imagine Stephen Davies waking each morning in this lonely room, starting his day with a ritual reminder of the fragility of life. A ritual which must have started hopeful, become increasingly weary, and ultimately pointless.

He flipped them open in turn and found each of the compartments empty, other than those for Sunday which contained a succession of pills and tablets of different colours, shapes and sizes. Caton reasoned that if he filled the boxes every Sunday night for the whole of the following week, this seemed to confirm that his routine had only been disrupted, fatally, sometime after he had risen on the Saturday, and before he was dumped in St John's Gardens.

He turned his attention to the wardrobe, which held a number of jackets, trousers, jeans and vests, sweatshirts and jumpers, folded neatly on the built-in shelves. The en suite bathroom, resplendent with

Villeroy & Boch matching bowl and toilet, yielded nothing other than to confirm single occupation; one toothbrush, one safety razor, one flannel.

Caton moved back into the hall where Harry Johnston stood ramrod tall and clearly uncomfortable, and opened the door into the bathroom. He flicked the light switch. The room was bathed in a soft and reassuring glow from downlights. An empty soap holder, a tub of bath salts, a bottle of shower and bath gel, a loofa, two clean towels and a white cotton dressing gown on the back of the door waited in vain. He switched off the light and headed into the living room.

As with the rest of the apartment, it was tastefully furnished in a minimalist style. Lots of black and white, and chrome, matching the clean lines and stainless-steel door furniture. Several abstract paintings brought splashes of colour to the walls. A thirty-two-inch flat-screen television, iPod hi-fi unit and a wireless-ready laptop the only personal touches apart from a white leather two-piece suite and a glass-topped table with four matching chairs.

He glanced in at the narrow galley kitchen, knowing that Stuart would already have searched it. Smart, bright and inviting, with its granite tops, wood and stainless-steel units. He slid open the door to the second bedroom, expectant, and the room gave the impression of never having been lived in; not a photo, book or single belonging. He walked to the end of the living room and stepped through an open door onto the balcony, where DS Stuart stood waiting for him.

'Hell of a view,' she said, looking out over the canal.

Caton followed her gaze. The cathedral-like spire of the Town Hall stood out starkly against the white-topped apartment blocks, their tinted windows burnished red and gold, their lower floors deep in shadow from the dipping sun.

'Did you find anything?' Caton asked.

She turned to look at him. 'Not a thing, sir. It's like he was a hermit. How about you?'

'Not really. Just probable confirmation that he was here on the Saturday morning.'

'So a wasted journey really?'

'Not entirely. At least we know he was living alone.'

He looked out over the city, slowly putting on its evening face.

'I wonder if our man is out there watching us.'

He took a breath of the cold evening air and blew it out slowly, like a jet trail in a summer sky.

'Well,' he said softly, 'whether you are or whether you're not, we're coming for you.'

'Did Mr Davies have any visitors?' Caton asked the concierge as they made their way back down the street towards the entrance.

'I never saw anyone enter or leave with him, and certainly no one came asking for him. Kept himself to himself did Mr Davies. I can ask my colleague, but I'm sure he'll say the same.'

Caton and Stuart shook his hand, thanked him for his help, and retraced their steps down the ramp and onto the darkening towpath.

Chapter 15

'Where the hell is Eden?' Caton asked, putting his mobile back in his pocket and starting to climb the steps up to street level.

'Don't tell me the Alternatives have started reading philosophy, sir,' DS Stuart teased.

'Don't be daft, Jo. I have a job persuading them to pick anything that's been on the Booker list. No, it's Sergeant Peake. He's just sent me a text message: *I'm in Eden* – wherever that is.'

She laughed and pointed diagonally across the road.

'It's a bar just over there, on Canal Street, where Metz used to be.'

He looked nonplussed.

'I take it you don't get into the Village much then, sir?'

Caton wasn't sure if she was serious or sending him up. They waited for the stream of traffic down Princess Street to pass.

'You'd be surprised,' she said. 'Most of the new bars are straight, but lesbian and gay friendly, and there are nights when almost half of the people in the Village are straight; mainly groups and couples.'

The traffic eased and they hurried across.

'It's a continuing source of controversy. There are those who want to keep it an almost wholly gay and lesbian community, and others who believe it should be integrated, and that in the long run stereotyping the area will make it harder to break down homophobic attitudes.'

'And what do you think, Jo?' he asked as they crossed the bridge and turned onto Canal Street.

'I doubt there's much anyone can do about it,' she said. 'The commercial owners of the newer pubs and clubs are just interested in profit, whoever it comes from. The privately owned ones will continue to cater for lesbian, gay, bi, transsexual, transgender and transvestite customers. The important thing is to make sure everyone works to cut out discrimination, and hate crimes in particular. The trouble is, that with it being such a well-defined area, it's bound to be a magnet for some mindless idiots and voyeurs. Although, to be honest, hen parties are the worst.'

She stopped opposite the Manto Bar and turned to face the canal, where a pretty green and white wooden bridge led across to the far bank.

Eden turned out to be a large red-brick converted mill. A black fire escape snaked up the frontage, giving access to an art gallery on the first floor and safe exit from the floors above. The main restaurant bar appeared to be on the ground floor, and in the cellar. Moored alongside, a large open-topped barge set out with tables and chairs, and sporting a white sailcloth awning, was already beginning to fill up with early evening customers. An earnest young man in his late twenties waved up at them.

'There's Darren,' she said, and started off across the bridge.

Sergeant Darren Peake pushed back his chair and rose to meet them.

'Hi, Jo,' he said with a broad smile. He offered Caton his hand. 'DS Stuart and I did our Sergeant's exam together,' he said by way of explanation. 'But I don't think we've met, sir. Although I did see you give a presentation at Hough End last year.'

Sergeant Peake, a good few inches shorter than Caton, had a firm handshake that matched his broad frame. His light brown hair was short and wiry. Despite his age, flecks of grey were evident around his temples, betraying the constant wearing of helmet and cap. This evening he wore a brown bomber jacket, roll-necked pullover, khaki chinos and Gore-Tex shoes. He saw Caton appraising him.

'I try to avoid wearing my uniform when I come here. It's one of the things the liaison committee was strong on. There was a time not so long ago when police vans would cruise round the neighbourhood and park up waiting for trouble. It felt like we were targeting the gay community, rather than protecting them.'

'But with such a concentration of bars and clubs there must still be a higher than average incidence of drink-related crime,' said Caton, recalling a time when he was one of those officers helmeted up and sitting in the dark and sweaty confines of a blue van waiting for the violence to kick off.

'That's true. It's just that we try to be a bit more sensitive about it. Fewer vans, more foot patrols, the occasional mounted patrol and specially trained community support officers. And it's paying off.'

He pushed his half empty cup aside.

'I was just having a coffee while I was waiting, but we'd better get off. I've tracked down your Mr Davies' company, and they won't want to be hanging around.'

He started to lead them across the gangway and towards the bridge.

'Company?' said Joanne Stuart. 'He actually owned a company?'

'Well, it's a partnership really. There are four of them, including him, all designers of one kind or another, and they have a couple of freelance workers who do stuff on a consultancy basis, plus a regular supply of students from the Metropolitan University. Quite successful by all accounts.'

'How did you get on to it, Sergeant?' Caton asked.

'Your collator said it was a graphics design firm somewhere in the area, and there are just a couple, so it only took one phone call. They're expecting us. I haven't told them why.'

Mancunian Designs was smaller than Caton had expected. Three rooms on the top floor of what must have been two terraces knocked through, provided an open-plan area set out with conventional computer work spaces, and larger desks on which drawings and plans were set out. Pinboards took up much of the wall space, displaying posters, photographs and a range of other artwork. Three large Velux windows in the open roof space provided much-needed extra natural light during the day.

A young woman glued to a computer screen near the door looked up anxiously as they entered. Two men in their late thirties, and an older woman in her mid forties, were gathered around one of the tables, deep in conversation. The woman spotted them in the doorway and came over.

'I'm sorry, I didn't see you come in,' she said, the words flowing in a torrent. 'You must be the police officers. I'm Trish Herd. This is Angela, a real treasure; she's just joined us for a month from the university.'

Before they could introduce themselves, she had taken Caton by the arm and was sweeping him towards the centre of the room.

'This is Jeremy,' she said, touching the taller of the

two, well over six feet, in conventional white shirt and grey trousers. 'And this is Julian. Julian is our expert in all things Web and multimedia. We call him Flash Julian.'

Julian smiled self-consciously and tugged at his Fat Face T-shirt.

'You wanted to talk about Stephen,' she continued. 'I hope he's alright?'

Caton was relieved that Peake had told the partners nothing. First reactions were often crucial.

'I'm Detective Chief Inspector Caton. This is Sergeant Stuart and this is Sergeant Peake, who rang you,' he said.

'Mr Peake, I know,' she gushed. 'We met at his Village Bobby surgery last year when we had a series of break-ins. You were really helpful,' she said.

'You still haven't got a security lock on the front door, though,' Peake replied.

That took her back, but she recovered quickly.

'But we do have an alarm, and mortice locks on the door up here,' she countered.

'Is there somewhere we can all sit down?' Caton asked.

She led them to the farthest end of the room, where a sofa and easy chairs were grouped around a glass-topped coffee table liberally patterned with coffee rings. Three gaily coloured mugs, a plate with three Jammie Dodgers and a half eaten muesli bar sat on the table.

'Please excuse the mess, we've just had a meeting,' she said. 'Would you like a drink? It'll only take a moment.'

'No, thank you,' said Caton, waiting for the others to take their seats and then sinking into one of the easy chairs. 'I'm afraid we've got some bad news.' He paused briefly, gauging their reactions. 'Mr Davies is dead.'

'I knew it! Didn't I say?' Trish Herd said, looking at her partners. She turned back towards Caton. 'We haven't seen or heard from him for over a week, and that's not like Stephen. But he was beginning to sound so hopeful. That new treatment he'd started at Christie's.'

Jeremy and Julian nodded their sympathetic agreement.

'But we all knew it was a last resort, Trish, and so did Stephen,' Jeremy said.

'I'm afraid Mr Davies didn't die from his illness.' Caton's voice cut through the conversation.

They turned to look at him, surprise etched on their faces.

'We believe that he was murdered.'

Their faces paled as one. Trish Herd's hands flew up to her face, tears already welling up. In that moment, Caton decided these were witnesses and not suspects. Hours of police work would eventually confirm that, but right now instincts came no more powerfully than this.

'We need to ask you some questions,' he said. 'If you don't mind, I would like you to speak with Sergeant Stuart, Ms Herd. I will speak with you, Jeremy, and Julian, I'd like you to go with Sergeant Peake.'

He looked over his shoulder at the student still glued to the computer, although Caton doubted she could have missed the anguish with which Davies' death had been greeted.

'Angela only started with us at the beginning of the week, Chief Inspector,' said Jeremy. 'She never met Stephen.'

'In that case, let's separate and get on with it. I'm sure we would all like to get this over as quickly as possible.'

Twenty minutes later, they had finished and were comparing notes in the stairwell on the ground floor, having closed the office door securely behind them.

'So all three of them are agreed on the following,' Caton said. 'He was a quiet, unassuming guy, who had no enemies. He had been living with HIV for twelve years and found out he had full-blown AIDS four years ago. He knew that he was going to die, and the only hope was this new treatment that was being trialled at Christie Hospital, and he'd been coming in part time three half days until a fortnight ago. A week before he was found in St John's Gardens.'

'That's right, sir,' Sergeant Peake agreed.

Caton looked up expectantly at DS Stuart.

'Yes, sir,' she said. 'And according to the two male partners, he hadn't dated – at least not in the full sense – since he first discovered he had HIV.'

'But all three of them are heterosexual; how would they know?' Caton asked.

'First off, when you've worked together for as long as they have, you get to know. It's like a family. Secondly, they are adamant that he'd actually told them that was the case, and everything about his demeanour confirmed it. What was it Julian said to me?'

DS Peake turned the pages of his notebook until he found the words he was looking for. He read them verbatim.

'"Before he found out he'd got it, he would always tell us about his latest partner. And he wasn't one for casual flings. So sometimes we actually got to meet them. There were only three or four in all the time I'd known him, which is over twenty years".'

'Twenty years?' Caton asked in surprise.

DS Peake looked up. 'They were at university together, sir. They met the other two and set up the company a year out of college.'

'Carry on,' said Caton.

Peake continued to read. '"And then one day he came in and told us he'd been diagnosed. He was gutted. But to be fair, you'd never have known until recently. He put a really brave face on it, but there was never any mention of boyfriends after that. And none of us ever saw him with anyone, until last spring".'

'Which was when he met this American … Aaron Novak,' said Caton, checking in his notebook.

'Anglo American actually,' said DS Stuart. 'Apparently, his mother was English, so he's got dual nationality.'

'Which is good news for us, because otherwise he'd have had to go back to the States by now,' said Peake.

'But according to Jeremy, that all fell apart in August of this year,' said Caton, 'and Davies seemed to have taken it really hard.'

'That's right,' said DS Stuart. 'It coincided with the sudden decline in his health.'

'The question is which came first, the chicken or the egg?' Caton wondered out loud. 'Well, there's only one way to find out. Julian reckons that he spends most nights in one of the bars near here. Is that right?'

'That's right, sir,' said DS Peake. 'Apparently, ever since they broke up, he seems to haunt the Village, always on his own, and spends most of his time in the Rem.'

'The Rem? What is that, a cyber café?' Caton asked.

The two sergeants laughed. 'No, sir, it's the *Rembrandt*, one of the original bars in the Village. It's on the corner of Sackville Street and Canal Street; you must have passed it on your way to meet me.'

'I know where it is. I was a regular visitor at weekends, together with the heavy mob. I hope it's improved.'

'The Rembrandt never was a problem,' said DS Stuart, 'just the lunatic fringe that hung around the edge of the Village looking to cause trouble. Right now it's really popular, and as safe as any of the bars. In summer it opens right onto the canal; it really buzzes.'

Caton put his notebook in his inside pocket.

'DS Stuart, I want you to get on with that list of Stephen Davies' clients. Start with the most recent. And ask the collator to task someone to run CRO and background checks on the partners, and on Mr Novak. DS Peake and I will see if we can find our Mr Novak. I'll see you back at base in the morning.'

The bartender pointed to a table in the corner, by a large window that looked out onto the canal. A young man Caton reckoned to be somewhere in his mid twenties sat cradling a bottle of beer, and staring blankly out onto the street and the waterfront beyond.

'He practically lives here. Comes in first thing, comes back for an hour at lunchtime and then gets in early before the evening rush. Always goes for the same table.'

He paused to place two glasses on the overhead rack.

'Bloody nuisance really. He's no trouble, but all he does is sit there on his own staring out of the bloody window. You can see he's a good-looking guy, so he gets plenty of approaches, but he just ignores them. All the regulars find him a bit weird and steer clear, but that's three prime seats buggered half the time. I wanted to bar him, but the boss says there's a history and to leave him be. If it was up to me...'

He turned to serve a customer who was clinking a coin impatiently on the bar. Conversation over.

Caton studied the young man. He wore a light grey sweatshirt edged in pink, over a turquoise-green long-sleeved T-shirt. His tight-fitting dark-blue jeans, secured with a blue snake-pattern belt, met a pair of white-laced purple sneakers. Over his left shoulder a broad grey strap held a lime-green and orange bag nestled against his right hip. Broad shouldered yet lithe, he had strong features – a square face with a high forehead and firm jaw – and thick blonde hair, gelled to give a windswept appearance, with short layers around the perimeters of the hairline. Although his face was in profile, and partly in shadow, Caton could see him working in television, or possibly as a male model.

They walked over and sat down at the table facing him, their backs to the street. He took a swig from the bottle, put it down and focused his gaze between and beyond them, as though neither of them were there. Caton saw heavy eyebrows above liquid brown eyes, rimmed red, with dark shadows beneath them. A mouth tightly set, the lips downturned. A day's stubble traced the template of moustache and beard. This was a handsome face, full of despair.

'Mr Novak? Mr Aaron Novak?' said Caton quietly but firmly. 'I am Detective Chief Inspector Caton, this is Sergeant Peake.'

The eyes flickered to Caton's face, and then to DS Peake's; startled, and suspicious, in turn. They had his attention.

'We understand that you were acquainted with Stephen Davies?'

The young man's face came alive, suffused for an instant with what Caton could only interpret as joy, and then, almost as quickly, dissolving into a mask of anxiety.

'What do you mean, *were*?' His tough New York accent strained through the tightening muscles of his throat and neck.

'I am afraid we have some bad news for you, Mr Novak,' Caton began, but before he could finish, a cry – somewhere between a scream and a wail – came from the young man opposite as he half rose from his seat, grasping the table, his face deathly white.

Caton and Peake reached out to stop him, but he was already crashing forward across the table, knocking over the bottle, spraying them both with Czechoslovakian beer.

They stood with their backs to the window and watched through the open door of the en suite as Aaron Novak sipped a second glass of water. It was a stroke of fortune that the Rembrandt was also a hotel.

'What are we going to do with him now, sir?' DS Peake asked softly.

'Take him back to his flat, and get the partners to keep an eye on him. They're only a block away, and at least they had Davies in common. He'll need to talk it through with someone. You can check on him from time to time, maybe arrange some victim support. We'll need a proper statement, in the morning; there's no point the state he's in. We'll have to treat him as a suspect, though, until we've ruled him out. He's the only one with anything approaching a motive at this stage. But if he's acting, he should get an Oscar. There'll be the funeral in due course, poor beggar. But he's young, he'll get over it.'

'I'm not so sure, sir,' said Peake, his whisper barely audible. 'In his twenties, three deaths in under a year and lovelorn. He's a classic case for young male suicide.'

Caton nodded. The story had emerged between gusts of weeping that gave new meaning to the phrase 'gut-wrenching'.

Novak had flown into Manchester from New York

in February, following the death of his mother and sister in a fire in the Bronx. His father had drowned his sorrows in booze, and the son had taken advantage of his dual nationality to escape to England. The father had always had difficulty accepting Aaron's sexuality, and the Gay Village had become a kind of safe haven for the young man in more ways than one, and he found no difficulty getting on to the books of an agency in Manchester. He met Stephen Davies in early April through a photo shoot he was doing for one of Stephen's corporate clients. The attraction was instant, mutual and intense.

Stephen had been suffering from AIDS for over three years, and the last thing he wanted was to begin a relationship that would add to his own sense of guilt, and ultimately cause pain to his partner. But he was unable to help himself. Emotionally the two of them were equally vulnerable, and they met a need in each other, in a space which was safe and where they could each be themselves. In any case, Aaron claimed, the chemical attraction was so strong that the force which pulled them together would always have been irresistible.

They agreed from the outset that they would never fully consummate their relationship, at least not until Stephen was better. This was a hope that both of them dared to entertain in the heady days of that spring and early summer.

At first, their love for each other seemed to work like a tonic for Stephen, who appeared to grow stronger and happier, and more positive in general. They visited art galleries and museums together, frequented restaurants and bars beyond the Village, even had a week away in a cottage in the Lakes. Aaron had even begun to accompany Stephen on his appointments to the hospital and, when his schedule permitted, would sit with him during the long spells of chemotherapy. And then, in July, Aaron began to notice a gradual slump in Stephen's shoulders, long periods of silence on his part, their conversations becoming one-way, and a general cooling in their relationship.

Suddenly, in the first week in August, Stephen told him that he believed he was dying. That he didn't regret the months they had had together, but that he could not bear the thought of Aaron watching him wither away. He wanted Aaron to remember him as he had been, and to move on with his life. When Aaron had pleaded to be allowed to continue to support him, whatever the outcome, Stephen had admitted that he felt it would be harder for him to come to terms with the time he had left while worrying about Aaron. It would be a final act of love, he said, for Aaron to let him go. And with that, he had walked out of his life.

Aaron had not given up easily. The following day he went to Stephen's flat, only to find that he had moved. He called at his workplace, but Stephen refused to see him, and when he had caught him on the way to work, the distress it clearly caused Stephen had been so great that Aaron had backed off.

In the months that followed, Aaron had caught glimpses of him most days through the window in the bar, on his way to and from work. On one occasion he had even begun to follow him, to find out where he was staying, but had been overcome by shame and turned back. And then suddenly, just over a week ago, Stephen had disappeared. Aaron had begun to fear the worst. And now they had confirmed it. Only the truth was far worse than he could have imagined, and now he blamed himself for not having been there to protect him.

'It doesn't get us any closer to his killer, does it, sir?' said DS Peake.

'I don't think it does,' said Caton. 'At the very least I thought we might get some clue as to where he might have met the perpetrator. All we've got is the vaguest possibility that it might have been a fellow resident, or one of his clients.'

'Or someone he met at the hospital?' Peake added.

For some reason, that hadn't occurred to Caton.

'Or the hospital,' he agreed. He began to cross the room. 'Come on, Mr Novak, it's time we got you home.'

'Do you think he'll be alright?' asked Caton, looking up at the balcony of Novak's flat above the Via Fossa, a stone's throw from the Rembrandt.

'God knows,' said DS Peake. 'That's a third-floor balcony, and he's got the sleeping tablets he's been using for the past five weeks. If he wants to do it, we're not going to be able to stop him. We can hardly section him, can we?'

'The poor beggar,' Caton said as they started to walk back along the centre of the street, avoiding the cheerful throng blocking the pavements on either side.

Outside the City Art Gallery they waited for a tram to pass, snaking its way up Moseley Street; a glow-worm packed with office workers, late-night shoppers and early evening starters. Caton thanked Peake for his help and set off with Joanne Stuart towards the GMex car park, leaving behind the hustle and bustle of the Village, the lights twinkling on the surface of the canal and the young man, exhausted by grief, in his lonely flat.

Chapter 16

Albert Stephen tapped the syringe three times, squeezed the plunger and watched the liquid spurt out and down, in a gentle arc, onto the cellar floor. With his left hand he tightened the tourniquet on the rough sleeper's upper arm. He bent closer, searching for a viable vein. It was becoming harder, not least because the veins had shrunk, and narrowed, as the organs fought for the remaining fluid in his body. Finding a thin line of blue, barely palpable, he inserted the needle and emptied the syringe. Withdrawing the needle, he knocked the sharp into an empty baked bean tin.

He was concerned that this was all moving faster than he had planned. Six to eight weeks was what the textbooks had said. But he realised now that he had failed to factor in how weak and undernourished his victim had already been. The combination of the sedatives and the total absence of food and drink was straining the man's heart. His pulse was thin, thread-like and irregular, and his breathing laboured. He was going to die soon, perhaps before it would be obvious that he had starved to death. No matter, Albert Stephen decided; let them work it out for themselves. In the meantime, he would bring forward the next stage.

He put the syringe into his trouser pocket. Grasping the tin in his left hand, he began to climb the stone steps leading up to the hallway.

'…If the looking glass gets broke, Mamma's goin' to buy you a billy goat…'

The building resembled a great ocean liner, the cabins on its upper decks regimented rows of brilliance cutting through the darkness as the ship sailed on into the mouth of the storm.

'I've got to stop reading Conrad,' Caton muttered to himself as he switched off the engine. Although, he reflected, had Conrad spent some time away from the merchant marine and wandered instead the streets of Manchester, he would have found as much to fire his creative spirit, by turns dark and dangerous, bright and wondrous, as he had on the high seas.

He climbed out of the car and glanced at his watch as he headed towards the entrance – 6.15 p.m. He had quarter of an hour before she arrived. Just long enough to check his emails and catch up with progress on both enquiries. He swiped his access card, waited for the door to click open and entered the building.

The incident room was quiet. According to Ged, the office manager, most of the team were either out on a job or had left for the day. Joanne Stuart had made her own way to the Town Hall to meet the caterers for her post-partnership party; Gordon Holmes had yet to return from his meeting with the lorry driver. According to the incident room manual, DS Carter had survived his second round with the redoubtable Mrs Obong, with a partial result … the eyes were spot on.

Caton recorded his own two visits in the manual, had a word with the allocator and was on his way back to his room when Ged called him back.

'Chief Inspector. There's a Kate Webb waiting for you at reception. Do you want them to bring her up, or will you go down for her?'

Caton looked at up at the incident room clock. She was ten minutes early.

'Get them to bring her up please, Ged.'

'Do you want me to arrange some drinks, sir?'

'No, thanks. I've got a supply of instants in my room. I've actually bought a kettle. But don't tell anyone,' he said, playing the conspirator. 'It hasn't been PAT tested by the health and safety bods yet.'

Ged raised her eyebrows, grinned and turned back to the phone.

Caton hurried back to his office, irritated that he had been unable to sort his emails and clear his head. He hated to be under-prepared. He was bending down taking a plastic box with assorted drink sachets out of a cupboard when the knock came.

'Come in,' he called, straightening up, box in hand, and banging his head on the shelf above.

The door opened, and a face he recognised from the front counter staff appeared around the door, grinning like a Cheshire cat. Mike something or other, recently retired from local government and now working part time with the police support staff.

'Miss Kate Webb, Chief Inspector,' he said with an exaggerated wink, stepping back and pushing the door gently open.

Caton rubbed his head with his free hand and was trying to decide if being over sixty was sufficient excuse for that kind of familiarity, when in she walked.

For the second time in less than thirty seconds, he was stunned. He had been expecting a dowdy, studious type with heavy glasses and a tweed suit; at best, an eternal student in fading jeans and baggy pullover. Kate Webb was neither.

She wore a fitted navy trench coat, unbuttoned, the belt hanging free, revealing a pretty blue and white polka-dot top, and a navy button-fronted skirt that finished at the knees revealing perfectly proportioned legs and slim ankles. A pair of red and white spotted shoes, with a three-inch heel, brought her to within a couple of inches of Caton's six foot one. Her oval face was framed by a cascade of rich auburn hair that ended in a short ponytail on the collar of her coat. Long, slim eyebrows accentuated oval green eyes that sparkled gold reflections from the halogen lights. Her skin was pale, on the verge of translucent, picking up the rich shadow from her hair. Her lips, full and pink, parted as she advanced towards him.

'Chief Inspector, I'm early, I know. I'm so sorry. The traffic was much lighter than I'd anticipated. I hope you don't mind?'

Mind? He registered that she was offering to shake his hand, and that his own was still clamped to the top of his head. Flustered, he dropped his hand and grasped hers. It was light, cool and firm. A shot of static arced between them, and their hands leapt apart.

'God, I'm sorry,' he said, even more embarrassed. 'That was me ... rubbing my head. I banged it on the shelf just before you came in.'

Her face broke into a wide smile. 'You mustn't let work get to you like that,' she said. 'I can recommend yoga, and a nice cup of camomile.'

They both began to laugh, the ice broken.

Caton put the sachets down on the coffee table and crossed behind her to close the door.

'Can I take your coat, Miss Webb?' he asked.

'I can manage thanks,' she replied. 'And it's Kate, if that's alright with you?'

'In which case, I'm Tom in here, and Chief Inspector in front of my team, if that isn't too confusing?'

'I think I can manage that.' Her voice was light, almost musical, with a lilt he couldn't quite place.

She slipped out of her coat and draped it over the nearest of the chairs grouped around the table. Long, slim, sensuous arms emerged from her sleeveless top. She shook her ponytail free from her shoulder with a movement that ran a shiver up his spine.

I'm losing it here, he thought to himself. He pulled out one of the chairs for her to sit on, and did the same for himself.

'Please, Kate, take a seat.'

He plugged the kettle in and switched it on, fumbling with the switch. Pull yourself together, man, he told himself.

'Would you like a drink while I fill in the background, and then I'll take you through to the incident room and you can have a look at the evidence and exhibits we've got so far?' he said.

'That would be great, I'll have a decaff' coffee if you've got it, or failing that … a camomile tea. It's been a hard day.'

He caught her mischievous grin, and they both burst out laughing again.

As she cradled the mug in her hands, Caton found himself checking her hands for rings.

'So, there's just been the one so far?' she said.

So she was single. Twenty-eight … thirty at the most? Maybe she was divorced. After all, he no longer wore his wedding ring.

'Just the one, Tom?' The concern in her voice brought him out of it.

'I'm sorry,' he said, 'I was miles away there for a moment. You were saying?'

'There has just been the one murder?'

'So far as we know,' he said. 'But you can see why I asked for a profiler. I may be a novice when it comes to this kind of MO, but I know what the training manuals say.'

She smiled. An open smile, no edge, no guile. 'That makes two of us I'm afraid,' she said. 'But as soon as Professor Stewart-Baker gets back...'

'No,' Caton cut her off a little too quickly.

He could see that she had picked up on it, felt himself beginning to blush and hurried to recover. Get a grip, he told himself, you're behaving like an adolescent.

'Now that I've briefed you, let's see where this takes us, shall we?' he said.

He put his mug on the table and got up.

'Let's go through to the incident room.'

She seemed as relieved as he was to break the awkwardness of the moment. As he brushed past her to open the door, the subtle scent of honeysuckle and jasmine fired a memory from deep in his past. His mother was calling from the kitchen; he was with his father in their garden, tidying up the borders after an early summer rain. For the first time in years, he felt a wave of tranquillity washing over the ever-present sense of loss.

Kate Webb held the small transparent bag closer to the light and turned it slowly in her hands.

'This isn't white,' she said.

'Sorry?' said Caton, coming over.

'It's not white, Tom. This is a palomino.'

'Are you sure?'

'If it was a real horse, I'd say this was a Danish palomino, and that would probably make this colour officially cremelo.'

She handed the horse to him. He examined it closely.

'You're right,' he said. 'This is closer to cream than white.'

'What made you think it was white in the first place?'

He had to think about that. 'It was how the pathologist described it at the post mortem, and in his report. I suppose we never questioned it after that.' He put the bag back down on the table. 'Does it make a difference?'

'Everything someone does who goes to this much trouble makes a difference,' she said. 'The clown outfit; displaying of the victim; how and where it was displayed; this horse; each one of them has a meaning, something he is telling us.'

'So chasing a white horse around the Web has been a waste of time,' he said, as much to himself as to her.

'Not necessarily, but I'd start looking at pale, and palomino as well, if I were you.'

'Duggie will be over the moon. He had thirty million hits on the first one.'

Caton started to lead her back towards his office.

'I've shown you everything we've got,' he said. 'Incidentally, where did you learn about horses?'

She flicked her ponytail. 'I was mad about horses. With other girls it was ballet, boys, pop stars, even soccer. With me it was horses. Daft really, because we were never going to be able to afford a pony, let alone a horse. I started mucking out at some stables in Teddington, where we lived, so that I could get free lessons.'

He opened the door to his office and followed her in. She sat at the table while he went to plug in the kettle.

'I'm sorry,' he said, 'I'll have to get some more water.'

'Not for me,' she said.

'In that case I won't bother either.'

He put the kettle back and flopped into a chair.

'You won't believe this,' she picked up where she'd left off, 'but I used to go to Thames Ditton, watching a boy I fancied at school playing rugby for Teddington, and that's how I discovered the Metropolitan Police Mounted Branch training school at Imber Court. I went to an open day, and then I persuaded them to let me help with the mucking out.' Her face lit up. 'Did you know they were started in 1760 to deal with a plague of highwaymen, and their uniform was the first one to be issued to any police force anywhere in the world? You should have seen their ceremonial turnout. And the horses were adorable. I was in seventh heaven. All I wanted to do after that was join the mounted police.'

'So what happened?'

She smiled wryly. 'A combination of things really. My teachers told me I would be limiting my chances, that I had a bright future. Then one of the policewomen I really admired at Imber Court told me much the same thing. Said she loved her job, but she didn't really think it was for me. Because I was into everything to do with the police at that time, I was watching *Cracker* on TV. It had just started when I was doing my GCSEs. Even then I knew it was exaggerated, but it was the first time I realised there was such a thing as a profiler. I was hooked.' She grinned again. 'And here I am.'

Caton smiled back. Thank you, Jimmy McGovern, he thought to himself.

'So what do you think?' he said. 'Does our Mr Bojangles fit a profile? More to the point, is he going to strike again?'

She leaned her elbows on the table, steepled her fingers to support her chin and looked at Caton thoughtfully. Now she was cool, focused and very professional.

'It's not as simple as that,' she said. 'There aren't sets of profiles sitting around on shelves that we can dust down and measure up against a given MO. Every single perpetrator has a unique profile. What we try to do is to get as close as possible to what that profile might be. Obviously there are characteristics, motivations, triggers that we know are commonly associated with random, multiple or serial murderers. But there aren't any templates. Think of it as a kind of e-fit. You don't start with a photo and work backwards. You build up the likeness piece by piece, from a database of shapes, and sizes, colours and tones. Well, that's what *we* do; only we are dealing with the mind.'

Caton nodded. 'Fair enough,' he said. 'But can you hazard an educated guess? Are we likely to hear from him again?'

She leaned back in her chair and placed her hands flat on the table.

'I'm afraid that's not very hard to answer,' she said softly. 'The display, the horse, the trouble he's taken to leave the body where he has, the fact that he knew much of this was on camera. He's on some kind of a mission, and he needs us to understand. So until we do understand … oh yes, we'll hear from him again.'

It sounded like she'd already appointed herself a member of the team, emotionally and intellectually at least.

'What was the focus for your PhD, Kate?' he asked.

'Is this an interview, Chief Inspector?' she replied, frowning slightly.

'Not at all,' he rushed to reassure her. 'You are licensed as a profiler, and that's good enough for me. No, seriously, I'm genuinely interested.'

The frown was replaced by a wide smile. 'Well, just remember that you asked for this,' she said. 'The title was: *To what extent do existing models of offender behaviour provide a basis for the construction of models for the drivers of serial murderers, in Britain, based on the characteristics of those murderers?'*

'Drivers?' he asked.

'Yes, it was a bit clumsy,' she said. 'Basically, the things which drive them to commit the murders, and the way in which they commit them.'

'Why in Britain?'

She grinned. 'Because there was no way the university was going to fund me to swan off to the USA to interview serial killers. And anyway, there are real cultural differences between us and the States that probably affect some of those drivers, added to which it was a reasonably unploughed field over here.'

'Interview them?' He had difficulty hiding his surprise.

'Naturally. How else was I going to find out what drove them? Most of them are vain, egocentric narcissists. There's nothing more they like talking about than themselves. Like most men I suppose,' she said half seriously. 'And before you ask – because every man I've met since I started this work has asked – what a young woman was doing interviewing a load of seriously sick and dangerous weirdos, ask yourself why you do what you do. Because the answer is almost certainly the same.'

There was a challenge in her voice and behind her smile that warned him to be honest. She was feisty, liberated and nobody's fool. He realised that he was enjoying this conversation in ways that he had not done with another woman in years.

'I won't pretend that it hadn't crossed my mind,' he said. 'But I can assure you that was where it was going to stay. There's just one thing, though. You mentioned models. I thought you said there was no such thing as a template.'

'Very good,' she said.

To anybody watching this, Caton realised, it could easily be seen as intellectual foreplay. It certainly felt like it.

'That's the trouble with words in the English language,' she continued, 'they have too many possible interpretations. On the other hand, that's what makes our language so rich, and so much fun. In my use of the word, a template is a cut-out you can simply lay down and draw around, or copy. A model, however, is a representation, an ideal, a sort of mock-up to be tested, not an exact copy.'

'So when do we get see your model for our Mr Bojangles?' he asked.

'Give me a day or two,' she said. 'I'll ring you.'

'Let's hope he gives us a little longer than that,' said Caton, rising and leading her towards the door.

It was 9 o'clock when he got to the apartment. Too late for the gym. In any case, he was exhausted; and yet his mind was buzzing. He opened the fridge and realised it was time to visit the supermarket. There was a Tupperware containing half a can of baked beans. He checked in the bread bin, relieved to find a couple of bagels, and fished a small can of tomatoes from the cupboard. Beans and tomatoes, and a dash of Worcester sauce, on a toasted bagel, washed down with a glass of milk. Could be worse. He opened the fridge again. No milk. He pulled a bottle of Budvar out from the chiller compartment and wearily closed the door.

Twenty minutes later he had polished off his meagre feast and was sitting reading his emails. Amazon was telling him that people like him who had ordered *The Serial Killer Files: The Who, What, Where, How and Why of the World's Most Terrifying Murderers* by Harold Schechter had also ordered *Serial Killers:*

The Method and Madness of Monsters by Peter Vronsky.

It depressed him to think that there were other people out there who might be reading these books for pleasure, rather than work. He pressed delete, and considered the offer from Oddbins: six bottles of champagne for the price of five. Maybe, when they'd put this investigation to bed, that might just be an offer he'd take up. He pressed delete again. Scanning the remaining seven emails, he realised that not one of them was personal in any way. He marked them all, pressed delete and watched as they disappeared. *You have no messages,* said the screen. It may as well have added *Saddo!*

He came out of his email and shut down the computer. He looked at his watch. Twenty minutes to leg it up to the Sainsbury's Local on Quay Street before it closed. A breath of fresh air, and the promise of more than a stale bagel for breakfast, might just clear his head.

As he began to jog up Liverpool Street, his mind still on Kate Webb, he failed to connect the silver-grey Mercedes parked opposite the Castlefield Hotel with the car that had followed him, unnoticed, from the station, always one or two vehicles behind.

Chapter 17

Fresh from a good night's sleep, and a breakfast of scrambled eggs, bacon, toast, fruit juice and yoghurt, Caton fairly bounded into the incident room. Gordon Holmes looked up from his desk.

'You're looking sprightly this morning, boss,' he said, grinning broadly. 'Wouldn't be anything to do with the latest of Caton's Chicks, would it?' he added innocently.

'What the hell are you on about, Gordon?' Caton responded, though he had a pretty good idea.

'It's what Division are calling the bevy of attractive young women on our team. It seems last night's addition more or less confirmed it; apparently, you've started a harem. She's a right cracker by all accounts.'

'For God's sake!' Caton exploded. 'Haven't they got anything better to do with their bloody time?'

Everyone in the office looked up. The boss had made it clear from the outset he didn't like swearing in his team, never mind sexist innuendo. Holmes was as surprised as any of them by the strength of his reaction. Truth to tell, Caton had surprised himself. Holmes tried to make light of it.

'It's only a joke, boss; you know what they're like.'

Caton knew only too well. It was like a family in more ways than one, with all the ribbing, the petty jealousies and the claustrophobia that went with it. He hadn't planned to have three stunners on his team, but that wouldn't make any difference. He knew what people on the outside would make of it. He tried not to think about the kind of jokes that would already be circulating. Still, best to just grin, bear it and make sure he didn't give them any ammunition.

'You're right, Gordon,' he said. 'It's wishful thinking on their part; just because they don't have our magnetic personalities.'

Holmes laughed along with him, but he knew the boss had been rattled. He couldn't wait to meet this consultant investigative psychologist.

'How did you get on yesterday, Gordon?' Caton asked him, changing the subject.

Holmes leant perilously back in his chair.

'The missing driver looks like a blank, boss. He's still got the ramp on his lorry, and he claims he was in bed in Newcastle, in a guesthouse, on the Sunday morning when our friend was making his own delivery in St John's Gardens. He says he wasn't alone in bed either. Seems like it's a regular run, and he's got a thing going with the landlady. Bit reluctant to tell me at first, but when I pointed out that we were talking about a murder enquiry, he soon fessed up. It checks out with his logbook and tachograph. I've got someone from their murder squad checking it out. A quid pro quo for that favour we did them on the Clarendon case.'

'I suppose it means we'll have to widen the search area for the ramp. How many did DC Wood say had been sold in the UK?'

'A hundred and seventeen altogether. We've just eliminated nine of the ten sold in the Greater Manchester area.' He paused and looked at Caton quizzically. 'But surely, boss, our best lead is the guy Soaper sold his one to. He matches all the other descriptions. Do we really have to track down the others?'

'You're right,' Caton agreed. 'But until we know for certain, we'll have to track them all down. No need for you to get involved in the legwork. I need you to bring me up to date on Operation Panda. Superintendent Gates is bound to want an update soon.'

'Did you get anywhere with the profiler, sir?' Holmes asked as they made their way towards Caton's old office, to which the Operation Panda files had been relegated.

Caton looked sharply at his DI, but it was clear from Holmes' face that he was either a bloody good liar or Caton was becoming paranoid. Probably both.

They'd finally decided how to breathe some life into Operation Panda when there was a knock, and DI Weston poked her head around the door.

'You asked me to let you know, sir. DS Carter and DS Stuart are both here.'

'What time are you due at the hospital?' Caton asked.

'11.30, after the consultant's rounds.'

'In which case, you three go through. We'll be with you in a minute. And get someone to sort the drinks out please, Sarah.'

'Okay, sir.' Her head disappeared and she closed the door behind her.

Caton turned back to his other DI.

'So you reckon we've got about five months before the Serious and Organised Crime Agency start to crawl all over this one?'

'I'd have thought so, boss. That's the feedback I'm getting from NCS liaison anyway. The National Crime Squad, and the part of the Immigration Service we're dealing with, have been diverted to some extent in preparing for the changeover. But sometime early in the New Year they're going to want to get back up to speed on our part in this investigation, if only because the new commander of SOCA is going to have to show the Home Office that the Agency can hit the ground running. And let's face it, Operation Panda has it all as far as the Agency's remit is concerned: drugs, prostitution, illegal immigration, people trafficking, fraud, copyright infringement on a massive scale...'

'And murder,' Caton added. 'Let's not forget murder; that's the only reason we were involved.'

Holmes put the evidence box he was holding back onto a shelf, dusted his hands and turned to face Caton.

'Wouldn't it be better if we just handed it straight over to the NCS now? The Agency will probably take it off us anyway in April.'

'I'm sure you're right, Gordon,' Caton replied. 'Call it pride, but I'd love to have a final crack at it. If we don't get Bojangles sorted fast, it will all be academic. We'll have to admit we don't have the time or the resources to do it justice.' He opened the door, and added as he was leaving, 'And this room will empty faster than a steam room invaded by a skunk.'

Gordon Holmes stepped into the corridor and locked the door, pondering the sudden shift in his boss' manner. Something was definitely going on.

By half past ten the team had brought each other up to date. DI Holmes was chairing the briefing, and Caton had asked Joanne Stuart to recount their visit to The Lock and the Gay Village; as much to allow him to run over it in his own mind, as to give her some proper airtime. He realised that he had hogged most of the questioning during those interviews, and just hoped she didn't think that his asking her to handle the briefing was patronising. But then DS Stuart was much tougher than she looked, and if she had been offended he would have been the first to know.

'We've got a possible description which matches the man who dumped the body, and the man who bought the Ramp 2 Roll from Soaper, so...' DI Holmes began counting off on his fingers. 'We widen our trace on the purchasers of the ramp; we need to find the van, and the young lad that was sent in to collect the false plates from Gerry's; we speed up the collation, analysis and follow-up to any responses from the public to the description; track down and interview anybody who knew, or was seen with, Stephen Davies in the weeks before his disappearance...' He paused and looked around the table.

'Incidentally, nobody's said anything about his family. Have they been contacted?'

'Sorry, I should have told you,' said DI Weston. 'He was an only child. His father had a heart attack and died three years ago. His mother is living with her sister in Norfolk. They're travelling up to Manchester later today and staying overnight. I said I'd accompany her to the morgue in the morning. We still need a positive ID. I gather you didn't ask Novak if he'd come in and do that, sir?' she asked Caton.

'I know, I should have done,' he said. 'But to be honest there was no way he was up to it.'

DS Stuart nodded in agreement. 'I was going to get DS Peake to bring him in today, but if the mother's on her way, and the dental records are conclusive, I think we can wait.'

'I've lost track now,' said Holmes. 'What have I missed?'

'The profiler's suggestion that we look at pale, and palomino, horses,' DS Carter offered.

'Thanks, Nick,' said Holmes. 'I guess we've got

everything covered, except the boss has asked me to breathe a bit of life into Operation Panda, so somebody is going to have to make sure we get the door-to-door and street enquiries up and running around the Gay Village, between the Palace Theatre and the Hacienda on Whitworth Street, and along the parallel stretch of the Rochdale canal either side of The Lock. Given it's a towpath, we just need someone by each of the bridges. They can use the e-fit, and the photo of Stephen Davies from Novak's flat.'

He sat back in his chair and looked across the table at Caton.

'I think that's about it, boss.'

Caton checked his watch as they began to gather their papers and push back their chairs.

'DI Weston,' he said, 'I've got some paperwork to get through; can we meet up in the car park at quarter past? It's only going to take us ten minutes to get down there.'

'It could take us as long to park, though. Can we make it ten past instead?' she replied. 'I don't think consultants like to be kept waiting.'

Sarah Weston had been right; they had to park three streets away. It was dead on half past as they hurried to the consultant's office. They arrived at a small but cosy reception area, surrounded by comfortable seating. Coffee tables were well stocked with a range of magazines. A hot drinks machine and a water dispenser filled one corner. Caton was surprised that there were only four people waiting and one ahead of them in the queue. They hung back at a discrete distance until the window was free.

A pleasant-looking woman in her mid fifties, with a practised smile, welcomed them.

'Next, please.'

Caton leant close to the window and showed his warrant card discretely.

'DCI Caton and Detective Inspector Weston. We have an appointment with Doctor Winstanley.'

Her smile evaporated, and her face showed genuine concern.

'Of course, that dreadful thing with poor Mr Davies; I'll let him know you're here.'

She picked up the phone and made the call.

'Doctor Winstanley will see you now,' she said. 'If you go down the corridor, it's the second on the left.'

'Thank you, Mrs…?' said Caton, fishing.

'Mrs Jackson,' she replied. 'You're welcome.'

'When we've finished speaking with Doctor Winstanley, perhaps we could have a word with you, Mrs Jackson? In the meantime, it would be really helpful if you could be trying to remember anyone who accompanied Mr Davies here, or whom he may have struck up an acquaintance with?'

'That's very easy,' she said. 'I can tell you now there was only ever one – a Mr Novak. He started coming with Mr Davies last May, and more often than not would be with him throughout his chemotherapy treatment. It was very touching really. Then he suddenly stopped coming.'

'When was that, Mrs Jackson?' Sarah Weston asked.

She thought about that. 'It was just after I came back from my holiday in Dubrovnik. So that would be about the second week in August. Mr Davies arrived for a new regime, and Mr Novak wasn't with him. I was tempted to ask where he was, but Mr Davies looked pretty low, so I didn't.'

'Thank you, Mrs Jackson,' Caton said. 'You've been very helpful.' He placed a card on the counter. 'If you remember anything else, please don't hesitate to ring this number.'

'Do come in.'

Winstanley advanced to meet them. He was dressed in a blue and white check shirt, with a yellow tie covered in characters from The Simpsons. His shirt jacket lay over the back of his chair, on top of a long white lab coat. He was a striking figure. Six foot in height and approaching fifteen stone, he was deceptively light on his feet. Could have been a rugby player, Caton speculated.

They introduced themselves and the consultant pumped their hands firmly in turn, taking just a little longer over Sarah Weston's.

'Good to meet you … shame it had to be under these circumstances. Terrible business… I'll do what I can to help … only got ten minutes though, I'm afraid.'

His words fired at them like bullets.

'We don't see it taking that long, doctor,' DI Weston said as he gestured them to take a seat. 'Just a few questions about Mr Stephens, if we may.'

The doctor picked a weighty file up from his desk.

'Fire away,' he said.

Sarah Weston opened her notebook.

'How long had you been treating Mr Davies?' she asked.

'I've been … had been treating him for the past two years. He was first diagnosed as suffering from AIDS…' He consulted the file. 'By Doctor Habid in July 2003. But he had been HIV positive quite some time before he developed AIDS.'

'And what kind of patient was he?' she asked.

'Intelligent … very positive … completely cooperative … willing to try anything… In many ways the perfect patient.' He paused, reflecting for a moment, and put the file down on his desk. 'Until we started the new regime.'

'In what way did he change?'

'It's difficult to put my finger on it. He suddenly seemed to lose interest in the treatment. Before, he always wanted to know what the trials had proved ... what sort of results there had been ... what he could do to help. This time he didn't want to know. Frankly, it was such a change in him that I was concerned.'

'Did you raise it with him?'

'Of course.'

'And what did he say?'

'That he was getting tired of fighting ... that he just needed to take a back seat for a change, and let the treatment work.'

'And did you believe him?' Caton asked.

He thought very carefully about it before he answered.

Measuring his words, and deliberately slowing down his speech, he said, 'Actually, I did. At first I thought his relationship might have broken down. A Mr Novak had been accompanying him.'

He looked up and saw them both nodding.

'They were very close ... you would have to say in love. But when this new treatment started, Stephen was always alone. I actually tackled him about it. He said that it wasn't fair to build up Aaron's hopes – his name was Aaron...'

Again they nodded.

'And then dash them down again.'

'Did that surprise you?' asked Sarah Weston.

'Not really. It happens; usually when a patient begins to sense that they may not make it after all. It isn't necessarily that they don't want their loved ones to suffer; it's just as likely that it makes it harder for them to deal with approaching death, having to witness the growing sadness and the pity in the faces of those who come to visit them.'

'Isn't that selfish?'

The doctor straightened his tie. 'I wouldn't like to judge. Sometimes it's easier in a hospice, or with home support, where both parties can be helped to build a safe emotional bond through which to deal with the inevitable. Stephen hadn't quite reached that stage.'

'But his condition was critical?' Caton asked.

'Oh yes. This treatment was a last resort, and he knew it. He had always wanted the whole truth.'

'Which was?'

'That without the treatment, he had less than three months to live. With it, we might be able to extend that by between nine months and a year.'

'And the odds of that happening?'

'Based on the most recent trials, twenty per cent.'

A silence descended on the room for a moment as Caton and Weston reflected on how they would have responded to such news. DI Weston cleared a frog in her throat.

'Just for the record, Doctor, what was this treatment exactly?'

He had no need to consult the file. 'It was a special trial involving a GSK protease inhibitor, together with ritonavir and combivir. We have high hopes for it, possibly bringing patients significant remission, but in Stephen's case, I'm afraid it came too late.'

Caton saw him glance at the clock on the wall opposite his desk.

'Just one more question, if you don't mind, Doctor,' he said. 'Apart from Mr Novak, can you think of anyone else with whom he may have developed an acquaintance beyond that which you might expect; other patients, nurses, hospital porters, anyone at all?'

Winstanley looked surprised, but appeared to give it a lot of thought.

'No, I'm sorry,' he said at last. 'You see, apart from

the spells of chemo' and recovery from the radiography, and some invasive investigations, he was never admitted to a hospital bed. There was hardly time to develop a strong acquaintance. But I'm not the best person to ask; I suggest you speak to the day ward sister. Janet, my secretary, will arrange that.'

He closed the file pointedly and began to put on his jacket.

'And now, if you'll excuse me, I do have patients waiting.'

They closed their notebooks and got to their feet.

'Thank you very much for your time, Doctor,' Sarah Weston said, shaking his hand and giving him one of her winning smiles. 'We know how precious it is. And in case you think of anything else, here is my card.'

He took the card and put it on his desk. Caton shook his hand, and the two of them began to leave.

'There is one thing I remember ... it may be nothing.'

They turned to face him.

'It was about three weeks before he disappeared ... or rather, missed his appointment. I was passing the café in Waterstones, on my way to the loos, and I spotted Stephen in conversation with someone at one of the tables.'

'Did you get a good look at this person?' DI Weston asked.

'I'm afraid not; he had his back to me. Stephen had a coffee in front of him, and a paperback it looked as though he might have been reading. It was open and turned over so that you could see the spine. Not that I could read the title from where I was.'

'The man, Doctor, is there anything you can remember about him?'

'I don't know; probably in his forties or fifties ...

dark hair, black or brown. I've no idea how tall he was because he was seated and leaning forward across the table. He had on a big brown duffel; he could have been almost any build under that.'

'Is there a possibility you might have seen him before?' Caton asked.

'No, I don't think so; hard to say really.'

'But it wasn't Aaron Novak?'

'Oh no, definitely not. Too old, and wrong colour hair.

'And this was the Waterstones on Deansgate?'

'That's the one. I generally pop in when I'm in town.'

'Could you help us with the date at all?' Caton asked.

The consultant glanced at his watch and huffed a little, but reached for his desk diary and flipped through it.

'Here it is. Must have been the Saturday morning; only day I got into town that week. 22nd of October. Would have been about 11.30, I guess.'

'That's really helpful, Doctor, and if you think of anything else…' said Caton.

'I'll give DI Weston a call.'

I bet you will, thought Caton as they left the room.

'When you speak with the ward sister,' Caton said as they waited for Mrs Jackson to become free, 'ask her to put together a list of all of the people who came into contact with Stephen Davies more than once, and get Mrs Jackson to let you have a list of anyone who had access to Stephen Davies' records. If you get any grief, ask to see the senior hospital manager.'

'What about the DPA, sir?' Sarah Weston asked.

'We are not in contravention of the Data Protection Act unless we ask for names, addresses or other details held on their computers. There's no reason they have to use their records for any of this, just their memories and common sense. We don't need to know anything about the reasons why patients are here, so there is no patient confidentiality involved. If you still have a problem, which I doubt, point out that there is a murderer on the loose, and he could be right here in this hospital. That should do the trick. As soon as you've got some names, ask the allocator to set up interviews, starting with the hospital staff. When he briefs the team, tell him they mustn't show that e-fit to the witnesses, or discuss the description, until after the witnesses have racked their brains. How much time did they spend with Davies? Did he talk to them, and if so what about? Did he mention anyone else? Did they see him with, or speaking to, anyone else? You know the drill. And I want a background check on everyone on that list.'

'Everyone, sir?'

'Everyone. We're clutching at straws here. For all we know there may be an accomplice, in which case the description and e-fit won't help. I know it's time-consuming, but you and I both know that's what routine police work is all about, and in the end that's how we solve most of our cases, contrary to what the films would have us believe.'

'That and the mistakes perpetrators make,' she added.

'That too, Sarah, that too.'

'What are you going to be doing, sir?' she asked.

'I think I'll get up to Waterstones and see if they have any CCTV tape for the 22nd of October. If they do, there's a good chance we can identify this mystery man entering or leaving the shop.'

They didn't. There was plenty of surveillance alright, but as with most retail stores there didn't seem to be much point in keeping tapes beyond the normal stock check period. It was a significant blow, and the rest of the day dragged as he ploughed through a mound of paperwork, waiting for some kind of breakthrough. It never came, and Caton realised they had hit the doldrums that seemed to affect all but the simplest of investigations. Perhaps the profile Kate Webb was working on could breathe some life into the case. His ruminations were rudely interrupted by a knock on the door. It was DS Carter.

'Boss ... you wanted to know what kind of response we're getting from the e-fit,' he said.

'Come on in, Nick, and sit down; I could do with a break from this lot,' Caton replied.

'It's not going to take that long, I'm afraid. The street interviews haven't thrown anything up so far, and the telephone response to pictures in the paper are running true to form. He's been seen at Manchester Piccadilly, Manchester Airport, The Triangle, The Trafford Centre and the Odeon Cinema at the Printworks – where apparently his eyes were glowing in the dark. Three people reckon it's the devil incarnate; one woman claims he's been stalking her for the last two years, and now he's started hovering over her bed at night; we've had an offer from a clairvoyant who reckons he can help if we let him see the victim's body; and an interesting observation from a jeweller on Cheetham Hill. Apparently, he says the eyes are the exact colour of a gemstone that's only found in one mine in Nevada. It's called Orvill Jack turquoise, after the mine owner.'

'No surprises there then,' Caton said. 'We might need to think about a clairvoyant at some stage, but if we do, I think we'll choose our own. You can't afford to ignore the sightings, however bizarre they might be. At least all those places have good CCTV coverage.' He paused for a moment and rubbed his head where the bruise was still annoying him. 'That jeweller may be on to something. You remember those firms you checked out that do coloured lenses?'

'Yes, boss.'

'Why don't you contact them? See if any of them have had any strange requests. Or if any of them do lenses like that, or know of any that might.'

Carter left, and Caton got up and poured himself a mug of water from the kettle to help clear his head, before tackling the quarterly monitoring report that had been sitting in his pending tray for the past fortnight. I can't wait to see what the profiler has come up with, he thought to himself as he settled back in his chair. We've got evidence, but no real suspects, and no motive. This is the best hope we've got right now.

As he picked up the report and looked absently at the first set of targets, he knew there was more behind the expectation he had for tomorrow's meeting; in truth, he couldn't wait to see Kate Webb again.

Chapter 18

It was a dry, crisp morning. Caton waited patiently to turn off Oxford Road and into the car park on Burlington Street, alongside Alfred Waterhouse's magnificent Whitworth Hall, its walls, buttresses and blue-topped spires gleaming gold and red in the morning sun. He watched as gaggles of students made their way towards the students' union building, just as he had done two decades earlier. He envied their easy camaraderie, their youth and the boundless opportunities ahead of them.

Those had definitely been the best years of his life to date; the friendships, the sport, the MadChester scene, the demos, even the learning. Then, he remembered, we worried about Terry Waite, Northern Ireland, the Lockerbie Bombing, whether the Iran/Iraq war would escalate, Black Monday, Apartheid, the Palestinian–Israeli conflict, Section 28, if Morrissey or New Order would make it to number one. Now, they probably worry about global warming, AIDS in Africa, Iraq, Afghanistan, the Palestinian–Israeli conflict and how to pay off student loans, afford a house and save for pensions. I don't think I'd swap after all, he decided as a break appeared in the traffic. He swung into the narrow street and up to the barrier.

Caton wondered how Kate Webb had managed to wangle him a parking permit, right here in the heart of the Owens complex. He picked the campus map off the dashboard, locked the car and set off on foot to cross Oxford Road and find the Henry Fielding Centre of Psychology and Policing.

She met him at reception and took him up to her office. Her ponytail bobbed from side to side as she led him up the stairs. Her step was light, athletic, everything about her exuding a sense of vitality. Halfway down the corridor on the first floor, she unlocked a door and ushered him in.

The room was deceptively small, almost half the size of his own. The reason it seemed larger at first glance, Caton realised, was down to the way a large table desk had been shunted up against the windows to make room for a flipchart and three display panels on a telescopic stand. There was a comforting smell of fresh bread and freshly brewed coffee.

'I hope you haven't had any breakfast,' she said, crossing to the table where a cafetière sat alongside two mugs, two cartons of juice, a couple of paper plates and a bag of croissants. 'I always pick something up on the way in when it's a breakfast meeting or an early start.'

'Brilliant,' said Caton. 'But I will pass on the juice; it's the only thing I did manage.'

'Help yourself. There's milk and sugar on the way, and you've a choice of pain au chocolat or almond.'

She watched him hover, undecided.

'Go ahead,' she said, teasing him. 'It's not a test.'

'That's the trouble with psychologists,' he said. 'You can't tell when it is and when it isn't.'

They sat side by side on the edge of the desk, cradling their mugs.

'Don't worry,' she replied, 'I'll let you know when it is.'

She smiled at him over the rim of her mug as she put it to her lips. A logo ran around the centre of the mug: *THE HOME OF... red and proud... www.redandproud.com.*

He considered himself warned. No place for ginger jokes.

'What did they say when you told them you wanted to become an offender profiler?' He took a bite out of his croissant. 'At your faculty interview.'

'I didn't...' she said, wiping a crumb from the corner of her mouth, '...tell them. I figured they'd think I was some kind of weirdo. It was hard enough explaining why I wanted to do Criminology in the first place. I mentioned that I'd been working at Imber Court, became interested in police work, then read a bit about psychology and liked it, and that led me to apply.'

'Did you tell them about *Cracker*?'

'Funnily enough, they asked if I watched it. I said I did, but I played it down a bit. We had to take Psychology, Crime and Criminal Justice as a compulsory course unit in year one, and it just rolled on from there. It was only when I'd done my Masters that I overtly pursued the profiling. I met someone from a research group at the Metropolitan University, and they helped me with my PhD and preparation for my accredited status. Through them, I was also lucky to be able to work with several eminent forensic psychiatrists who let me accompany them into secure institutions. So now I'm part of a network, and although people have different styles and approaches, it's great being able to bounce things off each other; especially when it's my first real live case.'

'But that's only going to be a small part of your work, surely?' Caton said, picking up his mug.

'Not even that, really. We have to squeeze it in, almost like a hobby, which is why you find it so hard to get a profiler when you need one. I can justify it, to an extent, as part of my research, but I earn my bread taking seminars and tutorials, delivering lectures and writing. I also do some consultancy for the Greater Manchester Strategic Health Authority – mainly with the South Manchester PCT – on offender behaviours.'

'Now I feel guilty taking up your time,' Caton said.

She stood and wiped her hands on one of the paper serviettes alongside the plates.

'Well, you've no need to. Firstly, because I think it's important; secondly, because I'm learning so much from it; thirdly, because I'm not sure this is going to be all that helpful to you; and finally, because I'm afraid you'll have to fit in with me, and not the other way round.' It was a statement; neither an apology nor an explanation, simply a matter of fact.

Caton noted again how quickly and comfortably she moved from relaxed and friendly to focused and professional, establishing a clear line between work and anything else. Something he realised others would recognise in him. He wiped his mouth and hands on the remaining serviette, crumpled it on the plate and watched as she opened out the display stands like a concertina.

Each panel was covered with various Velcro-backed pieces of plain white card. On some of the cards, photos had been fixed; on others, diagrams had been drawn or text written in felt-tip. Exclamation marks and question marks punctuated the text. Thin strips of coloured wool linked cards to one another in an apparently random web. It reminded him of the incident room.

Leaning forward to get a better view, he was startled to find that one cluster of photos on the first panel consisted of the cross in St John's Gardens as it now was, and three eerie black and white historical pictures: one of the old church, long since pulled down, and two depicting thousands of gravestones, laid end to end, covering the entire area between Byrom Street and Lower Byrom Street. Further down were photos of the front and rear entrances to The Lock, the canal towpath, one of the Gay Village and one of Christie Hospital.

Among the diagrams on the second panel was a rough sketch of the horse they had found on Stephen Christie, and the words 'palomino', 'gullet' and 'inserted'. Most of the textual comment appeared to consist of lists or questions too small for him to read. It was obviously not for presentation, rather an aide memoir, or work in progress.

'You've been busy,' he said, trying to keep from his voice the surprise he was feeling.

'Don't worry,' she said, misinterpreting his guarded tone, 'I put this lot away in my storeroom cupboard every night, and lock the room when I go out.'

'No, seriously,' he assured her, 'I wasn't expecting you to go to these lengths, or this quickly.'

She smiled. 'I think you'll find most offender profilers turn their office into a mini-incident room. If it works for you, why not for us?'

She finished checking that the stands were stable and turned to face him.

'Shall we get started?'

Caton nodded. 'Fire away.'

She stood with one arm across the top of the flipchart, the other on her hip.

'So, what exactly do you want to get out of this?'

'We have some evidence, no real suspect and no motive. I'm hoping you can help us consider what the evidence tells us about motive. Can we narrow down the kind of person we might be looking for? Do you think he's done it before? Is he likely to do it again? And if so, who might be his victims?'

'Well, I can have a go at some of that, but you do realise that this is going to be really tentative. I'll probably raise as many questions as answers. I've got only one incident to go on. To be honest, I wouldn't even have considered touching it, except that it does have some bizarre features, and I do think there's a high probability he will strike again.'

'Fair enough,' Caton said. 'I've done the training, and read the literature. I know the limits of what we can expect. Profiling is as much educated guesswork as most of what we do. Another tool for us to use; not a holy grail.'

'Good,' she smiled knowingly, 'because there's a saying amongst accredited profilers: if you get it wrong, they'll blame you, and if you get right, they'll take the credit.'

'That's not what I said.'

'No, but just so long as you understand, I don't really care who takes the credit, but if you take what I have to say as gospel, then neither do I expect to take the blame.'

'That's a promise.' Caton smiled back. 'Hopefully, I'll be able to do something about the "credit" bit as well.'

'Time will tell,' Kate said. 'How much do you know about Activity Theory?' she asked as she prepared to turn back the first page of the flipchart.

'I read something on it when I was doing my MA.'

Her eyebrows rose, just enough to tell him she had some stereotypic ideas about policemen.

'An MA, really? What was it in?'

'Crime, Law and Society – two years part time. I did it here as a matter of fact; well, at the university, but not in this building.'

'That will save us some time.' She planted her feet a little wider apart and folded her arms. 'Go on then.'

'Is this a test, Ms Webb?' he asked pointedly.

'Ouch.' She laughed loudly and flipped back the first page of the chart.

There was a heading at the top of the page: *Activity Theory: Five Principles.* Below it were five bullet headings with some short paragraphs under each.

'So I don't need to go through all of this in detail?' she said.

'Just a quick revision will do fine,' Caton said.

She pointed to the first bullet, *Goal-directed.*

'Everything he does is directed towards a single purpose. We have to find out what that is.'

She pointed to the second bullet, *Hierarchical.*

'Everything he does is meticulously planned, and is only going to change in response to unforeseen, unplanned changes in the context he finds himself in.'

'Like the jig he did when Roberts and Riley turned up out of the blue,' Caton observed.

'Exactly.'

She pointed to the third bullet, *Internalization & externalization.*

'This is more complicated, but let's just accept that whatever's going on outside his head – his external behaviours – is inextricably linked to what's going on inside his head.'

She checked that he was still with her.

'This fourth one – *Mediation* – is a typical academic construct. It's basically saying that all human activity is supported by tools and artefacts; things like language and signs, and machines and instruments – in this case the rolling ramp, the clown outfit, the horse – that we create, or use, to control our behaviour.'

She checked with Caton again.

'...*Neither hand nor mind alone suffice; the tools and devices they employ finally shape them,*' he said, almost to himself.

She stared at him, and this time her surprise was undisguised.

'Francis Bacon,' he said.

'The pioneer of the scientific method,' she said. 'He'd have made a great profiler.'

She turned back to the chart.

'The final principle is *Development*. The theory requires us to analyse human actions in terms of the context of development. This is where it gets tricky, because the activity is actually the context.'

She saw him frown.

'Think of it like this; our perpetrator abducts, kills and displays another man, in a public place that was formerly a church and mass graveyard. In the course of doing that, he uses drugs, a van, a particular kind of ramp and he wears a clown outfit. All of that is both activity and the context within which he operationalises the activity.'

She stepped away from the chart to use her hands to better effect, stabbing the air for emphasis.

'The really important thing about all of this is that the internal and the external contexts are – for all of us – fused at the same time ... it's unified.'

'So how our man is acting is a direct expression of how he is feeling, and who he is inside,' said Caton, hoping he'd got it.

'Even more than that,' she said, 'they are one and the same. And it all comes out in who he selects as his victims; how and where he abducts or attacks them; how he kills them; how he disposes of the body; and how he seeks to evade justice.'

'That's all very well,' Caton agreed, 'but what if he's schizophrenic? Will what one personality does actually tell us who the other personality is?'

'I'm disappointed,' she said. 'You're falling into the trap of popular belief. Schizophrenia has nothing to do with split personality. Although since it comes from the Greek for shattered, or split mind, you could be forgiven for thinking that. People with untreated schizophrenia typically experience delusions, hallucinations and are disorganised in their thinking. Do you think such a person could carry off what our perpetrator has managed?'

'Not a chance,' Caton replied.

'What people crudely refer to as split personality is actually called dissociative identity disorder, or DID. It used to be called multiple personality disorder.'

'Okay, so what about DID? Does activity theory still hold true then?'

'Absolutely. It would still hold true, but for each of the personalities separately,' she said. 'But although these so-called personalities must routinely take control over a person's behaviour for a diagnosis to be made, there's a lot of controversy over whether or not they are personalities at all, or simply altered states of consciousness.'

She detected a gleam in Caton's eye.

'And before you ask if Bojangles could be suffering from DID,' she said, 'I'll tell you. Yes, it is possible, but that doesn't mean we couldn't build up a useful profile.'

'And is it likely?' Caton asked.

'In a word, no. It only affects about one per cent of the population, and more importantly, it isn't associated with the kind of highly organised, confident, controlled behaviour we are witnessing here. Quite the opposite. That doesn't mean he may not have suffered from DID to a lesser degree in the past, because the triggers that might explain his behaviour are the same as those which are believed to cause DID.'

'You'll have to explain that,' Caton said.

'Well, it's closely associated to post-traumatic stress disorder and, as you'd expect, is found in people who have suffered trauma – most often at a sensitive stage in their childhood. This can range from repetitive, overwhelming and sometimes life-threatening trauma such as might come from extreme abuse – sexual, physical or emotional – or that experienced through war, torture or disasters such as the tsunami.'

'Or kidnapping,' Caton added, remembering a case a few years back.

'Or kidnapping,' she agreed. 'When a child has suffered, or is suffering, something like that, they often find refuge by switching off. It's commonly been described as "going away in their heads". When that turns out to be effective in cutting themselves off from the pain of the experience, they begin to resort to it in the face of any challenges, and so it becomes a pattern of behaviour which can continue long after the original threat has passed. In an extreme form, it becomes socially and emotionally disabling.'

'And it never results in violence towards others?'

'I don't know about never,' Kate replied. 'The most common symptoms are panic attacks, phobias, depression, mood swings, sleep disorders, flashbacks, obsessive compulsions, eating disorders, amnesia, time loss, trances... The list is endless. As far as violence goes, the main tendencies are towards self-harm.'

She paused for a moment to consider the implications.

'But yes, a small minority are driven to violence towards others.' She returned to the flipchart. 'But I still doubt that's the case here; it's all too meticulous, too well planned.'

She looked at her watch.

'We'd better get on,' she said. 'Would you like another drink?'

'No, thanks. But don't feel you have to rush it. This is too important. I've got till lunchtime.'

She looked relieved. 'In that case, if we crack it by then, perhaps you'd like to come across to the Refectory and have a light lunch?'

'Sounds good to me,' he said without a moment's hesitation.

She flipped over the first sheet and revealed a set of numbered bullet points, seven in total, headed *Salient Case Details*.

'As far as we know,' she began, 'we only have this one incident involving this predator, so from a profiling point of view the most important details are limited.'

She pointed to the first of the bullets.

'First, we have the cause of death. We know it was an administered overdose, the victim already had a terminal illness and the method chosen was apparently painless. Why choose this method? Why select a dying man – assuming he knew Davies was dying? Was there a deliberate avoidance of pain? Next, we have the choice of place. It's more or less central in the city, it's on the site of a former graveyard, those buried there died – among other things – from cholera and typhus; plagues of their period. Is there a connection with the fact the victim had AIDS – often referred to as a plague of our times? Why in such a prominent place? Thirdly, we have the deliberate displaying of the victim. This involved significant risk. Does the man get off on the risk of discovery? Does the place have such a high level of importance that it's worth the risk?'

Her finger stabbed at number four.

'The costume – this was presumably for disguise, but it seems it was also about performance. Is there a reason for this particular costume? Whatever the answers, it suggests narcissism and arrogance. Fifthly, we have the eyes. These are so startling we have to ask, are they likely to be real? Probably not, given the rest of the disguise, and the way he chose to cover his tracks with the van and the costume. So, are they another part of the disguise, a distracter? Or do they have another purpose, a special significance for the perpetrator? Number six, the horse; this is an artefact that must have a special significance, meaning or message. He is clearly playing a game, challenging us, trying to tell us something.'

She moved her finger to the seventh and final bullet, and tapped three times on the chart.

'And finally, everything suggests that he knows this city. He either lives here, or works here, lived here, or worked here. I'm fairly confident that he's still here, not least because he wants to see what you are going to do next.'

She dropped her hand to her side and looked at him expectantly.

'That's really impressive,' he said. 'All you've had was an hour and a half at the station, and I doubt I'd get a better summary from any of my team.'

She allowed a small smile to curl the edges of her lips, something he found really sexy. So much so that he forgot what he was about to say.

'So?' she said.

'So ... what conclusions do you draw from all that?'

She flipped the next sheet over to reveal yet another set of bullets. They were headed *Tentative Conclusions*.

'Note the word tentative,' she said firmly, and then began to reel them off. 'He's controlling, he takes risks so he may be an adrenalin junkie, but that doesn't necessarily mean he goes in for bungee jumping and white-water rafting. On the other hand, he also seeks to minimise risks. He's intelligent and competitive. He may have a trace of empathy – the choice of killing, the lack of sign of abuse of any kind; in a bizarre way it feels a bit like euthanasia. Again, on the other hand, he must be cold and calculating, using a human being – albeit one who is dying – for his own ends. Alienated, we would call it. He probably works alone. He is a victim in some way.'

'Victim?'

'We're looking at causality here, not excuses,' she replied. 'He's likely to have suffered trauma of some kind – loss, abuse – or perceive himself to have been the victim of persecution, denial, exclusion. At the very least, he has at some point – probably in childhood – experienced or sensed weakness. In a normal family that will have been overcome by affection, love, opportunities to exercise responsibility, to be praised, a sense of security and a feeling of being respected and trusted. In such an environment that child becomes a coping person. In a dysfunctional family that's unlikely to happen, so he grows with that sense of weakness, or more likely has it reinforced. He's going to have real difficulty trusting people. His relationships with others will be flawed. And that will make him even more hateful.'

'So, low self-esteem, self-hatred, hatred of others?'

'That's it, except if he's going to be able to cope in an adult world he has to find a way of living with all that. If he can't, he'll probably turn to drink or drugs. He might get into pornography, he might obsess on food and become morbidly obese – although we know

233

that's not true in this case.'

'And if he does find a way of coping?'

'It's likely to be through finding ways to control others, through manipulation, intimidation or bullying. That will make him contemptuous of others – especially those he controls – and build his own sense of importance.'

'Surely he'll be able to develop some relationships?'

'He'll probably try to, but if he fails, either because he's rejected or because it doesn't feed his ego, he's going to become even angrier. The rage will build up inside, and he'll have to find a way to release it. And when he finally does, he'll get a climactic rush of adrenaline – almost orgasmic. But, just like an orgasm, it will be momentary, and each successive one will lack the thrill of the first. So he'll desperately seek to rediscover it, and the frequency of his attacks will increase. And then he'll realise that the greater thrill is in the preparation, the capture, the execution and the ease with which he can get away with it. All this feeds his sense of omnipotence. He's finally found a way of coping.'

'But why give us clues? Does he want to get caught?'

'That's a possibility. If he has the slightest trace of moral principle he may be feeling a sense of self-loathing at the same time that he's feeling godlike. On the other hand, he may just enjoy taunting us, and the clues could turn out to just be distracters. Of course, there's always the possibility that it's more complicated than that.'

'And is that what you think we have here?'

'I don't know. But I think it's possible.'

'So where does that leave us?'

'Clinically? At the very least, borderline personality disorder – far more likely to be a severe personality disorder. In terms of the beginnings of a profile – and bear in mind this is about as sketchy and tenuous as it gets…'

She flipped the chart for a final time, and revealed a single paragraph in italics.

White Caucasian male, 35–55, intelligent, with a good knowledge of the city; lives and/or works locally. May have been abused. May have been in care – adopted, fostered, in a council home – or equivalent. Could have a criminal record related to precursor activity. May have been an underachiever – or paradoxically a high achiever – at school. Likely to be employed or self-employed. May be homophobic or paradoxically gay [rejected]. Likely to be outwardly charming. Will be a practised liar, but also a loner – no real friends, no clubs or groups, no evidence of belonging.

Caton read it through several times.

'That probably narrows it down to about five thousand men in Manchester, and that's not including the seven boroughs that touch the city boundaries,' he said.

'But how many within a one-, two- and then a three-mile radius of where the body was found? A tenth of that?' she asked.

Caton nodded. 'The only problem then, is how we identify them. And it's not as though we've got any fingerprints or DNA.'

'I know,' she said. 'But it's as good as it gets at this stage.'

She paused, as though uncertain about whether to commit herself further.

'Can I suggest what you might think of doing next?'

'Go ahead,' said Caton; 'you've been doing a good job so far.'

'Well, I'm sure you are already on top of all of this … but, with the profile as just another tool – as you put it so elegantly earlier – there are some things you might want to think about. There's usually a learning curve. Try to connect him to precursor behaviours. Try to find out if the motive might be personal, homophobic or simply egocentric. Work out what that horse is supposed to tell us. Look for patterns in his modus operandi, although I accept that only becomes possible with further incidents, and I'm not suggesting we wish for that. Follow the geographers' principle of nearness, and the psychologists' principle of least effort; it's likely that you'll find him within a relatively narrow radius of a circle whose centre is between the victim's house and work, and where he was left.'

'What kind of precursor behaviours?' Caton asked.

'That's a hard one. Possibly stalking – in person, by phone or over the Net – cruelty to animals as a child, attempted suicide; to be honest I don't know. I'm sorry. I did say there wasn't a lot to go on at this stage.'

She flipped the pages of the chart back to the beginning, and came and sat beside him on the edge of the table, trying to gauge his response.

'There's no need to apologise,' Caton said. 'I didn't expect a miracle, and to be honest you've exceeded my expectations. Can I take those sheets with me?'

'I can do better than that,' she said, crossing to her desk and taking a data key from the top drawer. 'It's all on here.'

She handed him the key and took a lilac padded windcheater from a hook on the back of her door. Smiling, she opened the door invitingly.

'Now, shall we have some lunch?'

Albert Stephen moved the pasta hypnotically around his plate. Ribbons of golden olive oil and black balsamic came together in swirls of bronze that separated out as quickly into little puddles. He counted himself lucky that he had been able to find a place on a table with an unrestricted view of the lifts. It had been his first stroke of good fortune since losing the policeman when he turned off Oxford Road into the one-way street with the manned barrier. Albert Stephen had been forced to park in the Aquatics Centre multi-storey car park two blocks away, and by the time he returned, Caton had disappeared. His second piece of luck was spotting them preparing to cross the road towards the Refectory where he had been loitering. He had just had time to duck into the Food Hall and join the queue. A surreptitious glance caught them entering the Refectory and making for the lifts.

He glanced at his watch. It had now been over three quarters of an hour. On several occasions he had been asked, by students desperate for somewhere to eat their lunch, if he had finished. He would really have liked a glass of water, but there were none on the table, and he didn't want to risk missing them. Ten minutes later, his patience was rewarded.

The woman stepped from the lift, closely followed by Caton. It was the first time that he had seen her face close up and from the front. A band of steel tightened around his chest, and his pulse began to race. He dropped his fork and grasped the edge of the table with both hands.

'Are you alright?' The student sitting opposite him leant forward, concerned that this older man might collapse across the table.

Albert Stephen ignored him. He watched as the two of them made their way towards the long glass doors. She walked tall and confident, light on her feet, her short glorious auburn ponytail swaying gently from side to side; just as he remembered his mother's had before their world fell apart. As soon as the doors closed behind them, Albert Stephen pushed himself up. His chair clattered to the floor behind him. He hurried up the steps and hung back at the long glass panel beside the doors.

He watched as Caton climbed into his car. The young woman bent for a moment, her face close to the open passenger window. Then she stood up and waved as the car set off. She began to walk along the pavement towards Oxford Road, but turned suddenly to climb the steps towards him.

In a panic, Albert Stephen spun around and, spotting several notices beside the lift, moved across as though studying them. He thought he caught a faint scent of jasmine as she passed close by. It reminded him of the stephanotis he had bought the first time his mother came home from hospital. The tightness around his chest began to ease, and his pulse began to slow. He took a few deep breaths and slowly turned. He watched as she went through the doors on the opposite side of the hall and headed down the steps. He waited until she had passed from sight, and only then did he head for the doors.

None of this had been lost on the young man who had first become concerned by Albert Stephen's demeanour. He had watched as the man hovered by the doors; had seen him turn suddenly, making a pretence of reading the menu for the staff dining room; he had seen him watch the woman as she crossed the Refectory; and he had no doubt that she was now being followed. Had he not been a fresher with less than a term under his belt; had he listened carefully to the talk by the police liaison officer during the induction programme; had he been a woman perhaps, alarm bells might have been ringing in his head. As it was, here was a man – an older man granted – who was clearly infatuated. She was, after all, a cracker. He turned his attention back to his friends, with a tale to embellish.

Chapter 19

Caton closed the spellchecker and pressed save. It was finished, and two days ahead of schedule. The quarterly report was probably his least favourite, and most thankless, task. The fact that it had now been linked to performance-related pay made not a jot of difference to him. The statistics could always be given a gloss, but ultimately they spoke for themselves. With two major investigations on the go, both of them resource greedy, and neither of them appearing to go anywhere, he was not looking forward to the review. It was unlikely that Chief Superintendent Hadfield, or the assistant chief constable for that matter, would make allowances for the fact that his team had been set up to deal with just such cases. Results and resources were the only things they would be interested in. With a sigh, he took the remaining folder from his in-tray. It was the latest progress report on the Bojangles investigation. He opened it, and began to read.

Ten minutes later he had been through it twice. It had not made comfortable reading. They had reached, he realised, the plateau that seemed to characterise every single investigation, other than those like the domestics that practically solved themselves; and he didn't get any of those any more. Now it was a frantic charge uphill, a long slog across a top that seemed to be going nowhere, and then, if you were lucky, a quick sprint down the other side when you least expected it. He looked at the ominous number of documents in his pending tray and decided he needed a break. He had to talk to someone, anyone, before the walls began to close in on him. Then it came to him. It had been a week since he reported back on his visit to the university. The response from his senior officers had been mixed, but broadly favourable. DI Weston had been openly impressed. Nick Carter and Joanne Stuart had been pretty objective and measured in their appraisal. Gordon Holmes had been grudging in his praise. What he had no idea of, was how it had gone down with the rest of the team. He picked up the phone and called the office manager.

'Ged? Is DI Holmes in?'

'I think so, sir. He's certainly not signed out. I'll see if I can find him.'

'When you do, let him know I'd like a quick word.'

Two minutes later, Gordon Holmes knocked and popped his head around the door.

'You wanted a word, sir?'

'Come in, Gordon, and take a seat. I was wondering what kind of reaction you got when you distributed that briefing note based on the profiler's suggestions?'

Profiler, Holmes reflected, not Kate Webb, or even Ms Webb. Was there some kind of cooling off going on?

The chief looked like he had been taking uppers when he came back from the university. Now, he looked positively down.

'It was about what you'd expect,' he replied. 'To start with, there was a general air of scepticism. Wood was downright dismissive; "load of bollocks" was his expert opinion, expressed just sufficiently sotto voce for everyone to hear. But Duggie Wallace and his guys were quite enthusiastic; reckoned they could use some of it as another filter when they're working though their analyses. And when DI Weston came in, and told them in no uncertain terms that she thought there was some mileage in it, you'd be surprised how people started nodding.'

'By people, I assume you mean the men?' said Caton.

Holmes laughed.

'And what about you, Gordon?' Caton asked. 'I know what you said in here, but what's your feeling about it now?'

Holmes folded his arms. 'To be fair, a lot of it is common sense, and we'd all had similar thoughts about the kind of person who would pull a stunt like this. But you've got to admire the way she's pulled it together, given it a bit of structure. And I must admit, it gets you thinking when you're talking to witnesses, and looking at possible suspects; so long as it doesn't narrow our vision too much.'

'Fair comment,' said Caton.

He was interrupted by the phone. It was Helen Gates.

'Good morning, Tom,' she said. 'Are you tied up with anything in particular?'

'Nothing I couldn't postpone, Ma'am,' Caton replied, putting his hand over the receiver and letting Holmes know he would get back to him.

'Is there someone there with you, Chief Inspector?' she said.

'I'm sorry, Ma'am; it's just Inspector Holmes … he's leaving as we speak.'

'Not on my account I hope?'

Holmes closed the door quietly behind him.

'No, Ma'am, we'd just finished. What can I do for you?'

'I'd like you to come over and give me a progress report before my meeting this afternoon with Chief Superintendent Hadfield and the ACC Crime. You can bring the quarterly report with you. I'd like to make sure I'm well briefed before Tuesday.' She paused for emphasis. 'I take it you have finished it?'

'Of course, Ma'am.' Caton smiled to himself; worth another brownie point, if he'd bothered to collect them.

'Right then; I'll expect you shortly.' She put the phone down first.

Caton printed off two copies of the quarterly report and picked up the Bojangles folder. He knew exactly where Operation Panda was up to; stalled again. He took his coat from the stand behind the door and went to collect his copies from the printer, and to let Ged know where he was going. He had wanted a change of scene, and now he had got it.

Superintendent Gates put the folder back on her desk

'So give it to me again, in summary.'

'We've had nothing of any substance from the e-fit,' Caton began, 'nor from the questionnaires around The Lock and the Gay Village. The person Davies met in Waterstones remains a mystery. Then there's the van. We've widened the search area for garages and lock-ups, but you've seen the budget figures, and I doubt you're going to approve more officers?'

One look at her face was enough.

'The same with the ramp,' he continued. 'We've extended that to cover all of the models imported to the UK, although my money is on the one that Mr Soaper sold. Sometime soon I will have to discuss with you whether we ask the public to help us with the van, the ramp and the clown costume. They are the only physical clues we have.'

Gates wriggled uncomfortably in her seat. 'You mean *Crimewatch*?' she said.

Caton shook his head. 'I'm not sure we're there just yet. But flagging the three together in the local press might be a sensible first stage.'

'What about including the e-fit?' she asked.

'I don't think so,' he said. 'I've a strong feeling that's a major distracter. It's just too bizarre and too scary. If there was anyone wandering around looking like that I think we'd have known about it by now. Although we could release it in black and white,' he added as an afterthought.

He stopped for a moment, making a mental checklist before continuing.

'And then there are the possible contacts at the hospital. That took a while, but now we've got a list of names, I have a small team of carefully selected officers carrying out interviews. You can understand how delicate that is. Apart from the hospital staff, everybody involved has a reason to be anxious. There are those who are very ill, their partners and friends, and in some cases relatives recently bereaved.'

Helen Gates thought about that. 'What about the profile?' she asked. 'How are you using it exactly?'

'Well, it's not exactly a profile, Ma'am. Ms Webb was careful to point out that she had too little to go on to provide us with that. It is a useful basis on which a profile could be constructed, with some more data.'

'Well, we can't sit around waiting for another victim to turn up, can we?' she said, an edge creeping into her voice. 'So what exactly are you doing with what she has given you?'

Caton counted to three before he replied. He understood the pressure Gates was under, and the frustration of being one step removed from the investigations, but it didn't make it any easier to take.

'The Criminal Intelligence Analysis team are factoring it in to all of our data collection and analysis,' he said calmly. 'And the rest of the team have been well briefed and know that I expect them to use it as a reference point in all of the interviews and work on the ground.'

Gates knew from Caton's measured response that she had let her frustration show, and tried to make up for it.

'Well, it seems as though you are doing everything possible at the moment, Tom; let's hope there's a breakthrough soon. The press have been quiet for the past few days, but I still have the chief executive of the council ringing me every other day. It's not been good for the image of the city. Just let me know if you make any progress at all, and I can get him off my back.'

The meeting ended amicably. Caton took his leave, and headed back to the station and his mound of paperwork.

At precisely the moment that Caton drove out of Chester House, Albert Stephen coasted into the drive of the house, parked behind the high yew hedge, armed the car and let himself, unseen, into the house. He sensed that something had happened. The alarm was functioning as normal and the panel was clear. He keyed in the code and set about checking each of the downstairs rooms. Then he climbed the stairs and entered his study.

The CCTV monitor screens flickered down at him, their pictures ghostly grey. Everything appeared normal. The rough sleeper lay on his back, with his head turned slightly to the left, just as he had been when Albert Stephen left the house. And then it struck him; it was the silence. He walked over to the desk and turned the volume on the speaker controls to maximum. There was a steady sound like wind in a tunnel, or surf rolling onto the shore. The rough sleeper was neither snoring nor breathing. He turned the volume down and toggled the zoom control on the CCTV monitor. He thought he could detect a greater pallor on the sunken cheeks and on the skin stretched tightly, mask-like, across the protruding facial bones.

He retraced his steps, this time making his way into the pantry just off the kitchen. From a large plastic box on the second shelf he took a pair of surgical gloves, a surgical mask, a white coverall with elasticated hood, waist, wrists and ankles, and a pair of blue polyethylene overshoes. He put them on, walked back to the cloakroom beneath the stairs and unlocked the cellar door.

Even before he reached the bottom step Albert Stephen knew that the man was dead. He took a small mirror from one of the shelves and held it to the lips, blue and cracked, drawn back across the rotten teeth. He placed two fingers on the carotid artery in what he knew was a futile gesture.

He untied the straps that secured the man to the bed. Taking a reel of hose from a hook on the wall, he turned on the tap to which it was connected and moved to within two metres of the bed. He opened the nozzle until he had a steady jet of water, with which he proceeded to sluice down the body and the table. After a few minutes, he turned off the hose and tap, and began to sweep the water and debris towards the drain set in the concrete floor.

Ten minutes later, he had re-clothed the body using the clothes it had originally worn. Pulling a sheet of plastic wrapping from another reel attached to the wall, he slid the body onto it, rolled it onto its side, pulled the knees up towards the chest, and proceeded to wrap the plastic over and under twice, before slicing it with a Stanley knife and tying the centre and both ends securely with thin rope.

He stepped back, admiring his handiwork. It would do. He looked at his watch. It was just approaching mid afternoon; far too early to set out for the lock-up beneath the railway arches. He decided to wait until the latter end of the Friday evening exodus. There would be sufficient traffic to blend into, but less people likely to notice him arriving. In any case, they would all be intent on getting home for the weekend. No matter that the man had expired two full weeks earlier than he had expected. Albert Stephen was ready. Humming softly to himself, he started up the steps.

'If that looking glass gets broke, Mamma's gonna buy you a billy goat. If that billy goat don't pull, Mamma's gonna buy you a cart and bull...'

Caton checked the time. It was 3.35. He looked at the pile in his out tray with grim satisfaction. None of it would make a lot of difference to either investigation, but it had to be done, and he reckoned that another hour and a half would leave his desk clear for the first time in a fortnight. It would be piling up again by midday on Monday, but at least he could face the weekend with the illusion that he was getting somewhere. He knew just how Sisyphus must have felt each time he reached the top of the mountain, only to see the rock falling back down the other side. The phone rang. It was Kate Webb.

'Tom. It's Kate. I hope you don't mind me ringing you at work, but you might just be able to do me a favour.'

He leant back in his chair, relaxing a little for the first time that day.

'Kate. If I can, you know I will.'

'It's just that…'

She paused for a moment, as though uncertain as to how he would take it. Then, suddenly emboldened, it came out in a rush.

'I was going to the theatre this evening with a friend, but she's pulled out at the last moment. It's too late to get the money back, but actually it's just a couple of banquettes at the Royal Exchange, so it's not about the money. It's just never quite the same going on your own. And I wondered … if you're not doing anything … and if you like the theatre, if you'd like to join me?'

'I'd love too,' Caton began.

'Only it seems such a waste … and it's got a really good write-up. It's the premier of a play about an Italian family ice cream firm in Ancoats. I know a few people who have been and they all say it's hilarious…'

'Kate,' Caton interrupted the flow, 'I'd love to come.'

There was a pause as she let it sink in. 'You would? That's brilliant. Only … we'd booked a table too, just pre-theatre dinner at Café Istanbul, on Upper Bridge Street…'

'I know where it is, Kate. That would be fine. What time have you booked it for?'

'Six; the play starts at 7.45, and it's only a spit away, isn't it? But you need to be there at least ten minutes beforehand to get a choice view; you know what it's like with the banquettes, a real free-for-all. But they're used to theatre diners; an hour and twenty should be fine.'

Caton looked at his watch. Two and a quarter hours; plenty of time to finish off here, nip home, get a shower and walk the quarter of a mile to Bridge Street.

'Okay,' he said. 'How about if we meet up at the Bridge first and have a quick drink? It's virtually opposite, and there's a great atmosphere on a Friday night.'

'Brilliant.' He could hear the relief in her voice. 'I'll see you then.'

'I'll look forward to it,' he said. 'And, Kate, thanks for thinking of me.'

Well, that's a surprise, he thought as he replaced the phone. But then again, maybe not. They had got on really well over lunch in the staff dining room in the Refectory, and several times in the intervening week he had almost plucked up the courage to pick up the phone and ask her out for a drink. That was the trouble with being single in the city, especially at his age. He had forgotten how to be impulsive. It just felt too important, too meaningful. How would she interpret it? He wasn't even sure what it might mean to him. And there was always the possibility she would say no. And they were working together. Wouldn't that make it even more difficult, whichever way it went? Left to his own devices he doubted he'd have had the courage to make the first move. He wondered if there really had been a friend who'd let her down. Frankly, he didn't care. He returned to the document in front of him.

Better crack on. He checked the last line he'd written on the screen and began to type. As he did so, he smiled to himself. Thank God, he thought, for female emancipation.

The next time Caton looked at his watch, it said 5 o'clock.

'Bugger!' he said out loud.

Right in the middle of the rush hour. He had already convinced himself that he was never going to make it. He logged out, grabbed his coat and hurried from the office.

He was tempted to use his blue light, but in the end, a combination of luck and just about every rat run he could think of brought him to within a couple of hundred yards of the apartment in just twenty minutes. And then everything stopped moving. Both sides of Liverpool Road were at a standstill, and with the double parking, even an ambulance – lights flashing – would have found it impossible. To cap it all, a light sleet began to fall. The last thing he needed was Kate waiting alone in the pub, wondering if he'd stood her up, surrounded by the mainly male Friday night drinkers. He switched on his hands-free and accessed the address book. It was a good job they'd exchanged mobile numbers – ostensibly for professional reasons, but even then he had harboured hopes. He found and dialled her number. Just when he thought it would switch to voicemail, she picked up.

'Hi.' She was breathless.

'Kate? It's Tom. I'm sorry, but I'm running behind. I'm stuck in traffic within sight of the apartment, but I don't think I'm going to make the Bridge. How about if you drive over here and come in while I get ready? That way, we can walk up together.'

'You were lucky to get me, Tom,' she said, recovering her composure, 'I was halfway out the door. But that's fine. What's your address?'

Up ahead, the traffic slowly began to move.

He was just about to get in the shower when the bell went. Sod's law. He wrapped a towel around him and padded to the entry video phone. It was Kate. He pressed the button.

'Come on up. I'm just getting in the shower, so

make yourself at home, and I'll be with you in five minutes.'

He grabbed his newest pair of black trousers and a casual white linen shirt from the wardrobe, scooped up a pair of pants, took them through to the bathroom and dived into the wet room just as heard her enter the hallway.

Kate's coat was beginning to drip onto the wooden floor. She slipped it off, folded it inside out and looked around for somewhere to put it. The lounge and study area were clearly out, so she went through into the kitchen diner and settled for dropping it over the back of one of the chairs. The kitchen was neat and clean, and gleaming. A half full glass of water on the table was testimony to the speed with which he must have hurried to get ready.

She went back into the lounge and, in one quick sweep, took in the functional decor: comfortable sofa and easy chair; thirty-two-inch plasma widescreen and hard disc DVD rewriter/player; office area with computer, flat screen, small bookcase and an iPod music player. Functionally male, but somehow far more neutral, and much tidier, than her previous experience of the lairs of lone city males. She pushed open the door to what turned out to be the bedroom.

A fitted wardrobe ran along one wall. A Hessian blind was raised above the single window, through which the lights from a converted warehouse winked across the canal basin on Potato Wharf. A king-size bed dominated the room, with a light grey polycotton duvet, Egyptian cotton sheets and matching pillows.

She recalled a close encounter she had had only months before. The guy – a barrister no less – had invited her back for a coffee. While he was making it she took a peek in the bedroom. The prints on the duvet featured a naked man and woman, full size – in every respect – lying side by side. Across the man's chest were emblazoned the words 'Stud muffin'; the face was a photo print of the man making the coffee. The woman's head was missing, presumably waiting for the next lucky lady to wake up in the morning and find him taking a photo for his trophy album. How do I pick them? she asked herself; so much for a Master's in psychology and criminology! She was out of there before the coffee had started to percolate.

She wandered back into the lounge and sat down on the sofa. A remote lay on the coffee table. She picked it up and idly pressed the play button. Beside her were the TV listings for the week. She picked them up and started to leaf through them. Suddenly, beautiful haunting music flooded from the speakers. On the screen a young woman was playing a brass instrument, backed by a motley band of men accompanying her with undisguised admiration. She recognised, but could not name, the tune. She settled back against the cushions and let it wash over her.

Caton turned off the shower and pulled the bath towel from the ring on the wall. As he started to rub himself dry, he too heard the exquisite haunting sound of the flugelhorn. He broke out in goose bumps, less from the sudden change in temperature than from the emotional connection that it had for him, and the thought of Kate Webb waiting in the lounge. He finished drying, stepped into the bathroom and pulled on his pants, trousers and shirt. As he opened the door into the lounge, he heard the bandleader's immortal words.

'And she calls that, wobbly!'

Kate turned as he came in to the room.

'That was beautiful,' she said. 'I'm sure I've heard it before – what is it, Tom?'

'Rodrigo's Concerto d'Arangues,' he said. 'It was written for Spanish guitar, although Sarah Brightman recorded a sung version some years back – En Arangues con tu amor. That's probably where you heard it.'

He wiped his forehead distractedly with the towel.

'Rodrigo was supposedly inspired by the honeymoon he spent in Arangues with his wife.'

'His honeymoon? But it's so sad,' she said.

'Yes, it is.' There was an awkward pause. He pointed to his bare feet. 'I'll just get some shoes and socks on, grab my coat and we can get off.'

'You're okay,' she said, smiling. 'Take your time. They are holding the table, and we'll easily make it with ten minutes to spare.'

Caton was entranced by how beautiful she looked. Her hair was loose, cascading around her neck and lying soft upon her shoulders. As she moved her head, the light from the candles picked up natural highlights of gold and bronze. Her green eyes flashed and sparkled. The midnight-blue jersey dress accentuated her classic figure. He was reminded of Botticelli's Venus in the Uffizi: beautiful, strong and vulnerable.

Even before his second glass of wine Caton found himself opening up to her gentle probing. By the time they set off for the short walk to the theatre she knew about his parents' death on the winding road in Greece. How he had been pulled alive but unconscious from the wreck, and had woken six days later, otherwise unscathed, in the hospital in Istanbul. How his mother's sister and her husband had become his legal guardians and taken him in; the only condition being that he should move from the comprehensive school near to his parents' former home in Chorlton to Manchester Grammar, where his uncle was an Old Boy and member of the governing body.

She even managed to get him to talk about his marriage. How he had met Laura at university, and how their marriage, even before she graduated, had started so well. The long hours they worked – he as a young PC on shifts, and she as a junior doctor at the infirmary – meant that some weeks they passed like ships in the night. When she finally succumbed to the charms of a handsome, womanising, cardiac consultant – who, much to the surprise of his colleagues, left his wife for Laura, divorce was inevitable. Caton admitted to having been hurt terribly by her betrayal. But, over time, he had come to accept that it was he who had pushed for them to marry, and he who had sought the emotional blanket of home and family. For neither of which was she really ready. He no longer felt bitter.

About Kate, he had learned much less. Father a plumber; mother an assistant manager at the Co-op; three younger brothers whom she had helped to raise; an apparently happy childhood in an unassuming semi-detached in Teddington; the first of her family to make it to university. She was currently unattached, whatever that meant.

The play was every bit as good as the reviews had promised. Normally Caton would have felt exposed, sprawled on the banquette at stage level, his long legs perilously close to the actors as they played in the round; conscious that everyone in the theatre would have a clear view of him. With Kate alongside him, her laughter and natural ease so infectious, he had quickly relaxed and enjoyed the play. In any case, he loved the Royal Exchange. It was the combination of the intimacy of the theatre itself, the history and grandeur of the building that housed it, and the fusion of old and new. In particular, he marvelled at the way in which it had survived and recovered from the IRA bomb as yet another metaphor for the courage, and heart, and spirit of this city.

The sleet had cleared by the time they left the theatre, but the cold was damp, and there was a biting easterly. She linked her arm through his and snuggled close as they crossed St Ann's Square, leaning forward into the wind; two characters in a Lowry print. It felt good to Caton, and reassuringly familiar. They chatted as they walked, about the play, Manchester and student days.

Before he knew it, they were standing at the steps to his apartment. He hesitated, desperate to get this right. He glanced nervously at her upturned face, softly smiling, eyes wide and encouraging.

'Coffee?' he ventured.

'Whatever,' she replied, squeezing his arm and laughing playfully.

He was helping her out of her coat in the hallway when their eyes met again. She tilted her head invitingly, and Caton found himself kissing her on her lips. As the coat fell to the floor, Kate wrapped her arms around his neck and melted into him. Without a moment's thought, he scooped her up into his arms, shouldered open the door to the bedroom and kicked it closed behind them.

Chapter 20

Albert Stephen picked the cardboard stencil up from the workbench and held it close to the front parking light of the van. He had taken the precaution of working in this half-light since he arrived, and it was good enough; as was the stencil. He opened the passenger door and laid the stencil in the passenger foot well alongside the can of paint. He closed the door, walked round to the driver's side and climbed in. He looked at his watch. It was a quarter to midnight. He switched off the van lights, angled the seat back to a comfortable incline, leant his head on the back rest and closed his eyes. He knew he would not sleep, but there was nothing more to do but wait.

Caton woke with a start. Kate lay beside him, facing away towards the window, one arm on top of the sheet, her hair fanned out on the pillow behind her. Apart from her breathing, soft and rhythmical, nothing stirred. He sat up carefully and looked around the bedroom. From the feeble halo around the blind, it was not yet dawn. Twisting gently to his left to avoid disturbing her, he pressed the snooze alarm on his bedside table. It was 4.46 a.m.

He lay back on the pillow and stared at the ceiling, feeling strangely refreshed, as though he had been swimming in a mountain stream. He smiled, recalling the events of the night before. The feverish passion with which they had first devoured each other; and then, much later, the slow, gentle exploration, which had brought them to the same explosive climax, moulding their bodies together as wave after wave shuddered through them. No way should he be feeling this alert. Exhausted, sated, he would have expected, but not alert.

It was clear that Kate would sleep on for a while longer, but when she did wake, what then? It had been totally unplanned; certainly on his part. Not that he regretted a moment of it. Right now he was unprepared. Ever since the divorce, on those occasions when he had ended up in bed with a woman, they had both known in advance exactly where they stood. No expectations of something strong and lasting. A comfortable arrangement that met mutual needs for human comfort and sexual release. Even now, he blushed at the thought of some of those liaisons.

Everything in his upbringing and education had counselled against casual sex; probably why they had been relatively few and far between. And from a professional point of view he had always felt it important to be careful whom he got close to, let alone allowed into his bed. There were some who might say that he had already overstepped that mark.

He thought about it. Kate was not part of his team, not even on the force. She wasn't a witness or a suspect, and it was unlikely her contribution would ever be given in evidence. So it was just a question of whether he might allow their relationship – there, now he had said it, their relationship – to affect his judgment when weighing her advice.

He thought about that for a moment and dismissed it; not a problem. But still he had no idea what he was going to say to Kate, except that it had been fantastic, and that he would like to see her again. He sensed that would be a poor, inadequate response. And yet he was anxious that if he really told her how he felt, he might just scare her off.

He sighed and turned on his side, one hand underneath his head, the other mirroring hers on top of the sheet. Instinctively he drew his knees up, cradling her soft warm body in his. She stirred briefly, wiggling her bottom and shoulders, and sighing contentedly. Caton fought the natural desire this awoke in him and gradually melted into a deep, untroubled sleep.

'Tom! Wake up.' Kate shook him firmly.

His eyes flickered open, focused. An insistent buzzing tone invaded the room.

'God, it's my pager.'

He leapt out of bed, scrambled across the floor and searched frantically beneath the duvet for his trousers. He located the pager and unclipped it from the belt. Kate suppressed a giggle behind her hand.

'Sorry,' she said. 'It's just, you look so funny.'

He crawled back to the bed, switched on his side light and read the message.

'It's Superintendent Gates,' he said. 'I'm sorry, I'll have to ring her.'

'Do you want me to go next door?' she asked.

'It's alright,' he said. 'I'll use the landline.'

He pressed the snooze alarm; 5.27 a.m. He had been asleep just forty minutes, and this time he felt anything but fresh. He pulled on his trousers and went out into the lounge.

Kate could tell from the expression on his face that it was bad news.

'Bojangles,' he said. 'It looks as though he's struck again.'

'Where?' she asked, suddenly wide awake.

'In the Northern Quarter; corner of John Street and Hilton Street. I've got to go, I'm afraid.'

She pushed back the sheet, unconcerned by her nakedness, got out of bed and began to search for her clothes.

'I'll come with you.' It was a statement, not a request.

'Hang on, Kate,' Caton began. 'I'm not sure that's such a good idea…'

'Nonsense,' she said as she looped her arms through her bra straps. 'It's a great idea. Think about it, Tom. I'm the accredited profiler working on this case. What better way to get inside the perpetrator's head than to see first-hand the scene that he's set up for you?'

She was right, of course. His objection had nothing to do with her being at the scene. That was easy to rationalise. What would be less easy to explain was their arriving together, and her still in the clothes she had worn the night before.

She was way ahead of him.

'It's alright. I'll come in my car, and give you five minutes head start.'

She gave him a serious smile and gently brushed him aside as she made for the door.

'Is it alright if I use the bathroom first?'

Caton sped up Mangle Street. The morning was dry and cold, just above freezing. An angry motorist beeped his horn as Caton nosed out, spied his chance and accelerated across into Tariff Street. A quick left and he was heading up Hilton Street towards the police line. A motorbike patrolman walked purposefully across to his car, ready to send him on his way. Caton retracted the driver's window and flashed his warrant card.

'Morning, Chief Inspector,' the patrolman said. 'Perhaps you could back your car up close in to the kerb and make your way on foot from here? SOCO's instructions, sir,' he added apologetically.

Caton parked up, slipped on his protective overshoes, gloves and all-in-one, and walked over to the patrolman.

'There'll be a Miss Webb from the university arriving soon. She's with us on this one. Can you send her across when she arrives? And make sure she gets a Tyvek suit.'

'Certainly, sir.'

Caton ducked under the police line and crossed towards the small plot of land that marked the corner where John Street and Hilton Street met. A twenty-metre cordon had been taped out with another cordon inside it, at the centre of which a small white screen had been erected. Inside the outer cordon, the usual suspects were gathered. He spotted Jack Benson – presumably the senior crime scene investigator on this one too – a photographer and several SOCOs. This time all of them were wearing protective outfits, hoods up. The directive from Headquarters had followed on from a coroner's recent high-profile statement to the press about a bungled case in another force down south some months before. Chief Superintendent Hadfield was determined there would be no accusations that crime scenes had been contaminated by FMIT officers.

Inspector Gerry Sarsfield spotted Caton and came across.

'Morning, Tom.' He lifted the tape for Caton to duck under. 'Looks like your man has been at it again. I wish he'd choose someone else's patch for a change. Failing that, perhaps he could wait till I'm off duty.'

He saw Caton looking towards the screen.

'Apart from erecting the screen, and taping the area, no one has been allowed inside the search cordon pending the arrival of the SIO; I take it that's you?'

'Looks like it, Gerry. Are you sure it's our man?'

'You can make your own mind up,' Sarsfield said, lifting his face mask into place and heading off towards the inner cordon.

He lifted the tape for Caton to pass under and indicated a narrow strip of pavement, bounded by parallel lines of tape.

'Mind how you go.'

The tapes led them straight to the screen on a small patch of land backed by trees that partly hid a concrete-clad multi-storey car park to the rear. This remote corner was dominated by a huge sculpture. Behind a low set of railings separating it from the pavement, a painted steel brush soared ten feet above the two large blocks of stone on which it rested. Against the blocks was propped a matching steel shovel. At the foot of the sculpture – behind the screen – lay a body, curled in a foetal position, wrapped in a thick, dirty trench coat. To all intents, a rough sleeper, sleeping. Beside the feet, the bizarre image of a black horse, approximately a foot in length, had been painted on the pavement. A twenty pence piece and a ten pence piece lay between the horse and the victim's feet.

Caton pointed to the coins. 'Someone's idea of a joke?'

Sarsfield shook his head. 'The guy who reported it, apparently. Thought it was street art, and then had second thoughts. Turned back, and as soon as he realised the guy was dead rang 999. Had the sense not to touch anything.' He paused and looked down at the body. 'What do you think then? Is it him?'

'It certainly looks like it. Or a copycat.'

Caton stepped beyond the screen and looked around. Jack Benson was heading towards them accompanied by the photographer and a woman he assumed was the doctor. As they entered the inner cordon he could see that it was Jean Hope, the pathologist who had assisted Sir James Flatman at the post mortem on Stephen Davies. Beyond the outer perimeter he could see Gordon Holmes and Kate Webb climbing into their Tyvek suits.

'Good morning, Doctor,' he said, stepping out of the way. 'He's all yours.'

Jean Hope nodded grimly, and ducked behind the screen.

'I'll get back then,' said Sarsfield. 'I'll hand over the Crime Scene log to your lot now they've arrived, and make sure the traffic diversions are sorted.'

'Thanks, Gerry. You've done a good job,' Caton told him.

'I wouldn't like to think it's going to become a habit,' Sarsfield grimly replied.

'Is it him?' Holmes enquired.

'Early to say, but it's certainly looking that way,' said Caton. 'He's left his calling card.'

'Another plastic gee-gee?'

'You'll see for yourself. This is Kate Webb, by the way.'

'I know,' he said, accompanying it with a none too subtle wink that neither he nor Kate could possibly miss. 'We've introduced ourselves.'

Kate's rich auburn hair framed her face beneath the hood. Her cheeks were bright with cold, her green eyes full of professional concern, as much, Caton guessed, because she was conscious that Holmes was watching them closely.

'Can we see the body, Chief Inspector?'

'Not a problem. But we need to stay out of the way

while Dr Hope completes her examination and the photographs are taken. She'll be using a Dictaphone, so we should keep our voices down.'

He led them back behind the screen. Their view was blocked by the photographer. They circled, and came in from the other side.

The pathologist was kneeling beside the body, speaking into the recorder. The photographer took a number of shots over her shoulder. Jack Benson stood by, paper and polythene evidence bags at the ready. Holmes was staring at the painting of the horse.

'How did he have time to paint that?' he asked.

'It's spray paint,' said Benson. 'Must have used a stencil.'

'Is this how the body was when it was found?' asked Kate.

'More or less,' said Benson. 'Head tucked in, knees drawn up. Looked like he was sleeping. A security guard on his way to Piccadilly Gardens found him and rang in.'

'What time was that?' asked Caton.

'Quarter to five, according to Inspector Sarsfield.'

'Did he see anyone, hear anything, see any vehicles?'

'I don't know, sir. You'll have to ask him yourself. I think he's with a uniformed officer in a patrol car on Oak Street.'

'Gordon,' Caton said, 'can you do that? And get things moving on the traffic cameras and CCTV. There are plenty around here. We must have him on film.'

As Holmes started back, Kate pointed to the sculpture.

'What's the significance of this?' she asked.

'I've no idea, but I can tell you what it is,' said Caton. 'It's called New Broom. A Glasgow artist, Tom Wylie, was commissioned to do it to celebrate the regeneration of this part of the city – the Northern Quarter. It was unveiled in the summer, about six years ago. I was working the city centre at the time. Council dignitaries, guests and passers-by were handed brooms and invited to "sweep it open" instead of cutting the usual tape; supposedly symbolic of sweeping the city clean. Then it was formally handed over to the City Council's Operational Services.'

'And the first one was at the foot of a cross in a former burial ground. There must be a connection,' Kate said.

'The only one I can see is the fact that they are both sculptures of a sort.'

'And both owned by the City Council,' she added.

'That and the horses,' he said, not to be outdone.

'Heart attack.' Jean Hope sat back on her heels. 'That's the most likely cause of death, at this stage.'

'Caused by?' Caton asked.

'Difficult to say. But there's no immediate evidence that it was induced by someone else … unless he was frightened to death. No, more likely that his heart just gave out. It doesn't look as though he's eaten for weeks. Or had anything to drink, for that matter.'

'So he could have just laid down here to sleep, and died.'

The pathologist got to her feet, rubbed her knees, straightened up and turned to face Caton. The same serious brown eyes he remembered from the mortuary.

'In which case he must have done so sometime yesterday; he has been dead for at least sixteen hours, possibly longer.'

'He was placed here?'

'Almost certainly. Unless it really has reached the stage where people walk past dead bodies on the street. More telling is the pooling just visible at the waistband, which strongly suggests that he was flat on his back when he died. I can't tell you for sure until I've conducted the post mortem. The good news is that I should be able to manage that later this morning.'

Albert Stephen stood on the raised platform at Crumpsall Station and waited patiently for the next Metrolink tram to arrive. He merged well with the group of passengers waiting with him. In common with a number of them, his anorak was zipped all the way to the top. His face was well hidden beneath the fur-lined hood, and by the scarf wound several times around his mouth and nose.

The tram was characteristically punctual. Ten minutes later, they were swinging into Piccadilly Gardens. He noted the police barriers across the entrances to Tib Street and Oldham Road, the yellow diversion signs and the Saturday morning shoppers frustrated to find the traffic ground to a halt.

It took him less than fifteen minutes from leaving the tram at Piccadilly Station to retrieve his Peugeot estate. He was back in the house in Whalley Range a little before 7 o'clock, the car parked safely out of sight at the rear.

Despite the fact that it was a Saturday, most of the team had already made it in. Kate had gone home to change, but was anxious to sit in on the mid-morning briefing, and Caton had agreed to that. She had after all present at the scene of crime; on the other hand, he knew he wasn't fooling himself, even if he could the others. Carter, Stuart and Caton were watching the CCTV. Holmes was with DI Weston in the major incident room.

'It's too easy, boss.' DS Carter pointed at the video screen. 'He wants us to know how he did it, just like the last time.'

If anything, the pictures were sharper than before. Slightly better lighting, or one of the newer cameras, was Caton's guess. The disguise was different this time, too; gone were the clown costume, wig and silly shoes. This time he wore a full-length anorak with a furry hood; beneath that, a dark-coloured balaclava. Most startling of all was the van. Although the pictures were in black and white, it was evident that the van belonged to Manchester City Council Operational Services. Or at least it was badged as such. And the registration had checked out, too. It was cloned. The original City Council van was not a Ford Transit, and in any case it had been locked away in the workshop where it was undergoing repairs. No sign of the ramp and roll either.

The van had pulled up at the pavement alongside the sculpture. They saw the driver open the rear doors and haul out a large package bound in a sheet of plastic. Three quick slashes with some kind of blade and the sheeting was pulled out from under the body, leaving the pathetic bundle huddled where it was shortly to be found. They watched the driver throw the sheeting into the van, lean in and return to the pavement holding a piece of cardboard and a can.

'Benson was right. It was a stencil,' Caton said to no one in particular.

They saw him hold the board close to the floor, spray back and forth with the can four times, check, make one more pass and return to the van. He threw the board on top of the sheeting, closed the door and drove off.

'No little dance for us this time, then?' Carter said bitterly.

They ran the tape for a second and a third time, but failed to spot anything new. They were about to compare notes when Duggie Wallace burst in, waving a computer printout.

'They're horsemen!' he exclaimed. 'It's not about the horses, it's about their riders.'

They looked at him expectantly.

'As soon as I put pale and black together, it came up trumps. It's the Apocalypse; the Four Horsemen of the Apocalypse.'

'Of course,' said Caton. 'The Revelation to St John the Apostle. Why didn't we think of that?'

'It wasn't that obvious,' Wallace said. 'Not until we had two to go on. But now we have, there's an obvious connection with his victims.'

He had them on tenterhooks.

'Duggie, get on with it,' Carter prompted.

Wallace placed the printout on the table and stabbed at it with his finger.

'The four horsemen appear one by one when the Lamb – that's Jesus – opens the first four of seven seals on a scroll. The first is a white horse, its rider wearing a crown and carrying a bow; that's supposed to represent conquest. The second is a red horse with a rider carrying a large sword; that's war. The third is a black horse, and the rider carries a pair of scales...'

'Representing justice?' Carter guessed.

Wallace ignored the interruption. 'Representing famine.' He paused, building up to the climax. 'And the fourth was a pale horse, whose rider was named Death, and Hell was following close behind. And get this. Despite what the translations say, the horse isn't really pale at all – at least not as in palomino. It's actually a sickly greeny-yellowy colour from the Greek chloros, as in chlorine. Just like the colour of a really sick or dying person. This represents disease or plague.'

He stood back, waiting for their congratulations.

'If that's what he's basing it on, he's doing it in reverse order,' Carter observed.

'And he obviously hasn't picked up on the chloros part. That horse was definitely not greeny-yellow,' DS Stuart chipped in.

'But the plague connection works,' Caton said thoughtfully. 'St John's burial ground, and Stephen Davies dying of AIDS. That fits. And going by what I saw this morning, I'd say the black horse does as well. The victim was starved.'

'That's really twisted,' Joanne Stuart said.

Carter grimaced. 'I think we'd already come to that conclusion.'

They were still considering the implications when Gordon Holmes walked in.

'You are not going to believe this, boss. The fire brigade have had two call-outs this morning. One to a lock-up garage under the railway arches in West Gorton, the other to a patch of wasteland between Harpurhey and Moston. They got the first call at 5.30 a.m. They reckon the fire must have been raging for at least an hour, but there was no one around to see it. They say it would have been self-contained for much of that time anyway. Apparently, it's completely gutted. There are indications that it's been used as a garage-cum-workshop. The other one was also spotted just after 5.30. It was an abandoned van, a Ford Transit, also completely gutted. They're pretty sure they were both arson. Uniform arrived at the Moston one at the same time as the fire brigade. One of the licence plates had been blown clear, and guess what?'

Joanne Stuart fed him the answer. 'It's a City Council registration – Operational Services?'

He corrected her. 'To be precise, it's our man's cloned City Council registration. The officer that arrived at the Gorton fire knew we'd been searching garages and lock-ups, wondered if there might be a connection and rang it in.'

'Another good day for uniform,' Carter muttered.

Caton motioned Holmes and Wallace to join them at the table.

When they were seated, he said, 'We need both of the fires treated as a crime scene.'

'We've set that in motion, boss,' said Holmes. 'DI Weston is liaising with SOCO, the fire service and the pathologist. And Ged is contacting all the personnel we've been using to search for the van, to tell them to come in asap. We need to work out how he got from Gorton to the Northern Quarter, from there to Moston, and how he left the scene of the van fire. And, if he has been using that lock-up since day one, someone must have seen something. There'll be a hell of a lot of work to do on the ground. The allocator is waiting for us to hand him the specific actions. I hope that's alright,' he added as an afterthought.

'That's fine,' said Caton. 'We don't have any option but to the throw everything at it, before the trail gets too cold. I'll deal with the overtime issue later. DS Stuart and DS Carter, I'd like you to coordinate the work of the teams in the Moston and Gorton areas. DI Holmes will carry on pulling it together here as evidence and information comes in from you and from the Northern Quarter. DI Weston will attend the post mortem.'

He turned to Duggie Wallace.

'Mr Wallace, you'll have plenty to occupy you as all this data comes in, but I'd like you to put together everything you have on these horsemen, and make a record of the Web addresses you've used. There's an outside chance the perpetrator may have used the same ones. And I'd like you to brief Ms Webb as soon as she gets in.'

He noted, and ignored, the subtle shift in body language around the table at the mention of Kate Webb.

'What are you going to do, sir?' It was a genuine question from Holmes. No edge to it.

'I'm going to let Superintendent Gates and Detective Chief Superintendent Hadfield know where we are up to. Then I'm going to check on progress with Gordon, and see how Ms Webb thinks this may affect her profile.' He looked around the table. 'Keep DI Holmes informed of your progress, and I'd like us all back here at 13.30 for an update.'

He pushed his chair back from the table. When he spoke, his voice was sombre.

'If Mr Wallace is right, there are two more horses yet to come. One of them promises war, and the other conquest. Whatever this maniac has planned, we have to find him, and soon.'

Chapter 21

'Albert Stephen … don't! I'm such a mess!'

His mother raised her left hand towards him, trying to block the shot. With her right hand she flicked her auburn hair free from her shoulder. She secretly loved to be photoed or videoed, but always pretended, coyly, to hate it. She wore the electric-blue dress which he loved so much because it set off her hair, and eyes, to perfection. She leant on the stone parapet, looking back across the Seine towards the Eiffel Tower.

The camera shook, and he recalled the emotion that he had felt at the time. He felt it now. Brushing the tears from his eyes, he waited for her to turn back and smile broadly at the camera; waited as the picture zoomed in on her amazing eyes; watched as the image of her face, in close-up, held steady; continued to watch, long after it had faded to an empty screen.

He switched off the video and placed the remote control on the arm of the chair. The holiday in Paris had been his treat for her, to celebrate his new job at the Town Hall. Strictly speaking it was in a nearby high-rise office block, but his mother always referred to it as the Town Hall. The video camera was his treat. New to the market, he was the first in the office to own one. Mother was so proud of what he had achieved. Which was why, when the job had been taken from him, he had kept it from her. Two years of getting up at 7 every morning. Donning his office clothes. Sitting down to the breakfast she had prepared. Collecting the packed lunch so lovingly put together. Kissing her goodbye and then returning from a day spent in the Central Library, to share with her the eagerly awaited stories of internecine office intrigue and intransigent problems solved. The latter, at least, held some twisted vestiges of the remembered truth. And then, before he had time to put it all right, she was struck down and it was too late. He sometimes wondered if she ever believed that he had actually been granted compassionate leave to care for her. There were times in those final months when he sensed disappointment in those dimming, pain-filled eyes. On those occasions the nagging pain inside him grew, fit to explode.

Albert Stephen rose from the chair and crossed to his desk. He launched the Access software and selected a folder simply called *Gangs*, and a file named *Key Players North and South Manchester and Salford*. A list of names, complete with street names, addresses and known associates, appeared. He checked the file date: 16th October 2006. Eleven individual gangs were represented. There were one hundred and thirty-two names representing approximately twenty-five per cent of all of the gang members known to the police. The average age was twenty-one. Almost half of those listed had addresses within one and a half miles of where Albert Stephen now sat. He had read somewhere that residents in this neighbourhood were one hundred and forty times more likely to be shot than residents anywhere else in Greater Manchester. Those statistics were about to rise.

Caton's morning had been hectic. His first task had been contacting his superiors, and fending them off with assurances that he knew it would be hard to substantiate. At least there had been no problem in getting the approval to pull in some more officers from across the Force Major Incident Team, and to authorise overtime. Kate had arrived shortly before noon, and he had sent her through to Wallace to bring her up to speed on his Four Horsemen theory. And now, a plate of cheese and pickle sandwiches on the table between them, they had just finished viewing the CCTV footage from the Northern Quarter.

'So at least we have the beginnings of a pattern,' she said, sipping her coffee. 'And some significant changes in his behaviour, too.'

'Significant how exactly?' he asked, picking up a sandwich and taking a bite.

'Well, there are things that he's done which are common to both victims and dump scenes…'

'*Dump* scenes?' he interrupted, spluttering a small spray of soggy particles into the ether.

'I'm sorry,' she said, 'I've been reading too many American articles. But at least it's relevant in this case.' She rephrased it in a gently mocking tone. 'The sites where the perpetrator chose to display the bodies. Is that sensitive enough for you?'

'Point taken,' Caton said, wiping the table with his paper napkin.

'Things such as his choice of public statues or monuments to display the bodies,' she continued. 'Then there's the fact that he's taken quite a risk to use these sites in the city centre. In both cases the victims are male and in a similar age bracket. The fact that both of them were killed sometime before they were dumped. The fact that he's used the same van.' She took another sip of coffee. 'Then there are the things which are different this time.'

'Such as him ditching the clown outfit and going

to all the trouble of cloning the van in City Council livery and registration plates?' Caton suggested.

'Exactly.' She picked up a sandwich and examined it, before taking a bite. 'And then there are a couple of unknowns. We don't yet know if he used drugs to restrain or capture his second victim. We don't even know if he was responsible for his death, or how; and we don't know if this victim was gay.'

'Well, we should get most of those resolved by the post mortem,' Caton mused.

They concentrated on their sandwiches for a moment. Caton was the first to break the silence.

'Look, Kate,' he began, 'I know this isn't the time or place, but about last night...'

There was a knock on the door.

'Come in,' Caton almost yelled in frustration.

Sarah Weston arrived on cue. She looked from one to the other, picking up on the awkwardness in the room.

'Would you like me to come back, sir?' she asked, only adding to his embarrassment.

'No, Inspector, it's fine,' he said, regretting his overreaction. 'In fact, we were just saying we could do with the post mortem results.'

'Well, you're in luck, sir. I've got the initial findings here,' she said, tapping her document case against her thigh.

Caton looked at the clock. It was almost 1.30pm, the time he had asked the team to meet.

'Perhaps you could round the others up?' he asked. 'Then we can get started.'

'Already done,' DI Weston replied, pulling a chair out and plonking herself down. 'They're right behind me; just topping their drinks up.'

Caton tried to hide his irritation, but Kate Webb had clearly sensed it because his shin received a gentle kick beneath the table. When he looked up, her lips silently formed 'It's alright.' She shot him a brief encouraging smile.

Sarah Weston, busy unloading her document case, still caught the exchange from the corner of her eye. This room is getting too small, Caton decided.

All of the chairs were taken, and Kate Webb had been introduced. He asked DI Weston to go first. She distributed a single sheet of A4 paper for each of them.

'Preliminary findings only,' she explained, giving them time to scan it. 'We'll have a detailed report by tomorrow.'

When she was sure they had all finished, she began.

'Key points,' she said. 'We have a male, somewhere between forty-five and fifty-five years of age. At the moment the best estimate is that death occurred between twelve hundred hours and eighteen hundred hours prior to the discovery of the body.' She looked up from her papers. 'That will be pinned down to within an hour or two by tomorrow.'

She returned to her notes, and continued.

'The victim's underlying state of health – as evidenced by his teeth, bones, hands, feet and so on – is consistent with him being a long-term rough sleeper. There's no evidence that he had had any significant medical intervention – including dental work – in the recent past. Death was from a massive heart attack. In this case, although the arteries were heavily furred with plaques, he didn't appear to have a myocardial infarction. It seems most likely that a blockage was caused by a spasm of the heart muscles themselves. The victim also had multiple organ failure, which would have put critical strain on the heart – probably triggering the muscle spasm.'

She looked up to emphasise the importance of the

next part, which she recited from memory.

'Although the liver showed signs of cirrhosis, and there was pre-existing kidney disease, the doctor is certain that the multiple organ failure, and therefore the heart attack, were caused by starvation.'

'But isn't that consistent with him being homeless?' Holmes asked.

'We don't know that he was,' Caton replied. 'In any case, when did we last hear of a rough sleeper dying of starvation in the North-West, let alone Manchester?'

'That's what the pathologist said,' Sarah Weston added. 'Pneumonia, influenza, TB, alcohol poisoning … almost anything except starvation.'

'What about AIDS?' Kate Webb asked.

They turned to look at her, as though they had forgotten that she was present.

'Only wouldn't it be significant if he was HIV positive, or had AIDS – just like the first victim?'

'Good point, Kate,' Sarah Weston said, oozing female solidarity. 'We are going to have to wait for the test results for that. We do have some toxicology results, though – fortunately, they took samples first thing. There are traces of morphine administered intravenously, within the last twenty-four hours, and there are a number of recent injection sites that suggest he may have received regular doses over the past few weeks, and possibly longer.'

'Why morphine?' Carter asked.

'We all know that it's used for pain relief, and the pathologist suggested there may have been some pain associated with the organ failure, and to some extent from the body's reaction to starvation; stomach cramps and the like. But it's also used for sedation. In this case it might have served both purposes.'

'What about Rohipnol?' DS Stuart wondered out loud, a millisecond before everyone else.

'There was no evidence of any other drugs – incapacitating or otherwise. Although it's unlikely that there would have been any need over the past week or so given the weakened state that he was in. And...' She paused while she consulted her notes. 'There were marks across his ribs, upper arms, stomach and thighs, consistent with him having been restrained while lying on his back. The body was definitely moved into the foetal position in which it was found after death had occurred – almost certainly before rigor mortis had set in, so probably within three to four hours. That's all we have from pathology so far. Incidentally, Kate asked about HIV/AIDS; well, there is no evidence of sexual activity. Not that that's the only way to become infected.'

She put the papers down on the desk and pulled out a small notebook.

'SOCO are working on the samples taken from the dump site, garage and van. They're not holding out a great deal of hope.'

At the mention of the dump site, Caton registered another little dig at his shin. He carefully avoided Kate's eyes.

'They are also running tests on the rope and polythene, and DI Holmes has people trying to track down likely suppliers,' DI Weston concluded. 'That should be easier with the rope because of its specialist nature. We've started with places like the YHA, Blacks and Snow & Rock,' Holmes added.

'What about the fires?' Caton asked.

'The fire service has confirmed arson,' Weston replied. 'Both fires were started with an accelerant – they think petrol. There was a small canister of propane gas in the lock-up. Thank God it didn't explode. A spare can of petrol had been left in the van; that did explode. It was probably that, or the tank going up, that blew the registration plate off.'

Carter and Stuart had little to report. The house-to-house enquiries were under way, but most people would have been fast asleep in bed, and the only ones who might have seen anything would still be at work.

'There is one thing, sir,' said Carter. 'It's always possible he jogged across the spare land, cut round the back of the old Monsall Hospital site and caught the Metrolink. If he did, the station and the trains are well covered by CCTV. I've got a couple of officers on to that.'

'Okay,' Caton said, turning to Gordon Holmes. 'What about you, Inspector?'

Holmes opened his notebook and milked the moment.

'I have a name for the victim,' he said evenly, as though it was to be expected that he would. 'We got it almost straight away, from a visit to the Barnabas Centre on Oldham Street.'

Caton glanced at Joanne Stuart, who nodded that she was having the same thought. It was in the heart of the Gay Village, almost equidistant between The Lock apartments and the design studio where Davies had worked. They had passed within a few metres of it.

'They recognised the description straight away, and it was confirmed by our own Rough Sleepers Unit,' Holmes was saying. 'In fact, he's quite well known to them. Thomas Hoolock; aka Whistler. Some of the tales he told suggested he had been a solicitor, others an estate agent, and others a store manager. Alcohol and a woman allegedly put him out on the streets; no surprises there then. His real name and origin are unknown. He's been homeless and rough sleeping in Manchester for about five years. Had a short spell selling *The Big Issue*, but couldn't keep to the discipline. Similarly, did spells in hostels. He was offered a flat by the City Council just before the Commonwealth Games. He turned it down. He migrated down to Stockport when the heat was turned up, but arrived back early in 2003. Had a route he used to follow meticulously around the city centre. We're following up on that. He always slept in one of three places. Dropped out of sight about four weeks ago, but everyone's a bit hazy about that. We're trying to get a handle on it, see if we can establish exactly where and when he was last seen.'

'Hoolock. That's an unusual name. Have we been able to get any trace on that?' Caton asked.

'Nope. No such name in the UK phonebook. He probably made it up or adopted it,' Holmes replied. 'It's a form of monkey – a Gibbon. It's also the name of a band that won the national final of the Battle of the Bands in 2001.'

For the second time they turned to look at Kate Webb. She flushed slightly.

'I only know because I was there. It's a student thing.'

'Is that it, Gordon?' Caton asked, giving her a chance to gather her thoughts.

'That's it for the moment, sir,' Holmes replied.

'In which case, I am shortly going to ask Ms Webb to share her thoughts on how this might throw a little more light on our perpetrator. But first, I'll give you my feedback.'

He proceeded to tell them about his conversations with Gates and Hadfield. Of the extra resources he had brokered, and the increasing pressure being brought to bear by the chief executive; this time through the Police Authority, as well as directly. He had also had the press office wanting something innocuous to give Larry Hymer, who really had the bit between his teeth, threatening a headline such as *Killer Strikes Again; New Broom needed at GMP?* All in all it meant that they would have to consider every possibility, including the psychological profile. He looked across the table where Kate sat calm and collected, her folder open in front of her.

'Which brings us to Ms Webb,' he said.

Kate was conscious of the fact that this was the first time she had addressed the whole of the senior team. They were vastly experienced officers. All of whom had probably decided there was something going on between her and their chief inspector, and who would be judging her on two levels: both professionally, and as someone on whom Tom Caton could be risking both his professional and personal reputation.

She took a deep breath, and began.

'You have all seen the salient features analysis I provided, and the very tentative beginnings of a possible profile. Based on what I observed at the crime scene this morning, the CCTV footage and what you've shared here this afternoon, I suggest that there have been some reinforcements of those analyses, and also some things we can eliminate.'

She looked around the table. They watched her closely. Neither sceptical nor encouraging, giving nothing away. If she was expecting feedback, she realised, she would have to give them something concrete.

Over the next five minutes she repeated the observations she had shared with Tom about the changes to the salient features. Now came the test.

'You'll be wondering what all of this means in terms of the profile. Well, there are certain things that are now less tentative, that have been strengthened by the pattern in his behaviours. We now know that he is targeting adult male victims, in a common age range.

Given that there does not at this stage appear to be an obvious connection between the victims, it is less likely that his rage is directed against them personally. This not only suggests that he has a reason to hate and/or fear adult males, but the age range gives us two possible target groups. If the cause of his hatred, jealousy or fear is recent and current, then the real object of his rage – the causal factor – is more likely to be someone who has wounded him, caused him deep traumatic emotional pain. A serious blow to his self-esteem. Possibly a male partner, someone he fantasises over or possibly a family member. If, however, the causal factor was at some stage in his childhood, then it is almost certain that it would have been a family member; father, stepfather, grandfather or uncle. Then again, it could have been a non-familial adult male with whom he came into regular contact. Such as a babysitter, teacher, family friend, someone who ran a club or team, a coach or youth leader.'

She could see that they were following her. The women were nodding; Carter appeared to be processing what he had heard. Holmes, she could tell, was barely suppressing the desire to say *that narrows it down then*. She pressed on.

'If the assumption that the horses are all about the Apocalypse is correct, then we may well be looking at a religious influence; warped either by fanaticism or by delusion.'

'Can we go back a stage?' Carter asked.

Caton was about to intervene, but Kate got in first.

'Certainly,' she said, pleased to be getting some feedback at last. 'Fire away.'

'If the cause is way back in his childhood, why would he only start killing in his middle age?'

'Good point. It would only be because something happened to bring to a head all the pent-up rage and anger that he has carried with him all those years. We call that a trigger incident. Failing that, it could be that something that was holding him back from taking action – something acting on what Freud would have called the conscience part of his super-ego – was suddenly removed. If we could find out what that was, we would be that much closer to catching him. The reality is that we're unlikely to find out until we do catch him.'

Carter sat back to think it through.

'There are two other elements that I believe have been strengthened,' Kate continued. 'The first is the sense that he is both controlled, and needs to control. The second, and this is born out by the repetition of his use of morphine to both sedate and control pain, is that whilst he is clearly using his victims to release his anger and to make some kind of statement, he doesn't seek to brutalise them, or cause them unnecessary pain. That suggests some trace of empathy, or at the very least the ability to distinguish between the person or persons against whom his rage is directed, and his victims.'

She looked around the table. She still had them with her. Caton risked a glimmer of encouragement in his eyes. She was on the home straight.

She directed a question to DI Holmes. 'Detective Inspector, have any of the victims' contacts suggested that he might have had gay sexual preferences?'

Holmes shook his head. 'If anything, the reverse; apparently, he was forever pestering the women rough sleepers and female volunteers.'

'In which case, it is beginning to look as though his actions are not directed against gay men per se. His behaviour may be homophobic in the literal sense, but not in a sexual one. I think we can eliminate that at this stage; as we can the clown costume. It is unlikely that it has any connotations beyond a flamboyant form of disguise. It made us sit up and take notice. It formed a distraction and used up time and resources. But it has not been repeated. The van has also served its purpose, which suggests that whatever he has planned next will not require that form of transport.'

She checked her notes, flipping forward to the final page.

'Perhaps the most significant new element has been the use of the City Council badging. He must have gone to some lengths to acquire and prepare this transformation; again, at considerable risk.'

She looked at Caton.

'I assume there was always a possibility a Council worker might have recognised the anomaly in the make of van, and that the police cameras might have picked up the fact that the plates were not originals?'

'Correct on both counts,' Caton replied.

'This suggests that there is something significant about the City Council, possibly even Operational Services. Both the cross in St John's Gardens and the New Broom Sculpture are owned by the City, and are the responsibility of Operational Services?'

Caton nodded.

'So you may want to add that this person might well have a strong grievance against the City Council. Possibly someone who has been fired, evicted, sued...
'

'Given an ASBO,' Holmes chipped in, treading perilously close to the border between serious and flippant.

'That too,' she said. 'There are plenty of adults in the city who have been served ASBOs, and you shouldn't underestimate the impact of apparently minor interventions as potential triggers for the seriously disturbed.'

Holmes retreated back in his chair, conscious that Carter and Stuart were smirking.

'And that brings me to possibly the most important piece of confirmation. We now have two victims and two victim dump sites, and I am using that as a technical term,' she added quickly. 'The sites where the van was prepared and abandoned, and, most importantly, the homes of the victims. I use the term home loosely of course in the case of Mr Hoolock. That gives enough reference points to make geographical profiling so much more reliable.' She looked around the table again. 'You all know about geographical profiling?'

They nodded in unison. Of course they did; FMIT had its own software.

'What you may not know,' she continued, 'is that there is an increasing number of conflicting perspectives, each with their own computerised programmes. Some analysts believe that over time the dump sites will move ever closer towards the perpetrator's home base. Some believe that the victim is likely to have been travelling towards the perpetrator's home; others that the perpetrator travels towards the victim's home. In the first case the perpetrator's home and the dump sites will be in close proximity; in the second case the reverse will be true. In either case, the perpetrator is likely to live within a one-mile radius of a circle or – in an alternative theory of an angle or sector of that circle – from the centre of the cluster of dump sites, or the victims' homes.'

Kate could see that she had lost Holmes and Stuart. She took a sheet of paper from her notes, leaned back and held it up, such that all of them could see it. A rough diagram showed the Town Hall marked as the centre of a small map, to the south-west of which a cross marked St John's Gardens, and to the north-east of which – almost in a straight line – another marked the second dump site. To the south-east a cross marked Stephen Davies' apartment. Kate had joined the crosses to form a rough equilateral triangle, with the Town Hall almost at the centre of the base. Out to the east of the city, on the fringe of the map, a cross marked the burnt-out lock-up.

'I am going to urge some caution in relation to all of these theoretical predictions in our case,' she said, 'because it looks as though our perpetrator is choosing the dump sites not simply to dispose of the bodies, but rather to make a point. In essence, depending on which theory you subscribe to, there is a better than fifty per cent probability that our perpetrator lives within one of two circles, or sectors of a circle, whose centres, or point of origin, are either the Town Hall or Stephen Davies' flat. And both theories would strongly point towards it lying within a sector covering the south and east of the city.'

She placed the diagram on the table, marked out two overlapping sectors, each with an angle of approximately ninety degrees, and sat down.

The room was silent as Carter, Holmes and Stuart leant forward, mentally mapping the delineated area into a 3D landscape. City Centre South, St Georges, Hulme, the University Precinct, Moss Side, Greenheys and Whalley Range. Caton caught DI Weston's eye. She nodded what he assumed was her approval.

'Thank you, Ms Webb,' Caton said, his tone carefully measured. 'If you can let Inspector Holmes have a copy of your summary he'll make sure it's circulated, and also that Mr Wallace takes account of them in his multivariate analyses of the databases his team is searching. It seems to me,' he continued, 'that apart from the routine work that's already in hand, we need to get a list of anyone in the recent past with a real grudge against the City Council. All of the categories Ms Webb has suggested, plus any more we can think of; including any direct threats they may have received. If we can cross-reference those against the geographical profile zones, that might start to narrow down the likely suspects. We can always widen it over time if we have to.'

If nothing else, Caton reflected, it might prove to the chief executive and the leader that we are on the case. It might also give them something else to worry about. But he kept that to himself.

Chapter 22

'Can I have a word, boss?' Holmes asked, hovering.

Caton was caught between two stools. Only he, Holmes and Kate Webb remained. He desperately needed a moment alone with Kate, but he didn't want to make it obvious to Holmes, who he sensed was well aware of the situation and for some reason was determined to make it hard for them both.

'No problem, Gordon,' he responded, heading towards the door. 'I'll just show Ms Webb to her car.'

He opened the door for the two of them and stepped out into the corridor. Holmes muttered something about seeing him in the incident room, and turned away. Kate waited until the two of them were in the car park before she spoke.

'I think your detective inspector may be a trifle jealous,' she said playfully.

'Of me, or of you?' Caton asked, knowing full well.

'Oh, definitely of me,' she said. 'Doesn't want anything to break up the happy family.'

'He's got a family of his own. A wife, and a boy and three girls.'

'There you go, then. Maybe he sees you as a surrogate son.'

She opened her car door, climbed in and lowered the side window. Caton placed one hand on the roof and leaned closer.

'I'm going to run it all by Professor Stewart-Baker,' she said. 'If that's alright with you? He's sort of mentoring me, with this being my first case.'

'That's fine,' said Caton. 'Although you seem to be doing okay on your own.'

Her eyes flared briefly. 'Don't patronise me, Chief Inspector. Neither of us will know if I'm within a hundred miles of getting this right until you've caught him.'

He knew she was right. He hadn't meant to patronise her, she was doing fine. But she was right, he wouldn't have made the same comment to Professor Stewart-Baker.

'I'm sorry,' he said.

Her voice softened. 'Forget it. I'll also put the data we have into some of our geographical profiling software. I'm sure your guys will do the same. It won't hurt to check out those predictions I made – they were rough and ready to say the least.'

He resisted the temptation to contradict her.

'Thanks.'

She looked directly into his eyes, her smile beguiling.

'I had a wonderful time last night. I know it was probably as much a surprise to you as it was to me, but if you feel the same, I'd love to see you again.'

'I'd like nothing more,' he said, suddenly tongue-tied.

'I know this will be a busy weekend for you,' she said in a rush. 'And in any case, I'd agreed to go down and see my parents tomorrow. Next week is going to be really heavy. I've got a pile of end-of-term assignments to mark and a couple of lectures to prepare. Perhaps we could arrange something towards the end of the week? Thursday evening would be good. I've booked Friday as leave for DS Stuart's do, and I've got the whole of the weekend free.'

'That would be great, Kate,' he said. 'Let me arrange something this time.'

'Fine. Call me.'

He could feel a thousand eyes watching him from the windows of the incident room, and resisted the temptation to lean in and plant a kiss on her lips. She wound up the window, started the engine and drove away, sending him a flutter of a wave as she pulled out onto the road.

There were only two pairs of eyes at the window. They belonged to DI Weston and DI Holmes.

'He's got it bad,' Holmes opined.

'Hardly surprising,' Sarah Weston said. 'And if you ask me, it's about time.'

'Just so long as it doesn't affect his judgment,' Holmes added grudgingly.

As Caton began to turn towards them, Sarah pulled Holmes away from the window.

'Of course it will,' she said. 'That's a definition of infatuation.' She gave him a knowing look. 'Just so long as it doesn't affect our judgment too.'

Caton was not surprised to discover that DI Holmes had forgotten what it was he needed to see him about. Reassured by the bustle of purposeful activity in the incident room, he went back to his office. Initially he found it hard to concentrate on the task in hand. His mind was a whirl of emotions. He was reassured by Kate's reaction, but felt anxious about the implications. Above all, he remained elated by the way the previous evening had gone. If I have to have flashbacks, he decided, best to have them about a night like that.

Every time he closed his eyes, the images of the bodies commingled. Stephen Davies, helpless on the mortuary slab; Tom Hoolock, curled pathetically on the cold, hard pavement; and Kate – long, smooth, warm and sensuous – poised above him on the bed. He found it intensely disturbing that the killer's work should infest his brain in such an insidious manner. Over dinner, Kate had suggested, albeit gently, that the death of his parents at such a vulnerable age must have left him with some issues. He wondered now if these images were part of that, or if every detective, SOCO, traffic officer or paramedic was similarly affected.

He poured himself a glass of water and picked up the phone. He asked Ged to see if Superintendent Gates was available. He secretly hoped that she was not.

Sunday passed quietly. There was a skeleton staff processing data, but Caton still felt he had to be there. The labs were closed, so there was nothing from that front. The most significant piece of evidence appeared in a report from Nick Carter. It was almost certain that their man had bought a ticket from the ticket machine at Crumpsall Station for the 6.14 – the first tram of the day. The company had provided a list of all credit card purchases, although Caton doubted that Bojangles would make such a stupid mistake.

Unfortunately, the machine had been emptied of cash long before they got to it, so fingerprints were out of the question. The CCTV tapes had been retrieved from the tram – the number 1018 Sir Matt Busby – and from both stations.

Caton had sat and watched their man arrive at Crumpsall, purchase his ticket, wait on the platform, enter the tram head lowered, face obscured, and leave it at Piccadilly. He had watched as the man crossed the station concourse, descended the escalators and negotiated Fairfield Street, before disappearing into the maze of backstreets and industrial units.

Caton found it doubly infuriating that their quarry should deliberately allow them this voyeuristic opportunity, knowing full well they would be overwhelmed by a sense of impotence. The only shred of comfort was that they could now be a little more certain about his height – although that proved to be no more than a confirmation of their original estimate.

The follow-up interviews with Metrolink and Mainline station employees, and passengers returning to Crumpsall on the evening trams, had yielded nothing they could use. Eventually, he gave it up and went home.

Monday proved equally uneventful, apart from Larry Hymer's wheedling attempts to get a new angle for the evening edition. The detailed pathology report added nothing of significance to DI Weston's version, and forensics had drawn a blank so far on all three sites and the burnt-out van. Certainly there was nothing that brought them nearer to the perpetrator. Enquiries continued apace to track down the source of the climbing rope.

On Wednesday, Holmes had a call from Dicky Lounds confirming their suspicion that the City Council plates had also been supplied by Gerry Nelson. Nelson hadn't bothered to mention it, because he hadn't specifically been asked about that particular licence number. Holmes suspected that it was also because these plates would have been more evidently intended for a fraudulent purpose. It was irrelevant now. The damage had been done.

Caton's phone beeped and he picked up a long-awaited text message from Kate.

Hi Tom. How R U? Reeli sori but forgot am tydup 2moro Eve. Jo S has askd me to her civ partnership & recep on Fri.

Sed U'll be there. We cud go somwre aftwards? B in tuch.

K. Xxx.

Caton was relieved to receive the message; disappointed about Thursday evening. He wondered if they could manage to extricate themselves from DS Stuart's reception early, without giving offence and adding fuel to the rumours that he suspected were already rife. He was still trying to decide where he might take her when Ged rang to tell him that the Town Hall had just emailed her a first list of the dismissed and aggrieved.

He was already annoyed that it had taken so long, especially given the pressure that was still coming from the chief exec's office. When he opened the file he discovered that they had only sent the ones that had involved the City solicitor. The terse note which accompanied it implied that it was going to be a long haul getting a comprehensive list of the others from the individual departments. Now he was angry.

One mile, nine hundred and sixty yards, due west, Albert Stephen placed the last of the notes in a flimsy white self-seal envelope. He wondered if the police would be able to trace them back to the ink-jet printer. He had no idea if printers carried an individual footprint in the way that manual typewriters of old had done. He vaguely remembered a film on television from the sixties which had been solved in just that way.

He gathered the envelopes, checking that each of them had a different name scrawled across the front, and stuffed them into the inside pocket of his great coat. It didn't really matter if they could. Nor that they would probably be able to pin the handwritten names down to him. By the time they did, it would be too late. It would only be a matter of time before they put two and two together, but right now he was in control, and he only needed a few more days.

One by one he closed the open files on his computer screen. The first was the list of key players; the second, the names, locations and connections of the five young boys he had cultivated carefully over the previous two years. A purchase here, a gift there, no favours asked in return, until now. The third was an Internet map of a section to the north-east of the city. When those files had been closed, there was one remaining. He sat and stared at the photo, oblivious to the passage of time. Despite the fact that it had been taken with a telephoto lens, the image was crisp and clear. Head turned slightly, hair lifted gently by the wind, revealing the long pale curve of her neck; it had captured Kate Webb as she waited patiently to cross Oxford Road.

At 9.30 Thursday morning, Caton was on the phone when Ged knocked twice and stuck her head around the door. That she failed to wait for him to invite her in was singular enough, but the look on her face was enough to cause him to make his apologies and end the call.

'Ged. What on earth's the matter?'

'I'm sorry, sir, but Superintendent Gates has just been on the phone. She was steaming. She said – and I quote – "Get Caton. I don't care what he's doing. My car will be there in four minutes, and he'd better be out on the pavement waiting".'

'Caton. Not Chief Inspector, or Mr?'

'No, sir. Just Caton.' She looked at the clock. 'And that was a minute and a half ago.'

Caton grabbed his coat from the back of the door.

'You'll need this,' Ged told him, holding up his umbrella.

It had not rained for almost a week, and was hitting back with a vengeance. He clipped his mobile onto his belt and headed for the car park.

He found himself in a queue for the exit. Ahead of him, officers donned bulletproof vests as they shuffled towards the door. Outside, vans and cars were lined up in the pouring rain with their engines running. He saw two authorised firearms officers climbing into an armed response vehicle, and behind them two dog handlers loading their German Shepherds into a van.

As he reached the pavement, a traffic car screeched to a halt beside him, the bow wave soaking his trousers and mocking the parade-ground shine on his shoes.

Helen Gates, red faced, beckoned him to join her in the back. No sooner had he closed the door than they were off, the g-force pinioning him to his seat. He struggled to get into his seat belt.

'What's going on, Ma'am?' he heard himself say.

'You may well ask!' Gates bellowed above the noise of the sirens. 'It's your bloody Bojangles. He's starting a war out there.'

'The red horse.'

'What?' Gates demanded.

'It's the second horseman, astride a red horse, bringer of war.'

'Precisely!'

She thrust a slip of paper at him, approximately ten centimetres by six. A message was printed across the centre.

They comin for you – Gooch 2 – less you take them out first Cheetham an broughton they toolin up north of the river in the cemity in philips Park 10.30 in the morning tomoro tusday This is serius man!!!!

In the bottom right-hand corner, a red horse – the size of a postage stamp – reared up on its hind legs. She passed him an envelope.

'It was addressed to one of the Doddington crew lieutenants,' she said. 'It looks certain that Gooch Close got one too. All the indications are he's sprayed them across the city; same message, different order. He's trying to engineer unholy alliances, and set gang against gang. If we don't stop this, it'll be more like a bloodbath than a war.'

Caton hung on to the roof handle as the car overtook a recalcitrant driver on the wrong side of the road and sped across the Pottery Lane junction with Ashton Old Road. As soon as they crossed into Alan Turing Way, the driver cut the sirens. Caton noticed that the roads had become eerily empty, the only noise above the engine the swish of their wake and the clack of the windscreen wipers.

'How did we get hold of it?' he asked.

'Sheer fluke. Drug Squad were watching the supermarket car park off Moss Lane. Saw a lad on a mountain bike – early teens – pass this to a younger boy with a mate, both on mountain bikes. The older one rode off towards Greenheys. The younger ones were obviously arguing about what to do with it when three youths in their late teens jumped them, grabbed the envelope, their mobile phones and what looked like a couple of packages from the inside of their windcheaters. The young lads fled. The Drug Squad waited for the youths to leave the car park and then nabbed them. Apart from the phones, some cannabis and a small quantity of crystal meth, they found the envelope and the note.'

'When was this?' Caton asked.

'Twenty-one hundred hours last night. Drug Squad put their feelers out and got a confirmation late last night from one of their informants that the Cheetham Hill gang were in a panic, and there was talk on the streets that they'd called a truce with the Salford Lads, and all the parties were tooling up.'

'Gerry Nelson,' Caton muttered to himself.

'About the same time,' she continued, 'one of the kids on the Multi-Agency programme reported a sibling being approached to take a similar message to a gang leader of the Longsight Crew. The assistant chief constable decided to take no chances and called everyone together. The operation was planned overnight. Divisions, Tactical Aid Unit, Armed Response Unit, Drug Squad, Operation Xcalibre team. It was only half an hour ago, when Chief Superintendent Hadfield showed me that note, that we made the connection with your man.'

She seized the grab handle on her side with both hands and clung on for grim death as the car swung into the National Cycling Centre car park and screeched to a halt.

'Have you any idea what he's started here?' she asked, taking a deep breath and fighting for composure.

The driver's passenger turned to address her.

'This is as far we go, Ma'am. The active zone starts at Fairclough Street, this side of the park. You'll have to walk up from here. Someone's coming to meet you.'

Someone did. It was Dicky Lounds; windcheater hood pulled tight, the rain dripping from the end of his nose. At his ingratiating best.

'Ma'am, sir, if you'd like to come with me. We can only go so far. It's like the Somme up there.'

They set off, with every step carving swathes through the stream of water that ran towards them. Up ahead, small groups of officers hurried to their appointed destinations.

'Someone's made a balls-up somewhere along the line,' Lounds said for no obvious reason, although Caton had a pretty good idea it was aimed at him.

To her credit, Helen Gates held her counsel.

'What's the operational plan?' Caton asked.

Gates strained to hear him above the rain drumming on his umbrella.

'The first priority is to keep them apart,' she shouted. 'The second is to avoid bloodshed, especially anything involving innocent bystanders. The third is to try and make sure they don't regroup somewhere else. Anything beyond that will be a bonus.'

On Fairclough Street, at the southern border of the park, the police helicopter swooped low overhead, skimming the trees, heading north-west towards the cemetery. Through the driving rain, Caton could make out a mobile communications room, two police horseboxes, a mobile video unit, three ambulances, and sundry cars and vans parked parallel to the road.

'Gold Command is at Chester House, Silver at Bootle Street and Bronze is running the operation on the ground here from the Comm's room,' Lounds told them. 'You'll find them in there, including,' he added ominously, 'the deputy chief constable.'

He turned away towards Bank Street, leaving them to climb the steps into the van.

The Communications room was packed. A bank of screens fed live coverage from static vans and handheld video cameras. Instructions were being continuously relayed to separate command points and officers on the ground. To the fore, Caton spotted both the assistant chief constable Crime Operations and the assistant chief constable Specialist Operations.

'I hope the terrorists and armed robbers haven't got wind we're all tied up here,' Caton said to no one in particular.

Helen Gates fixed him with an icy stare.

'Hope? You'd better pray,' she said, before moving off to join Chief Superintendent Hadfield, who was deep in conversation with the deputy chief constable.

Caton edged closer to the screens. In one he could see a group of seven young men – four white, two of Asian appearance and one of mixed race – lying face down in the road, spreadeagled, heads turned sideways to keep their mouths clear of the water pooling around them and filling their hoods. Circling them stood members of the Tactical Aid Unit, vigilant, as one by one the captives had their hands secured behind their backs with plastic cable ties. Beyond this group, members of the Armed Response Unit were emptying magazines from an array of weapons into a metal box, prior to loading them into a van.

'You wouldn't believe what they've got already.'

Caton found Mark Watts, a colleague uniformed chief inspector from A Division North Manchester, at his shoulder.

'Small bore shotguns – Berettas and Merkels – single-shot and semi-automatic pistols. Two Kalashnikovs, a Mac 10 and at least a dozen converted replicas and reactivated handguns. Just like the amnesty all over again.'

'Where are we up to exactly?' Caton asked him.

'Well, the area was pretty well staked out by 9 o'clock this morning. The first lot turned up about twenty past, obviously trying to get there early to set up an ambush on the others. We let the first couple of groups through, mainly to avoid a shoot-out with rush-hour traffic, although a fair bit of that had been diverted. Any that arrived after that were basically blocked in back and front, and surrounded by Firearms before they knew what hit them. We think the Longsight Crew and Pitt Bull both sussed we had it staked out and turned back. Doddington haven't turned up. They never got their personal invite because the Drug Squad intercepted it. Word is they thought it was a wind-up. But it looks like most of the rest are here.'

'Who is this?' Caton asked, nodding towards the screen.

'We think it's some of the Cheetham Hill Gang and some of Higher Broughton. They had to have been shit scared for them to team up.'

'Has anyone been hurt?' Caton asked.

Watts pointed to another screen where a stretcher was being loaded onto an ambulance.

'Couple of the kids from the Longsight Soldiers panicked and started shooting. Our lot returned fire. One lad, about fifteen, is critical; another, younger, has a shoulder and a chest wound. Officially, he's seriously injured. That's why the deputy chief's here. We'll have to refer it to IPCC.'

An internal inquiry, and the Independent Police Complaints Commission, was going to tie up God knows how many officers over the next six months. Caton had already realised that there was no way he was going to avoid some of the fallout.

'How many have been arrested?' he asked.

'Nineteen at the last count.'

Caton pointed to the two central screens, to which most of the attention in the room was directed. One showed the backs of a large number of armed officers crouching in a long crescent behind an assorted jumble of gravestones. The other, a line of officers similarly armed, moving slowly forward in a broad arc.

'What's happening here?' he asked.

'Ah, that's the two groups that got through. Gooch parked behind the baths and were heading west when they realised we were behind them. Some of them legged it towards the reservoir and the area around Bank Bridge. The rest have got themselves trapped in Tulip Valley, between us and the Medlock.'

Caton tried to visualise what the River Medlock would look like after all the rain that had fallen overnight and this morning. At one time little more than an industrial sewer, the fast-flowing clear water was now behind iron railings, channelled in a deep, two-metre-wide, open brick channel. Not exactly a threat to life, even in spate, and probably fordable; especially with the Armed Response force on their heels. But the trees and railings would make it heavy going.

'Trouble is,' Watts continued, 'the rest of the Salford Lads from Lower Broughton and Ordsall were laid up in the cemetery, and now they're headed towards the river from the north. If the two of them meet up, it could end up like the Battle of the Little Bighorn.'

'I thought that most of Gooch Close got sent down in May, after they clashed with the Longsight Crew in the Infirmary?' Caton remarked.

'Three of them were jailed, three were given ASBOs, one got community service and one was given three months but released because he'd already spent more than that on remand. Five of the Longsight Crew went down, but with the time they spent on remand, plus time off for "good behaviour", most of them will have been released just in time for this. Ironic, isn't it?'

Ironic, was not the word Caton would have used. Suddenly, the tension in the room rose palpably; everyone stopped talking, other than those at the microphones. Pictures were coming in from the helicopter. On one screen it was just possible, between the trees that lined both banks, to make out a straggle of young men, some of them barely in their teens, standing indecisively on the banks of the rapidly flowing swollen river. Caton counted seven. It looked as though they had already ditched their weapons. Two had partially climbed down the side of the gully and were testing the depth of the water, one leg at a time. One of them looked up at the helicopter. Suddenly, a taller and older member of the group spotted something through the trees and railings on the opposite bank, and pointed. All of their heads went up. They froze, like rabbits in the presence of a hawk. The helicopter pulled back, the camera swivelling to capture another group of nine or ten men advancing between the gravestones towards the river, from the north. One of this new group raised what looked like a semi-automatic towards the helicopter, which instantly banked hard right and climbed rapidly, the camera losing focus for several seconds.

When the picture returned, the smaller group on the south bank had scattered, running left and right along the brick-lined bank, pursued by armed officers. The two who had entered the water stood waist deep, their arms raised as officers, having vaulted the railings, gesticulated at them from the bank. In the cemetery the gang members were either on their knees or already lying face down on the sodden grass, except for one, his back to the advancing officers, who, having reached the railings, flung his weapon into the foaming river, before turning arrogantly, arms splayed on either side, palms open, to face them.

A muted cheer rang through the mobile unit. The DCC congratulated his assistant chief constables and turned to speak briefly to Martin Hadfield. The chief superintendent turned and came across to Caton, with Helen Gates in tow.

'I'm glad you made it, Chief Inspector,' he said, his manner anything but friendly. 'If only so that you could see how close we came to a complete bloody, and I mean bloody, disaster. I think it's time you caught this clown, don't you?'

For a moment Caton wondered if he intended the term clown to be ironic or literal. He decided that this was not a good time to ask. He had also noted the way that Hadfield had tried to distance himself from the responsibility. The phrase 'hung out to dry' came to mind. Caton considered himself a reasonable man. Fair enough, he decided; it is about time I caught him.

Chapter 23

Caton spent the afternoon chasing progress. He was mindful that it wouldn't help to pass on his own frustration and sense of urgency to a team that was already working flat-out. It was not just about piling on more pressure. They had all heard the latest updates, seen the midday news. They knew it was their man behind it, even if, for now, that had been kept from the media. What they needed was a steer, not a battering.

He recalled another phrase from *The Art of Possibility* by Maestro Benjamin Zander, the conductor of the Boston Philharmonic Orchestra, and his wife Rosamund. Something about a leader being a master of distinctions.

He needed to unlock the voice in their heads that would guide them to spot, amongst the reams and screens of data, the one significant clue that would lead them to the perpetrator. He had a gut instinct that Kate's profile – however tentative she continued to claim that it was – held their best chance of narrowing it down. Several times throughout the afternoon he had tried to contact her. Her office told him she was giving a lecture, then had two tutorials – all in another building – and was intending to head straight home. He left a succession of messages on her mobile phone.

It was 6 o'clock in the evening when she finally

returned his calls from her landline. He was in the canteen watching the news with a dozen or so officers from Division. She sounded out of breath.

'Tom, it's me. I'm sorry I didn't get back to you sooner; I forgot to charge my battery. I've got the news on. It's him, isn't it?'

'Yes, it is. But they're keeping the lid on that for now. Thank God.'

'Sounds like a good move. Assuming publicity is what he's after, that's going to make him very, very angry. More chance he'll make a mistake, or come out into the open.'

There was a pause, followed by a strange scratching sound.

'It also means he's likely to step up a notch, escalate.' Her voice was suddenly muffled.

Caton looked at the mayhem on the screen. *How the hell*, he wondered, *is he going to improve on this?*

'Where are you?' he asked.

'I'm at home. Drying my hair. I've just had a shower.'

Caton's pictured the scene. It threatened to derail his train of thought big time. He pulled himself together.

'We need to meet to talk about this. I really need your advice.'

'I'm sorry,' she said. 'I'm in a hell of rush. It's my best friend's hen party. I'm late already.'

He heard the hum of a hairdryer.

'We'll have to do it now. I'll put the phone on speaker.'

'Give me a minute,' he said, 'I need the privacy of my office. I'll ring you back.'

He sat down behind his desk and made the call. She answered immediately. The hairdryer had stopped, but he sensed she was moving around the room. The rustling of clothes told him she was dressing.

'I'm running out of options here, Kate,' he said. 'We have to narrow it down faster. Is there anything you can add to what you've already given us?'

'Well, I've been giving it some thought,' she said.

He heard the rasp of a zip.

'And I did run it past Professor Stewart-Baker as I promised, and he concurs. The two things that struck me as most significant are the horses and the dump sites. That's because those are the things which seem to be most significant to the perpetrator.'

She opened a drawer, and he heard the sound of beads clanking together.

'He's running out of options too, Tom. First disease, then famine, now war; he only has conquest left, whatever that means. The most common interpretation put on the rider of the white horse is that he represents Christ; as judge, conqueror, avenger. My hunch – and it is only a hunch – is that is how the perpetrator sees himself; a sort of Christ figure. That would free him to behave in ways which his supposedly normal persona would not.'

She stopped talking and he heard a door opening, followed by the sound of boxes being moved. Shoes, he decided, in the wardrobe.

'Are you still there, Tom?' she called.

'Go ahead, I'm listening.'

Her voice became more distinct as she picked up the phone, switched off the speaker and sat down on the bed.

'So, if we assume that he's judging or avenging – the conquering bit would be the conclusion or result rather than the motivation – the question is...' She paused, inviting him to respond.

'Who is he judging or avenging?' Caton said.

'That brings us to the dump sites and the battleground,' she said.

'Each of them owned and managed by the City Council.'

'Correct. And who stands to lose most from this train of events, aside from the victims who look increasingly like unconnected tools, a means to an end?'

'The City Council, or more accurately, the image of the city,' Caton decided.

'And the reputation of the police,' she added, as if he needed reminding. 'Although I have the feeling that's simply an inevitable consequence rather than the aim; otherwise, he would have dumped the bodies on your doorstep. He's proved that he can do it more or less anywhere he wants.'

'You don't need to rub it in,' Caton said miserably.

She switched back to the speakerphone. He heard her cross the room and the clack of a hanger being plucked from its rail.

'I'm sorry, Tom, but I really do have to go. We'll be back late, so I won't ring you tonight.'

She threw the hanger on the bed and slipped her coat on.

'I'll see you at Joanne and Abbie's do at the Town Hall tomorrow, and we can take it from there.' She hesitated. When she spoke again, her voice was somewhere between entreating and demanding. 'By *it*, I mean whatever you have planned. Not more of this. I'm assuming we can try and park it for a day and a half?'

The last time Caton had heard that, expressed in almost exactly those terms, was the day before his first wedding anniversary dinner, for which he was nearly two hours late. Six months later, Laura had left him.

'Of course,' he said as convincingly as he could.

'And, Kate, I really appreciate this. Thank you. And have a great time tonight.'

'You're welcome, Tom. I'll see you tomorrow. Bye.'

Albert Stephen had also been watching the news. His initial elation had given way to confusion, and then anger. There had always been the possibility that the police might find out, but he had not expected it, nor that they would have been so well organised. There had been no mention of either of the previous victims, nor the symbols he had left, and neither of them had been linked to the morning's events. What made it worse was that both the police and the City Council were presenting it as a triumph.

He had watched, with rising fury, the deputy chief constable and leader stand side by side on the steps of the Town Hall, giving the clear impression that this was a victory for joint planning and long-standing intelligence work. A sizeable number of arrests had been made, weapons seized. The heads had been struck from a number of these gangs just as Hercules had destroyed the many-headed Hydra, and Perseus, Medusa's Gorgon. A warning had been posted that Manchester would not tolerate this kind of insidious disorder. The streets of this proud city would be that much safer for decent hard-working citizens.

He fought to control the rage that had built inside him. His stomach churned. The familiar belt of steel began to tighten around his chest. He lurched into the bathroom, ran the cold tap, filled the bowl and immersed his face. When he could hold his breath no longer, he collapsed onto the toilet seat, taking great intakes of breath, exhaling slowly and rhythmically as his mother had taught him. The water ran in rivulets from his hair, forehead, nose and chin, soaking his trousers.

Friday morning broke fine, dry and a little warmer than of late. Caton had been summoned to a meeting at Chester House to start at 10 o'clock. Knowing that it would be more of a crisis meeting than a summit, he arrived early. The conference room was already half full. People stood around drinking coffee and eating tiny Danish pastries. Caton would have given anything for a bacon barm cake.

Hadfield and Gates were already there, as were over half of the Command Team. The assistant commissioners for Crime Operations and Special Operations he had been expecting to see, and the assistant chief constable Territorial Policing, who had responsibility for the twelve divisions, was not a surprise. More ominously, the assistant chief constables for Human Relations and Internal Affairs had turned up, too. In one corner, the head of the Force Drugs Unit, as it was more formally known, was deep in conversation with the head of the Firearms Unit and a tall man in his mid forties that Caton did not recognise. In another corner, he could see the chief executive of the City Council talking to the head of the MMAGS team. The first initiative of its kind in the country, the Manchester Multi-Agency Gangs Strategy had been having impressive – if deliberately low-key – results. Targeting the siblings of current gang members, its primary task was to divert them away from gang membership, and show them alternative routes and opportunities.

'How are you, Tom?'

Caton turned to face Chief Superintendent Bill Tyrer, commander of the newly created Metropolitan Division. Tyrer had been at the training school at Bruge with Caton, and they both knew that had Tom been ambitious for promotion, they would, at the very least, have shared the same rank. Tyrer was a tough, hard-working, no-nonsense policeman with an instinct for force politics. Caton had a great deal of respect for him.

'Not bad. Though right now I could do without all this,' he said, inclining his head towards the babble behind him.

'You and me both. Incidentally, Tom, your Bojangles has worked a treat on our crime figures. Murders apart,' he added dryly, 'all the activity your lot has generated on the streets, and round the industrial estates, seems to have scared a load of our regulars off. Mind you, they're probably cursing you in the other divisions.'

Before Caton could respond, someone clinked a spoon against a glass and people began to take their seats. Bill Tyrer headed towards the top of the table.

Caton chose a seat at the bottom end, and checked that his mobile and pager were switched off. He noted with amusement how many were jostling for places, the most prized of all those facing the two doors; old habits die hard.

The assistant chief constable Crime Operations was chairing the meeting, and invited quick introductions around the table. When it came to Caton's turn, all eyes were on him. Some he knew were just curious about how he must be feeling, and what kind of fist he would make of it. Others – not least of whom the chief executive of the Council, head of the Force Drugs Unit and his own boss Hadfield – he could sense boring holes through to the back of his head. The last to introduce himself was the mystery man. In his early fifties, he was well built, hair beginning to thin, relaxed and confident.

'I am Chief Superintendent Pat Mayhew, National Crime Squad. Here by invitation, and in an observer role,' he said smoothly.

For now, Caton decided.

Introductions over, ACC Crime Ops brushed a few crumbs from the front of his uniform and began the meeting.

'Everybody has a copy of the agenda, and you all know why we're here. On one level, yesterday was a disaster. Armed gangs re-enacting Gunfight at The OK Corral on the streets of Manchester; roadblocks everywhere; complete disruption to the city, with gridlock on all of the arterial routes for over an hour, and fifteen-mile tailbacks on the M60 and the M62. And let's face it, it could have been an absolute bloodbath.' He paused for effect. 'World coverage to boot. Not a good image for the city.'

To the right of the Chair, the chief executive nodded vigorously. Took the wind out of his sails, Caton reflected; smart move.

'On the upside,' the ACC continued, 'this was an exemplary operation, with the full cooperation of the City Council, and the emergency services. Thirty-one arrests were made. Eighteen guns have been retrieved so far, including a number of mint-condition semi-automatic and automatic pistols and rifles from Eastern Europe. The park and cemetery are still being scoured, and officers from the Underwater Unit are searching the Medlock.'

'Rather them than me,' muttered the female superintendent on Caton's left.

'We have also seized assorted knives and machetes,' the ACC continued.

The head of the Tactical Firearms Unit raised his hand.

'We suspect,' he said, 'that a number of these guns have been rented or supplied on loan for this occasion, at very short notice. The likelihood is that they will have been used in other scenarios, and not just in the

GMP area. Given the length of the sentences some of them could be facing, we may just get the odd source, and through them, a handle on a number of unsolved cases.'

Another hand went up. It was the head of MMAGS.

'The trouble is,' she said, 'that by taking out so many of the hierarchy of three of these gangs, we've created a vacuum which the others will try to fill, and a new and younger, inexperienced leadership usually means more careless violence and vendettas than before. More drive-by shootings, safe houses raided, kidnappings.'

There were nods around the table. The head of the Force Drugs Unit seized his opportunity.

'We've been here before. This is still a sticking-plaster job. In the long run we aren't going to sort this until we improve the education, leisure time and long-term job prospects for these kids. Work on the absent father syndrome, look at the whole legal framework around substance abuse and cut out the easy money that comes on the back of the drugs.'

The chief executive raised his hand.

'Well, the City Council has gone a long way to get the infrastructure right. In most of the areas where these gangs operate we've regenerated the housing, built new supermarkets, supported small business start-ups, developed the health and social amenities, doubled the Connexions Service.'

Not to be outdone, the chair exercised his prerogative and clawed it back.

'And for our part, we are catching them and locking them up as fast as they come back out again. And the research shows that the older they get, the less likely they are to continue in the gangs.'

The head of MMAGS leant forward. 'So the answer

is to lock them up till they grow out of it?' she said, leaving them to decide if it was a serious suggestion or a veiled criticism.

'Only if the prison service can keep them apart, and do some proper rehabilitation,' the head of South Division offered.

It was all getting out of hand, Caton observed. Then it rebounded in his direction.

The ACC Special Operations put his hand on the chair's arm and said ominously, 'We have Chief Inspector Caton with us, Bob.'

All eyes turned in Tom's direction. He topped his glass up with still water, took a sip and waited for the onslaught.

Research always paid dividends. Albert Stephen got through first time.

'Rachel Jazrawi. How can I help you?'

'Rachel.' He never uses Mrs, or Miss, to avoid offence, unless such a term is offered first. 'Good morning. This is Detective Inspector Holmes. I have a message for Kate Webb from Chief Inspector Caton. It's very urgent.'

'I'm sorry, Inspector, Ms Webb is on leave today.'

His heart began to pound. This wasn't happening. It could not happen.

'Will you be able to contact her?' he asked, holding his breath as he waited for the reply.

'Oh, yes, I'm sure she'll still be at home. I'm not able to give out her home number or her mobile, but I can contact her for you if that would be alright?'

He breathed out slowly. Better than alright; perfect.

'In which case, could you tell her that Chief Inspector Caton needs to meet with her urgently, straight away? It is in connection with the case she is working on.'

'Well, I don't know if she'll be…' the administrator began.

'I'm sure she will,' he cut her off. 'When you tell her it really is a matter of life and death.'

'Well, I suppose in that case…'

'The chief inspector will be waiting for her at the Town Hall, by the Reception. I will ring back in three minutes to make sure she has received the message. And I nearly forgot. Chief Inspector Caton is having problems with his mobile phone, which is why he asked me to ring. She won't be able to contact him direct. Thank you, Rachel,' he said, and replaced the handset before she had a chance to respond.

Albert Stephen remained in the phone box, much to the annoyance of the woman laden down with shopping bags, desperately trying to control two young boys, whose idea of fun was to blow raspberries at him and kick chunks out of each other. He rang back as the second hand hit twelve, and received the reassurance he needed.

Three minutes later, he was climbing the steps of the Town Hall, resplendent in his blue blazer and grey flannels. Every inch the official city guide.

'You look terrific,' Abbie called out through the open door to the en suite bathroom.

Joanne Stuart took one last look in the mirror. The pale cream suit was just right, and the ideal complement to the apricot one that her partner had chosen. Peaches and cream, everyone's dream. The sun was shining and the sky was clear. It was going to be a perfect day.

Kate had woken late and had a long, leisurely bath, letting the bath salts purge the excesses of the night before. And now she had to rush to get ready. She tried Tom's mobile again to no avail and left a second message. In the kitchen she threw down a glass of orange and cranberry juice, rinsed the glass under the tap and wiped her mouth with a piece of kitchen roll. She stopped momentarily to check in the hallway mirror that her lipstick had not smudged, flicked her hair behind her ears, set the alarm and left.

'I bet you're glad that's over, Tom?' Bill Tyrer said as he followed Caton out into the corridor. 'Thought you handled it really well, by the way. I bet you were surprised to find the chief super from the NCS in your corner?'

'Doesn't want to end up taking any of the flack himself,' said Caton. 'My guess is they won't want it referred to them, simply because there's not a lot more they could do that we aren't already doing.'

He stopped by the lift.

'You go on, Bill; I've got to check my calls.'

'I'll see you later, Tom, and remember, if there's any more I can do…' Tyrer stepped into the lift, followed by some of the others.

Caton decided to take the stairs, checking his messages as he went. The first was from DS Stuart, reminding him that the ceremony was at 1 p.m. in the Lord Mayor's Parlour. The second was from Gordon Holmes. He gave an address in Whalley Range and urged Caton to get over there straight away. His voice was charged with excitement; the reason, he left to the end.

I think we've found him!

The next two messages were both from Kate. The first simply said, *I got your message, I'll meet you there.* The second, *I'm leaving now.*

He looked at his watch. It was only 11.45 a.m. She's keen, he thought to himself. He switched off his phone, took the remaining stairs two at a time and hurried out towards the car park.

Kate asked the taxi to drop her by the Central Library and made her way quickly towards Albert Square. The Christmas market was at its height. A mass of people thronged between the brightly lit and festive stalls. Immediately in front of her, on the southern fringe of the square, the Stockport Youth Brass Band was playing a selection of carols, and she had to fight her way through the proud parents and appreciative spectators.

She climbed the steps into the entrance hall and searched for Caton. He was not by the Reception desk. The sculpture gallery to her right was full of glass cases offering modern jewellery for sale as part of the annual Dazzle exhibition. She wove her way around the display. There was still no sign of him. She took her mobile from her bag, tried Caton's phone again and then decided to ask at the Reception desk if there were any messages for her. The two women on the desk checked their screens.

'Sorry, love, no. But you might try Mr Allardyce at the porter's desk. It's just down there.'

Increasingly anxious, Kate hurried to the glass-encased box by the Lloyd Street entrance.

'I'm expecting to meet a Chief Inspector Caton. Has he left a message by any chance? My name is Webb.'

'Certainly, miss,' the porter replied with a friendly smile. 'Mr Caton has just rung down to say that he'd like you to join him by the Princess Street Staircase, on the fourth level. Here, I'll show you.'

He produced a floor plan of the Town Hall and traced the route.

'Go straight back in the direction you've just come

from, past the entrance and the Reception desk, the Reception Room and the Banqueting Room, and climb the spiral staircase on your right until you get to the fourth level. When you step off the staircase, Mr Caton should be waiting for you.'

She thanked him and set off. Through the open doors of the Mayor's Parlour she caught a glimpse of the caterers setting out champagne glasses. In less than an hour, Joanne and Abbie would be exchanging their vows.

Chapter 24

The street was deserted, apart from three parked cars, the furthest of which, some fifty yards away, Caton recognised as belonging to his team. DC Wood stepped out from behind the yew hedge into the empty driveway and directed him round to the rear of the building.

He pulled up behind Holmes' Mondeo, in front of which he glimpsed an ageing Peugeot 406 estate. As he climbed out, Wood caught up with him.

'We've to go in by the back door, boss,' he said conspiratorially. 'In case he comes back. Don't want him driving straight out again.'

'If he does, the team are waiting for him, surely?' Caton said as they crunched across the gravel.

Wood's shrug was noncommittal. 'Even so...'

They made their way through a scullery lined with shelves, on which tins of food were stacked in rows in what appeared to Caton to be height order, each row containing ever smaller tins.

The kitchen had an antiseptic smell to it. Above the cheap plastic table and chairs, an ancient wood and iron kitchen maid hung incongruously, a solitary tea towel fluttering in the draft they had just created.

The passage from the kitchen to the hall was long, dark and cold. They passed a door beneath the stairs that was open inwards, and Caton could see the first of a flight of stone steps angling downwards. DC Wood hurried past and led him up the stairs, urging him to take care where the green and gold Axminster carpet had become threadbare. Holmes, grinning from ear to ear, met them on the first landing.

'It's definitely him, boss. We've got him. John bloody Soaper. Right under our noses all the time.'

Caton was confused. 'But I thought he lived in that refurbished warehouse over towards New Islington?'

Holmes grimaced. 'So he does. That's the address he gave, and that's where I visited him; seems he still lives here as well.'

Caton peered into the room to his left. It had all the appearance of a study. SOCO were working on the computer, and going through filing cabinets and cupboards. On the CCTV screens above the desk he could see the empty driveway, and more SOCO moving around what appeared to be a basement cellar.

'How did you get on to him?' he asked.

'It was a combination of things. Duggie Wallace was working through a list of databases using some of the search criteria from the offender profile Kate Webb gave us. His mother appeared on the list of patients who'd been in the hospital at the same time as Stephen Davies. His own name turned up on the Child Protection Register. Then, beggar me, Soaper's name leapt out from the latest list they sent over from the Town Hall. It wasn't on the first list because technically he hadn't been dismissed; he had been forced to resign.'

'What had he done?' Caton asked.

'Apparently, he'd been sending abusive emails to some of his colleagues, and some kind of rant to the politicians. Crafty sod had been covering his tracks by using other people's terminals when they were on a break, in the canteen or having a smoke.'

'So how did they catch him?' Caton wondered out loud.

'Their Human Resources called Barton Street nick, who set a camera up through a peephole in the side of a filing cabinet. Worked a treat. Got him on day two.'

'So why wasn't he dismissed?'

Holmes rubbed the side of his jaw, as though checking his shave. A habit, Caton reflected, that had almost become a tick of late.

'Seems he worked for them for years. Never previously put a foot wrong. And they reckoned he was suffering from stress – something he vehemently denied. In the end they gave him a choice. Go quietly, or they'd dismiss him on grounds of gross misconduct.'

'His conduct's become a damn sight more gross since he left,' Caton observed grimly. 'Did they hear any more from him?'

'Apparently, he made some vague threats at the time, but it never came to anything.'

'When did all this happen?'

'Just under three years ago.'

'And when did his mother die?'

'Last February.'

While Caton thought that through, Holmes concluded his report.

'So he fitted the profile alright. Your phone was down, and I was just about to get a warrant for his other place when Wallace spotted that the address on the City Council file was in Whalley Range. Bang in line with the geographical profile. Looks like he left it in his mother's name, at least for the purpose of the land registry and council tax. If he was sole executor it would have been easy. Explains why he hadn't replied to the note I shoved under his door on my last visit to Ancoats. Soon as Duggie told me about it, and I couldn't contact you, I decided to come straight here and check it out. The rest, as they say, is history.'

'You said he was on the Child Protection Register?'

Holmes took his notebook out from his inside pocket.

'Not strictly the CP Register – it didn't exist in those days. In 1964 the school nurse raised a concern – signs of sexual abuse. It was referred to the Children's Officer, but the father was on the Council and nothing came of it. But they kept it on file. And because it wasn't on the computers, it crept under the clean-up they had when the Data Protection Act came in.'

'How did we get it so fast?'

Holmes rubbed at his chin again. 'You can thank Duggie Wallace's team for that. For the past four days he's had two of them trawling through all of the files covering the period from 1955 to 1970, just about covering the childhood years of anyone who could have fitted our age profile. When Soaper's name came up at the hospital, they realised it was on their list, too.'

'What's in the cellar?' Caton asked.

'Come and have a look for yourself.'

Kate felt a distinct chill that she assumed was emanating from the polished granite steps and pillars of the tortuously winding staircase. Clutching her bag, she reached the landing and searched the wall on the corridor that faced her. The sign read Level Four. As she stepped into the long, dark vaulted corridor, a man in a blue blazer and grey trousers emerged from an alcove set back between two office doors. He came towards her, smiling warmly.

'Miss Webb? I'm Albert. Chief Inspector Caton had to go on ahead. He asked me to wait for you and bring you on up.'

Kate felt both disappointment and surprise. She had been certain that Tom would be there. This man was shorter than her, in his mid fifties, of medium build, with brown hair and brown eyes with a hint of green flecks. It struck her that his hair was almost auburn, just a tone lighter than hers. He pointed proudly to the large oval badge pinned to his right lapel. A white outer surrounded a blue inner on which the words 'Blue Badge' and 'Registered GUIDE' were surmounted by a red rose.

'I'm a Blue Badge Guide,' he proclaimed. 'Have been for over fifteen years.'

Before she had time to protest, he had taken her right elbow and was guiding her down the corridor, deeper into the Town Hall, towards the east of the building.

'It's not to be taken lightly you know,' he continued. 'You have to train for at least a year. Then you have a test. And only then are you accredited by the Institute of Tourist Guiding.' He looked neither at her nor to the left or right. 'I know every inch of this building. The walls reek of history and architectural excellence.'

The door to one of the offices opened and a young man stepped into the corridor clutching a sheaf of papers.

'Hi, Albert,' he said as he passed them.

'Hi, Harpreet,' her guide replied, without breaking step or ceasing his flow of conversation. 'You should have seen us in 2002. The build-up to the Commonwealth Games, the Games themselves, it was amazing. We were rushed off our feet. But we didn't mind. So many people, from all over the world, and so appreciative.'

They reached the stairs and he set off at pace that surprised her. Three floors later they arrived at a door set in the wall, which Albert opened with a key. He ushered her through and locked the door behind them. Ahead of them a set of stairs headed up and out of sight. Kate suppressed her instinct to panic.

'Where is Chief Inspector Caton?' she asked, hoping the strength of her voice would mask her anxiety.

Albert Stephen stood between her and the door.

He smiled, pointed up the stairs, and in a soothing voice replied, 'Up there of course. He's waiting for us.'

Caton stood on the cellar steps and looked around the depressing basement room. Two scene of crime officers were inspecting the plastic-sheeted iron bedstead. Another officer was dusting the shelves, and the items on them, for fingerprints. The final member of the team was taking digital photographs as directed by her colleagues. Two matching pairs of leather straps hung miserably from the sides of the bed frame. Caton pointed to the film of cement dust on the steps and floor.

'This is the residue we found on Stephen Davies' shoes. Presumably they were scuffed when he was dragged across the floor and bumped up these steps.'

'That's about the size of it,' Holmes agreed. 'Thank God he kept them drugged. With any luck they wouldn't have known much about it.'

'What work did he do for the City Council?' Caton asked.

'He was an IT specialist, apparently. Bloody good by all accounts. And if you want corroboration of that, I can tell you he's hacked into the road traffic and public order camera systems. Not difficult, given that he was part of the team responsible for setting them up, and keeping them updated.'

Caton turned to look at his inspector. 'Which is

how he managed to lose us each time.'

'Precisely. And what's more, he's also hacked into all of the Multi-Agency files at the Town Hall.'

'This is how he knew who and where to contact the gangs?'

'Bingo. Clever little bastard, isn't he?'

DC Wood appeared at the top of the steps.

'Sorry to bother you, boss, but SOCO want you upstairs; sounds urgent.'

The officer looked up from the computer as they entered the study.

'I think you should have a look at this, sir,' he said. 'He's got your name and home address flagged in his email address book.'

Caton bent over to see. The details were accurate. His pulse began to race.

'Scroll down for me, slowly.'

They had almost reached the end of the list when his fears were realised. Kate Webb's home address and office phone number stared back at him.

'And there's this, sir.'

The technician clicked open a pictures file minimised on the menu bar. An album consisting of nine photos appeared. The first three were of Longsight Station from different angles. The next three were of Caton, leaving the station in his car, walking up Liverpool Road just yards from his apartment and leaving the mortuary with Joanne Stuart. The final three were all of Kate: leaving Monsoon with a shopping bag in each hand; waiting to cross Oxford Road; and, most disturbing of all, a close-up of her head and shoulders in which she appeared to be looking directly into the camera.

'Christ!'

Caton tore the mobile phone from his belt and switched it on, frantically accessing his messages.

There was just one voice message from Holmes repeating his earlier message, and a new text message, from Kate. He opened it.

I'm Here. Where are U?

It was timed at 10.30 a.m. He looked at his watch. It was now 11.50 a.m. He tried her mobile number. It was switched off. With a growing sense of apprehension, he rang her office. It was three long minutes before Rachel Jazrawi came to the phone.

'Kate?' she said. 'But I thought she was with you. You asked her to meet with you, didn't you?'

Caton fought the temptation to shout. 'No, Rachel, I didn't.'

'It was Inspector Holmes who rang on your behalf. Said you needed to see Ms Webb right away. A matter of life and death, he said.'

'And you gave her that message?'

'Oh yes. She wasn't best pleased at having to rush, but she said she would get there as soon as possible.'

Caton took a deep breath. 'Where was that exactly?'

'Why, the Town Hall, by the Reception.' She paused for a moment, sensing the tension in Caton's voice. 'There's nothing the matter is there?'

'No, Rachel, nothing's the matter. Thanks.'

He ended the call, the knuckles on the hand that held the phone showing white. He turned to Holmes, who had clearly grasped the tenor of the conversation.

'He's got her, Gordon,' he said. 'The bastard's got Kate.'

Chapter 25

Kate knew this was all wrong. There was no way that Caton would expect her to come up here alone with a stranger. If his mobile was out of action, he of all people would have had no problem borrowing another. And this man could easily fit her profile. It was a bit late to start rationalising it now, she decided, but not too late to think of a way out. There would be a door at the top. If he asked her to go first, she would slam it behind her, lean against it with all of her weight and yell for help. If he went first, she would pull the door closed and hang on for dear life … and then what?

Two steps from the top he told her to stop. Kate began to turn slowly, debating whether she should attempt to kick out and send him tumbling backwards down the stairs. She was brought up short by the sharp jab of a knife in the small of her back.

'I don't think so, Miss Webb.' The voice had changed. It was soft, cold, hard-edged. 'Don't turn around. Just use your left hand to hold your handbag out to the side.'

She felt him take it, and heard it drop onto the step behind her.

'Good,' he said. 'Now, ever so slowly put your hands behind your back and you'll be fine.'

She did as she was told, and felt him bind them

roughly with what she took to be duct or parcel tape. She sensed him bending to retrieve the handbag, the knife never wavering. He grunted slightly as he straightened up, and she caught a whiff of the mothballs she remembered from her grandmother's wardrobe. He pushed her roughly up the remaining steps and ordered her to turn and face the side wall. As he reached for the handle of the door with his left hand, he used his right to thrust the knife harder into her back.

She heard the door swing open. Bright sunlight flooded into the stairwell. He pulled her sideways onto the roof. Kate stumbled and, unable to break her fall, landed heavily on her side. Winded, she took a moment to catch her breath. He kicked the door closed behind them, and stood above and behind her, daring her to escape.

She sat up, her eyes adjusting to the light. She realised that they had just emerged from the secondary tower at the apex of the triangle that made up this neo-Gothic building. It was colder up here, made worse by the strong breeze racing around the perimeter.

They were on a small level terrace from which the two sides of the triangle radiated. Kate was surprised to find that buildings, not visible from the road below, occupied the inside of the roof space. Three of them ran the entire length of the right-hand side, parallel with Princess Street, each with windows in the low sides, above which steep blue slate roofs were punctuated by impressive stone chimneys. To the left, a similar, more uniform row of buildings had shallower tiled roofs, many of them with skylights. It felt like a small village up here, in a wind tunnel. Ahead of them, just visible above the cathedral-like roof of the Great Hall, rose the spire of the tower that housed the great bells and the clock.

She wondered if these buildings were occupied, or simply used for storage. She contemplated screaming for help. In that moment of hesitation a broad strip of tape was pulled tightly across her mouth and fastened roughly, pulling her hair in a bunch against the nape of her neck. As she fought to breathe through her nose, the panic threatened to constrict her throat. Again, the reek of mothballs. His breath brushed her ear and cheek.

'Not yet, Miss Webb. Not yet.'

He pulled her roughly to her feet and pushed her to her right, then forward towards the front of the Town Hall, along the surprisingly broad walkway, slightly sloping, that ended abruptly in a sheer drop to the inner courtyard below. At intervals, where the stone gutters ran into the lead Victorian drainpipes, grotesque gargoyles stared out into space. The Town Hall extension on the other side of Lloyd Street towered above them.

Kate could see the long row of windows in the blue tiled roof space, and the windows on the floor beneath. She reasoned that if she could see them, then someone must be able to see her.

Albert Stephen watched her head turn and saw her attempt to glance surreptitiously at the office windows high above them. He smiled. *Not as bright as she thinks she is, pretty Miss Doctor Psychiatrist.* He pressed the knife a little harder.

'I hope they do see you, Miss Webb. Here, I'll give you a hand, since you appear to be a little tied up at the moment.'

He turned her to face the extension building and waved enthusiastically with his free hand from which her bag swung to and fro. Her heart missed a beat as someone came to one of the windows, looked out, waved back, did a double take and disappeared.

A moment later the woman returned, accompanied by a second woman and a man. Kate found herself noticing that the women were so much taller than the man, and wondered why her mind should find that relevant at a time like this. Her captor waved again, and then began pushing and pulling her towards and away from him like a rag doll. When he stopped, Kate looked up at the windows again. The man had disappeared. One of the women had a hand to her face in evident shock. The second was trying to open the window.

'You see,' her captor said, 'I need them to know that you are here. The only reason for the tape over your mouth is that I don't want you alerting anyone who might be up here, until we reach our destination. Behave yourself, and when we get there I shall remove it. Do you understand?'

Kate looked into the cold brown eyes. She fought to control her breathing and to appear calm. She nodded.

'Good.' He prodded her, a little less roughly she thought, towards the flag tower in the opposite corner. 'Not far now.'

Lights flashing, siren wailing, it took Caton less than three minutes to reach Albert Square. He pulled up at the corner of Lloyd Street, drove onto the pavement, flung open the car door and raced into the Town Hall side entrance, taking the steps two at a time.

The women on Reception remembered Kate and directed him back to the porter's lodge. His worst fears were quickly confirmed. She had been seen going towards the staircase; she had not been seen leaving. Suppressing the overwhelming instinct to charge on up to the fourth level, he went back out into the square. The officers he had requested from

Division were already there. Sarsfield came over to meet him.

'What the hell's going on, Tom? My commander's here, and he's not best pleased. Chester House said it was a High Priority.'

'It's our serial killer,' said Caton brusquely. 'The one who nearly trigged the gang war. I think he's inside there somewhere, and he has our forensic profiler with him.'

'Christ,' said Sarsfield. 'Are you taking on command of this one?'

'I'm Bronze Commander for now. But for how long, depends. Can you get half of your shift to take up positions at all of the entrances? Tell them to look out for a woman in her thirties, five foot nine, with auburn hair to her shoulders. She may or may not be accompanied by a man a few inches shorter. He's not to be approached, but they have to report it straight away, and they mustn't lose sight of him, or her. I'm going to get security to sound the fire alarm and evacuate the building. Get the other half of your team to move everybody away from the square.'

Sarsfield looked at the heaving mass of people weaving their way slowly between the craft stalls, the delicatessens, and the food and beer tents of the Christmas market.

'There must be a good few thousand people here, Tom, and God knows how many inside.'

'I know,' said Caton, 'but I don't see any other option.'

'Won't it alert him to the fact that we know he's here?'

'Don't worry about that,' said Caton wryly. 'He already does.'

He looked around the square and up at the Town Hall clock, his mind working overtime.

'I think he wants an audience.'

'Well, he's certainly got one here. Is he armed?'

'I'm sorry, Gerry,' Caton said, 'I don't know, but we have to assume that he is.'

'I bloody hope not,' Sarsfield replied, grasping his radio and heading off towards the impatient cluster of police and community support officers.

'But what about the jewellery?' the security officer demanded, pointing to the rows of glass cases full of the Dazzle exhibits.

'Those cases are locked, aren't they?' Caton responded. 'And what would happen if there was a fire, or a bomb alert?'

The head porter nodded. 'You're right; let's just do it, Tony.'

His companion ducked into the office.

The alarm sounded almost immediately. Caton was impressed by the speed with which people began to head for the two exits. As he reached the steps leading out into the square, he came face-to-face with Nick Carter, Joanne Stuart and her partner, Abbie.

'What's going on, boss?' Carter asked as the press of people pushed them towards the glass doors.

'I'm sorry, Joanne, Abbie,' Caton said. 'I'm afraid this could take a while. Soaper is in here somewhere, and he's got Kate with him.'

Soaper? They looked at each other, bemused. Before any of them could respond, Caton's mobile phone rang. He turned away and flipped it open. It was Kate's number. He hurried out of the doors and moved away from the mass of people exiting the building.

'Kate, is that you?'

The voice, when it came, sent a chill through his blood.

'Miss Webb, or should I say Doctor Webb, is not

330

available at the moment, Inspector Caton. She is a little tied up.'

Caton fought the urge to call him a bastard, to threaten him. He counted to three and drew on every ounce of his training. He tried to project calmness, empathy and confidence.

'Whatever's happened, we can resolve this,' he said. 'But I need to speak with her. We have to know that she is safe.'

The voice was mocking. 'Come, come, Inspector. Of course she isn't safe. She is unharmed, however, apart from a slight fall. But you don't get to speak to her, let alone see her again, until you have given me what I want.'

Caton ran through a mental checklist: make sure he actually has the hostage; build rapport; establish if this is a negotiable situation; find out what it is he really wants; and then, if it's possible, find a way to give it to him without risk to the hostage or being accused of encouraging the taking of hostages at some point in the future; then, and only then, worry about actually arresting the bastard.

'Mr Soaper,' he said. 'It is Mr Soaper, isn't it? Mr John Soaper?'

'Very good, Chief Inspector. Only you must call me Albert Stephen, and I shall call you Tom. That's the way it works, isn't it?'

Caton ignored the jibe. 'Tell me, Albert Stephen,' he said, 'what is it you want? It must be important for you to have gone to all this trouble.'

'Oh it was no trouble, Tom, I assure you,' he chuckled to himself, before adopting a serious, measured tone. 'Listen carefully. I want the leader of the City Council up here, together with the press. I want newspapers and television. You have fifteen minutes.' The threat hung in the air.

Caton took the time to think it over before replying. It was, in any case, best to extend the conversation for as long as possible.

'Albert Stephen,' he said, 'where is up here exactly?'

'Where are you *exactly*, Tom?'

'I'm immediately in front of the Town Hall, by the main doors.'

'Excellent. If you step out a little further and cast your gaze up towards the roof, you will see me. And, since you've been so cooperative, I'll let you see Doctor Webb, too.'

The human tide was still pouring down the steps, and Caton had to push his way through them and duck under the cordon that Sarsfield's team had already set up. He turned and looked up.

A huge inflated Father Christmas clung incongruously to the left-hand side of the imposing clock tower. Immediately to its left, standing on what Caton assumed must be a ledge or parapet, bordered by an intricately decorated wrought-iron railing, stood the man he now knew to be John Albert Stephen Soaper. Kneeling beside him was Kate, her arms behind her back, a tape of some kind across her mouth. Soaper waved his right hand, clutching his mobile phone, and then returned it to his ear.

'What, no wave, Tom? I am disappointed.'

Behind Caton, people who had already been pushed back to the farthest limit of the market began to murmur and several began to call out, pointing up at the Town Hall roof. Carter and Joanne Stuart joined him and stared aghast at Soaper and Kate Webb. Caton fought to retain his composure. Don't personalise this, he told himself.

'Please remove the tape, Albert Stephen,' he said. 'Now that we know where Doctor Webb is, it serves no purpose. Then we can discuss your needs.'

'You are in no position to issue me with instructions, Tom. I have a knife in Doctor Webb's back, and, in case you have not noticed, we happen to be astride two precipices.'

Caton cursed silently. Rule five: never argue with a hostage taker.

'You are quite right, Albert Stephen,' he said, 'I put that badly. What I meant was that it would be easier for me to convince the authorities to consider your demands if you were to make this gesture of good will.'

There was a long silence on the other end of the line. Caton could see Soaper staring down at him. His adversary placed the mobile phone in his jacket pocket and grasped the crown of Kate's hair. He raised his left arm and brought it round to the front where she and everyone below could see it. A mass gasp came from the crowd, still moving backwards between the stalls.

Caton watched nervously as Soaper sliced through the tape at the side of her mouth and peeled the tape back from both sides, leaving it hanging from the hair which now framed her pale face. Soaper raised the phone to his mouth.

'And now, Tom, it's your turn. The leader, and the press. And, Tom, it's you I want to speak with from now on. Just you. You have fifteen minutes.'

He took the phone away from his face and the line went dead. Soaper squatted down behind Kate, one arm around her neck, the other out of sight behind her back.

Caton turned to face Carter and Stuart.

'I can't negotiate with Soaper and command this operation. I want you two to stay with whoever picks up the command and the secondary negotiator. Nick, you can brief them about Soaper, his profile, Kate, everything. It's vital that they know as much as possible. DI Holmes is at his mother's house where he kept his victims. I want you, Jo, to establish continuous contact with him. Relay back to Nick everything and anything he comes up with. The secondary negotiator will relay it to me.'

He looked at Abbie, pretty and crestfallen in her apricot trouser suit and cream corsage.

'I'm sorry, Abbie, but since there's no way you'll be going back in there for some time, Jo is going to be better occupied this way.'

She grimaced. 'What they say about marrying the job,' she said, 'I didn't expect it to turn out this literally.'

Kate sucked the air in through her mouth and tried to order her thoughts. She knew that she had to establish a relationship – better still, a rapport – with her captor. She knew his name, having heard him give it to Tom. That was a start. She also knew what he was asking for. Now she needed to find out why. As she started to cast her mind back over the profile, the breeze began to gain in strength. She tipped her head with difficulty against the restraint of his arm and looked in the direction from which it came. A bank of grey clouds, their undersides tinged with pink and purple, were moving in from the north-west. Her knees were aching and her back was becoming stiff. She shivered, dropped her shoulders and lowered her head in a vain attempt to escape the cold.

Soaper misread her movements, mistaking them for a sign of submission or despair. He bent his head to hers, the midday stubble like sandpaper against her cheek.

'That's it, Kate,' he whispered. 'Everything will be alright. Tom will make it so.'

Helen Gates was waiting for them outside the command post in Mount Street.

'This is becoming a habit, Chief Inspector,' she said dryly.

Behind the van a row of vehicles had pulled up, and Caton could see the Tactical Aid and Tactical Firearms Units awaiting instructions.

'You had better come inside and brief me,' she said. 'ACC Specialist Operations has taken over as Gold commander at Chester House. Silver command is being set up at Bootle Street, and Chief Superintendent Hadfield is on his way here.'

Inside the command post, plans of the Town Hall had already been brought up on one of the computer screens. On a second screen was a continuous real-time transmission of the front of the Town Hall, showing Soaper and Kate Webb cocooned together on the narrow parapet. Caton brought Gates up to speed.

'You realise you can't continue to negotiate with him?' she said. 'It's too personal. You'll have to hand over to the negotiator with the Tactical Aid Unit.'

'I'm sorry, Ma'am,' he said, 'that's not possible. Contact has already been made. He's chosen me, and refuses to speak with anyone else.'

Gates arched her eyebrows.

'I completed the Kidnap and Extortion SIO training, and the Negotiators course at Wybaston last year,' he reminded her. 'The guidance states that it would be too dangerous to change midstream. In any case, it would take too long to brief someone else.'

'You realise you can't retain Bronze command and negotiate at the same time?' she said, accepting defeat.

'Yes, Ma'am, and I wouldn't wish to. But I strongly suggest that we get the Tactical Aid Unit to enter the building covertly, to secure all exits from the roof. He's chosen his spot carefully. There is no way they could mount a surprise assault without putting Ms Webb at risk. We should place a Firearms expert rifle officer on top of the extension building behind us, on top of Heron House directly facing Soaper's position, and according to the plans we should be able to get one above him, in the Bell Tower. I would also like a rifle officer to accompany me up to the flag tower pavilion, here.'

On the second of the screens he pointed out a tower in the form of a truncated pyramid, some twenty metres from Soaper, crowning the south end of the building.

'That's a matter for the Firearms incident commander,' she said, 'as you very well know. But I'll put it to him. But you're not going up there, Tom.' There was a mixture of authority and concern in her voice.

'I don't have an option,' he said. 'I have to see what he's doing, where Doctor Webb is, and negotiate accordingly. I can't do that in here, or out there in the square with the world looking on and him playing to the gallery. We get up there through the attic above the old Council chamber, and there are three chimneys between him and us. There's no way he'll know that I'm there.'

'Then how will you be able to see him?'

'We'll take a technician from the Tactical Aid Unit with a wireless video link to the other cameras. When the rifle officer requires line of sight, it will be a simple move to the left or right of the chimney.'

Gates pointed to the live feed. 'You can track him from in here,' she persisted.

'The secondary negotiator will be able to do that,' Caton countered. 'Together with the Bronze commander and the Firearms incident commander. I will be a second, closer pair of eyes. In any case, you know the primary negotiator needs to be able to focus with the minimum of distractions. Do you really think that would be possible in here?' He could see that he was close to convincing her, or at the very least to wearing her down. 'It isn't personal, Ma'am. It's the City Council he's after, through the Leader. I don't believe he is going to harm Doctor Webb. I promise you, I can handle this.'

He looked at his watch.

'There are eight minutes left to his deadline. We have to sort this now.'

Caton entered the building accompanied by two members of the Firearms Unit, a technician from the Tactical Aid Unit and a police video cameraman dressed in jeans and a red anorak. All five of them wore identical black behind-head microphone speaker communication units. The rifleman had a dedicated line to his commander, and Caton a dedicated line to the secondary negotiator. For the time being his communication with Soaper would have to be through his mobile phone. It was a worry to him that he would have no way of knowing the intentions of the Firearms Unit. Those were the rules. The tactical units had been deployed. Cameras were in place. The leader was on his way. Communications had been tested and were operational. He would simply have to trust to their professionalism.

Caton admired the composure of the rifle officer striding confidently one step behind the Town Hall facilities manager, who was at the head of the group. The force deliberately avoided the term sniper, because it implied lethal force. Yet the reality was that in a hostage situation, apart from deterrent, intent to kill was the only justification for firearms. Soaper had not used a knife or any other weapon in the death of his first two victims. The profile Kate had prepared talked about a vestige of empathy with his victims.

Would Soaper really use the knife? Caton nursed the thought for a moment, and just as quickly dismissed it. A shot to immobilise a hostage taker was not what they were trained for, and wounding would enrage Soaper and almost certainly result in Kate's death. For the first time the enormity of it began to sink in. This man ahead of him might pull the trigger, and ultimately the decision would be his alone. Kate's life was in his hands. But then, it was in Caton's too. If he could negotiate her release there would be no question of a misdirected bullet, or a tragic ricochet. The problem for Caton was that despite what he had said to Gates, it was both professional and personal. His feelings for her were already so strong that he questioned his ability to separate the two. He knew that this was precisely what Soaper was banking on. Perhaps Helen Gates had been right all along.

They had not moved for over five minutes. Soaper had remained silent. Although there had been little more than a murmur from the crowd, pushed back to the margins of the square below, she felt their presence. In the distance, the wail of an ambulance and the steady hum of the traffic beyond the cordon reminded her that life was carrying on as normal out there. In her mind's eye she could picture the scene, like a vast film set. Try as she might, she could not prevent herself from playing out the different ways in which it might end. Her thighs were going into spasm. The pain was intense.

'I'm sorry, Albert Stephen,' she said as calmly as possible, 'I've got cramp in my legs. I don't think I can manage this much longer.'

She felt him tense at the sound of her voice and sudden use of his name. After what seemed an age, he spoke to her softly.

'We are going to stand, very slowly. No sudden movement please, Doctor Webb, you do not wish to fall any more than I do.'

She felt him shift his grip to the collar of her coat and begin to rise. He pulled her firmly to her feet. A buzz of anticipation rippled through the crowd and for a moment she found herself glancing down towards them. The sensation unnerved her, but neither could she close her eyes this close to the edge. She raised her head and fixed her eyes on the transmission mast above the Granada Television building. Seize the moment, she told herself.

'I am not a real doctor, Albert Stephen,' she said. 'I never use that title.'

For a moment she thought that he wasn't going to reply.

'You're a psychiatrist,' he said. 'A shrink.'

She felt a twinge of relief, and just as quickly suppressed it.

'Actually, I'm a psychologist, not a medical practitioner. I study behaviour. I try to understand why people behave as they do. Help them that way. Not treat them with drugs.'

He lapsed into silence. She wondered how he would be processing that. Had he ever been treated before, and if so how, and by whom? Would he be feeling more or less hostile towards her? It was clear that he was not going to respond. Rather than allow the conversation to falter, she decided to take a chance.

'I heard what you asked for, Albert Stephen, but I don't understand why. What do you want to achieve? I may be able to help.'

She felt the grip tighten on her collar and then slacken, tighten and then slacken, tighten and then slacken. The pressure of the knife in her back remained constant. There was a battle going on inside him. She tried hard to soften her tone, encouraging, prompting.

'What is it you want, Albert Stephen?'

'They have to admit it, in front of me, in front of everyone, in front of you.'

There was a subtle change in the tone of his voice. Almost as though he was speaking to himself, or some third person. Not to her.

'Admit what, Albert Stephen?' she asked, trying to mirror his tone.

'That they were wrong. That they could have ... should have stopped him.'

'Stopped who, Albert Stephen?' She wondered for an instant if she should stop using his name, but there was a rhythm to it, and she didn't dare to break the spell.

'You know who.' His voice sharpened. 'Him.'

'Why didn't they stop him, Albert Stephen?'

'Because he was one of them.' There was bitterness in his voice that chilled her beyond the effects of the freezing wind. 'A counsellor. He said the nurse was wrong. That I must have done it to myself. That I was a problem child. And they believed him. They wanted to take me away.'

Kate felt him beginning to shake. She wondered if perhaps he was crying. She was trying to decide what to say next, but when he spoke she was glad that she hadn't.

'But you didn't let them. You sent him away.'

He let go of her collar and encircled her chest with his arm. It was less a restraint she felt, more an embrace. The pressure of the knife had eased a little, as though he had relaxed. Kate instinctively responded in the role that he had now accorded her.

'Of course I did, Albert Stephen,' she replied. 'Because I love you.' Kate would never know why she had said it. But it was too late to change it now. She felt his shoulders begin to shake.

His voice came in bursts, as though he was having trouble breathing.

'You were so proud of me. And then they took my job away. I tried to hide it from you, but you knew, didn't you? And it killed you.'

She had no idea how to respond.

'It wasn't your fault, Albert Stephen,' she tried. 'It was not your fault.'

Chapter 26

Caton stepped cautiously onto the flat pavilion roof. One by one, the others followed him until all four were crouched with their backs to the vast stone chimney towering above them, masking them from the hostage and the hostage taker. The rifle officer and his buddy hunkered down in a huddle, lost in their own secret world.

Several metres further on, two smaller chimneys that served the Mayor's Parlour formed another barrier. Their arrival was recorded by the camera positioned at a window high in the roof of the extension building, and captured on one of the two screens on the equipment held by the technician. On the second screen they could see Kate and Soaper, standing three metres below them, no more than fifteen metres away. Much closer than Caton had estimated. He had a momentary flashback to the reconstructed footage of Craig and Bentley on the London rooftop, and the fatal consequences of a misinterpreted shout: Let him have it!

In his earpiece Caton heard the voice of Jared Coleman, the secondary negotiator.

'Echo One. This is Echo Two. Indicate with your right hand if you can hear me.'

Caton raised his right arm, thumb extended vertically.

'I copy that, Echo One. We have a concern here that even with those chimneys between you and the suspect, with the wind coming from behind, it will be too risky for you to negotiate with him from that position. And if you whisper, he will wonder why. He will know you are up there somewhere. Do you copy that?'

Caton repeated the gesture. He was not convinced that they were right, but he wasn't prepared to find out by trial and error. He signalled to the bogus TV cameraman to maintain his position. Then he and the technician withdrew to the first landing below the pavilion roof. Caton checked his watch. It was time.

He checked the camera feed. Soaper and Kate were still on their feet. Soaper's right arm was now around Kate's chest, and his head was buried between the nape of her neck and her right shoulder. He could see Soaper's left arm pressing into her back, just below the midline. There was no indication that he was ready to make contact. Caton checked that his mobile was still on and the signal good. The technicians had connected it to a charger unit attached to his belt. Caton had an idea.

'Echo Two, this is Echo One. Over.'

'Go ahead, Echo One. Over.'

'When he comes online, I would like to give him sight of the television cameras, but out of hearing range. Can you arrange for them to come up to the middle of Lloyd Street, between Tampopo and the Rajdoot? Over.'

There was a long pause, during which he knew that Hadfield and the Tactical Aid Adviser would be weighing up the pros and cons of his request.

The response was positive.

'On your signal, Echo One.'

High on the flat roof of Heron House, immediately

across the square from the Town Hall, November One made himself comfortable. Beside him, his buddy was busy checking the rucksack; they could be in for a long haul. Through his scope he could see the subject clearly, his arm around the woman's neck. There was no sign of a weapon, although he understood there to be a knife pressing into her back. If it came to it, he would need more than supposition before he squeezed the trigger.

November Two eased open the window in the same office in the extension roof from which Kate and her abductor had first been spotted. The entire building was empty now except for the rifleman and his buddy. Down to his left, he could see November Four crouched behind the chimney on the flag pavilion. His colleague, he realised, had no possibility of a line of sight on the suspect unless he stepped out from behind that chimney and stood on the extreme edge of the pavilion. From his own position, however, he had a clear view of the subject's back. He could see the left arm pressing into the woman's back and caught a glimpse of steel as it caught the sunlight. He had a clear target of the subject's head, but since the woman was the taller of the two there would be no possibility of a shot while the two were close together. And the crowd would be within range of a missed shot until they had been pushed back as far as Deansgate. This was going to prove very tricky indeed.

November Three followed his buddy up the narrow spiral stone staircase that led from the clock face room. Having already passed through the bell room and seen the twenty-three-bell carillon, he had asked his commander to make damn sure someone stopped them chiming the hour. Even with his ear protectors on, he had a sense it would be deafening.

He stepped out onto the north-facing balcony high above the clock. Up here the wind was strong enough for him to have to make corrections for it. They crawled clockwise around the balcony on their hands and knees until he had sight of the subject through the stone balustrade. He was some thirty metres below them, and ten metres to the south. Between them and the subject, the giant inflatable Father Christmas clung perilously to the tower.

Because the subject and the woman were in profile, he reckoned that of the three riflemen he had the best chance of a shot, with the least risk to the woman. But it would only need either of them to move a fraction as he squeezed the trigger and the bullet could pass through the subject and strike the woman in the head or upper body. The balcony was narrow, and he realised he would have to move to one of the corners before he could get into any kind of firing position, and remain covert. Even with the wind travelling from the subject, every move would have to be conducted with the greatest care. This was turning into a nightmare.

Caton was trying to recall what he knew about the suspect, starting with Kate's profile. He desperately needed a hook to hang onto as he tried to get inside Soaper's mind. He was no further forward when Coleman's voice came through again, crystal clear.

'Echo One, we have the following from Inspector Holmes. They've found a pair of contact lenses, and a photo, in the suspect's bedside drawer. The photo is of a very attractive woman in her late forties. There are other photos of her in an album in the study. He believes it to be the suspect's mother. She has long red hair and green eyes flecked with brown. He said to tell you *Orvill Jack*. He said you would know what that meant. Over.'

Cold as it had been on the flag pavilion it felt oppressive down here, and the stab vest was tight beneath his jacket. Caton wiped the sweat from his brow and where it stung his eyes.

'Do you copy that, Echo One? Over.'

'I copy that, Echo Two,' Caton said. 'Over.'

With the channel open, he could hear a murmur of voices in the background. Then Coleman's voice again.

'Echo One. That hair, the eyes, is that a connection between the suspect and Dr Webb? Over.'

'Yes,' said Caton. Though I've no idea, he thought to himself, if that's good, or bad, or what the hell to do with it.

'Why did you choose those men, Albert Stephen?' Kate felt emboldened to ask him gently. 'What had they done?'

'Nothing,' he said to the ether. 'They had no future. They were a symbol of this Council and its hypocritical policies. They talk regeneration, but they fail to deal with poverty, the plague that is AIDS, the menace of the gangs that thrive on the trade in drugs and prostitution and illegal immigration.'

His voice began to rise, quietly but fiercely impassioned, almost preaching. He swung her body through ninety degrees, taking in the skyline with its jumble of gleaming towers from the Openshaw campus to the Beetham tower.

'Their regeneration is about buildings, and glass, and steel. The rest they brush into the corners. New houses for single professionals, penthouses for the rich. ASBOs to muzzle the troublemakers, and nothing to deal with the conditions that create them. They wouldn't save me or you from him. You had to take it on yourself. Now they have to admit their sins. You said they would have to. One day. You told me that.'

Kate fought to communicate a sense of calm.

'But didn't you feel something for those two men? Or for the boys who could have been killed in the park?' It was a statement of fact, not an accusation.

His voice was quieter now, distant and reflective.

'Those boys will be dead at each other's hands long before their appointed time. And neither of those men had a future. The only options offered by this Council are dispersal or disappearance. Mine, at least, was an honest cleansing.'

A police siren sounded briefly in Cross Street. It was enough to jolt him from his reverie. Soaper removed the arm around her chest and replaced it with the one holding the knife; this time across her upper chest, with the edge of the blade against the side of her neck, the point just below her right ear. With his right hand, he took her mobile from his pocket and instant redialled.

Caton felt his mobile vibrate and waited ten seconds. Long enough to knock his confidence, fast enough to show willing. He pressed the receive button.

'Is that you, Albert Stephen?'

'Tom,' Soaper rasped, his voice betraying his irritation. 'Why has it taken you so long?'

'I misunderstood,' Caton replied, his voice level, neither apologetic nor dismissive. 'I thought you would be contacting me after the fifteen minutes were up. I was beginning to get worried. But, you are right, my superiors needed time to consider your requests.'

'Demands, Tom, not requests.' He paused to let it sink in. 'So, where is the leader? Where are the press? I want them now.'

'The press are already here, Albert Stephen, in the square. You only have to look down and you'll see them.'

347

On the screen he saw Soaper look up and out across the square. One of the cameras zoomed in and Caton could see the confusion in his face, and the tension in Kate's. He watched as Soaper put the phone to his mouth.

'I can't see them.'

No Tom this time, Caton noted. He counted to three.

'If you look diagonally across to your left you will see them, Albert Stephen. On the pavement, just past the sign for the Indian restaurant, Rajdoot. The BBC, and Granada, and the Manchester Evening News. Just as you asked.'

He watched as Soaper adjusted his grip on Kate and turned through forty-five degrees. The phone came up to his mouth.

'They are too far away. I need them up here where I can talk to them. Now!'

'I'm not sure that the authorities will agree to that, Albert Stephen.' Caton's voice was firm and reasoned. 'They will expect you to at least put away your knife. They have told me that there is no way they can allow you to be filmed with a knife at Doctor Webb's throat. And it would not do any good for the credibility of whatever it is you want to say. I'm sure you can see that.'

'Be careful, Echo One,' he heard in his earpiece. 'You don't want to push him into a corner too soon.'

The camera zoomed closer. Caton saw the resolve flood back into Soaper's face and cursed himself for his impatience. Soaper pulled Kate closer to him and raised the phone.

'I want them up here where I can talk to them. And the leader has to be here, too.' His voice was calm and cold and determined. He sounded very much in control.

348

'I'll have to try to get authority for that,' Caton responded, back to playing for time – for the one break they would need.

'Then get it.' It was a dismissal.

Caton watched on the screen as Soaper put the phone back in his pocket and began to push Kate along the parapet towards the nearest of the two smaller chimneys, out of the field of vision of the camera on the Town Hall extension.

'Shit,' Caton allowed himself.

Momentarily panic began to spread its icy tendrils, until the camera positioned on Heron House picked up transmission. Soaper was leaning back against the chimney, Kate against his body. They were both in shadow, and it was impossible to tell what either of them might be thinking.

It was warmer here, out of the wind, but Kate knew this was a bad turn of events. His whole manner had changed. He was tense, anxious and determined. She was torn between the need to know what kind of risks she might need to take if it all fell apart, and the instinct to try to calm him. She took a slow, deep breath.

'I'm sure Tom is doing his best,' she said, testing the water.

The silence weighed heavy. She could not decide if he was thinking it over or ignoring her.

'He would be a fool not to,' he said at last.

'But it isn't down to him,' she replied. 'They may not let you see the Leader; they may not allow the media up here.'

This time the response was immediate.

'They will!'

He sounded to Kate like a wilful child.

'But what if they don't, Albert Stephen?' Her tone was that of a patient mother.

349

The response when it came was all the more chilling because of the matter-of-fact way that he said it.

'Then I shall have to kill you.'

It lay between them like a gulf. A gulf she knew she had to bridge.

'I don't think you can, Albert Stephen,' she finally managed. 'I am not part of this. Nor am I like the men you chose.'

The silence became oppressive.

'What would your mother say if you did kill me, Albert Stephen?'

She felt him tense and relax, tense and relax, tense and relax. She pressed on.

'And if you did, they would never listen to you then. There would be no one to tell how you have suffered. This would all have been a waste.'

There was still no response. She searched desperately for the right words and tone.

'Let me be your mouthpiece, Albert Stephen. Let me tell them what happened to you. How they failed your mother. How they failed you.'

Caton's conversation with Coleman, and through him with the commander, had been short. The leader was making his way up to the pavilion roof. He would be safe enough, and there would be no one to hear whatever admission he might or might not make. The police cameraman in the red anorak would be convincing enough at this distance. It was their best bet; their only bet. And Kate's only chance. He rarely prayed, but he was praying now.

The pavilion felt that much smaller with the five of them up there. The leader, shorter than Caton remembered, was clearly prepared to do whatever was asked of him. He repeated the instructions Caton had given him. Rehearsal over, Caton pressed redial.

This time it was answered straight away.

'Is that you, Tom?'

On the screen they saw him straighten up and move out from the shadows, bringing Kate with him.

'Yes, Albert Stephen.'

'And what was their answer, Tom?'

Caton thought he detected a tremor of anxiety behind the practised coldness of the tone.

Caton replied with, 'The leader is up here on the roof, with me, and a BBC cameraman.'

They watched Soaper turn and look back towards the east, away from the square, scanning both sides of the triangle in vain.

'Where?' he asked. 'Where are you?'

'We are up here on the pavilion tower, Albert Stephen, behind you. You will have to move back to within a few metres of the bell tower and then you will be able to see us.'

They watched as Soaper shuffled back along the parapet, dragging Kate with him.

On Caton's signal, the three of them moved to the extreme edge of the pavilion.

Soaper turned and pulled Kate with him; still his shield.

'Very good, Tom,' Soaper said, a smile crawling across his face. 'Now step back and let the other two come forward.'

Caton stood his ground.

Projecting all the determination he could muster, he said, 'I am not empowered to do that until you release Doctor Webb.'

Kate felt Soaper's hesitation.

'My hands are tied,' she told him. 'I can't escape. This is what you wanted. Take it.'

There was silence while he thought it through.

'Kneel down in front of me, Doctor Webb. And

don't move. If you do, you will leave me with no choice. Do you understand?'

Kate nodded her head. His grip loosened. He stepped back one pace, his knife dangling in his left hand, the right clutching the mobile to his face. She bent one knee to the parapet, and then the other. To maintain her balance, she twisted her body and clutched with difficulty the low iron fence beside her.

High in their eagle's nests, three of the rifle officers had a clear shot. They sensed they were entering the termination stage. They had been cleared to use their own judgment.

Behind Soaper's head, and less than twenty metres above him, Caton could see the dark outline of the officer on the bell tower balcony. It would be impossible to miss the shot. Unless, Caton realised, Soaper fell or dived forward, knife in hand, towards Kate. With the steep angle there was always the possibility of a ricochet. The risk would be too great. In any case, he knew that none of them would fire without a reasonable belief that Kate was in imminent danger, especially with the whole world watching. He needed Kate to move another yard.

Soaper's voice cut across his thoughts. 'That is the best I can offer, Chief Inspector. Now step back.'

So it was Chief Inspector now, Caton reflected. He saw Kate raise her head and stare straight at him. Saw the slight movement of her head, inclined to the right, and then repeated. He nodded his understanding, hoping to hell she knew what she was doing.

'I can't do that, Albert Stephen,' he said, 'unless you step away from Doctor Webb. Then the camera will be switched on and I shall step back. But I need your word that when this is over, you will throw down your knife and release Doctor Webb.'

Soaper seemed to hesitate, and then made one step backwards. There was now a metre and a half between the two of them. Soaper raised the knife level with his waist and thrust it out in front of him. With his right hand he put the mobile phone back into his pocket.

'Very well, Chief Inspector,' he said, projecting his voice almost to a shout. 'But if you fail to keep your side of this bargain, be certain that I shall kill Kate.'

The sudden and calculated use of her name jolted Caton. So he's made it personal at last, he realised. That makes it even more dangerous, and yet that much easier. He made sure that Kate was looking straight at him, took a deep breath and nodded slowly as he spoke.

'I don't think you want to do that, Albert Stephen,' he said. 'There are armed police above and behind you. If you move towards Doctor Webb, you will be shot.'

In the bell tower, high above Soaper, November Three bellowed, 'Armed police. Stay where you are!'

Soaper turned instinctively at the sound and saw the muzzle of the rifle pointing directly at him. The fourth rifleman stepped out from behind the chimney stack and took up position beside Caton.

'Armed police. Stay where you are!'

Soaper whirled to face them, startled and bemused.

Kate rolled sideways, used her hands as a fulcrum and launched herself over the iron guard rail.

Caton watched her perilous slide down the tiled roof, between two Gothic dormer windows and out of sight. Frantically he searched the screens. The camera high on Heron House lost focus as it zoomed in. When the picture cleared he was relieved to see her crouching behind the stone balustrade that lined the narrow balcony running the length of the roof.

Soaper stood transfixed, trying to work out how he

had allowed this to happen. The riflemen were still shouting, but he did not hear them. Kate's voice floated up to him, pleading.

'Albert Stephen, listen to me. You will still be able to have your say. The leader will see you. Everything you say will be reported. I can tell them, Albert Stephen. Your mother would want you to come down and tell everyone how you have suffered. Do as they tell you, Albert Stephen.'

He saw himself standing in the dock. Him, in the dock, not them. Everything twisted to protect the guilty. He saw himself in a tiny cell, curled into a ball, waiting in the dark. The same nightmare that had haunted him for as long as he could remember. He looked down at Kate five metres below him.

'You tell them,' he said.

Albert Stephen dropped the knife, raised his hands and began to walk slowly towards the pavilion, ignoring the increasingly urgent commands to stop. Shortly before he reached the first of the two chimneys, he stepped over the railings and out onto the ridge of the great stone window projecting three metres from the roof.

Kate watched him walk, one foot on either side of the rail along the ridge, until he reached the small cross-like decoration at the apex of the roof. Soaper stood there for a moment, looking out across the square, beyond the canvas roofs of the stalls, past the Albert memorial, to the vast hushed crowd that had momentarily halted its passage down Brasenose Street.

Kate pulled herself painfully to her feet and began to edge towards him, hoping to talk him down, knowing in her heart it was a fool's mission. She saw him raise his arms sideways like a preacher. A smile crept across his face and froze. Her stomach knotted.

No, she decided, not a preacher; this is a crucifixion pose. She thought she heard him begin to sing softly.

'If that cart and bull fall down…'

As Albert Stephen Soaper pitched forward, the rest of the words were lost in the screams of the crowd and the whistling of the wind between the chimneys.

Chapter 27

It had been the evening of the day following Kate's ordeal that she and Tom had finally been able to meet up.

Despite her protestations, Kate had been whisked off, at Tom's insistence, for a check-up and to get her away from the prying media. He had been busy until the early hours making and checking statements, and compiling a report. They had spoken several times on the phone.

With admiration she had watched him on the news as he handled the press conference, flanked by Helen Gates and Martin Hadfield, both basking in the reflective glory. Larry Hymer had tried to cast a dismal light on the proceedings by pointing out that two men had died, and a near massacre had only narrowly been averted, before Soaper had been cornered. This was a view Kate knew Tom openly agreed with, frustrated that they had always been a step behind. But Hadfield had swiftly stepped in to point out that it had been the quickest identification and capture of a serial killer in recent history. Never mind, thought Kate, that in the end he had wanted to be caught. The general tenor from the television and tabloids had been triumphalist. Chester House, however, was insistent that modest satisfaction should be the order of the day.

Tom had reserved a table tucked away in the corner of The Establishment. He reasoned that the clientele and general ambience of the restaurant would limit the likelihood that they would be pestered. He was right.

She thought that Tom looked tired, and somehow a little sad. She was reminded that there was an appealing vulnerability about him, and yet it was tied up with the issues from his past that would be better faced up to than buried. For a second she had a flashback to Soaper, standing alone on the narrow ridge tiles, devoid of hope. Sweeping it from her mind, she picked up her menu.

Later that evening, they made love in Tom's apartment. It had none of the violent passion of the first occasion. They undressed each other, turn by turn, item by item, kissing and caressing. Tom was gentle and considerate, tracing with his lips and blowing softly on the livid areas where her ribs and sides had broken her fall. Kate's climax, when it came, was long and languorous. As they lay together, staring through the window at the moon and stars, clear and bright in a sky that heralded a heavy frost, it was as though they had exorcised a nightmare.

Caton had not expected Kate to turn up, despite her insistence that she would. It was less than a week since she had stood bruised, bound and emotionally drained on the balcony immediately above this room, and had watched Soaper plummet to the street below.

It was the earliest the registrar had been able to reschedule, and with all of the paperwork that tying up Operation Bojangles had entailed, Caton had been relieved. At least it had now been possible for all of them to attend. Even Gordon Holmes, sandwiched between Nick Carter and Sarah Weston on a window seat in one of the great stone bays, was entering into the spirit.

Caton watched Kate's face as Joanne Stuart and her partner Abbie took their places on the gold-embossed leather chairs to sign the partnership agreement at the long wooden table with carved spindle legs. An ornate oak screen and canopy rose – a perfect frame behind them. The lights from the candelabra picked up the natural highlights in Kate's hair, flashing gold and bronze against rich auburn. She had skilfully masked a bruise on her left cheek with a hint of blusher that accentuated the translucent paleness of her skin. Her green eyes sparkled. Small pear-like tears began to form in them. A familiar voice awoke in his head.

Christ, she is beautiful. Too beautiful for you. How are you going to hang onto this one, Tom? Have you got the balls for it? Sorry, Tom, no pun intended.

She sensed him gazing at her and flashed him a smile, her face lighting up. She dabbed her eyes with a tissue and turned back to join in the applause as the happy couple rose from their chairs and gave each other a long, lingering hug.

The leader of the City Council had insisted on providing a special buffet for Joanne, Abbie and their guests immediately following the rescheduled ceremony. Kate took Tom's hand and drew him into the procession of people moving steadily under the high roof of the adjoining Tower Room, above which November Three had taken up position, through the vast doors of the Reception Room, past the alabaster fireplace appropriately bearing, Caton reflected, the figures of Truth and Justice. They emerged in the Banqueting Room.

On the minstrels' gallery a string quartet was playing Albinoni's Adagio. Wistful, haunting and bittersweet, somehow appropriate in the light of all that had happened.

They each took a glass of champagne, and joined the queue waiting to offer their congratulations. Starting with the meal in The Establishment, there had been an unspoken agreement not to mention Soaper, but they no longer felt his presence as a rebuke that lay between them.

'Will he ever stand trial, Tom?' Kate asked, reading his thoughts.

The moment Caton had discovered that the canvas roof of the stall, whilst catapulting Soaper onto the stone flags of the pavement, had saved his life, that question had been uppermost in his mind. Right now it was academic; Soaper lay paralysed and in a coma in the hospital bed. If he survived, his faculties intact – and the odds of either were poor – he would never walk again.

'Would you judge him fit to stand trial?' he asked.

'Thank God it wouldn't be up to me,' she replied. 'But no, I wouldn't. And I doubt that any purpose would be served by it. He'll be held indefinitely in the secure hospital wing at Rampton.' She sipped her champagne thoughtfully.

'And would you visit him … a suitable case for study?' he asked.

'I don't know.' She creased her brow, and he brushed a wisp of hair away from her eyes, a gesture which normally irritated her and in time he would learn to avoid. 'In one sense it would be tempting,' she continued. 'But I don't know how objective I could be, and how he would take it; as an opportunity to purge himself and find some closure, or to start a set of mind games with me?'

They moved a few paces forward in the queue.

'What about you?' she asked. 'What have they got lined up for you?'

Caton had been hoping to keep it until later.

'I'm off to Shanghai with Gordon Holmes, the day after tomorrow,' he said. 'We could be away for a week or two. I'm sorry, I know you were hoping we could get away for a couple of days.'

'You were hoping to as well,' she reminded him.

The voice in his head appeared on cue. *There you go again, Tom.*

'You know what I meant, Kate. I was going to tell you, when the time was right.'

'Don't be daft.' She squeezed his hand. 'The time is never right with things like that. You can always tell me straight. I'll understand.'

Always. The word filled him with a sense of hope, tinged with the old anxieties. In the early days of their marriage, his wife had said she would always understand. His dread of history repeating itself had ended every relationship before it had begun. He had no idea how he would stop that happening again; he just knew that this time he had no choice.

'I was hoping to delay it until next month,' he said. 'But the powers that be want to get it done before the National Crime Squad muscle in. Operation Bojangles has apparently imbued me with an aura of invincibility at Chester House.'

'I'll put them straight,' she said, wrapping her free arm around his and pulling him close.

Albert Stephen Soaper lay naked on the bed, but for a modesty sheet and the straps that held him secure in the vain hope that the nerves in his neck might begin to repair themselves. The bandage around his head, and the mass of tubes and lines supporting his breathing, sustaining his body and monitoring his vital signs, made it difficult to see him properly. The nurse bent over his chest. Beneath his lids the eyeballs had been moving for several days.

These random eye movements were deemed to be a function of the trauma to his head and subsequent loss of control. But today she sensed they were of a different order. She turned to check one of the machines beside the bed and found the evidence she needed. She pressed a button to print off the reading. Along the top of the page the polysomnograph had recorded sudden short disturbances to the normal, almost flatline state. Immediately below it, the EEG printout showed significant peaks and troughs in parallel with what she was now convinced were not random, but rapid eye movements. REM signalled the lightest form of sleep and suggested that his brain was, at the very least, acting above a vegetative state.

She went to the nurses' station and paged the duty consultant.

Albert Stephen Soaper was flying. He knew that he was flying despite the fact that there were no surroundings to confirm it. He was flying in a bright white space. He felt a heady mix of exhilaration and calm. Somewhere a voice was calling him, singing perhaps. The words were indistinct. Albert Stephen Soaper didn't really care. He was flying ... he was free.

The nurse and the consultant approached his bed together. Albert Stephen's eyes were still closed, but he was smiling.

Her voice was like a mother's kiss, her singing as clear as crystal.

'You'll still be the sweetest little baby, in...n the...e town.'

Also by Bill Rogers

The Head Case

The Tiger's Cave

A Fatal Intervention

A Trace of Blood

Bluebell Hollow

The Frozen Contract

Backwash

A Venetian Moon

www.billrogers.co.uk

www.catonbooks.com